LITTLE
FIRE

WARRIORS OF THE FIVE REALMS

 1

HOLLEE MANDS

LITTLE FIRE

WARRIORS OF THE FIVE REALMS

HOLLEE MANDS

CONTENTS

Little Fire

Copyright © 2021 by Hollee Mands.

Editing and proofreading by Kelley Luna

Proofreading by Spell Bound

Cover design by Covers by Christian

For me.
And every soul out there with a story to tell.

THE FIVE REALMS

Once upon a time, we are told,
the five worlds were cast of the same mold,
Each identical in form and frame,
Yet varied in their creatures, none quite the same,
You see, the five gods once struck a charter,
Each to create a realm reflecting their splendor,
It began with Railea, the goddess of love, light, and sun,
Who created the first realm where mortal and immortal live as one,
Second was Ozenn, the god of chaos, order, and stars,
Who spun a world filled with magic so deep the land wears its scars,
Next came Thurin, the god of war, metal, and might,
Who built the third realm filled with creatures made for fight,
Fourth was Chonsea, the goddess of life, mercy, and sea,
Who fashioned a world where its inhabitants live free,
Last was Draedyn, the god of death, shadows, and moon,
His was a world much like a tomb,
Filled with frost and creatures none too sublime,
So it is told, once upon a time . . .

A CAUTIONARY TALE FROM THE
BARD'S COMPENDIUM

No archmage should be crossed,
No life is worth the cost,
Godly powers etched in their skin,
All are wise to heed their every whim,
Lord of the land and master of his domain,
Disobey one at your own bane.

A light breeze tickled the leaves, teasing the air with the musk of loam, moss, and the sweet scent of her. Declan stirred the lapping water with his feet. He loved sitting here by the pond with Freya, amid the playful splashes of warbling ducks and the distant trill of songbirds with the spring breeze caressing his skin. It made him feel safe.

She made him feel safe.

"Do you want to ascend one day?" The pages of the book on her lap rustled shut, and she fiddled their entwined fingers absently. "When you are fully grown?"

"No," he said. And because it was her, he admitted, "It scares me." He never needed to pretend around her. Freya never expected him to behave like an adult or a blooded warrior. She didn't expect him to act like anything but himself.

A young mage. A boy.

There was a soft splash, her feet kicking lightly in the pond before she said, "Well, I hope you do."

Declan swallowed. "Why?" Mages were said to lose a part of their soul during ascension—payment the gods demanded in exchange for such power. And he, of all people, knew it to be truth. He'd experienced firsthand the cruelty of an archmage.

"Then you'll be strong enough to stop whoever it is that keeps hurting you." The musical lilt in her voice hardened as she tightened her fingers around his. Declan dipped his head. He didn't tell her that even if he did ascend, he could never be strong enough to stop his own mother.

"It won't change anything," he murmured.

"Of course it will. No one hurts an archmage," she said. He could almost hear the pout in her voice. "And then maybe we won't have to meet in secret."

Declan nodded with a faint smile. If he ever ascended, he would most certainly leave the enclave and bring Freya with him. "If I ascend, I'll use my power to end the war in your realm. Then you can go home whenever you wish." He knew how she missed her father, who remained in the fae realm to fight the war.

She stiffened. "I want the war to end, but"—she jiggled their threaded fingers again—"I don't want to leave you."

Declan couldn't explain the bubbly rush in his veins at her whispered admission; he only knew it put a dopey smile on his face. The kind of smile that would have him beaten up in the enclave.

"But you'll come back to me. Won't you?" Every day, he counted the hours until their next meeting. She was the only person who had ever shown him care beyond the antiseptic walls of the enclave infirmary. The only person who worried if he hurt, or if he was sad. The only person who saw him for who he was, not merely the son of an archmage.

There was a long pause before she replied, "Always."

"If I ascend, I will rule a kingdom. Then I'll make you a princess," he declared, wanting to chase away the sadness in her voice. "You'll have a crown and everything." She giggled, and her unfettered laughter seeped through him like liquid sunshine, warming him down to the marrow. If it would make her happy, he would do everything he could to ascend. He would do anything for her—even if it meant losing a part of his soul.

She sidled closer. "Truly?"

He nodded. She would always be his princess.

She seemed happy, because the pages of the book rustled as she finagled to reopen it with one hand, her other still clasped in his. He never had a chance to read fiction books in the enclave; all he owned were textbooks on arithmetic, science, language, and history. But he loved her stories. Loved escaping into fictional worlds with her. Most of all, he loved listening to her voice.

He was so engrossed that he did not feel the prickly sensation that should have alerted him. Not until it was too late.

A telltale ripple shimmered in the air across the pond. Not a breeze, but a presence.

Freya gave a startled shriek. Her book slid over her lap to fall into the water with a wet plop. They scrambled to their feet, and she clutched his arms, her nails digging into his skin.

"*This* is who you've been sneaking out to see? She's nothing but a child!" Though Corvina's tone held more disbelief than derision, dread curdled in Declan's chest.

"I'm sorry," Declan stammered. His heart hammered like an executioner's drum as he nudged Freya behind him. His mother's chuckle was contemptuous—one often accompanied by bone-crushing punishments. The thought of such a thing happening to Freya caused cold sweat to trickle down his spine.

"We are friends," Freya protested from behind his back, fearless in her indignation.

"Friends?" Corvina laughed again, her voice a blade sheathed in silk. "Child, magekind will never be friends with you and your devious ilk." Her gown susurrated as she advanced like a snake slithering through the grass. His mother paused, and Freya's breathing turned ragged. A muffled scream tore from her throat.

"Mother, no!" Declan cried. Freya's agony reverberated on the psychic plane in choppy waves as she thrashed.

Help! Her mental voice rang in his mind. *Declan, help me!*

"Please, stop! Let her go, and I will never leave the enclave again. I swear it."

His mother only amplified her psychic torment. The invisible cords wrapped around Freya's neck constricted further, intent on suffocating and snuffing out the only warmth in Declan's life.

Freya's thrashing slowed, and the spark of her mind grew dim. *Help . . .*

Desperation solidified his fear into defiance. Moisture in the air congealed and crystallized into chips of ice, and Declan sent the shards hurtling toward Corvina like a hail of broken glass. But his attack evaporated into a swath of steam inches before his target.

"You can wield ice?" Corvina's voice hitched.

Declan tensed, his jaw clenching. He had tried to keep the progress of his abilities secret. "Let Freya go," he dared whisper. "Please, Mother."

"You would defy *me* for a fae child?" Fury oozed from her every syllable, her wrath churning around him in hostile waves. He released another burst of ice, this time forming a frozen wall to shroud Freya from sight.

"Run, Freya!" Declan cried. "Go!"

A torrent of flames seared his ice wall as hot vapor rose to cloud the air. When Freya remained motionless, he pleaded, "Go, Freya, please!" He could not hold Corvina for long—in fact, he was certain his mother was toying with him. Allowing his defiance just to test the extent of his strength. Corvina could easily set them all up in flames if she wanted. He hurled icicles shaped like daggers, deliberately showing off his abilities to buy Freya more time.

I'm scared, Declan! Freya's mental voice sobbed. *She's going to hurt you!*

Even now, warmth seeped through his veins. Freya was channeling her energies into him, compounding his strength. Amplifying his power.

I'll be fine, he lied. *Don't be scared.*

Heat flared. His mother sent firebolts slashing through the air. Declan fashioned another ice wall, wide enough to shield them from the incendiary assault. The hiss of sizzling ice told him the wall was crumbling.

Go, and don't look back. He swallowed his fear. *Be brave, Freya.*

With a heart-wrenching sob, the only beacon of light in his life turned and fled. Just before his mother tore through the pitiful wall of ice and shattered every bone in his body.

ONE

PRESENT DAY, VILLAGE ARNS, RAILEA'S REALM

Too fast, too close, *too much*. Evangeline Barre turned her cheek to evade the kiss and wedged a hand between herself and the broad chest pinning her against the counter. Her breaths shortened, and her heart thrummed a wild staccato in her chest.

"Please, Malcolm," Evangeline whispered, willing herself to stop trembling. Could he not tell she'd reached her limit?

His dark eyes clouded, but he didn't step back. Didn't release her. "You want this." His voice slurred, and his breath, laced with the yeasty scent of ale, made her stomach churn. "I know you want me."

Evangeline shook her head and swallowed her whimper. "Not like this."

He leaned in to leave a wet kiss on the base of her throat. "Come on, Evie," he implored. "Let me have you. I need to know you'll always belong to me."

But she didn't *want* to belong to him. The sudden clarity hit her like a slap. She should never have allowed herself to get embroiled with a man like Malcolm Fairsworn. She shot a frantic glance at the doorway. The shadows from the trees along the footpath had lengthened, beckoning through the small window of the apothecary with ghostly fingers.

He smirked. "Don't worry, beautiful." He nuzzled at her neck; his breath was damp heat against her skin. "No one is coming in at this hour." His chuckle made her insides contort. "Besides, I've already flipped the sign to *closed*."

She applied more pressure against him. "I can't."

His chest heaved, and his heart thudded heavily against her palm. His patience was short. It had grown progressively shorter as the months of their courtship lengthened. Gentle caresses transformed into groping, sweet kisses morphed into sloppy, tongue-grinding sessions she could hardly endure.

"Can't or won't?" he prodded, tone almost pleading.

Guilt, honed from previous lovers, loomed at her inability to meet his needs. His hand, warm and moist, traversed her inner thigh—far higher than he'd ventured before. Every hair on her body sprang up, as though an insect burrowed beneath her skin.

"You know I can't." She was no lightskirt. Far from it. She shoved at him this time, willing him to release her. It only served to fuel his impatience.

"After all these months, you're still trying to play hard to get?" His eyes narrowed, and a sneer formed on the face she'd once thought patrician. "Don't be a little tease. It's getting tiresome." He jerked her hand away, his weight forcing the blunt, wooden counter edge into her back. A hand roamed higher up her thigh, another ripping at the ties of her dress to grope at flesh even as his tongue delved into her mouth in a lewd parody of what was to come.

Fear ingrained so deep it felt nearly ancient roared to life in her ears. Panic seized her throat like a skeletal hand, choking every bit of air from her lungs.

No, no, no!

Evangeline bit down hard enough to draw a sharp tang of iron and a howl of pain from Malcolm's throat. He stumbled back, spewing profanities that made her ears burn. If he weren't blocking the doorway, she would have fled. Instead, she darted behind the counter, seeking refuge from the barrier of polished oak. Her sight never left him as she opened the drawers with fumbling hands and found the smooth contours of a glass pitcher.

"Get out," she spat, hating the quiver in her voice. Betrayal bubbled over her simmering anger. How could Malcolm do this to her? He knew how she felt about intimacy. He knew of the memories buried so deep they haunted her dreams as fragmented nightmares. He knew, yet how naïve was she to think he'd be different? Men would always be men.

Malcolm's eyes pinned her like a butterfly in a display case. With a jerky swipe of his forearm, he wiped the dribble of crimson from his curled lips. "I've had enough of your games. I'm not leaving until you give me a taste, you little bitch."

Evangeline flinched. Her best friend, Stefan, was right. Malcolm hadn't changed at all. She'd been willfully blind, choosing to believe he had matured since he'd become the village's chief constable. But the veneer of respectability Malcolm had acquired had been nothing but a polished farce. And she was nothing but a fool.

He lurched forward to seize her wrist and hauled her over the counter. Unable to break free from his bruising grip, Evangeline smashed the glass pitcher over his head with her other hand. The receptacle splintered on contact. Warmth welled in her grip, lubricating the brittle shards.

Malcolm's hand flew from her wrist to his temple. When he pulled it away, he stared at his bloodstained fingers. Rage deepened the color of his ale-flushed cheeks. "You—"

The door banged open. A woman stood in the entry, a slight figure against the darkened skies, but the sight of the worn woolen cloak and the shock of burnished red hair sent relief gushing through her.

Evangeline blew out a breath. "Mother."

Agnes Barre had always taken pains to keep the apothecary spotless, and now her jaw hung at the sight of shattered glass scattered on the parquet floor. When her gaze snagged on Evangeline's ripped bodice, her eyes flared. "Step away from my daughter, you degenerate scapegrace!"

Agnes barely moved, but Malcolm took an uneasy step back. Though her mother was wholly peaceful, no human in their right mind would stoke the ire of a mage close to a thousand years old.

But Malcolm proved more ale-addled than she'd thought, for he had the gall to sneer. "She attacked me," he declared, gesturing at the evidence trickling from his temple. "I can have her thrown behind bars for striking the chief constable!"

"*She* attacked you?" Agnes narrowed her eyes into slits before she shook her head. "Evie never did learn to properly bleed a chicken."

A shard of glass levitated off the ground to swivel in the air until its jagged edge was trained menacingly at Malcolm.

He took another step back. "You wouldn't dare. I will have you and your tease of a daughter run out of town."

Agnes's fists curled at her sides, and the still-levitating piece of glass jerked in ominous threat.

Evangeline snapped out of her haze and attempted to snatch the shard from the air before her mother could act on anger. The glass piece hovered firmly, unyielding.

"Mother, please." Evangeline shot Agnes a beseeching look. She wasn't worried about Malcolm's life. Her mother might be enraged enough to maim, but she was no cold-blooded murderer.

No, Evangeline was worried about *Malcolm's* threat.

Though Agnes was a powerful mage, Malcolm descended from a long line of Fairsworns, a family designated as vicegerents of Arns for so many generations that they had become the law. Added to that, Malcolm himself had weighty connections. As the chief constable, he communed frequently with battlemages and high mages alike. Malcolm was also vindictive enough to act on his threat without heeding the effect it would have on the villagers.

With the closest healer three days away on horseback, the villagers, particularly the ones hard pressed for coin, needed the Barre Apothecary as much as Agnes needed the solace and solitude offered by the community.

After a strained moment, her mother relented. The glass shard continued to levitate, but the sharp edge was no longer pointed in Malcolm's direction. Evangeline plucked it from the air with a sigh of relief.

Malcolm snorted and rolled his eyes.

Evangeline glared at him. "I'd get out of here if I were you."

"You can't throw me out," he said with a sneer. "This is *my* town."

"This is my shop," Agnes countered. "And I'm sure the governor"—Agnes raised a pointed brow—"your *father*, wouldn't be too happy to hear you've caused a scene in Arn's only apothecary."

Malcolm's face deepened into a shade of puce. For a terrible moment, Evangeline wondered if he would attack her mother. He never did tolerate reminders of his father's superior standing—Malcolm preferred to think of himself as a man of his own making.

To her relief, he retreated to the doorway, but not without

throwing Evangeline a treacherous glare. "Bitch. You'll pay for this."

A gnes settled Evangeline on a wooden stool behind the counter before scouring the drawers to produce gauze. Somewhat dazed, Evangeline blinked. Only when her mother reached for her hand did she notice the lacerations scoring her palms in angry, crimson streaks.

Evangeline grimaced. Small shards of glass were embedded in her skin.

"The loathsome swine." Agnes exhaled heavily, fury ripe on her ageless features. "How dare he hurt my child?"

It didn't matter to Agnes that Evangeline was already an adult. A woman of twenty-three years. To a being whose life-span stretched thousands of years, Evangeline would always be the little girl Agnes had found barely alive in the ravine thirteen years ago.

Her mother didn't lift a finger, but the jar containing double-boiled broadyew leaves unscrewed, as though opened by a phantom hand. Agnes leaned forward to scoop out a couple leaves and deposited them into the mortar. The pestle clanked against the mortar's edge as it ground of its own accord, thumping with an intensity that mirrored her mother's anger. Still, Agnes tended Evie's wound with a tenderness that caused her throat to constrict, and the incident with Malcolm regurgitated itself like bile she couldn't keep down.

"I'll make sure the governor hears of this," Agnes declared with a steel glint in her gray eyes as she added a scoop of minnowseeds to the mortar.

Evangeline chewed her bottom lip, trying to stem the tears

threatening to trickle. "Governor Fairsworn would never countenance complaints against his only son."

Agnes pursed her lips at the truth in Evangeline's words and deftly dressed her wound with the poultice she'd made. "He can't attack you and get away with it. Railea's tears, Malcolm is the chief constable! One who received a commendation from the lord archmage Thorne himself."

"Well, he was key to the capture of many slave-trade operators," Evangeline mumbled. It was the reason she had found Malcolm attractive. He was a venerated hero who championed the freedom of innocents—a cause that resonated deeply in her bones. But clearly, Malcolm's heroics were reserved for arresting those who chose to serve the insidious Unseelie cartel.

Fresh tears welled as Evangeline stared down at her bandaged palm and the glass splinters littering the ground. She'd been such a fool. She swiped angrily at her eyes with her sleeve-covered forearm. "It was my fault. I should have ended things between us weeks ago."

Handsome and suave, Malcolm had been patient at the start of their courtship. Attentive, even, when she spoke of her inexplicable fear of intimacy. *We'll work through your nightmares together,* Malcolm had said with a roguish grin, dusting her nose with the soft petals of a red rose. Eventually, she'd succumbed and allowed herself to forget the bully he'd once been who'd picked on smaller children when he thought no one was looking. She'd allowed herself to believe he'd changed and to be swept away by his persistent overtures. She'd believed him, too, when he'd said they'd go at her pace. But Malcolm had proven himself nothing more than a lecherous drunk.

And her fear had, once again, proven relentless.

"You need the help of a healer," Agnes murmured solemnly,

as though reading her mind. Not likely, since her mother's grasp of telepathy remained weak. Magekind was a psychic race, but most never mastered beyond one psychic ability. Agnes cupped her cheeks and emitted a weary sigh. "If only I had enough coin, you wouldn't need to wait for an apprenticeship."

Healers were rare, and most resided in the capital, where clients wouldn't have to scrimp and save for their services. Evangeline and her mother might own the only apothecary in the village, but in light of most villagers' shallow purses and Agnes's overgenerous tendencies, it did little but put food on their table.

Fortunately for Evangeline, healers took new apprentices every five years—and all apprentices had free access to the healer's services. Evangeline had failed in her application five years ago, and the five years before that because she'd been too young.

"Will you come with me to the capital if my application for an apprenticeship is granted this year?" Evangeline asked, even though she knew her mother's response. Agnes would never leave Arns. But the mere thought of leaving her mother behind weighed her heart down.

Agnes heaved another sigh of a being who had lived far too long and seen too much. "Sweetling, you know the village can't do without an apothecarist. The people rely on us in the absence of a proper healer." It wasn't Agnes's only reason, but Evangeline didn't pursue it.

Her mother shook her head with a forlorn smile. "No, you will have to go without me." The mage slipped an unopened letter from her dress pocket. Evangeline's eyes widened as she recognized the seal—the curlicue of the healer of Torgerson Falls was unmistakable. Agnes chuckled at her expression.

"This is why I came looking for you." Nudging the letter into her hands, Agnes urged, "Open it."

With the shaky fingers of her unbandaged hand, Evangeline broke the seal and scanned the contents with bated breath. Her vision was watery when she met her mother's eyes.

"My application. It's approved."

TWO

"P-please, my lord archmage." The miller knelt with his head bowed low enough to kiss the dirt. Damp patches soaked through the broadcloth tunic beneath his arms as he flattened his flour-dusted palms over the gravel path. "Have mercy."

When Declan remained unmoved, the human knocked his forehead to the ground repeatedly, as if the action would buy him clemency. A gust of wind whistled through the estate, and a flurry of fallen leaves danced through the courtyard as the heavy sails of the windmill began to rotate. The wooden turbine whirred seamlessly from its lofty stand overlooking a modest, pale-bricked gristmill flanked by large elm trees.

"Mercy?" said Killian, the commander of Declan's battlemages. Lips curling with unbridled disgust, the commander imparted another kick, and the miller went sprawling. "How dare you beg the sire for mercy after all the girls you've brutalized and sold?"

Killian flicked his wrist, and the miller squealed like swine in a slaughterhouse. Eventually, his screams ebbed. Shaking with whimpering pants, he cast a frantic gaze to the other human male in the vicinity as if to plead reprieve. Malcolm Fairsworn, the chief constable responsible for the miller's capture, took a step to the side, eyes carefully averted from the man's agony.

Declan watched with detached tedium as his commander compressed the man's ribcage with telekinesis, felt indifference even as the miller retched crimson-colored bile. Little did the human know he *was* receiving mercy. There would have been far more damage under Declan's hand.

The miller trembled, lungs whistling like an out-of-tune piccolo. He cowered on all fours and struggled for breath as his girth strained the waistband of his trousers. "I-I have n-no idea who the others are." A harrowing cough racked his frame before his face contorted with pain. "The fae keep their human operators separate in each village. Spread us out."

Of course they did. The Unseelie were a benighted, conniving race. What better way to attain a steady supply of human slaves than through the very hands of greedy mortals willing to betray their own? Humans could be such avaricious creatures.

Declan turned to the ashen constable. "Have you unearthed other operators?"

The constable blinked, as though he weren't sure the query was directed at him. Faint amusement crested within Declan. He'd expected tougher composition of the governor's son. Fairsworns, as memory served, had been made of hardier stock.

"Constable," Killian said, snapping the man from his daze.

Fairsworn straightened. "Yes, my lord . . . I mean, no, Lord Archmage." He cleared his throat. "The informant gave us no other names."

"And what of the miller's wife and child?" Declan added, inciting a wave of sobs from the miller, still on his knees.

"Please spare my family . . . my daughter . . . " He moaned.

Declan barely spared the man a glance. The miller had forfeited his life the moment he'd chosen to work with the cartel. But unlike Killian, Declan cared little for the miller's victims. The women sold were human, and likely contributed little to his lands. It was the miller's gall to betray his rule that engendered his ire.

"The women are in the house, my lord archmage," Fairsworn responded without prompting this time, his tone ingratiating. "Shall I retrieve them?"

Declan shook his head in response and nodded to his commander instead. When Killian warped, Fairsworn drew in a sharp breath and blinked rapidly. Teleportation was a rare ability, even for magekind.

Killian returned, materializing with a rotund woman and a fair-haired girl. The women stumbled to the ground, wide-eyed and whimpering. Declan couldn't tell if they were disoriented from warping or if they were shocked by the miller's roughened state.

"Reap his mind," Declan said to Killian. "When you are certain he has withheld no further knowledge, he will hang."

The miller did no more than groan. His fate was sealed. The girl scurried to her father's side while her mother stared. All color leached from her face. "Lord Archmage." She began to tremble. "I played no part in the trade!"

A dark chasm split the air like a lightning strike, and a man stepped nonchalantly out of the swirling sphere of shadows. Once, Declan would have annihilated Unseelie intruders on sight, especially one as lethal as the leader of a guild of cutthroat mercenaries. But Gabriel Blacksage had become an ally. The guildmaster didn't bother with human pretenses today, quintessential fae traits on full display—pointed ears, violet irises, and the slight show of fangs completed by the sheen that shrouded his skin like a dark aura.

Gabriel met Declan's gaze and dipped his head. "Archmage." The fae acknowledged both the commander and the constable with another nod before turning his attention to the cowering couple. "Ah, I remember you." He lifted a haughty brow at the miller's wife. "You're the one who knocked the wench back in place during the sale. I remember the imprint you left on the girl's face."

"I was just following my husband's orders." The woman wept, shrill and strident. She shuffled further from her husband, as if distance would free her from implication.

"You traitorous bitch," the miller hissed. He would have hit the woman if his daughter hadn't caught hold of his arm.

"Those girls . . . I took care of them. I loved them like my own," added the miller's wife, with her back turned to her husband and daughter.

As guilty as her husband. Gabriel's wry mental voice filled Declan's mind. *The girl they attempted to sell intimated the wife often took pleasure in inflicting little injuries.*

"Please spare me from the noose, my lord." She made the mistake of scurrying forward to clutch the hem of Declan's trousers, inciting a sliver of annoyance. Her life was as significant to him as an ant beneath his boot. Less, even. Ants did not betray his rule.

When he offered no response, she swallowed and blinked rapidly, fingers tightening over the fabric. "Please, I will do anything to be of use." She glanced up, eyes darting between him and Killian. "My daughter . . . she's young. Beautiful. She will serve you and your men."

A sob escaped the girl's throat at her mother's offer.

Declan arched a brow. "Your daughter's service in exchange for your life?"

The woman swallowed, seemingly uncertain if her offer had pleased or offended. Declan turned his attention to the girl. She appeared no older than sixteen summers, with a face and figure that would not be unwelcome in a man's bed. He returned his gaze to the woman, who nodded vigorously, a hopeful gleam lighting her eyes. "She will do as you bid, she will."

Declan did not even blink.

Fire caught the woman's pristine kerseymere frock, embers of red lapping up the pale-blue fabric with ravenous hunger. Violent screams reverberated through the estate, and the smell of burnt flesh defiled the air as the windmill's wooden sails continued to sweep solemn circles. A blackened stump was all that remained. If there was anything Declan despised more than disloyalty, it was a viper masquerading as a mother.

The daughter retched with her fingers digging into her father's arm. The man appeared an effigy of shock. Constable Fairsworn had moved to the side. His green-tinged expression contrasted with the Unseelie's, who stood with his arms nonchalantly folded as though watching a theater play.

Declan shot the guildmaster a mental query. *Has the daughter been involved in the trade?*

I do not know, Gabriel responded after a moment's pause. *I have not seen the girl in any of the couple's dealings. Although it is unlikely she knows nothing of her parents' transgression.*

Declan nodded at Killian, who stood grim and unfazed. "Reap the girl's mind."

The miller reanimated with the belligerence of a man who knew he would soon be dead. "The gods curse you, Archmage! My daughter is innocent!"

He lunged for Declan.

Killian snarled, and the crunch of snapping bones resounded. The miller crumpled before he could scream. The girl covered her mouth with her hands to muffle a cry and stared at Declan as though he were Draedyn in the flesh. Once, the fear and loathing brimming in her eyes might have troubled him, but now it bothered him less than a pebble in his shoe.

Reaping was a psychic assault on the human mind that often resulted in insanity. Human minds were weak. If the girl was truly innocent, she would be allowed to live. With her mind intact or not, Declan did not care.

Children often paid for the sins of their parents; this girl would not be the first.

Declan was about to warp off-site when two battlemages materialized before him, lips set in grim lines.

"Sire." The men dipped their heads, and one said, "We've just received report of an Unseelie squadron invading the village Arns."

Declan clenched a fist. This day was getting more distasteful by the minute.

THREE

"I'll kill him." The hammer struck with a sharp clang as though to punctuate the gritted statement. "I'm going to fucking kill him," Stefan Hanesworth repeated, his sky-blue eyes stormy with anger. He heaved the hammer high and brought it down swiftly as he fashioned the steepled end of an axe. Sparks flew as hammer collided with hot steel.

Evangeline winced, then conjured a light smile. "To be honest, I'm glad things ended." She met Stefan's glower so he could see the truth in her eyes. Apart from the lingering bitterness at her own foolishness, Evangeline was far from devastated. The end of the stilted relationship brought a strange sense of relief—she was released from Malcolm's subtle pressure to submit.

"Why didn't you tell me when it happened?" Stefan scowled as he grabbed a vise from the wooden rack and clamped the red-hot metal before dipping the tempered blade into the vat. Water gurgled and hissed; steam rose to add to the heat and humidity of the Hanesworth Forge.

Evangeline lifted a shoulder in a sheepish shrug. "I didn't

want to talk about it." Truthfully, she hadn't wanted Stefan to know. She didn't want him swinging fists on her account. Though it wasn't a secret she could keep for long. Barely two days after the incident, Malcolm had been sighted around the village flaunting a doxy on his arm.

Stefan wiped an ore-streaked hand over a dark brow, painting black stains across his forehead. He crossed his arms over his calfskin apron as he eyed both her satchel and travel sack with dubious eyes. "And you're going to allow that leech to run you out of town?"

Exasperation rose in response to the scowl on his face, stiffening her shoulders. "I'm not running out of town. You know how long I've waited for this opportunity." Evangeline folded her arms to mirror the blacksmith glowering down at her. "The healer of Torgerson Falls is the only one who responded to me."

Needing him to understand, she prattled on. "People say he's a halfbreed. A *halfbreed*, Stefan." Healers were rare, and halfbreed healers even rarer. Descended from the union of mages with the Seelie fae, a race long extinct, halfbreeds possessed both psychic and magical energies. Some were blessed with the ability to enhance crop growth, and some with the ability to heal wounds with supernatural swiftness. Evangeline hoped their abilities extended beyond physical wounds.

Stefan crossed the forge in two steps and wrapped an arm around her, wordlessly drawing her into his embrace.

Perhaps it was because his touch was platonic, but Stefan had never made her skin crawl upon direct contact. Even so, she usually shied away from it. There was something about being in a man's arms that made her shiver and her heart pound—and not for the right reasons. This time, however, Evangeline allowed the warmth and scent of male sweat, iron, and grime to envelop her, knowing Stefan needed the reassurance.

"I understand. I know how long you've waited." Stefan's voice was gruff as he spoke with his cheek resting over the top of her head. "I'm sorry, Evie. But I just . . . can't bear to see you leave."

Evangeline sighed into his chest and shut her eyes, trying to restrain the prickle of warmth behind her lids. She was not keen to replay her tear-drenched goodbyes with her mother from the morning, but Stefan was the one man she adored unconditionally. He was the other reason her heart weighed heavy at the thought of leaving Arns, no matter her excitement.

"I'll come back as often as I can to visit," she promised.

Stefan grunted his response but continued to hold her, the hug stretching longer than she'd prefer. Evangeline had started fidgeting when the back door opened unceremoniously, giving her the perfect opportunity to shimmy out of the friendly embrace.

"I say," said the man who filled the doorway. "I'm not interruptin' anythin' am I?" The older man blinked owlishly as he regarded Stefan and Evangeline with interest.

Evangeline managed a laugh. "No, Mr. Hanesworth. Not at all."

Stefan rubbed the back of his neck, the way he did whenever he was flustered, before shoving his hands into his pockets. "Evie's here for goodbyes, Pa. She's headed to the capital."

Mr. Hanesworth, a weathered replica of Stefan, ran a rough hand through his hair— sandy strands striated with white. He shot Evangeline a sympathetic glance. "Ah, I hope it's not because of what happened with the guv'nor's son, Evie."

Evangeline lifted her brows, but Mr. Hanesworth ambled

up to give her a fatherly pat on the back. "Your ma," he explained with a wag of his bushy brows. "Sweet girl like you deserves a better man if you're askin' me . . . " A wink. "Maybe you'll meet him in the capital, eh?"

Evangeline rubbed the sides of her arms and let out an embarrassed laugh. "Thanks, Mr. Hanesworth, but I think I've had it with men."

Stefan scrunched up his wholesome features and dramatically clutched his chest. "Ah, you wound me, Evie."

Evangeline couldn't help the chuckle filling her throat. "Goose. You're an exception, of course." Like his father, Stefan was a big man—his shoulders broad and arms heavily corded with muscle. Yet, to her, he would always be the boy with a sweet smile who had approached her on her first day of school. Stefan had been nervous, while Evangeline, diffident. Perhaps that was how they'd bonded, two socially awkward creatures.

Mr. Hanesworth lingered with expectancy in his eyes.

"What do you need, Pa?" Stefan asked, his face still bracketed with a smile.

His father grunted and rubbed the back of his neck in a move that perfectly echoed his son's. "The Dwyer widow needs someone to tend to 'er livestock. I told 'er I'd send you along when you were done 'ere."

Evangeline smiled. She would miss them both. The Hanesworth men might not have much, but they were always ready to lend a helping hand. Stefan stuffed his hands into his pockets, clearly unwilling to cut their farewell short.

"I'll walk with you," Evangeline offered. "The Dwyer Farm isn't far from the Traveling Wagons anyway." She wouldn't mind checking in on the elderly widow just before she left. Mrs. Dwyer was largely reclusive, but she sometimes ventured into the Barre Apothecary for smelling salts or a balm for her inflamed joints.

The wrinkle between Stefan's brows was quickly replaced by creases in his cheeks. "And I'll walk you to the Wagons after?"

Evangeline answered with a smile. A little detour wouldn't do her any harm.

The familiar vibrant chatter welcomed Evangeline and Stefan as they cut through the market square to the Dwyer Farm. It was early enough that the morning market was still in session. Cheery stallholders hawked their wares and bargain hunters haggled for the best prices. Spices and herbs scented the air along with the scintillating aroma of deep-fried crullers. Stefan rubbed a hand over his stomach as he eyed the food cart.

Evangeline smirked. "You never stop thinking about food, do you?"

"I'm thinking of *you*. I am certain you'll miss Mrs. Peppers's crullers," was his solemn retort as he ushered her toward the popular pastry cart.

Evangeline chuckled. "Oh, absolutely," she responded with a wry shake of her head.

As Stefan purchased his vice, Evangeline occupied herself watching a nearby street entertainer—clearly a mage—levitate feathers. Bright plumes swirled in perfect harmony, creating a tiny whirlwind of colors above the performer's head before settling gently into the outstretched hands of an eager child. The girl curled chubby fingers around the bouquet as she toddled toward her mother, waving the feathers with infectious glee. Evangeline applauded alongside the delighted crowd. She dug into her satchel for a coin and dropped it into the performer's upturned hat.

Stefan snorted, clearly unimpressed as he spoke between large mouthfuls of braided bun. "If I were a mage, I'd give the audience a real show by levitating knives."

"Or crullers straight into your mouth," Evangeline retorted.

Amusement tickled her throat like a wayward feather. Telekinesis might be a common mage ability, but most, like her mother, never gained the ability to do anything more than move one object at a time. It took considerable skill to move multiple items in concert, even if they were just feathers.

Stefan gave her a toothy grin that would make any hot-blooded woman blush—except Evangeline. Stefan was . . . Stefan. Evangeline accepted his offering and bit into the sweet, fried dough, savoring the soft, crumbly texture.

"But who needs telekinesis when I can do this?" He made a show of tossing a piece into the air before catching it deftly in his mouth.

Evangeline was laughing when alarmed cries filled the air.

She whirled around, looking for the source.

Stefan cursed.

She followed his gaze, and her half-eaten cruller slipped from her fingers. A shadowy *sphere* manifested in the middle of the square as though someone had taken a bucket of ink and splashed it into the air. The black stain hovered inches from the ground, an unnatural, amorphous blot growing larger until it was large enough to swallow a man.

Her breath snagged in her throat. She'd heard enough about the fae to comprehend what was unfolding before her eyes. A portal. An interdimensional gateway.

A squadron of soldiers spewed forth, clad in armor gleaming sleek and silver as they leapt from the inky portal to the cobblestone ground. Their helmets were shaped like curving beaks and shrouded their upper faces, leaving their jaws exposed.

Purple irises stared out of the eye slits. Unseelie. No other race possessed such a distinctive shade.

"Run, Evie!" Stefan shoved her to the side. Shrieks added to the chaos of the clamoring crowd. Some soldiers were armed with scythes, while others carried ornate crossbows. One raised his toward a stallholder and took aim, but no tangible arrow was deployed. Instead, shadows surged from the archer's forearms, followed by a crackling sound. The bolt of blackfire streaked through the air. Found its mark.

The merchant spasmed, his body juddering. He sprawled to the ground, clutching at his chest where black shadows crawled like oversized spiders.

Sheer terror secured Evangeline in place.

Stefan jerked her forearm. "Run!" he yelled again, snapping her from her stupor. Evangeline started, but she didn't know which way to go. The market was completely infiltrated, as though the god of chaos himself danced through the square wreaking panic and pandemonium.

A subtle crackling resounded again, so close that Evangeline ducked on instinct.

Stefan collapsed to his knees with a scream. A black stain bloomed on his thigh and spread like a growing spiderweb.

"No!" Evangeline dropped to his side, desperate to help him to his feet, but Stefan was already spasming. She grabbed hold of his forearm and startled—unnatural heat fevered his skin. The assailant stalked closer, his every step heralded by the subtle clink of metal against stone. Without giving her a single glance, he jerked Stefan up by the collar. Up close, Evangeline realized the metal plates of his armor were fashioned as feathers, his pauldrons shaped like outstretched wings, and his gauntlets tipped with protruding talons.

A silver eagle. And Stefan was his prey.

"No," she dared cry. "Please!"

Eyes of startling lilac narrowed as he hissed out words she did not comprehend. Hard, menacing words with an oddly musical cadence.

Smoky tendrils coiled around them, phantom fingers seeking to suffocate. It took her precious seconds to realize the soldier was creating *another* portal, with Stefan thrashing helplessly in his grip. Panic overwhelmed even her terror. Somehow, she knew with absolute certainty she would never see Stefan again should the soldier succeed in opening the portal. She would never see the boy who had been her very first friend, the boy who had taught her to swim and climb trees, the boy who had once pretended he didn't like sweet treats just so she could have his.

"Let him go!" Evangeline threw herself at the fae, grappling to free her best friend even as her heart threatened to escape her ribcage.

"Evie, get away," Stefan cried, wild terror in his voice.

She ignored him and reached out to claw at the soldier's eyes. She only managed to scrape his metal helmet. So she struck at his exposed jaw. He snarled, peeling back lips to reveal long canines that promised pain and whispered of death.

Evangeline flinched, but the blow never came. Her attacker staggered, blood leaking from his eyes and ears, before he slumped to the ground. She covered her mouth with a hand to stifle her shock. Blinked. More soldiers marched into view. Soldiers in black armor bearing the distinctive crest of a golden dragon.

Air gushed from her lungs while she pressed a palm over her heart. "Railea's tears, thank the gods."

Amereen's battlemages had arrived.

But her relief was short-lived. Her flesh tingled as though pricked by a thousand tiny needles. Glancing down, Evangeline drew in a stuttering gasp. Despite her fallen attacker, the amorphous inky tendrils continued to grow, coiling around her and Stefan like ghostly snakes bent on devouring them whole. She stared at her hands, and her breath stalled completely. She could see *through* them to the hem of her skirt and her boots. She was growing . . . translucent.

"Stefan!" She attempted to shove him from the dark sphere, but his body was a leaden anvil. "Help," she sobbed, her voice swallowed by the cries of a terrified crowd. "Help me, please!"

Then Stefan was plucked from her arms as though he weighed no more than a child. Evangeline sagged to her knees, but strong arms engulfed her, jerking her upright. The needling sensation intensified until every fiber of her being seemed to splinter. The last thing she heard before her vision disintegrated into darkness was her own screams.

Declan warped into the market square of Village Arns just in time to witness the chaos. Stalls were abandoned and wares trampled. People, humans and mages alike, ran frenzied across cobbled stone, trying to evade the Unseelie soldiers. Before him, an overturned handcart added rolling peaches and mushed grapes to the fray. The fae swarmed through the panicked crowd like a locust plague, their armor glinting silver as they terrorized the innocents with scythes and shadowbows—the quintessential crossbows of the Winter Court.

The darkness within him reared up with anger. First they despoiled his lands with slave-trade operators and now *this*?

Killian, heedless of danger, warped headfirst into the heart of the commotion to swoop up a crying toddler clutching a cluster of colorful feathers. An Unseelie raised his crossbow and took aim. The commander shifted to shield the child's body with his own.

Declan slammed a telekinetic shield into the air, nullifying streaks of blackfire before they met his commander's back. Killian wore no armor, and Unseelie magic could easily penetrate a leather cuirass.

Secure the square! Declan ordered. He fired a stream of mental commands to the men who had warped in beside him. The Unseelie king, Zephyr of the Winter Court, must have noticed the growing apprehension of his many operators seeded across Declan's lands like weeds. If Zephyr thought he could retrieve them by creating a distraction with this squadron of hell-raising soldiers, he was in for disappointment.

No soldier would return to the fae realm alive.

Declan sent an Unseelie crashing into the stone wall with telekinetic force. Exasperation gnawed at him. They were in the middle of a dense commercial square, and he couldn't set the attackers on fire without risking more damage or compromising the innocent. He would have to take them down one by one.

An indignant cry rose above the fracas. "Let him go!"

Declan turned to the source—a young woman. Slight though she was, she charged at a soldier grappling with an injured civilian. She pounced, clawing at the fae like an enraged kitten.

"Evie, get out of here!" cried the wounded man, struggling unsuccessfully to free himself from the soldier's metal talons.

Narrowing his eyes, Declan emitted a pulse of telekinesis and collapsed the attacker's lungs. Even though the Unseelie crumpled to the ground, the seeds of a portal continued to grow. Shadows coiled around the woman and her wounded friend, nebulous threads of darkness that signaled the beginnings of an interdimensional doorway.

"Stefan!"

Somehow, the terror in her voice tugged at Declan like a fishhook. Instead of fleeing, the little fool was trying to shove the man from the amorphous doorway.

In seconds, the portal would be complete. If it led back to the fae realm, the woman would face a fate worse than death. The foot soldiers in the Winter Court alone were depraved enough to leave her a ravaged hull. If she survived beyond that, slavery was inevitable. If she was too foolish to run, why should he care? Declan had a village square to defend. Fae soldiers to eliminate.

"Help," she sobbed. "Help me, please!"

Freya's voice, from so long ago, echoed in his mind. *Help me . . .*

Declan warped close to haul the wounded man out of the solidifying portal. But it was too late for the woman. She was turning immaterial.

The portal was tearing her out of this realm.

Sire!

Ignoring Killian's telepathic shout, Declan warped into the coalescing darkness and drew her into his arms just as the portal consumed them both.

FOUR

Evangeline sucked in a wobbly breath and exhaled shallow puffs. Her skin prickled from the sudden dip in temperature. She rubbed her eyes, trying to shake off the dizzying wave of disorientation. When the pinpricks of black finally receded from her vision, her knees shook. Gone were the cobbled streets of Market Square, the cluttered vendor carts, and the quaint shop fronts.

Sleet and snow replaced it all. Leagues and leagues of white carpeted the ground, stretching as far as Evangeline could see. Only a smattering of gnarled and twisted trees broke the near-barren terrain. It had been midmorning, but now, the heavens were painted in gloom, the final wisps of sunlight dimmed by dense clouds. Jagged mountains loomed over the horizon like rows of serrated teeth attempting to rip into murky skies.

A shiver skittered down her spine, borne from the sudden chill of her new surroundings and the innate sense of *wrongness*. A strangled cry crowded her throat. Where in Railea's name . . . ?

It took her another moment to realize she was standing *because* she was clinging to a solid wall of muscle, her cheek pressed against the solid plane of a man's chest. Stefan? But this man felt different. Leaner and taller. Much taller.

The assailant!

She recoiled with a shriek and stumbled backward into freezing slush. Dampness seeped through her skirt to compound the tremors racking her body.

"S-stay away from me!" Evangeline glanced around wildly for a weapon. Her travel sack and satchel must have been lost in the altercation. Unless she wanted to heave snowballs at the stranger, there were no other means to defend herself.

The man surprised her by shifting back, as if to give her space, and held his hands open in a gesture of peace.

"I am not one of the fae, little mortal." His voice was startlingly deep and unnervingly calm.

She blinked as her eyes adjusted to the feeble light. Indeed, the stranger wasn't wearing the silver-scaled armor of the attackers who had flooded the square. Instead, he was almost formally dressed—a coat over a crisp shirt, fitted trousers paired with riding boots. Save the muted gray of his shirt that matched the dreary sky, everything on him was a somber black, including the short strands of raven-colored hair.

The stranger's formidable stature paired with his emotionless scrutiny caused her to shrink deeper into the snow despite the chilling damp. "Who are you? Where are we?"

"A portal," was his only response.

A portal . . . ? Sudden furor tickled her throat, and a startled laugh leaked from her lips. "Oh, I get it now. This is one of my nightmares," she said, gasps of hysterics rising up like steam from a boiling kettle. She buried her face in her hands and began to rock. "Wake up. I just need to wake up."

Warm hands bracketed her shoulders. She ignored them and continued to rock herself as she tried to steady her pulse.

"Go away," she muttered, voice muffled by her hands. "You're just a figment of my imagination. This isn't real. Can't you see? I was just eating crullers with . . . "

Just as quickly, hysteria switched to trepidation. A ragged moan tore through her throat. "Stefan . . . " Goddess of mercy, what had happened to Stefan? This couldn't possibly be happening. Yet the cold seeping through her muslin dress felt all too real. She drew in a tremulous breath of frigid air and dug her nails into her biceps.

"Your friend should be safe. I pulled him out of the portal, but I couldn't get you out in time."

Her fear crept down a notch at the stranger's words, but before she could further process her predicament, an other-worldly screech rumbled through the skies—a nightmarish sound that raised every hair on the back of her neck.

"Wh-what in Railea's name was that?" Her heart battered against her ribcage. She glanced up, scouring the skies for the ominous source. Nothing but dense clouds clotting the heavens to mask the fleeting sun.

But the stranger clearly heard it, too, for he lifted his head to scan the firmament. Her gaze snagged on the strong column of his throat, exposed at the collar of his shirt. Even in the dim light, faint swirling lines and arcane symbols danced against his bronze skin.

Glyphs? She gulped. She had never seen them before but instinctively knew these symbols were no ordinary tattoos. A mage's ascension was said to be so violent the resulting power was etched into their skin.

The hairs on the back of her neck prickled. There had been soldiers in the square. Men who wore the sigil of the archmage who ruled Amereen. A golden dragon. The very same dragon stitched on this man's collar.

Her stuttering inhale drew his attention back to her.

"A-are we still in Arns?" As soon as the words left her lips, she recognized the idiocy of her question. It never snowed like this in Arns. "Are we still in Amereen?" she asked hopefully, even though deep down she already knew the answer.

"No."

An undignified squeak escaped her throat at his unvarnished response. Before she could pelt him with more questions, another screech echoed.

"What *was* that?" Her gaze darted across the skies.

Abruptly, he crouched before her. The edge of urgency in his voice cut through her panic like a blade. "Look at me, little mortal."

Eyes of brilliant green bored into hers, and her quailing heart stilled. For a moment, she saw the forest in his eyes. Lush and vibrant. Soothing.

"If you wish to see home again, you will compose yourself and come with me." His expression revealed not a hint of fear, and the sheer confidence in his words brought a sense of calm, like a lid thrown over a bubbling pot, momentarily stifling the myriad emotions vying for release.

"*Where?*" She wasn't about to argue. Every instinct screamed for her to flee, to seek cover. But they were in the middle of a snow-laden plain occupied only by lonely, far-flung trees.

His eyes tracked the horizon. "The mountains. Whatever is out here, I doubt it's friendly."

Though his statement echoed her own sentiments, it didn't soothe her. The mountains were not only leagues away but also appeared dark and foreboding.

Another screech resounded, this time loud enough to

propel her to her feet. In the distance, a shadow flitted through the layer of dense clouds, low enough to hint of wings larger than any bird's she'd ever seen.

Declan swallowed an oath when he recognized the demon in the sky. Arrowtail. The winged serpent confirmed his suspicion of their whereabouts. It explained the inexplicable leaching of his powers with every passing minute—as though the very ground exhausted him. To ensure the balance of power remained constant in each realm, the gods weakened every being who traversed a realm not their own. The more power they had, the faster the drain.

And as a being of such violent power, Declan felt the drain keenly.

The little mortal issued a loud gasp. Though it was far in the distance, the sinuous silhouette drawing lazy circles over stratus clouds could hardly be mistaken for a bird. "What is that ... thing?"

The arrowtail soared closer, and all color bled from her face to render it plain as parchment. "Railea's tears, we need to run!"

When he made no attempt to move, she grabbed his forearm and tugged. "Run!" she hissed before darting off like a rabbit seeking a burrow.

Declan narrowed his eyes. Foolish girl. Did she not realize her sudden movement across the barren landscape would only draw the arrowtail's attention? He sprinted after her, captured the crook of her arm, and jerked her to a halt.

"Stop," he commanded. Ignoring her protests and attempts to wrench herself free from his grip, Declan cast his gaze to the chain of mountains in the distance. He warped.

A wall of saw-toothed rocks covered by a smattering of white filled his vision. But the little mortal was nowhere in sight.

"*Fuck.*"

This realm rendered him weak beyond belief. He could no longer teleport bodily with her. Declan warped again, returning to his original location where the woman, wild eyed, whimpered at the sight of him. In relief or fear, he did not know.

"How did you just *vanish?*"

At her strident tone, the demon swerved in their direction, no longer aimless in its flight. Declan firmed his stance and drew deep into his marrow—there was no outrunning the arrowtail. The demon barreled through the skies to hover above them like a vulture circling carrion. Baring a rounded snout crowded with tiny rows of spiky teeth, it released an avaricious shriek before descending on what it must consider easy prey.

Declan emitted a burst of power, nothing but a weak flare of flames, but it served to throw the serpent off-kilter. The arrowtail flailed its wings—webbed constructs of spindly bones covered in thin, leathery skin—before swooping again. Declan released another burst of flames, this time singeing the demon's wings, which thwarted the creature's desire to make a feast of him. With a shriek of rage, the demon veered into the skies until the tip of its pointed tail disappeared into the clouds.

Only when he was satisfied the arrowtail would not return did Declan permit himself to shut his eyes against the wave of light-headedness. When he turned, it was to see the woman huddled on the ground, her mouth agape as if locked in a silent scream, her eyes glazed with shock.

"Calm yourself," he muttered. "Most demons are attracted to fear."

She blinked once. Twice. Snapped her jaw shut. After a long pause, she drew in a jittery breath as if to recompose herself. "That thing—demon . . . Is it gone?"

"For now. We should keep moving." This realm was filled with creatures far deadlier than the arrowtail.

Fine tremors continued to rack her slight form, but her next words were wholly unexpected. "Are you . . . " She swallowed tentatively. "Are you all right?"

Declan stared at her. Though he allowed no change in his expression, her query left him dumbfounded. He couldn't remember the last time anyone had asked him such a question. At his continued silence, her lids fanned down to hood her eyes and her lips quivered.

"Where are we?" she asked, her voice small but surprisingly steadfast.

"Somewhere in the realm of Draedyn's creation." After the appearance of the arrowtail, there was no longer any doubt.

Her eyes rounded. "Draedyn . . . the god of death?" She emitted an inarticulate sound, as though struggling for breath. "We're . . . we're . . . in the *shadow realm?*"

"Breathe," he commanded. It would not do for her to start swooning. "Until my men find us, we will seek shelter."

He had no doubt Gabriel would scour the realms to bring him home—the fae were the *only* creatures with the ability to traverse the five realms. And no matter their improbable alliance, he knew the Unseelie guildmaster was loyal to him to the bone. But it would likely take Gabriel days to track his psychic signature.

"You're an archmage?" Her whispered words sounded more like an accusation than a question.

Declan gave a curt nod, and her amber eyes widened.

Round and stark, they dominated her face. A pleasing one, even if it was pale enough to mirror their wintry surrounds. Awry strands of brown fought to escape a disheveled braid, adding to her bewildered expression.

The pragmatic gray of her plain dress and the lack of adornments in her hair and around her neck told him she was a commoner. Human. Only mortals traversed realms without suffering any noticeable ill effects, for they possessed no powers to begin with. Weak.

She continued to stare at him, clearly petrified.

Declan suppressed the urge to sigh. The fear she emitted would draw demons to them quicker than flies to raw meat. That, coupled with his diminishing powers, meant keeping them both alive in this demon realm was about as promising as cutting his veins open and wading into shark-infested waters. What in the five blazing hells had possessed him to warp into an imploding portal after a little mortal woman?

FIVE

Evangeline shut her eyes and willed the ground to split and swallow her whole. An archmage. She was in the presence of an *archmage*. One of the eight supreme rulers of her realm—beings so lethal they were said to kill with a mere blink of an eye. Her stomach churned, as though her half-eaten cruller vied for escape.

Like an imbecile, she stuttered her shock.

But he paid her no heed. He merely beckoned as though summoning a servant before trekking through the snow. Clearly expecting her to follow.

Evangeline couldn't make her legs budge.

As though sensing her incompliance, he swiveled around, his movements far too graceful for a man of his stature. Something flickered over his features—the first semblance of emotion she'd seen him wear. Annoyance. Her breath hitched. His expression told her he was not tolerant of disobedience, and it reminded her exactly who he was. The knowledge chilled her far more than the surreal notion of her current predicament.

"I am unable to warp *with* you," he said, as though it were somehow her fault. Retrospectively, she understood he'd teleported. It made sense now. Only the strongest of magekind possessed the ability. And despite her misgivings, he had returned to prevent her from becoming the repast of a giant flying snake.

It was on the tip of her tongue to voice her gratitude when he added, "You would be wise to follow me if you wish to seek shelter."

Without sparing her another glance, he strode toward the mountains that lay like shards of broken glass sticking out of the horizon. She had a wild impulse to run in the opposite direction, away from his retreating back, but common sense prevailed.

"Can't you do something to take us home?" Evangeline bit the inside of her lip. How did one even address an archmage? He might rule supreme in Amereen, but he was also the most private of the eight members of the Echelon. Not once had she heard of him—Lord Archmage Thorne—making a public appearance.

When he continued moving, showing no indication he'd heard her, Evangeline added hastily, "Lord Archmage Thorne."

He paused. When he turned, his expression was a blank canvas of regal lines and chiseled angles, save the sculpted softness of his lips. Thick slashes of brows gave him an air of severity but did nothing to detract from his appeal.

"Interdimensional portals can only be created by faekind," he said, as though that explained everything.

"Then how will we get home, my lord?" she pressed, her voice brittle to her own ears.

"Lord Archmage," he corrected before adding, "I have fae allies." His tone held such confidence that her shoulders sagged with relief. He gestured to the barren landscape.

"Unless it is spelled or warded, there isn't a single location within the five realms inaccessible to the fae and their portals."

"So we . . . wait?"

"It will take time for them to find me. Right now, the mountains ahead are our best chance," he said, dashing whatever kernel of hope had bloomed in her heart.

Evangeline swallowed. "How much time are you referring to, Lord Archmage?"

"Likely days."

Another whimper wormed up her throat. The healer of Torgerson Falls was expecting her in *five* days. Evangeline scrubbed a hand over her mouth to stifle the noise. Calm. She needed to calm herself. Perhaps they would be home by then. She might still make it in time. For now, she'd simply have to wait—she cast another frantic glance at her surrounds—and survive. Survive days in a realm where the air was so frigid her breath came out in puffs of white and snakes could fly. With one of the Echelon for company.

She didn't know which aspect was more terrifying.

The eight archmages of the Echelon were the supreme rulers of her realm, fabled to have powers that rivaled the gods'. Growing up, she'd heard many stories. She'd particularly enjoyed those of the benevolent Archmage Orus Isa who ruled the peaceful province of Teti Unas, and the righteous female archmage, Sonja Tuath, who ruled the fair lands of Yarveric. Archmages were generally venerated, but some were feared as much as they were revered.

And for good reason.

A few years ago, Evangeline had heard about a village girl in the distant province of Jachuana unfortunate enough to catch the eye of the archmage Dakari Chikere. *He set the entire village on fire. Razed it to the ground, he did,* a traveling gypsy had said. *Simply because the woman he wanted refused to lay with him, and the villagers tried to stop him from taking her.*

Lord Chikere was an infamous sadist, renowned for his abuse of women. Jachuana became a province where all manner of injustice against womenfolk was commonplace because its archmage both committed and condoned it.

And as for this archmage before her?

Declan Thorne, the archmage of Amereen, was rumored to be so lethal he scared monsters like Dakari Chikere. If Evangeline recalled her history lessons correctly, he had warred with the Jachuanan archmage to expand the borders of Amereen shortly after his ascension. Dakari Chikere had yielded eventually, but not before blood soaked the lands in rivers of red.

Now Lord Archmage Thorne's sight was fixed on her, disarming in its intensity. Evangeline opened her mouth but couldn't seem to find her voice. She swallowed nervously. "But I need . . ."

"Shelter," he concluded on her behalf. Curt and dismissive. He turned on his heel and resumed walking, apparently done with her queries.

I need to be in Torgerson Falls in five days, or lose my chance to make sense of my nightmares. She wanted to scream, but she snapped her mouth shut and swallowed her distress. She likely wouldn't see home again if she engendered his ire. And the archmage was already strides ahead, his back a retreating specter of black in the gloom and gray. Evangeline rubbed her arms and glanced up at the skies to reassure herself that no shadows lurked above. Nothing but ominous thunderheads.

Blustery winds whipped her dress as if to spur her forward.

Drawing in a bolstering breath, she trailed after him.

Evangeline panted as she bounded in the archmage's footprints. His pace was laborious, and she soon realized it was much easier to walk in his tracks than to trudge through the thick snow on her own. Only his paces were much wider apart than hers. So she'd resorted to taking tiny leaps behind him, which gave her ample opportunity to study his form.

It was every bit as unnerving as his face.

His aristocratic attire did nothing to disguise his warrior-straight posture and callous demeanor. If anything, the elegantly fitted coat only served to emphasize formidable shoulders and a ruggedly muscled physique. Despite the ankle-high snowbank, he plowed through with a smooth, rippling grace that reminded her of a prowling feline. A panther, perhaps.

A cold and sullen one.

"Lord Archmage, will we make it to the mountains before nightfall?" she asked between pants, needing to voice the questions brimming in her throat. The sun must have sidled down from its apex, for the gray skies had darkened to the color of wet slate. But the snowcapped mountains still loomed far in the distance.

"Unlikely," he said without breaking his stride.

Evangeline cast another wary glance to the skies and shuddered. "The attackers in the square," she began as she hurried after him, "were clearly fae . . . Could we be in the fae realm?"

"Demons exist only in the shadow realm."

A logical statement, yet her brows furrowed. "But why would the attacker's portal lead here?" To a barren valley in the basest of all the five realms.

"By killing him, I caused his portal to implode. That likely threw his intended destination off."

Evangeline blinked, trying to make sense of his words.

"That we landed here appears to be an effect of random chance," he added.

"*Chance?*"

"We could have landed anywhere in the five realms."

A dizziness filled her head at the prospect. "If we're here by chance, how will your men know where to find you?"

"Every mage exudes a unique psychic signature. My men will trace me telepathically."

Telekinesis, telepathy, teleportation, and telementation. The first two were commonplace, while the latter were almost outlandish. Teleportation was an aberration, while telementation—the psychic manifestation of the elements—was even more unheard of.

Evangeline eyed him warily as she recalled the burst of flames he'd directed at the arrowtail. The man clearly mastered all four. His psychic signature must be *unequivocal.*

"Your fae allies . . . " Evangeline had never heard of an alliance between psychic mages and the magic-wielding fae. "They will be able to find you based on your psychic signature alone, no matter where you are?"

"Theoretically, yes."

"*Theoretically?*" she parroted, unable to stifle her alarm.

Though there was no change in his tone, Evangeline sensed his annoyance as he answered, "Not if I were stranded in the Abyss."

Perhaps he could feel her blank stare boring into the back of his head or hear her unspoken questions, for he explained without further prompting.

"The Abyss is the buffer that separates each realm," he explained brusquely, as though it were something she should have known. "A place where time and space ceases to exist. There would have been no escape if we'd landed there."

The thought of being lost somewhere *between* worlds sent an involuntary shudder snaking down her spine, and she quickened her pace. A yelp slipped from her throat when she missed a step and found her leg lodged calf deep in the frost. Her ankle-length work dress did little to insulate her from the stinging chill, but she had serendipitously donned her leather boots in anticipation of travel—a small blessing that had her thanking the gods.

She was shaking snow off her boots when she realized the archmage had paused to slant her a sidelong glance. Though his gaze remained inscrutable, his strides shortened and his pace slowed.

"Thank you, Lord Archmage."

He did not acknowledge her gratitude.

Sudden warmth prickled her eyes, dampness distorting her vision. Evangeline couldn't help but feel like she'd been cast out into a turbulent sea on nothing but a raft—without oars. She scrubbed the wetness from her eyes and marched on. She would keep her head down and do whatever it took to return to Arns. Gods willing, she'd return in time to meet the healer of Torgerson Falls.

An eternity seemed to pass before the archmage came to an abrupt halt.

Evangeline flailed, nearly bumping into his back. "What?"

He held up a hand, signaling for her silence. She peered over his shoulder in confusion. Then she heard it. The slight hissing sound.

Pale white scales glinted in her periphery before the creature glided into their path, thicker than both her thighs combined and longer than a horse cart. Blood drained from her face even as her pulse spiked. Another arrowtail? But this creature was not only much smaller; it was also wingless. Where it lacked wings, two spindly appendages protruded from the creature's back. Arms. They were disturbingly humanlike, bent at what appeared to be elbows, ending with long fingers digging into the snow. And like the arrowtail, this creature had no hind legs.

"Calm," the archmage murmured without taking his eyes off the creature, and for a moment she wasn't certain if the word was intended for her or the pearlescent demon.

It reared up and propped itself up by its arms to regard them with unblinking eyes of filmy gray. A pink, forked tongue darted between the smooth seam of the creature's mouth before it hissed.

Evangeline's breath hitched.

Translucent skin unfurled from the side of the demon's head, flaring wide in warning. Its hiss deepened, but the archmage remained dauntless.

"Calm yourself, little mortal," he repeated, and she remembered his earlier words. Demons were attracted to *fear*. Evangeline forced herself to draw in a deep breath, willing her heart to slow. But how could she when the demon stared at her with opaque, hungry eyes?

The archmage took a single step forward.

The demon retracted its fanlike skin as though in capitulation before it reared back and slunk off, its arms skittering on the ground like a spider's legs while its long tail left ripples in the snow.

A foggy puff of white escaped Evangeline's mouth as she stared at the creature's retreating form.

"Come," the archmage said, resuming his pace as though he hadn't just stared down another demon large enough to swallow him whole. "The skies grow dark."

Evangeline followed close on his heels.

By the time they arrived at the foothills of the snowcapped mountains, dusk had well and truly fallen. Lit only by a waning moon, the colossal rocks and frosty crevices were layers of glimmering obsidian. Stray thickets, small shrubs, and an occasional gnarled tree interspersed with smatters of shimmering snow completed the inhospitable landscape.

"Are you able to continue hiking up the mountain?" The unexpected query jerked Evangeline from her morose musings. She nodded despite her protesting muscles. Perhaps it was foolish, but she wasn't about to appear weak before the strongest being she'd ever come across.

"We will find a place to rest as soon as possible," he said, as if judging her incapable of further exertion. It nipped at her pride, but she didn't argue. Even though he'd already slowed his pace, it was still strenuous. Cold seeped through her skin and crept into her marrow, weighing her limbs with weariness.

" . . . stealth. We don't want to alert whatever is lurking in these mountains to our presence."

She blinked. She was so close to exhaustion she'd missed some of his words. Her voice came out once again in an undignified squeak. "You think there are more demons living here?"

"Any creature living in the foothills, like the last demon we just encountered, is a bottom feeder. It's the ones that roam the terrain come nightfall we should be worried about."

She didn't argue with that.

The expanse of snowy ground narrowed to a steep trail of sleet and rock. Layers of frostbitten stone and pebbles lined the path, varied with dehydrated bushes and boulders acting as slippery obstacles intent on barring her passage. Her leather boots, pitifully damp from their trek, skidded for the umpteenth time. Her fingers, numb from the cold, finally lost their grip. A large hand clamped over the crook of her arm just before she hit the ground.

"You are about as graceful as a trampling elephant, little mortal." He glanced down at her without so much as a furrow in his brow, yet she had the strangest suspicion he was amused.

Unnerved by the strength of his hold, she snatched her arm away. "I have a name," she protested, a little testier than intended. She was aching, scared, cold, and hungry, and his reference—clearly how he viewed her—raised her hackles.

"It's Evangeline Barre," she snapped. Then she added, "Lord Archmage," wisely softening her tone as she remembered whom she was speaking to.

He tilted his head as if to study her. Evangeline dipped hers, suddenly thankful for the starless skies as heat rose to her cheeks. He might be an archmage, but he shared her predicament. The only difference was he scaled the foothill like a sure-footed mountain goat while she trampled. Like an elephant.

"Evangeline Barre," he said, as if testing the words. Perhaps it was a bad idea to give him her full name. On his tongue, it sounded exotic. More compelling than it should be. But he made no further comment, and she was too weary to attempt conversation, so they resumed hiking in silence.

The steady grind of the archmage's boots on the gravelly path and her clumsier crunches became a mind-numbing monotone before he halted unexpectedly and once again motioned for her silence.

There was no demon in sight.

Instead, his attention focused upon the myriad cracks in the rock wall ahead. Evangeline frowned. The slim fissures tapered into a larger crevice at the base of the escarpment, wide enough for a man's entry. Her shoulders tensed. Or a demon's.

"Let's keep moving," she whispered despite her weariness. Instinct told her the hellish and inhospitable hole harbored danger, not shelter.

The archmage clearly did not share her instincts, for his telepathic voice flooded her mind without warning. *It is already dusk, little mortal.*

A shiver wended down her spine, and a gasp eked from her throat before she could suppress it. She squeezed her eyes shut. Evangeline was rarely exposed to telepathic speech. Her mother's telepathy was nonexistent, and even mages gifted in the art rarely imposed their skill upon humans. The sudden intrusion of his voice—rich and husky—in her head did more than startle. It overwhelmed.

But *of course* he could communicate telepathically. The man was an archmage.

After dragging a few gulps of air, Evangeline trusted herself to open her eyes. He stared at her with tension tightening the corners of his mouth. Her heart rabbited. Railea's tears, she'd offended him. She parted her lips, but before she could utter a word, his voice flowed into her head again.

This is the only shelter we've encountered. It will serve. If he was annoyed, he made no remark of it. Instead, his voice was softer somehow, almost wary. As though he was whispering. Telepathically. Trying not to spook the human.

A hysterical urge to laugh wormed in her throat when a sword materialized in his hand with a flash of gold. She jolted. Its sharp edge gleamed even under the feeble light, adorned with gilded inscriptions in the old magerian script.

Gods, the man could make swords appear from thin air.

Stay here.

He crept toward the narrow opening. She craned her neck

and caught a glimpse of a dark, slender cave. It was as if they'd discovered an open vein leading into the mountain's core.

Disregarding his command, Evangeline shuffled closer. A few paces forward and she caught the unmistakable scent of death and decay. The contents of her belly churned. Her heart pounded in her ears, a symphony to the steady rhythm of trickling water from the recesses of the cavern.

Drip . . . Drip . . . Drip . . .

Her instincts urged her to flee, but the archmage had already disappeared into the stygian depths. She slunk closer. The cavern appeared empty apart from the slim stone protrusions that dripped from the ceiling like melting wax frozen in time. As her eyes adjusted to the dim light, an eerie cluster of creatures came into view.

Drip . . . Drip . . . Drip . . .

They appeared inanimate. Dead?

The archmage advanced, his sword ready, his steps stealthy.

One of the creatures lurched upright without warning, and Evangeline bit down on her hand to stifle a scream. Her flesh crawled. The thing—demon—was unmistakably humanlike, which made it all the more obscene. A gnarled and skeletal frame. An open chest cavity with protruding ribs. Tattered skin hanging like threadbare cloth. Empty eye sockets. And its mouth . . . No lips. No skin to shroud the sharp, crooked teeth sticking out of the gums that stretched in a wide rictus.

Drip . . . Drip . . .

The creature clapped its jaws together in rapid succession, creating a hair-raising clicking noise. She was about to beg for the archmage to run when movement caught her eye. The creature's brethren stirred like agitated wasps from a disturbed nest.

The closest demon charged.

The archmage struck out with his sword.

With startling dexterity, the demon somersaulted like a grotesque trapeze artist. Arms bent at an odd angle, it landed upside down, perched on the ceiling of the cave like a bat. Its fingers and toes were unnaturally long, miniature chisels of horror, tipped with sharp, crusty nails. The distinct click, click, click grew louder. More erratic. Frenzied.

Evangeline bit into her lip to smother her screams.

More demons lunged, but the archmage proved as adept with his sword as he was scaling slippery rocks. He dismembered each one with chilling precision, every move he made one of calculated efficiency. As he beheaded another, the demon on the ceiling scuttled in a jerky, hair-raising fashion and launched itself squarely onto his back.

"Watch out!" she cried, far too late.

It struck.

The sword clattered out of the archmage's grip, and the demon raked nails across his face, drawing crimson streaks in its wake. He flung the demon off with preternatural strength, then grappled with another that snapped a distended mandible at his throat. More circled like vultures, looking for an opening.

Without hesitation, Evangeline picked up the closest weapon available—a large, jagged rock—and hefted it toward the nearest demon. The projectile knocked it squarely between the shoulder blades.

Empty eye sockets stared back at her.

A flurry of furious clicking resounded before it leapt.

Evangeline stumbled onto her back. Sharp stones dug into her skin. Kicking the demon in the abdomen, she threw it off-kilter, but sharp nails sliced into her calf, ripping a shriek from her throat. Abruptly, the clicking silenced.

The creature's head toppled off in a bloodless roll.

The archmage loomed over her, sword in hand. Evangeline choked back a gasp borne of both relief and disbelief. The demons in the cavern all lay slain. Sidestepping the remains of the demon, he went onto his haunches beside her. Although his voice betrayed no hint of emotion, a glint in his eyes told her he was displeased.

"Didn't I tell you to stay outside?"

Her shoulders tensed. "I was trying to help you."

"*Help* me?"

She gestured at the bloody scores on his cheeks. He gave her an odd look. The second time she'd seen anything but reserve in his expression.

"I am immortal. My wounds heal quickly. Yours do not," he said, as if she needed the reminder. The claw marks at her ankles burned, and her back throbbed, while the wounds on his cheek had already stopped bleeding.

"I couldn't just stand by and watch them attack you," she muttered. "Why didn't you"—Evangeline lifted a shoulder, remembering what he'd done with the winged demon—"send them up in flames or something?"

The grim set of his jaw made her nervous.

"It seems I have completely lost the ability to use the elements."

SIX

The little mortal stared at Declan with her mouth agape. "Wh-what do you mean?"

"This realm has stripped my archabilities." He'd lost his ability to manifest fire and ice. The vital part of him, the part that made him an archmage, was utterly unresponsive —a humbling reminder he was no longer in his own domain.

The last time he'd been this weak, he'd been a boy of a hundred and twenty summers, under his mother's thumb and unable to protect the only person who had ever shown him care. The only person *he* had truly cared about.

At Evangeline's horrified expression, Declan felt the need to provide reassurance. "I still have access to some of my basic abilities." His telekinesis, although weakened, still functioned. And he had been able to summon his sword.

Breaking away from the concern in her eyes, Declan surveyed the cave. Evidence of the cave-dwellers' recent feed lay in the innermost corners—the source of the faint stench of decay, partially hidden by knurled rocks.

"Oh, gods . . . " She followed his line of sight, and her hands flew up to cover her mouth as she discovered the remnants of flesh and bones already in semiputrefaction. Turning paler than he'd thought humanly possible, Evangeline stumbled out of the cavern and retched, though she didn't bring up much. She returned and tucked herself into a little ball with her hands holding her knees, eyes adamantly averted from the bodies that littered the ground.

"We will find better shelter in the morning," Declan said. He was not eager to linger amid the stink and damp filth, either, but her enervated presence made it impossible for them to keep moving in the dark. Her response was a feeble tilt of her chin.

Agitation mounted in his chest. He was trying hard to keep her alive, yet she appeared careworn like parchment soaked in water. More, the wounds on her leg set his teeth on edge. They were no deeper than the scores on his face. Mere scratches. But on her? They appeared severe gashes. A desecration. It was like looking at the crushed petals of a tender bloom.

But Declan was no healer. So he turned away to address what he could.

Using telekinesis, he shoveled the offending bodies against the decomposing carcass. He debated moving the bodies out of the cavern, but a pile of dead cave-dwellers would likely draw unwelcome attention from the local inhabitants. And lethargy was a rising lull in his veins, as though the use of telekinesis now wearied him.

He walked along the perimeter of the cavern, searching for the steady drip of water that had first alerted him to the possibility of life within these walls. He soon found it, a small, precious dribble of fresh water. After he drank, he fashioned the steady rivulet into a sphere of liquid telekinetically suspended in air. Evangeline, who had descended into listless silence, was reanimated as her eyes tracked his movements with open fascination.

He nodded at her. "Cup your hands together."

She blinked with surprise but complied. The smile on her face as he transferred the liquid sphere into her hands soothed something inside him he hadn't realized was ruffled.

"Can I have more?" Her voice wavered, tone uncertain. In response, he directed more water, twirling the liquid tendril in the air for her benefit. "Thank you." She gave a little sigh of pleasure and shot him another small smile.

So easily pleased.

"You need a bandage, and the wound needs to be cleansed regularly."

She grimaced at the grisly pile in the corner and patted the edge of her wound. "And some antiseptic, or I fear it'll get infected."

He eyed the hem of her dress. Soiled.

He untucked his shirt and ripped off a strip from the hem to wrap it tightly over her wound. The resulting gratitude in her eyes was a warmth that trickled into his veins. She lifted her fingers toward his face, then jerked her hand back as though consciously checking herself.

"Does it hurt?" A hesitant question filled with concern.

He frowned. Yet another unexpected query. The last time someone had asked him such a question had been centuries ago. A little girl with sunlight in her voice.

"No." When his response did nothing to remove the concern in her eyes, he added, "It will heal." She did not seem convinced, but she lowered her sight and fidgeted with the makeshift bandage on her leg. Sighed. "If only there were broadyew leaves here. They grow freely in Arns and make an excellent antiseptic."

"Would you be able to recognize other plants with similar properties?" If he could find the source of fresh water, perhaps they would find more than dehydrated bushes.

Her nod held more confidence than he'd seen on her before. "I am an apothecarist, so I know a great deal about plants and their uses." She swallowed, her surety faltering. "But everything seems so different in this realm that I am not sure I'll find what I need." Her gaze skimmed the grazes on his face before returning to her calf. "But I'll try."

For the first time, he realized fine tremors ran down her arms. Where her sleeves ended on her forearm, gooseflesh mottled exposed skin.

He shrugged off his coat. "Put this on."

When she didn't move to accept, he draped it over her shoulders. It dwarfed her small, slender frame. She looked surprised, but she didn't repudiate his offering. Instead, she fingered the lapels of his coat before fixing large, amber eyes on him.

"Won't you be cold without it?"

He shook his head. "I never feel the cold."

He suspected his ability to manipulate both fire and ice worked in tandem on a subconscious level to regulate his body temperature. And perhaps he would soon feel the frigid sting of the air with his archabilities now stripped. But the frosty terrain had yet to impact him, so he had failed to realize she would have not only felt the cold but had likely suffered hiking through the icy plain.

She appeared to consider his response, then murmured almost wistfully, "It must be nice never to feel cold."

Declan didn't tell her his inability to feel the cold did not extend to his mental state. There, he was pure ice. He had no real capacity to feel warmth, not anymore. But it wasn't a bad thing. His thought patterns were often glacial in their clarity.

"Get some rest," he said.

In response, she burrowed deeper into his coat, a soft sigh escaping her lips. "We should be safe here for the night," he added. "No demon will venture into a cave-dweller's nest."

She made an inarticulate sound, and her eyelids fluttered shut. Her head rested on tucked-up knees, the delicate curve of her neck slightly exposed, framed by wisps of rich brown that escaped her braid. More than one color in her hair, he noted. The silken strands, ranging in shade from rich mahogany to turning oak leaves, coiled in a thick plait over her neck and rested over the soft swell of a modest bosom.

He tore his gaze away. What in hellfire was the matter with him? He should venture out, check the surroundings. Without her, he could possibly find better shelter, or maybe even hunt something for food.

But strangely, he didn't like the thought of leaving her here, vulnerable and alone.

Hunkering down beside her, he frowned. Something about her stirred things in him. Memories he'd kept locked in the deepest, most secret part of himself. Memories of a girl with a sunlit voice who had cleaned and dressed his wounds with meticulous care. A girl who read him stories of fantastical beasts and other fabled creatures even though he'd had nothing to offer her in return.

Evangeline stirred, and her head drooped. He shifted closer so her head rested against his arm instead. Despite the cloying stench of iron and decay in the air, she was close enough he scented wildflowers with a hint of cream.

She even smelled like *her*. But that was impossible.

Freya died centuries ago.

Thump. Thump. Thump. A woman's breathless sobs.

The prickly material abraded her skin as she curled into a fetal position on the bed, eyes squeezed shut. Her body convulsed as she heard the animal grunts in the other room and a woman's stifled screams.

"Come here, little girl." A lewd laugh.

Muffled cries she wasn't sure were her own.

Wake, Evangeline.

Evangeline woke with a start, with fear strumming her pulse and disconcertion dancing in her mind. She rubbed her eyes before the full impact of reality hit her. Railea, goddess of light, she had risen from one nightmare straight into another.

Well . . . not quite a nightmare.

Daylight softened the angles of his chiseled frame, his silhouette a picture of masculine perfection framed by unforgiving rocks. He was almost immaculate. The grazes on his face had disappeared overnight, and the only evidence of his current predicament were the slight shadows beneath his eyes and a night's worth of dark stubble. But the roughening of his features only made him more approachable.

More human.

More handsome.

Evangeline blinked. Handsome was almost too bland a word for him. In the soft light of dawn, the archmage was beautiful. Almost offensively so. Perhaps archmages were gods —how else could such beauty manifest in one man?

"You were having a nightmare," he said, drawing her from her unabashed scrutiny of him. Though he couched the sentence like a statement, there was query in his eyes. She must have fallen asleep and slumped against him overnight, and surprisingly he remained beside her, his body an unyielding wall of muscle and heat.

Evangeline scrubbed a hand over her face to remove the cold sweat misting her skin and focused instead on the reassuring warmth by her side. Earthy and unmistakably male, his scent was an intoxication that masked the reek of decay. Still seated beside him, she knew she should move away now she no longer had the excuse of sleep but found herself reluctant to put distance between them.

Evangeline blinked again, and shock had her biting into her lip.

She was utterly unfazed by his *proximity*.

"It's hard not to have nightmares stranded in this hellish world," Evangeline muttered. She hadn't had such vivid nightmares—to the point she could remember snippets of the terror—in a while. Though the dream had been distorted, as if she were viewing unwelcome pieces of her past through a morbid kaleidoscope.

She shivered, inadvertently moving away from him so she could wrap her arms around herself. He continued to look at her with such unwavering focus that she grew self-conscious. He reached out to brush wayward strands of hair from her face. The gesture felt strangely intimate. Warmth bloomed on her cheeks, but her stomach shared none of her sudden shyness, for it grumbled, vying for attention.

The heat on her cheeks intensified. Without a word, he siphoned fresh water from the crevice, twirling them into floating spheres before dropping them gently into her cupped palms.

Her lips parted with reluctant admiration. She had never seen a mage move *liquid*, much less shape it into watery orbs. It might be simple telekinesis on his part, but the effect was almost magical to her.

The moment they ventured out into the open, Evangeline almost felt compelled to return to the musty, horror-filled cavern. The skies were no less dreary this morning. Was it even morning? She couldn't see the sun. Shafts of sunlight lanced through thick clouds, dense as sheep's wool, heralding gale and thunderstorms. Her muscles throbbed, and the wounds on her calf protested at the slightest hint of strain.

Gritting her teeth, she forced herself to match the archmage's pace.

"How many more days will your men take to find you?" She had four days before her meeting with the healer.

"I can't be certain," he said, dashing her hopes. "But they will search until they find me." At the very least, she could find comfort in that.

Sighing, she eyed the sword now sheathed in a leather scabbard across his back. "How did you get it to materialize out of nowhere?"

He shot her an impassive glance. "I am an archmage, and yet you wonder?"

Undeterred, she said, "Well, I didn't realize archmages could make things appear out of thin air."

He raised a brow that finally broke the impassivity of his expression.

"Evangeline, I am an archmage, not a magician. Apart from the elements I control, I cannot create something out of nothing." They came across a small overhang of rocks, and he offered her his hand to help her down. She glanced up at him with surprise.

"The sword is a staverek, forged from metal fortified with my blood. The infusion of my essence allows me to summon it from any distance, even across realms."

"Staverek?" She winced as she hobbled up the increasingly steep incline, leaning heavily on her unwounded leg. "I thought it was a longsword." Evangeline had spent enough days at the Hanesworth Forge to recognize the weapons Stefan sometimes fashioned.

"Stavereks are longswords. Only weightier." He halted suddenly. "Your wounds are hurting." Not a question but an observation.

Already exhausted and utterly annoyed with herself, she shook her head even though the stinging pain on her calf screamed its objection. "I can continue." In the next moment, her worn soles glided gleefully over ice-coated rocks as if to spite her. He jerked her upward before she landed face first on the ground.

"I can carry you."

Evangeline blinked. "What?"

Before he could respond, she tugged free of his hold. "No." She didn't even enjoy hugging Stefan. It was madness to entertain the thought of allowing a man she barely knew—an archmage, no less—to hold her in his arms. If she couldn't even hold her own on the second day, would she survive long enough for the archmage's men to retrieve them?

He frowned at her in silent reprimand but didn't say anything else. He turned on his heel and continued the ascent. Then it occurred to her that the word *no* was probably not one he heard often.

They continued for another torturous stretch that reduced her to a pathetic, panting bundle. Overwhelmed, she blew out a harsh breath and fell to her knees, her muscles begging for a moment's surcease. Warmth oozed at her calf. Fresh blood was seeping through the makeshift bandage.

The archmage backtracked toward her. Though he'd been silent the entire time, he had slowed the pace to a snail's crawl, and even then, he had been yards ahead. She was unquestionably slowing them down.

"I'm . . . I'm sor-ry." She wheezed. "Need some time."

His gaze landed on the stained bandage, and he abruptly shifted the scabbard to his chest. "Climb onto my back."

She stared at him, astonished, even as he whirled around and went down on his haunches with his back toward her. While she was still processing that he was offering her a *piggyback ride*, he added in a tone that brooked no further argument, "Evangeline, I am strong enough to bear your weight, and it will be more efficient for us both if I carry you. We need to find food and shelter by nightfall, or we will be back in that cave tonight."

At the mention of food, her stomach almost yowled. She flattened her lips in frustration. He was right. But riding on an archmage's back?

The idea was so absurd it was almost comical.

At her continued hesitation, he turned to fix eyes of mesmerizing green on her in a silent command. What would he do if she failed to comply? Would he leave her behind? The thought of being stranded here, alone and defenseless, roused such panic it propelled her forward.

She circled loose arms around his shoulders and climbed onto him with as much grace and dignity as she could muster. A sigh escaped her lips at the immediate relief of removing her weight from her tender calf even as a nervous lump formed in her throat. She had never touched a man this way before. She'd embraced less than a handful of men in her lifetime and even then in fleeting instances.

Now, she was straddling him.

Oh, goddess of creation, the man was lean, hard muscle *everywhere*. He was also deliciously warm. Before she could get used to the position, he slid his arms under her knees and locked her into place. A sudden rush of fear filled her like rain spilling into an open well.

If he'd wanted to do anything deviant, he'd had the whole night in the cavern to try it. *He's just trying to help.* Evangeline rolled the words over and over in her mind, willing herself to relax. But locked in such an intimate position—with her legs wrapped around his narrow waist and her body flush against the wall of his stalwart frame—the fear that went hand in hand with her past trauma proved relentless. Just as it'd always been.

A shiver swept down her spine. She swallowed hard, trying to stifle her ragged breaths.

He loosened his arms, as though sensing her restlessness.

Struggling to calm the palpitations in her chest, Evangeline kept one hand slung around his shoulder and used the other to tug at the hem of her skirt. She pulled the fabric to cover as much of her legs as possible to satisfy her sense of modesty.

Thankfully, he remained still. Patient. When she finally stopped fidgeting, he tightened his arms once more and straightened to his full height. She was grateful he kept his palms facing down so he was not touching her unnecessarily. A small gesture, but it eased the rapid pound of her heart, soothed her inexorable fears.

As he adjusted to her weight, his muscles bunched beneath her, creating a mystifying sensation that drew warmth to her cheeks. Her fears ebbed, only to be replaced by a strange, foreign sensation—heat forming low in her belly.

Her breath hitched as he resumed the hike at a much faster pace without displaying even a hint of strain over her added weight. After an interminable moment, she began to relax, lulled by the heady scent of his skin and the easy rhythm of his gait.

"Thank you, Lord Archmage."

He might be inexpressive, almost frigid in his composure,

but he wasn't unsympathetic. Or dishonorable. He didn't need to protect or help her.

But he did.

"I'm really glad you're here," she whispered, needing to express the wave of gratitude that threatened to overwhelm.

This time, she got a brief nod of acknowledgment.

SEVEN

They traveled in a strange, companionable silence as the archmage scaled the highlands of the rocky mountain, wild, dangerous, and pristine in its untouched vastness. As they ventured higher, the skies darkened to an angry gray, while the snow covering climbed to the archmage's knees. Evangeline kept her eyes wide for any shrubbery or plants with medicinal properties, but to her dismay, it was even more barren here than it was down in the plains.

There was not a single hint of green. No signs of life.

Until a subtle glint beckoned from afar.

Evangeline tightened her grip around the archmage's shoulders. "Is that . . . a pond?"

Water. Though she'd drunk her fill in the cave, the arid surroundings had parched her throat. Seemingly spurred by her excitement, he hastened his pace, veering toward the promise of a shimmering oasis. As they came closer, Evangeline's enthusiasm dipped.

A river. A frozen one.

Even her unflappable companion seemed deflated. He released an exhale she construed as disappointment as he surveyed the length of the solid river.

"You can put me down now, Lord Archmage." She wasn't particularly keen to resume hiking. The heat of him was too comforting and his scent too soothing, but she was conscious she'd been riding on his back for what must have been hours.

There was no immediate response, but his arms flexed around her. Almost as if he, too, was reluctant to set her down. "We can't drink from this. And we will make better headway if you remain on my back."

"Aren't you tired?"

"You hardly weigh anything," he replied, continuing down the riverbank without a hitch in his stride. He'd taken a few more paces when she caught sight of tiny fractures shaped like pockmarks littering the ice.

She wriggled on his back. "Please, Lord Archmage, let me down."

When he complied, Evangeline shuffled toward the ice-encrusted edge and winced as she went to her knees. Needles seemed to prick her legs from her sudden animation, and a dull ache reminded her of the wounds on her calf.

Evangeline ignored it all.

She brushed the snow off the ice and scrabbled her fingers against the closest pockmark. The thin film of ice crumbled to reveal running water beneath. With renewed excitement, she plugged a finger into the hole, trying to make a larger opening.

"What are you doing?" The wariness in his tone caused her to withdraw her hand.

"Once, during a particularly cold winter season, the river near my village froze over, and because that was our main source of fresh water, the villagers drilled holes into the surface of the ice to get to the water beneath." She gave the ice an experimental thump of her fist. The tiny pockmarks had reminded her of the event, when they had carved holes large enough that even the forest animals drank from them.

His expression remained indecipherable, but his eyes tracked the pitted surface with obvious circumspection. "It seems too—"

Crack!

With a sudden spray of droplets, something large, something *monstrous*, lunged from beneath the surface, fragmenting large slabs of ice. Evangeline leapt to her feet.

Not fast enough.

A cavernous maw rimmed with rows of needlelike teeth was the last thing she saw before a slick, slate-colored appendage coiled around her hips and hauled her off her feet. She tumbled to the ground, face first, as the creature dragged her toward the river's edge.

The little mortal never got out a scream. Or maybe she did, but her cries were drowned by the behemoth's deafening bellow. It had no eyes. Only a mouthlike orifice brimming with slim fangs that was currently bared at its frantic prey. Declan lunged for her, but her hands slipped from his as the demon dragged her farther. But it didn't try to haul its prey into the water. It secured Evangeline firmly at the river's edge as a spindly protrusion extended from the orifice, dripping with sputum, poised like the tail of a scorpion.

Ready to strike.

With a low oath, Declan slammed a hefty dose of telekinesis into the demon's tubular head, knocking the creature sideways. It staggered and swayed, upending more ice as it sloshed about. Without giving it an opportunity to recover, he unsheathed his sword and warped close enough to hack into the tail still wrapped around Evangeline. Severed it completely. The demon released an ululating wail before retreating beneath the icy surface, bubbles rising in its wake.

The water stilled.

Evangeline sucked in rasping breaths as she stared at the severed slate-colored tail, now flopping bonelessly on the ground.

"Nerofidi," Declan muttered past his waning adrenaline. A freshwater demon that had likely drilled holes into the ice—for breathing purposes, perhaps. Or to lure prey desperate for water. He turned to the mortal and swallowed the uncanny surge of relief at seeing her unharmed.

Not really. Her calf was bleeding again.

He sheathed his sword, intending to pick her up, but he'd barely taken two steps when an insidious splash told him turning his back to the river had been a grave mistake. A flare of pain struck his shoulder, ripping through his linen shirt and driving deep into flesh.

Fuck! Instant numbness coursed through his back.

"No!" Evangeline's cry barely registered before something fleshy slicked around his torso and he went crashing headfirst into the river.

Ice water gushed into his lungs, shocking his system even as he thrashed. But his arms felt like the nerofidi's recently relieved tail. Boneless. Useless.

From the feeble shafts of light piercing the murky depths, it became apparent the appendage he'd severed was no tail, but merely one of the many tentacles extending from the demon's cylindrical head.

The nerofidi tightened its grip, dragging him deeper into the river.

True panic reared in Declan's chest when his lungs burned for breath. He couldn't warp. Not when his torso was slowly growing paralyzed. His strength had quickly dwindled, his arms deadweight.

He struck out telekinetically to loosen the creature's hold and kicked his way up to the surface. He took one gasp of precious air before something tightened around his ankle, tearing him back down into the depths. Water displaced the air in his lungs.

He was going to die.

Immortals might survive drowning, but only if their lungs were emptied of water. And he wouldn't have that chance if the creature devoured him while he was unconscious.

Evangeline would be left to fend for herself.

No. Declan had no qualms facing death, but he wouldn't leave the little mortal defenseless in this realm. As consciousness waned, he lashed out with his mind—the final weapon in his arsenal—cleaving the waters with a whiplash of mental energy. The bind around his ankle loosened; the waters turned inky.

Blood.

He was steeped in the demon's blood. He had managed to rend it in half. Triumph surged in his chest even as his lungs scorched for air. With a final burst of telekinesis, he propelled his body up to the surface. Declan flailed with enervated limbs, straining to keep his head above the water, but it was no use. The numbness from the demon's sting had spread to his mind, snaring his consciousness in cobwebs, dimming his vision. Water crashed over his head, and bubbles escaped his lips as he sank.

Evangeline stared at the river, willing the archmage to emerge once more. Willing any signs of life. But the waters remained deceptively calm. Time crawled at an agonizing speed as her heart pummeled against her ribcage. He was an *archmage*. Immortal. Surely he could free himself?

But the creature had struck him.

Railea's tears, what if he was already *dead*?

The water churned with swirls of black, as though someone had emptied an inkwell into the river. Then there he was, his head breaking the surface. He was alive! But her relief was short-lived, for he thrashed, as though struggling to stay afloat.

Could he not swim? Why wasn't he teleporting?

Evangeline charged to the river's edge. She had to help him. He was her only hope of ever returning to Amereen, and if he was dead, his men would never find him. She'd die out here. More, she couldn't possibly live with herself.

Without giving herself another chance to think, she dove into the river. Evangeline had spent many summer days swimming with Stefan in a tiny lake hidden in the forest surrounding Arns. She was adept in water. But nothing could have prepared her for the stinging cold or the sudden pain streaking up her calf.

Ignoring it, she swam to where the archmage floundered. She caught the edge of his collar and drew him close enough to loop an arm around him. Positioning her body beneath his, she buoyed him over her chest, trying to keep his head above the choppy water. She sputtered and coughed as mouthfuls of the river—blood laced with a vile tang of sulfur—made its way into her throat.

He had gone still, his body offering no resistance and no help.

Mages were not truly immortal. They died from fatal wounds. Drowning might not be a wound, but it was certainly fatal. Wasn't it? And the freshwater demon . . . where was it?

Was it lurking beneath them this very moment?

Evangeline refused to give into fear. She focused instead on attempting to swim on her back, using her legs to propel them toward the riverbank. But the gods were merciless. The waters churned. Pieces of ice swirled, as though dancing to a rhythm roiling beneath the surface. A heavy undercurrent caught her feet, trying to tug her down.

No matter how she defied the undercurrent with desperate pumps of her legs, the river's edge came no closer. Logic told her to let the archmage go. To save herself. Unconscious, he was too large. Too heavy. They would both drown.

But she couldn't let him go. She simply *couldn't*.

She let out a sob when her injured calf began to cramp. When her leg finally gave way, she submerged momentarily, and the archmage slipped from her hold. His head disappeared beneath the surface as though weighed down by rocks. Her horror lasted only a moment before water crashed over her head again.

The river was swallowing her, too.

EIGHT

E vangeline thrashed against the momentum of the undercurrent, fighting the swirling waters with futile strokes of her limbs. She was dragged under and slammed against something hard. Her hands scraped the smoothness of stone, but she was sucked down too rapidly to find anchor.

Just as her lungs began to burn, the river spat her out in a torrential gush. She caught a precious gasp of air before she was submerged again. The waters were distinctly warmer here, and less choppy. Evangeline kicked her legs, led only by instinct. She broke the water's surface and bobbed in place, trying to regain her bearings. Disorientation was a fog across her senses, followed by a fresh wave of terror. What had happened to the archmage? It was so dark she could well still be underwater if not for the blessed air filling her lungs.

When her vision adjusted, she realized she was no longer in the river but in a pool of some sort. In the place of gloomy skies was a natural ceiling of concave rock. Cracks patterned the timeworn walls, feeding stray shards of light into the cavernous room. A heavy waterfall cascaded from a crevice high in the rock. The river must have drawn her down a sink-hole, which emptied into this underground pool.

Her frantic gaze darted, only for dread to seize her chest.

A body floated nearby.

The archmage was drifting face down in the water.

Without the churning undercurrent to deter her, Evangeline reached him quickly. The pool wasn't particularly deep, and if she allowed herself to sink, she could touch its grainy surface with her toes. Drawing him by an arm, she half swam, half towed him across the pool. It was an excruciatingly slow process. She hauled herself over the edge first before dragging him up by the shoulders. He might not be burly the way Stefan was, but the archmage was still pure muscle. His drenched clothes added to his weight. The water gushed off him as she drew him over the ledge, bit by bit, using her knees as leverage.

The pool was no natural spring. Rather, the edges of the stone were whittled down to form smooth, curved edges. Man-made.

Another glance around her new environment sent a renewed chill down her spine, one that wasn't from the cold. The temperature had risen. In fact, it was almost warm. But urgency didn't give her time to ponder.

The archmage's skin was ashen, his lips bluish.

"Wake up," she whispered, patting his cheeks. Not a single flutter of his eyelash.

Railea's tears, his chest wasn't moving.

She rolled him onto his stomach and gasped. A gruesome, spindly protrusion was rooted in his left shoulder. She would deal with that later.

Now, she had to clear out his lungs.

She pumped his back with both her palms. No use. Her

motions were too slight. Evangeline clambered over his waist, using her body weight to aid the process. She didn't know how long she pumped, driven by fear and desperation and a wild panic. *Please don't die, please don't die, please don't die . . .*

The archmage finally emitted a gurgling cough, water dribbling from his lips, and relief swept her in dizzying circles. But his complexion remained pallid, and he made no other movement.

She rolled him onto his back and checked his pulse.

If he had one, she couldn't feel it.

With a frenzied sob, Evangeline put her lips against his cold, death-tinged ones and breathed into his lungs, willing him to reanimate.

"Please, Archmage," she whispered between breaths. "Wake up."

Declan could hear *her*. Freya's cries of distress. Screaming for him. He had to get to her. He tried to move, but his muscles were wooden. Useless. He'd always been useless.

Freya . . .

Air sliced through his lungs, forcing him to breathe.

Darkness retreated from his vision, and he was staring into eyes of liquid amber, so pure they were like crystalline fire.

"Oh, praise all the gods," she gasped. "You're alive!"

Declan blinked.

A slight weight rested on his core. It took him another slow blink to realize the little mortal was seated. Upon him. Her slender legs straddled his waist. And her soppy skirt was scrunched high, leaving an inordinate amount of bare skin exposed to his view. Swallowing, Declan dragged his gaze away from the display of creamy skin back to her eyes.

Wet tendrils of her hair kissed her face while her dress hugged her frame. Drenched and a little breathless, but she appeared otherwise unharmed. Relief caused him to drag in a deeper breath.

"What happened?" His words came out hoarse and his tone a whole lot weaker than he was comfortable with.

"I thought you were gone." At the fear threading her words, he reached for her, but his sluggish arm brushed against her bare leg. She pushed up and away from him abruptly as though she'd been branded.

As she straightened her skirt, he attempted to sit up, but his limbs weighed heavy, as though lead filled his veins instead of blood. And his head throbbed like his skull was fractured. He tried bending his knees to move his legs, but only succeeded in tiring them. Vaguely, he recalled her arm around him before he'd slipped beneath the current. She'd jumped in *after* him.

Foolish, foolish mortal.

She could have drowned.

He turned his head toward the sound of rushing water to see a gushing fall emptying into a pool. "Where are we?"

When he remained recumbent, she sidled close to lift his head onto her lap, as though sensing his need to get up. Using herself as an anchor, she drew him up so his head rested over her collarbone with his back propped against her chest.

"I think we may be in some sort of . . . abandoned temple," she murmured, stroking his hair from his forehead, handling him like a child.

Mortified, Declan resisted sluggishly, attempting to swat away her coddling hands.

"Stop it," she chided without bite in her tone. "Or would you prefer for me to lay you back on the ground?"

It was no hardship enduring her gentle ministrations, yet he despised it. It made him feel exposed in the worst possible way. Weak. But the feeling of vulnerability was worse if he remained on his back, so he stilled and allowed her to hold him as he studied their new environment.

The walls were uneven stone, etched with depictions of serpentine demons and mosaicked with pieces of dull tiles limned by lichen. The pool, nestled amid pieces of rubble—broken tiles, fallen columns, and fragmented carvings—stretched wide enough to be a communal bathhouse. And it was filling steadily with water he guessed came from the river that flowed high above the walls.

His telekinesis had done more than cleave the freshwater demon apart; it must have also damaged the riverbed, depositing them in this subterranean structure.

Instead of overflowing, the pool emptied into five canals fanning into domed openings carved into the stone walls—drainage canals that stretched beyond his line of vision. Yet shafts of light crept through cracks in the walls, illuminating swirling dust motes in his vision, which told him they were not trapped.

The canals would lead somewhere.

Scattered on the stone ground were broken pottery and clay vases, torn carpets, and other detritus that made him think of pagan worship and ancient ruins. But the carvings etched into the walls were what must have led to her conclusion about their current whereabouts.

As Declan studied them, he made out Draedyn, the god of death. The god was seated on a dais with a pack of wolflike beasts by his side. Lykosa. Before him was a procession of gliders, the humanoid race of demons who thrived in this realm. Gliders were depicted as regular people, only they possessed a long, serpentine tail in the place of legs. And in their arms, they carried humans, small enough to be children.

Children who were bound at the hands and feet, presented to Draedyn's dogs as sacrificial offerings.

T he archmage remained still and silent as he studied the wall's carvings while Evangeline wondered *who* had etched them into stone. She held him close, dimly aware of the indecency of their position, with him propped up against her chest. But she couldn't bear to push him away. For reasons that went beyond her own survival, she was simply glad he breathed.

That he lived.

And perhaps it was because his breathing remained ragged, or because he could barely hold himself upright, but she felt no fear or revulsion from cradling him in her arms.

"I should check your shoulder," she said when she judged him more alert. His movements remained sluggish, but he allowed her to lower him back to the ground onto his chest.

Even though she already knew what to expect, the sight of his gouged shoulder made her grimace anew. "The demon left a part of itself lodged in your flesh."

His breath came out in a soft growl. "Take it out."

She slid a hand down his front and urged him up. He shoved up to his elbows, his motions uncoordinated as she hovered over him, unbuttoning his shirt. Drawing the damp linen off his skin revealed the demon's black stinger, hard like the end of a lobster's tail, embedded above his left shoulder blade.

She clamped her fingers around the stinger and gave a gentle tug.

His hiss halted her instantly.

Evangeline winced. "I'm so sorry."

"Don't stop." His voice was strained, muffled against the ground.

She swallowed. The stinger was planted deep.

As though sensing her hesitation, he urged, "Take it out, little mortal. It is only hampering my body's ability to heal."

He was right. Remembering how quickly the scrapes on his cheek had knitted back together, Evangeline gripped the offending protrusion with renewed determination. Tugged. He made no sound this time, his body taut despite the blood welling at the edges of the wound.

"I'm sorry," she repeated.

He didn't even grunt.

Steeling herself, Evangeline pulled harder. Another fraction of the stinger extruded, but still it seemed firmly embedded. She continued to pry the stinger out, as gently as she could, until she realized it was *barbed*. The whole time, she'd been drawing fresh wounds through his shoulder by trying to rip the thing out.

And the archmage had remained silent through it all.

One look at his face and she knew he'd felt the pain. His body was taut, his jaw clenched tight, and his eyes firmly shut.

Merciful heavens, she was hurting him.

"I can't do this." Not without something to numb his pain.

He sucked in another strained breath. "It needs to come out."

With quivering hands, she glared at the blasted stinger. Perhaps she should rip it out quickly to spare him the pain. Then she remembered his sword. If she could make a small incision, it might make it easier to remove the stinger entirely.

"Your sword was lost in the river," she said. "Can you summon it?"

"You want to hack off my shoulder to rid me of the stinger?" There was a wry quality in his tone despite the threadiness of his voice. She pursed her lips. She needed a sharp tool to make an incision, but the archmage's sword was likely too heavy for her to wield anyway. When she told him of her intention, he shifted slightly to his unharmed side, cradling his palm with a look of concentration on his face. Gold flared from the glyphs on his skin, building up like molten lava to surge toward his palms, but instead of his sword, a wicked-looking dagger materialized in his hand.

"You'll find this more suitable to the task," he muttered, slumping back onto his chest when she took the dagger from him. Where his sword was unadorned lethality, this dagger seemed too ornate to be a weapon, its hilt studded with shimmering bloodred jewels.

"How many blood-bonded weapons do you own?"

"This is the *draga sul*. Not blooded to me. Rather, a magical artifact under my guardianship. But it is the only weapon accessible to me that is small enough for you to wield. Now, cut out the damned thing."

The dagger was hefty in her hand, but not too heavy for her use.

"Much better than the sword," she agreed, trying to keep her tone light.

She gritted her teeth and sliced the tip of the dagger through his flesh, carving out a clean line so she could remove the stinger without mangling more of his skin. Blood welled to obscure her incision. Her throat tightened, but she continued to run the blade down, wanting to do it as quickly as possible, knowing every lingering minute prolonged his pain.

The stinger turned out to be a spindle the length of her middle finger with a viciously barbed head that reminded her of the tip of an arrow. When it finally came loose, Evangeline hissed victoriously and threw the cursed thing as far as she could. It hit the stone wall featuring the grisly sacrificial procession, smattering the carving with droplets of blood before bouncing off to clatter behind one of the fallen columns.

She hurried back to the pool and scooped a handful of water to rinse the gaping wound in the archmage's shoulder. Prodding gently, she examined the injury for any remnants of the demon's barb. The bleeding had already slowed to a sluggish dribble, the deepest recesses of his wound knitting together before her eyes—the wonders of an immortal's regenerative abilities.

"It's done," she murmured as she withdrew her fingers.

The archmage released a shuddering breath, his body slackening like a released bow. His lashes feathered against his cheek. Evangeline slumped beside him, her own exhaustion stealing her breath. It would take his men days to find him, he'd said.

This was only their second day.

She had barely shut her eyes when a scuttling sound where the stinger had landed caused a fresh prickle of fear down her spine. Evangeline wiped her bloody hands on her skirt and reclaimed the blade. Ensconced in the shadows, staring right at her, were a pair of red, glowing eyes.

NINE

When Declan came to consciousness, the searing pain in his shoulder had ebbed to a dull throb. An involuntary groan left his lips. For the first time in centuries, his entire body *hurt*. His head remained groggy, his muscles wound too tight, his joints inflamed. Venom still coursed in his blood, dulling his body's natural ability to heal itself. He cracked his lids open. His vision swam with specks of white.

He shut his eyes once more to allow his thoughts to clear.

He would have drowned in the pool. The freshwater demon's venom would have kept him paralyzed and submerged long enough that his lungs would have suffered an irreversible, fatal intake of water. Five blazing hells, he would have died in the river had the little mortal not jumped in after him.

She'd saved his life.

The knowledge hit him like a stab of the demon's stinger in his gut. The *little mortal* had saved *his* life.

Declan peeled his eyes open again.

Why was it so quiet? The only thing he heard was the echo of the river, still pouring in a steady torrent into the pool. But where was she? As his eyes adjusted to the darkness, he realized light no longer spilled in from the cracks in the stone walls, telling him dusk had well and truly fallen.

Yet, flickering shadows danced, illuminating the macabre stone carvings. A fire. Where was the fire coming from?

"Evangeline?" he mumbled, his throat dry, his voice croaky. The little mortal was nowhere in sight. A foreign pang of emotion washed through him. Fear. Using the wall as leverage, he drew himself onto his legs, wobbly like an infant calf.

"Evangeline?" he called again, louder this time. There was a pitch of uncertainty in his voice that revealed something akin to panic. He didn't care for it.

"Where are you, little mortal?" he growled. He pushed past the grogginess in his head and reached out with telepathy to probe for her mind.

He found it—a shimmering glow on the telepathic plane, the only spark of life in the darkness of Draedyn's temple— just as her faraway voice met his ears.

"Lord Archmage?" She sounded unharmed, but afraid. "I'm in here."

Declan stalked in the direction of her voice, trailing past the pool, stumbling past the toppled columns to find a vestibule filled with a clutter of processional carvings and ruins. The antechamber emptied into a wide tunnel framed by an arched doorway. The tunnel was smooth and straight, its stone walls unadorned by carvings but lined with sconces that must have once lit the path toward a series of smaller chambers.

But the source of Evangeline's voice, the essence of her mind, and the flickering glow came from the furthest chamber, the one with the largest doorway at the very end of the tunnel.

Declan made his way toward it, his fingers displacing a film of dust as he passed. By the first doorway, ivory bones were piled close to the threshold. Femur bones. Human.

He peered into the second antechamber. It was sepulchral, but the flickering light from the main tunnel allowed him to see the manacles fastened to the walls. More bones lay heaped inside. He caught the roundness of a skull.

Disquiet rippled down his spine. "Evangeline?"

Silence. Urgency ratcheted in his chest, and he sped down the tunnel, ignoring the other chambers as he passed, his feet heavy on the tightly packed dirt floor until he arrived at what must be the main cella of the temple.

A bronze statue of an imperial god glared down at him with one eye from a disfigured face. Draedyn. Only the god of death had a face licked by hellfire. A mask of a horned skull obscured the other side of his face. The god lounged on his throne high upon the dais, overlooking an arena of sorts enclosed by a stone fence. Crumbled pillars engraved with acanthus leaves, ceremonial pottery etched with drawings, and other pieces of rock and relic lay in a sacrilegious heap on the ground.

Tension left his shoulders. There she was. Huddled with her back against the wall just paces from the entryway. Her arms were wrapped tightly around herself, and her chest heaved as she breathed in shallow gasps. In one hand she still clutched his blade as though it anchored her to sanity.

Declan was beside her in an instant. "What happened?"

She continued to wheeze, gulping air like she was in danger of drowning.

Breathe, Evangeline. He touched her telepathically without conscious thought, trying to penetrate the haze of panic, but was careful to keep his telepathic voice soft. He'd scared her before. *Calm down and breathe. In and out.*

He battled a wave of light-headedness and went to his haunches, reaching out with one hand to brush the stray strands of hair off her face. With the other he stroked her back the way he would a frightened mare until her breathing evened.

"Archmage." Her voice wavered as she looked at him with glassy eyes. "You're awake."

"What happened?" he repeated.

"I . . . I haven't felt s-such a-anxiety in a long time," she said when she could finally speak again, hands trembling like her speech. He remembered the way she'd held him propped up against her chest and now fought the urge to tuck her against his own. Instead, he forced his hands to drop to his sides.

"What terrifies you so?"

She took another trembling breath before shaking her head as though she couldn't speak. Then she gestured to the center of the arena. A large basin of tarnished gold stood bolted to the ground. It was the size of a bathtub, large enough to fit a grown man. Instead of water, it was filled with oil, and there lapped a modest flame—the source of flickering light that had illuminated the tunnels and bounced off the walls.

It took him a moment to realize Draedyn's was not the only statue in the chamber. Stone figurines of snarling demons flanked the god of death. More lykosa. Creatures that resembled a cross between a bear and a wolf with razor-like protrusions along the spine. They were portrayed with their lips peeled to reveal stone teeth, snarling at unseen prey.

Declan took in the crudely fashioned stone fence surrounding the basin and the manacles bolted closed. Fresh understanding tightened his lips. This was no cella. It was Draedyn's sacrificial altar.

Being chained so close, skin would blister and not burn; blood would simmer and not boil. It would ensure a slow and torturous death . . .

And evidence of such offerings cluttered the ground. Skeletons. The upper halves all appeared humanlike, but some had no hip bones. They had long, twisted spines that stretched out like a serpent's tail. But most were unmistakably human, with distinguishable pelvic bones attached to femurs and tibias. The most disturbing were their collective *sizes*. They were notably short. Small.

Children.

Distaste rose to the back of his throat. The young, the innocent, would always be the most vulnerable. Declan glanced down at the woman who embodied the very innocence he'd once been denied, a woman who was now curled up by the wall, inhaling uneven breaths. After confronting these remains, it was no surprise she was frightened. Yet, on the psychic plane, her mind emitted waves of rippling panic that seemed to overwhelm the shock.

It felt raw.

"The temple appears long abandoned, little mortal . . . Whatever happened here happened a long time ago."

She just shook her head, hands wrapped tightly around herself. Amid the ruins, she looked even smaller. Vulnerable.

Declan nodded at the smoldering basin. "How is there a fire here?"

She stared up at him blankly. He nodded again to the fire.

"It was getting dark, and I was afraid we'd be in complete darkness the moment dusk fell . . ." She gestured wordlessly to the rubble and debris around her. Not random detritus. She'd gathered pieces of flint and other stones.

The little mortal was proving to be a resourceful creature.

"But I had no firewood. Then I noticed the tunnel and

followed it down into this chamber. It had already grown so dark, yet the basin glowed. Then I realized there was oil in it. So I tried to make a fire."

When her words slowed, Declan nodded, urging her to continue.

She dipped her chin, clasping his blade with both hands. "When I managed to start an ember, I threw the tinder into the basin. The flames grew, and I was so pleased with myself. Then, the chamber lit up, and I saw . . . " She shuddered, curling deeper into herself. "I saw . . . "

But there was more to the story. His blade was not merely stained with red—his own blood—but the tip was also flecked with black. Demon gore.

"What else happened?" he prompted, gesturing at the dagger.

She exhaled and lifted a quivering finger, pointing to the far side of the burning basin. Then he saw it. Laid neatly among rubble where there were no bones was a small, furry creature.

Curiosity had him striding over to inspect it.

A rodent. Or he supposed it was the shadow realm version of a rat. It had the same ratlike head, the same furry body, and a scaly tail. The only difference was this creature was the size of a small dog, with boar-like tusks and hooves instead of claws. Black gore oozed from a small wound in its flank.

Declan returned swiftly to her side, filled with disbelief. "You killed it?"

She squirmed. "I really, really hate rats."

He gave her body a renewed inspection. "Did it hurt you?"

"It was trying to hurt *you*. I think it was attracted to blood. Before I found this chamber, I couldn't get you to wake up, and the thing kept skittering around the edges."

She wrinkled her nose. "So I pretended to sleep and

remained still enough the demon thought you unprotected. When it came for you, I drove the blade into its flank. Then I thought . . . well, if I could cook it, we could eat it."

If Declan hadn't perfected centuries of impassivity, his jaw would have hung. Even so, his lips parted. "You killed a demon rat," he said, suddenly humbled by her attempts to protect him. "Then decided it would serve as nourishment?"

She hung her head as though in shame, hand still not relinquishing his blade.

"I'm really hungry . . ."

Declan's lips twitched. Amusement tickled his throat. Another emotion rare enough it felt foreign. He sobered quickly when he noticed the bloodstained bandage around her calf that clung in tatters. The scores caused by the cave-dweller's claws still hadn't scabbed, reminding him she was mortal.

The demon rat could have severely injured her.

If he hadn't given her the *draga sul*, the creature might have even killed her.

Another thread of fear stitched in his chest at what *could* have happened while he was unconscious. He returned to his knees and reached for her leg.

She glanced up, startled. "What are you doing?"

"Checking your wound. Then I'll cook the rat."

TEN

The archmage tugged off Evangeline's boots unceremoniously to reveal her now ragged stockings before leaning closer to inspect her calf. His long fingers worked to loosen her makeshift bandage with a gentleness that contested her preconception of archmages. How could a being with such tremendous power be capable of such featherlike touches?

He ran a finger around the edge of her wound, sending a strange, frisson of warmth across her skin. Her cheeks burned, but it seemed she was the only one affected. He showed no expression as he studied her injuries. So close, she could see the perfection of his sculpted mouth, the bottom lip slightly fuller than the top.

Lips she now knew to be soft.

"How is your shoulder?" she asked. Apart from his bloodied shirt and river-slicked hair, all evidence of the man who had lain limp in her arms was gone, along with all traces of vulnerability.

"Fine," he said as he tightened her bandages, as though he'd been stung by nothing larger than a mosquito.

"Fine?" she parroted, incredulous.

"It will heal when the venom clears from my system."

Not fully recovered, then. "Let me see."

"No." His response was a little more than a grunt. Like that of an obstinate child.

She reached over to tug on the blood-soaked fabric at his shoulder. "Show me."

His long eyelashes flicked up, and his eyes, the color of springtime ferns flecked with shades of rich forests, bored into hers. His annoyance was plain.

"Remember to whom you speak, little mortal."

As soon as the rebuke left his lips, she flinched, and the hurt in her expression chastened him. Declan ground his teeth, suddenly feeling very much like the rear end of a mule. He forced himself to cough up words he hardly ever had cause to use.

"Thank you."

She glanced up at him warily.

"For helping me," he added. *For saving my life. For protecting me while I was unconscious.* But he uttered none of that aloud.

"I . . . should not have disturbed the ice," she said meekly. "It is my fault we are here."

"Indeed," he agreed, and she dipped her chin again. "You have led us to shelter."

Her gaze returned to his, blinking. Then a small smile lit her face, and he found himself transfixed.

"And dinner," she said with a teasing note in her voice.

She cocked her head at him, but when his expression

didn't change, the coaxing smile dropped from her lips. Declan hadn't smiled, but it didn't mean he wasn't amused.

To wear emotion on one's face was to bare a part of oneself to the world.

A weakness. A form of vulnerability he'd long ago learned to master.

"Does it still pain you?" she asked softly, clearly unwilling to let the matter rest.

"No," he lied despite the needling protest in his shoulder. It was pointless to dwell upon it. Acknowledging something only gave it more power, and pain was no different from any other emotion.

She seemed mollified, for she nodded and sighed at the sight of her own wounds, shallow compared to his, but no less tender.

"I wish I could heal like an immortal, too." As if immortality were a gift.

Immortality might ensure rapid healing of physical wounds, but it didn't make one immune to pain. Nor did it heal unseen hurts, the sort sustained in the heart. Being immortal only meant you learned to live with scars hidden beneath a mask of physical vitality. But Declan said nothing as he tightened the makeshift bandage around her calf, trying not to be distracted by the sight of her slender ankles. His fingers itched to remove the remnants of her stockings so he could stroke the feminine arch of her foot.

Abruptly, he drew his hands away, annoyed by his straying thoughts. He met her eyes only to realize she was staring at him, seemingly oblivious to the potent effect of her gaze. A charming shade of rose spread across her cheeks, and Declan had the strongest urge to breach the distance, to find out whether those pink lips were truly as soft as they appeared.

"Do you think Stefan is all right?" she blurted, disrupting his reverie.

He gritted his teeth. And she probably belonged to another man. He might be an archmage, but he would never poach on what was not his to take. He was not his father.

"I don't think his injury was fatal." Mortal or not, if Stefan received immediate medical attention, he would likely survive.

Worry continued to pinch her lips.

"My battlemages would have seen to the safety of the people in the square."

She nodded slowly before a contemplative frown overtook her expression. "Those soldiers . . . they were Unseelie, weren't they? Why were they harming innocents?"

He firmed his jaw. The fae were ostensibly attacking random targets.

One of them, Stefan.

Instead of answering her question, he said, "Tell me, little mortal." Because he couldn't seem to help himself. "This Stefan, is he your lover?"

Her eyes rounded, and she shook her head. "We are friends."

At her startled response, Declan's shoulders relaxed. "Do you know the sort of company he usually keeps?"

Her gaze widened further. Such expressive eyes. "What are you asking, Lord Archmage?"

He allowed silence to set in while annoyance flattened her lips and clipped her tone.

"If you're insinuating that Stefan"—she let out an indignant huff—"had something to do with the attack, then you're completely off the mark." She crossed her arms. "Stefan may appear a little rough, but he's a gentleman."

When Declan remained quiet, she curled her hands into

little fists. "He works at the village forge as a blacksmith. If he has spare time, he usually spends it doing odd jobs for the elderly. He is a good man, my lord archmage."

"Declan," he said. "My name is Declan Thorne." He rarely heard his name, and he had the sudden urge to hear it on her lips. She blinked, seemingly thrown by his correction. At her hesitation, he prodded, "He hasn't done anything out of the ordinary? Disappeared for stretches at a time?"

Her jaw tightened. Did she realize she was glowering at an archmage?

"*No.*"

He let the matter rest. Evangeline's loyalty to the man seemed concrete. If this Stefan had been involved in any unsavory activity, he would find out soon enough. In his absence, Killian, as lord commander, would assume authority. And Declan had no doubt Killian would investigate every individual in the square at the time.

It was as if the assailants had attacked due to King Zephyr's simple desire to wreak chaos. The Unseelie were abhorrent creatures, and the Unseelie king of the Winter Court had always taken perverse pleasure in causing pandemonium. But only a fool would think the attacks were random. And Declan was no fool.

"There has always been contention between the Echelon and the Winter Court," Declan murmured. Bloomed from a seed of discord Declan's father had sown when he'd decided to enjoy a taste of Zephyr's queen. "And in recent times the Unseelie king has encouraged the workings of his cartel, impinging on our lands, stealing our resources, and trafficking our citizens."

At the latter, Evangeline shuddered as though a draft had entered the room. Her eyes flitted to the bones by the foot of the basin, and her breath hitched audibly.

"These human bones came from *our* realm?"

"L ikely," the archmage said, giving voice to the nausea brewing in her gut. "After all, humans only exist in our world and Chonsea's Realm."

Evangeline had heard of the slave-trade cartel, of course. Malcolm had told her plenty of stories and his heroics. Only she had never known the fate of the trafficked victims.

"Are all the victims of the cartel sold as sacrifices?"

"No."

Her relief at his response lasted for a short while.

"What else are the victims used for?" she asked quietly.

There was a pause before he answered. "That would depend on *where* and to *whom* they are sold."

Evangeline shut her eyes to keep from viewing the remains of lost souls who had suffered unjust and unclean deaths a long time ago. "And you're aware of the cartel's operations?"

He gave a brisk nod. He was a man, she'd quickly realized, who spoke only when he had something to say. Otherwise he was quite comfortable remaining silent.

She was not.

"Are you working to stop the cartel?"

He gave another resolute nod, which eased the trepidation in her heart. Only a little.

"What about those who are still enslaved? What will you do to bring them home?"

Even though she lacked concrete memories, the ramifications of the cartel had always resonated with her. Evangeline understood what it felt like to be caged. To be held in chains. And to be held prisoner here, in this realm as barren and cold as it was uninhabitable, to be slave to . . . whatever demon they'd been sold to, had to be beyond a nightmare.

"Nothing."

The dismissive response rolled off his tongue so easily that she gaped. Then she licked her lips and rephrased her query. "Surely you have plans to retrieve them?"

He lifted a single dark brow. "No."

Evangeline released an incredulous breath. "You can't be serious."

"The Echelon," he said, "is working to stem the cartel's operations, Evangeline. But the cartel has been discreet. Employing nondescript operators and abducting only those no one would miss—making it extremely hard for us to track them."

He stared down at her, lofty in his stance. "If we were to start rescuing trafficked victims, it would only serve to tip off the cartel. The linchpins would disappear and crawl into their hiding places, and we would never be able to destroy the operation from the core."

She clenched her fist. "And that makes it justifiable? To knowingly abandon the people from our realm? Slaves to demons?"

A glint in his eye told her he did not care for her response.

"They are mostly human, Evangeline. They will expire soon enough. An interdimensional rescue expedition would require elite manpower. And we would need to hire the private resources of faekind to open portals. It is a foolhardy excursion to save the lives of those who would have been weak to begin with. They likely offer no real contribution to our realm. Their suffering, fleeting as it is, does not warrant such a vast expense of resources and energy."

She ground her teeth so hard that her jaw felt sore. What utter horseshit. "They are human. Just like me! Why are you helping me now? Why not leave me here to die? I will—how did you put it?—*expire* soon enough anyway!"

Her fervent outburst elicited nothing but the slight hardening of his lips.

"There is no real expense for me to help you, as I am already here."

She stared at him, unable to believe the cold, heartless way he rationalized his actions. As if everything he'd done so far was out of simple convenience. As if he considered the outcomes of all his actions based purely on the cost and benefit to his lands.

But of course he did.

Since he'd carried her on his back, she'd been warming up to him. Expecting him to act and think as if he had human scruples, but he wasn't human. He was an archmage. Why would he understand human suffering? He would live to see at least three thousand years, while she would be lucky to see a hundred. Her idea of an eternity was ephemeral to him.

"No matter what you may think, we are all people. Our suffering, fleeting though it may be to you and your kind, is real. It counts. It *matters*." Vehemence gave her voice a caustic edge. "Everyone deserves to be free."

His eyes darkened to midnight forests. "You're thinking of every individual as if they were born equal. They are not. And in the grand scheme of things, the slaves are a minute fraction of a greater populace. To expend such vast amounts of energy and resources to save the lives of the few—the weak—yields no benefit. No political or economic gain."

Evangeline clenched her fists.

He might have scaled a mountain carrying her on his back, saved her from falling prey to demons . . . but he'd just proven himself the most callous man she'd ever had the misfortune of meeting.

ELEVEN

"Be careful out there."

Declan paused. Those were the first words she'd uttered since their disagreement. "Get some rest," he said as he resumed his stride toward the tunnel. "You'll be safe in here."

She nodded once, barely glancing at him. Her flinty gaze and rigid posture told him she was upset with him. Angry. Their conflict continued to simmer in an open gulf between them.

Nursing his own displeasure, he hadn't attempted to bridge the gulf.

She'd tested his patience to the hilt. Never had anyone—much less a mortal—spoken to him with such boldness, challenged him with such open defiance, glared at him with such derision. As if she had the right to judge his decisions. To judge *him.* Had the conversation occurred in his court, she would have been severely punished for the insolence of her tone alone.

Yet her words abraded.

He'd replayed the conversation in his head several times over, and it only served to stoke his anger. He had always been slow to the combustive emotion, and he had been startled to realize that the real cause of his anger wasn't her insolence. It was her look of censure. It grated at him that she did not approve.

Why did her opinion even matter? She was but a mortal.

Disgruntled, Declan had settled down to skin the demon rodent only to discover the creature appeared an unpalatable food choice and was likely not safe for consumption even if cooked through. The black gore leaking from where Evangeline had punctured its gut puddled into a little pool crawling with maggot-like creatures. As a bottom feeder, its meat could harbor toxic properties. It would likely not harm him—but he wasn't willing to test it on Evangeline's human constitution.

Before he rounded into the tunnel, Declan cast her one final glance.

No matter his displeasure, he loathed to leave her in this grisly place. He could tell that the stiffness of her posture wasn't only from her disapproval of him. She remained fearful of her surroundings.

The sacrificial room posed a discomfiting setting, particularly with its various human remains. But Evangeline had jumped into a frigid river to brave a nerofidi and slayed a demon rat that would have sent most women, mages included, into a screaming frenzy. She was no coward. Yet the altar with its relics and dusty bones seemed to inspire an inordinate amount of fear in her.

He exhaled. She needed sustenance, and there was nothing else he could do for her. The temple would serve as far better shelter than the cave-dwellers' den. If he ventured beyond the stone walls of the temple, perhaps he would have better luck tracking creatures that didn't survive on carcasses and spoiled meat.

♦

Declan returned, crawling through the same canal he'd used for his exit, dragging his catch through the shallow flow of water from the pool. Red swirled and sloshed around his knees, dripping from the butchered meat.

He'd resorted to crawling through this canal—one of the five that flowed from the pool, and the only exit. It was large enough for him to move through, *if* he went on his knees. Beyond the underground temple, it wasn't the barren, snow-laden terrain he'd expected. Instead he'd found a thriving forest, albeit a frost-licked one.

The whole time away, Declan had kept his mind close to Evangeline's, listening for signs of distress. He wasn't probing her mind. He would never reap a human's mind without cause, but he could, however, sense the general state of any mind if he paid enough attention. And what he sensed from her was bone-deep exhaustion and a streak of defiant anger left over from their earlier dispute, interspersed with waves of anxiety and, most of all, worry.

He should have taught her to project her thoughts.

Declan's command of telepathy was strong enough that he could catch the thoughts of any non-telepathic being, should they direct them at him. The thought of hearing her voice in his mind . . . He hastened his steps.

Warping would have enabled him to traverse vast distances in a matter of minutes, but he no longer had that skill at his disposal. Perhaps it was the aftereffects of the freshwater demon, whose sting continued to pain him, or perhaps it was the continued effects of existing in a realm not his own. The gods were stripping him to the bone.

When Declan made it back into the pool chamber, he shouldered his kill, wincing at the soreness of his wound. He hauled his prey back through the tunnel. The smoky scent of the burning basin greeted him, a welcome contrast to the acrid tang of demon blood and the mildewed odor of an unused aquifer.

Still wrapped in his coat, Evangeline jumped to her feet, brandishing his dagger. When she realized it was him, relief swept over her features. Then her gaze flicked to his shirt, and her face paled.

"Are you hurt?" Again, she asked as if it *mattered* if he was in pain. All hint of displeasure left over from their previous disagreement seemed to have dissipated.

"The blood isn't mine."

She stared at the carcass on his back. "What is that?"

"Lykosa." The very creature depicted by the stone figurines lining the edges of the chamber. They thrived in the area. Before re-entering the canal, he had taken the time to remove the sharp spikes, embedding the pieces around the entrances of all five of the aqueducts. Lykosa were apex predators—its scent alone would likely deter other demons passing through the area.

"Things got a little bloody." He held out a hand for his blade. She returned the weapon with obvious reluctance as she stared at the cadaver and back at him.

"A little bloody?"

It was an understatement. His shirt was practically stiff with blood, but how else could he bring it back?

"Where is the rest of it?"

He'd made sure to disembowel his prey on site, wrenching out the innards and other unsavory parts so predators would be drawn to the bloody buffet. Far away from the temple. Away from Evangeline. He'd only brought back the meatier sections, leaving the rest of it strewn at the site of the kill as carrion. Declan gave her a brief account of his hunt as he dropped the carcass close to the smoldering basin and proceeded to carve out smaller sections of the meat. It felt strange recounting his actions. He hadn't done so with anyone in a long time.

"You disemboweled a demon with your mind?"

It was not done with finesse, but with brute telekinetic force that cracked bone and ripped muscles. Hence the slab of meat hardly resembled the creature it was.

Her eyes snagged on his collarbone, and he knew she was taking in the bruises on his skin—a result of the creature's rough hide chafing him while he hauled it back. The prime emotion emanating from the glowing warmth of her mind took a sudden, violent turn, and her breath came out in a hiss.

"You *are* hurt." Her fingers reached out to brush his skin in a gentle caress, uncaring of the blood and grime. It took him a moment to realize that the whole time, her worry hadn't been for her own predicament.

She had been worried about *him.*

"Let me cook," she offered. "Why don't you have a wash in the pool?"

He shook his head. "You'll get burnt cooking the meat this way." He'd intended to sear the meat skewered on the tip of his blade. The heat of the blade alone would be an uncomfortable temperature for humans.

"Here, we'll shave this down to a spike." She grabbed the

closest piece of splintered wood, one that had likely once been part of a chair leg, and gestured at it with industrious determination. "I can use it as a skewer for the meat." When he didn't comply immediately, she added, "Cooking will give me something to do. And you *need* to wash."

Strangely discomfited, he conceded.

The last thing he'd expected was to be the source of her worry. No one felt concern for an archmage. For it to come from a little mortal with wide, amber eyes and soft, sweet skin . . . a woman who dared judge him for his decisions. He wasn't entirely sure how it made him feel.

They made quick work of fashioning a makeshift hearth lined by pieces of pottery, using pieces of broken furniture doused with oil Declan transferred from the burning basin via telekinesis. Then he dipped lengthier pieces of wood into the basin to transfer fire to their makeshift fireplace.

When he ambled out of the chamber, she was already on her knees, gingerly hacking strips off his butchered catch.

He returned as soon as he was able, wearing damp trousers. He was weary and famished and . . . he was starting to feel the chill of the air.

The little mortal knelt close to the hearth, carefully turning the meat on the skewer as perspiration beaded her brow. Her eyes widened when she saw him, and color suffused her cheeks before she quickly dipped her chin and looked away.

Declan knew what a woman was thinking when she looked at him that way, and he was male enough to feel smug satisfaction. Pleased though he was, he remembered his decency and pulled on his coat, which she'd folded neatly on the ground.

Evangeline didn't strike him as a prude, but she was clearly not the promiscuous sort, either. In fact, she seemed excessively reserved when it came to touch. Not the sort of woman who had ever drawn his interest. He preferred his women experienced and forthcoming.

Yet, wreathed in her delicate fragrance that lingered on his coat, it felt like he was wrapped in a little swath of sunlight.

TWELVE

A prickling sensation ran down Declan's spine, stirring him from slumber.

Danger.

From the light streaming through the crevices in the rock wall, he guessed it was close to midday. Sweeping out with his telepathic senses, he felt the flicker of two sentient minds slinking through the canals.

"What is it?" Evangeline mumbled sleepily when he roused her. The somnolence quickly cleared from her eyes when he told her what he sensed.

Declan walked out of the tunnel into the pool chamber to intercept them. He wasn't surprised the gliders had come. The ceaseless fire from the burning basin would have deterred other demons, but clearly not those of the humanoid race.

Unlike him, they seemed to navigate the tight channels with little difficulty. It occurred to him then that the channels were no drainage canals—they *were* entrances. Just not made for people with legs.

Evangeline gasped from the threshold of the tunnel when the first glider exiting the canal came into view. Out of what had become habit, Declan brushed against her mind and sensed apprehension.

Don't worry, little mortal. I won't let them hurt you.

She glanced up at him, anxiety the chief emotion clouding her eyes. She opened her mouth but shut it again in favor of shoving her thoughts at him.

Declan's lips twitched.

He'd spent hours last night coaching her to project, but her thoughts remained foggy and faint. A soft, sweet hum he couldn't decipher without diving into her mind.

Clearly, projecting one's thoughts wasn't as simple as he'd assumed. Gabriel and the handful of other non-telepathic beings he'd come in occasional contact with made it seem easy. Evangeline's inability to do it only highlighted the feebleness of the human mind.

But Declan was determined.

He strained to listen and finally caught a single word.

. . . Scared . . .

Trust me, Evangeline.

The gliders stopped several paces away, staring at him with vertical irises. Just as in the carvings on the walls, their upper halves were human, save the odd eyes and pale skin that hinted of their ectothermic nature. In place of legs, their lower halves were coiled in a distinctly serpentine tail covered in iridescent scales. The gliders undulated their lower halves briskly as if to shake off the water from the canal while regarding them with unblinking eyes brimming with hostility.

Declan stationed himself firmly before the tunnel where Evangeline lingered and held his stance. It was pointless to hide her presence. If they hadn't already spied her lurking in the tunnel, they would have sensed her through their innate ability to detect body heat.

With arms crossed over a bare chest matted with scales, the one with a tail of variegated green broke the hostile silence with a snarl. "You have disrupted the overhead river and disturbed Draedyn's slumber." Green Scales gestured at the waterfall still steadily pouring into the pool. "Now water overflows."

Spoken in the demon tongue, the glider's words carried the echoes of a primal hiss. These were warriors, judging from the crossbows strapped to their backs. Deadly enough they were confident in approaching foreign intruders on their own.

Declan gave them a nod to acknowledge his misdeeds. "It was not my intention. But we were seeking shelter."

Wary surprise flickered in serpentine eyes. "You speak our language like a native."

Declan had made a point to learn all major languages of the five realms. Fluency was a useful political tool in a world where interdimensional travel was a rare but true possibility.

"Who are you, and why are you in the House of Draedyn? Why are you in our lands?" Green Scales demanded when Declan did not respond.

"We are only passing through. We do not intend to stay beyond what is necessary." Gliders were about as civilized as wild wolves. They wouldn't hesitate to tear out throats if they detected the slightest hint of weakness. "Grant us temporary sanctuary, and I won't give you any trouble."

A contemptuous snort came from the second glider, who undulated in place, a seemingly derisive gesture as he unfurled a gleaming black tail. But Green Scales spoke again. "How dare you make demands of us when you trespass *and* hunt in our lands?"

So they'd noticed his handiwork. Declan gave them a rare smile not meant to mollify but to unnerve.

In response, Black Tail nocked an arrow while Green Scales, the apparent mouthpiece of the duo, repeated, "I will ask you again, landwalker. Who are you, and why are you here?"

Declan allowed the symbols of his ascension to show, gold rising to pulse beneath his skin. Every creature across all realms, with the exception of those in Chonsea's Realm who existed in blissful ignorance, would know of Railea's archmages and the power they commanded.

From the incredulity of their expressions, it was clear the gliders understood the significance of his markings, but to their credit, they did not back off.

"I have no quarrel with your kind, no cause to harm you," Declan said.

Black Tail spoke for the first time, his voice scratchy and sly. "How intriguing. A warrior of the goddess of light . . . " He turned to Evangeline, and his beady eyes nictitated. Once. Twice. "And his human slave." A forked tongue darted from his lips.

Though she could not have understood the glider's language, the fear radiating from her mind peaked. Declan angled his frame so that he broke the glider's direct line of sight to her. The more verbose of the two sneered, revealing slim fangs. "And what is Railea's archmage doing in our realm?"

Declan issued no response. He owed them no explanations.

"You may be master of your domain, but this is our realm, Archmage. And Draedyn weakens every other creature who enters it." He let out an antagonistic hiss when Declan remained unmoving. "Even the mighty fae require our alliance when they do business here."

Declan had always known the Unseelie had contact with shadow realm clans, but to hear common warriors speak of it with such flagrant knowledge caused disquiet to rise in his chest. "What sort of alliance do you have with the fae?"

Another contemptuous sneer. "Your arrogance to presume that we would answer your questions is stifling, Archmage. We do not answer to you."

Declan levitated Black Tail two paces off the ground. The glider launched his arrow while his tail thrashed furiously like an exhumed earthworm. The arrow halted inches from Declan's face. He plucked the offending projectile from the air while the bow in the warrior's hand snapped in half.

"Even Draedyn," Declan murmured in a dangerously cold voice, "cannot fully weaken an archmage. You will answer my question. Tell me the nature of your alliance with the fae, and I will let you and your comrade go."

Green Scales watched, stupefied, as his companion struggled in the air against unyielding invisible bonds. At the warrior's continued silence, Declan stretched his telekinesis to wrap smoldering air around the stunned glider in silken threat.

"We are supplying them with low-level demons in exchange for slaves." The male hissed. Lowering Black Tail to the ground but not releasing either of them, Declan frowned.

"Who, exactly, are you liaising with from the fae realm?"

No answer. He tightened his hold.

"The eldest Unseelie prince," came the choking gasp. "He always comes alone!"

Prince Zenaidus himself. A direct link to the Winter Court. It was unlikely that Zenaidus would approach demon clans without an order from his father, Zephyr.

"We don't know any more about that arrangement—it was

struck between our chiefs and the Unseelie prince. Now let us go, Archmage."

Judging them to be telling the truth, Declan loosened his chokehold and released them. The gliders recoiled swiftly the moment his power slid away, unconcealed loathing in their eyes.

"We will grant you ten sunrises within these walls. Ten and no more. You are not permitted to cross the perimeters of our villages or hunt near our borders; otherwise, we will attack. Our numbers are legion and will supersede even your mind control, Archmage."

Declan gave a curt nod. "A fair deal. And what if I wish to meet your chief?"

Another hiss of laughter. "No one meets Chief Ulrik without proffering some kind of token." Green Scales shot a lecherous sneer at Evangeline's direction. "You seem to already have such a token at your disposal. Chief Ulrik never turns down a pretty new slave."

The gliders erupted in a bout of lewd, hissing laughter. "If she behaves well, the chief might even be persuaded to grant you better hospitality for your time here."

Declan clenched his fists, suppressing the urge to strike out with his hands.

"She is no bargaining chip."

"Then we hope for your whore's sake no other creature feels the need to assuage their curiosity about landwalkers."

With that, the warriors dipped low with an uncanny grace to slither on their chests, making their way out of the temple through the same canal they entered.

Seated beside the makeshift fireplace, Evangeline stared glumly at the crackle of fire as it lapped at firewood. It had been four days, and still no sign of the archmage's men. One more day and the healer of Torgerson Falls would see her tardiness and likely select another in her place. She would have to wait another five years for the next opportunity. Bitterness caused her throat to constrict.

"Five more years," she whispered to the crackling fire, blinking away the tears. Five more years of being tormented by nightmares that were too disjointed to make sense.

She shook her head.

She had much to be thankful for. At the very least, the wound on her calf had begun to scab, and thankfully, it did not show signs of infection. That was a miracle in itself, but Evangeline suspected it had to do with her dive into the river. The freshwater demon's blood was distinctly sulfuric, which may have staved off an infection. How strange for such a vile creature to have blood with antiseptic properties.

Also, the gliders had not come back.

She had no clue of the conversation that had taken place. She spoke no language other than the common tongue, but she caught enough of the body language and knew that she'd been the subject of the lewd dialogue at the end. When she'd asked, the archmage hadn't given her the details.

He had merely said, "They won't give us any trouble. You're safe here."

Evangeline's thoughts wandered back home. Agnes would be beside herself with worry right now. Or did she think Evangeline already dead? Was her mother mourning her right this instant? Her thoughts jumped to Stefan, and trepidation gnawed at her chest. No matter his burly stature, Stefan was still human. Could he truly recover from the insidious black magic that had caused him to spasm? Ugly visions of Stefan dead on the market's cobblestone square constricted her breathing.

What are you thinking about, little mortal?

She jumped.

The dark richness of his telepathic voice jerked her from her broody reverie while igniting a wave of strange flutters in her belly. The man looked regal even with his arms full of pieces of wood he'd undoubtedly harvested from the broken furniture around the temple.

He dropped the pile of tinder by their makeshift fireplace. Even though there was enough oil in the basin to last them for days, they had kept their hearth burning. Evangeline had no wish to move any closer to the grisly basin and the bones around it than necessary, and the fireplace made it easier to keep warm. Faint cracks riddled the stone walls, and though they relieved the chamber of excess smoke, they also allowed drafts into the temple.

"I'm worried about my family and friends," she replied aloud, too weary and dispirited to attempt projecting her thoughts. "For the grief they must be feeling at my disappearance." She wet her lips, deciding not to disclose her lost apprenticeship for fear of inciting unwelcome tears.

A piece of what was once a pillar levitated paces from the ground, sliding silently to barricade the entrance of the chamber. Ever since the gliders had left, the archmage had used the heavy stone piece to seal them in the altar chamber when they got ready for the night. And he had done all that without so much as a flicker of an eyelash, another demonstration of the staggering power at his disposal. It required far more focus and concentration for an average mage to move heavy objects, while the archmage made it look effortless, even though he'd claimed his abilities were weakened. To think he could also control the elements. The extent of power he wielded was almost beyond comprehension.

And to make him all the more unnerving, it was near impossible to decipher his thoughts. She had only ever seen tiny flickers of emotion in the time they'd spent together, but it was always cleared away so quickly he could well be an ice sculpture.

Yet she was no longer as scared of him as she should be.

"I'll take you back to Amereen," he replied, following her cue for verbal speech. The archmage's expression remained stolid, but his words were soothing, no matter the lack of feeling in their delivery. If Declan Thorne, one of the eight rulers of Railea's Realm, said he would take her home, she believed him.

Despite his powers and his ascetic veneer, the archmage —*Declan*—had never made her feel threatened or uncomfortable. Not even when she'd flagrantly disagreed with him.

In fact, he made her feel inexplicably *safe*.

And that in itself was an incongruity, for she had never felt truly safe with any man. Not even Stefan, whom she adored.

"Do you think your family is worried about you?" she asked, wanting to know more about the enigma before her.

"No." He tossed two pieces of tinder into the crackling fire. She thought that was the only response she would get until he added, "Lex is my only family. And he is not one to worry."

Only one person he considered family. For a being with a lifespan of three thousand odd years, that was a rare form of loneliness.

"Are you not on good terms with him?" she prodded. Declan mirrored her posture as he settled beside her, eyes on the fire.

"Lex is my half brother. We are on congenial terms—but

he knows better than to worry. I am an archmage. When I die, my battlemages will feel it."

Evangeline raised her head in surprise and turned to face him. Battlemages were the elite guards of archmages, but . . . "I didn't know battlemages could sense an archmage's death. Is your brother one of your battlemages?"

"No, Lex decided he was better suited as councilor." Slight emotion flashed in his eyes, but before she could decipher it, he continued, "Battlemages are blood bonded to their archmages. To be a battlemage is to be utterly loyal to the archmage you serve.

"In the event of my death, my battlemages would fall and suffer a period of unconsciousness. Amereen would be vulnerable to siege, for I have no heir. No regent. There would be no peace until the Echelon laid claim to my lands."

Involuntary shudders plagued Evangeline. Archmages were highly territorial. So much so that they skirted the line of genocide whenever they warred. And wasn't Declan the archmage who had slain every one of the guards in the Amereen Court when he'd first come to power?

She didn't dare ask.

Instead, she braved another query. "How does the blood bond ensure the loyalty of your men?"

He was silent for a while, and she wondered if she'd crossed an unspoken line. He shifted as if to make himself more comfortable. "To be a battlemage is more than pledging one's life. It is to be a living vessel of an archmage's power. The blood bond allows me to channel my strength into them in battle. Conversely, it gives me the strength to drain them at will."

"*Drain* them?"

"Don't look so surprised, little mortal. No archmage needs to siphon strength unless in dire circumstances. On the rare occasion archmages war against each other, for example. Victory may come down to the caliber of one's battlemages."

Evangeline swallowed, nauseated. "But a battlemage *has* betrayed an archmage before. I've heard the villagers talking about it . . . or is that just another rumor?" She recounted a story of an archmage who had broken every bone in one of his battlemage's body when the man had the audacity to cuckold him with one of his lovers.

"Ah, Alejandro does have a penchant for torture," was all he said.

She eyed him warily. "So it's true?"

His grim smile raised every hair on the back of her neck. "Archmages do not take betrayal lightly. But from Alejandro, it was an act of mercy."

Her eyes widened. "Breaking every bone in a man's body is considered an act of *mercy*?"

"Tradition dictates the battlemage who commits the betrayal be flayed for daring to touch what belongs to his archmage. Fortunately for him, Alejandro didn't particularly care for the woman. She was one of the many ayaris he kept for amusement."

Evangeline wrinkled her nose. She had heard of the sacred Keep, where immortal women trained for years to be an archmage's ayari. Glorified bedmates.

The archmage gave her a ghost of a smile. "Trust me, little mortal, broken bones are a lot less painful than the flaying of one's skin."

She stared at him, gooseflesh rising over her arms. "And how would you know?"

He raised a brow in response.

"Have you had your bones broken and your skin flayed?"

"On numerous occasions."

She flinched at his forthright admission. "You're an arch-mage. Who could have hurt you like that?"

His eyes were shuttered when he responded. "I wasn't born an archmage, little mortal. And physical torture . . . it isn't as uncommon as you think. After all, mages eventually heal."

Disbelief left her mouth agape. She'd been raised by a mage. Her mother and the mages Evangeline had encountered had never made light of torture. "That is no excuse."

He merely shrugged. "It is unfortunate for the battlemage, but Alejandro will forgive him. Eventually."

Evangeline couldn't stem her shock. "You mean this battlemage is still . . . alive?"

"Of course. Battlemages are infinitely stronger than a common mage. Broken bones eventually knit together, and even with repeated punishment, his body will continue to heal itself, so long as Alejandro ensures his vital organs are not destroyed beyond repair."

Her heart went out to the faceless battlemage, healing just to be broken again. She shuddered convulsively. "That's . . . absolutely barbaric."

It was on the tip of her tongue to ask him about his own experience, but she decided against it. Their friendship, if she could even call it that, was nascent at best. It wasn't ready for such personal stories to be shared, especially not when his usually impenetrable eyes now took on a haunting quality.

"What happened to the ayari?" she asked instead.

He shrugged, gazing into the crackling fire. "I do not know. But if I were to hazard a guess, the woman suffered a fate no less agonizing than her lover's."

A faraway howl resounded, dragging Evangeline from the dismay at Declan's response to the horror lurking beyond the temple walls.

"Don't worry, little mortal," he said, appearing not the least bit perturbed. "Lykosa hunt for prey out in the open. We're safe in here."

Wrapping an arm around herself, she shifted slightly closer to him. A man who was likely more lethal than any demon in this realm. The irony was not lost on her. But despite the unearthly howls echoing through the tunnels, her shoulders relaxed.

At least he kept the monsters at bay.

THIRTEEN

The little mortal was becoming an unwelcome distraction. One that superseded the ache festering in his shoulder, a constant reminder of his weakened state.

Declan heaved a breath of frustration and edged two paces away, increasing the space between himself and the slumbering woman. She lay on her side, curled in sleep and completely oblivious to the danger she was in. The sight of her, soft and vulnerable, stirred the deepest, darkest part of him. A part that yearned to reach out and close the distance between them.

Evangeline was exquisite. Not beautiful in the overt way of some women. Her body was petite and her frame too slight. Yet she was easily the most enthralling creature he'd ever met. And gazing into her guileless eyes . . . it was to drown in pools of liquid sunshine.

He frowned.

He had only ever associated Freya with the sun. But then again, Freya had been slight, too. Her hands small.

I'm sorry. Those had been Freya's first words to him. It had been centuries, yet he could still hear her. The sweet, lyrical voice of a girl of eighty-three summers. Sometimes, if he allowed himself to remember, he could still feel her tiny hands caressing his forehead. So gentle, as if he were made of glass. *I've tried healing you as much as I can . . . but I can't fix your eyes,* Freya had said.

As if it were her fault he was broken and sightless.

As a boy raised in what seemed like complete darkness, Freya had been his beacon of light. And after all this time, it seemed he was still trying to catch a little piece of the sun for himself. When he had first brushed against Evangeline's mind, he had been fascinated. Never had he seen such a glorious mind—a conflagration of light. Only her blaze wasn't blinding to a man's eye. It was warm and beckoning. Kind. And the darkest part of him wanted nothing more than to push itself into the amber flames. To possess.

Evangeline's hair, released from her braid, fell in soft waves over the slope of her cheek to curl over her neck and shoulder. His coat acted as her blanket, but it did nothing to hide the tempting curve of her hips. His fingers itched.

Declan stood abruptly, disgusted with himself.

It seemed he had lost more than his archabilities; he was missing self-control as well. He ground his teeth. He would venture outside. Remove himself from her presence until he regained some semblance of self-restraint.

He was about to lift the barricade from the entryway when she let out a disturbed moan. Her features twisted with distress, and her fingers clenched and unclenched. She whimpered, and the agonized sound made him want to dive into her mind and slay her demons.

He gave her a gentle shake instead. "Evangeline."

She continued to whimper, thrashing with more urgency.

Wake up, Evangeline.

Her eyes snapped open, unfocused. Abject fear was etched into her face. Unable to stop himself, he reached out to brush a stray strand of hair from her clammy forehead. His fingers trailed down to caress her flushed cheeks.

When she didn't repudiate his touch, he pulled her into his arms, cradling her to his chest. He half expected her to push away, but she burrowed into him instead. A quivering bundle of feminine warmth who positioned herself against the right side of his chest, as though trying to keep her weight from straining his injured side. The darkness within him purred with pleasure, luxuriating in her nearness. Even the ache in his shoulder seemed less intense with her proximity.

"What plagues your dreams, little mortal?"

She shook her head, so he simply held her.

As the fire retracted to glowing embers at the hearth, Declan worked his fingers into the rich fall of mahogany, stroking until he felt tension leave her body. She pillowed her head against his chest and rested an open palm over the top of his heart.

As the first light of dawn crept through the crevices, she fell back to sleep, curled up against him with such trust that he stilled in response.

Declan swallowed hard. A seed of emotion, one he'd brutally stamped out centuries ago, niggled at his chest. Discomfited, he shifted and tried to lower her back to the ground. Until she sighed and snuggled closer, causing the side of his lips to lift. His arms tightened around her. He might lack empathy, but he knew he held warmth and goodness in his arms. She was everything he had never been.

Everything worth protecting.

E vangeline woke still swaddled in Declan's arms, the strong and steady beat of his heart a soothing lullaby in her ear. *I'm being held by a man.* The thought was so aberrant, she blinked for several seconds trying to determine why she felt no fear. No hint of the inevitable panic that seized her when a man got too close. More, she felt absolutely *no* desire to break free from his embrace. She drew in a deep breath. The masculine scent of him was now familiar. Comforting, even.

Even in sleep, he looked no less devastating. Perhaps he appeared a little less dangerous, with those enviably long lashes fanning over chiseled cheeks. Of their own volition, her fingers lifted to trace the perfect slant between high cheekbones and a stubble-roughened jawline.

His lashes lifted, and she was staring into a clear meadow on a summer's day. His usual mask was undone, tempered by the haze of sleep, and she was looking into the world's best kept secret. There was emotion on his face. A soft tenderness that stole her breath away.

Home.

Evangeline blinked, the moment fractured by the sheer absurdity of her thought. Her cheeks heated. She hoped she hadn't inadvertently projected the word at him. She pushed off his chest with more force than intended.

"I'm sorry," she blurted, further flustered by the realization that she'd lain in his arms the whole night. "I didn't mean to sleep on you like that." She didn't know what she should have said, but she knew the words were a mistake the moment they were out.

When she looked up, the mask of impassivity slid across his features so flawlessly she questioned if she'd imagined the tender moment.

He stood and made his way to the exit.

"Where are you going?" she asked, nervously scrunching the fabric of her skirt in her hands.

"To get us a drink of water," he said, but he didn't turn back.

"Declan—" She swallowed. His name had slipped from her lips.

He stilled and turned to view her. His lips parted as though he wished to speak but didn't quite know what to say.

"Thank you for comforting me last night," she murmured. He shut his mouth and gave a curt nod before the pillar slid silently out of his way.

Evangeline sat by the edge of the pool, contemplating the tumbling waterfall and icy water with a shiver. Over the last few days, they had taken turns by the pool tending to their ablutions. Declan had always remained in the altar chamber when it was her turn, which appeased her need for privacy.

Thought of the archmage roused complicated emotions within her.

What *had* happened, exactly?

How had she slept so comfortably in his arms?

The splish-splash of the water seemed to taunt her. But she hadn't had a proper wash in five days. The squalid odor of the smoky altar room and the tang of overcooked demon meat was most certainly infused in her pores by now.

Gritting her teeth, Evangeline shed her clothing, waded waist deep into the pool, and fastidiously scrubbed herself. As she dipped lower into the water, goosebumps broke out over her bare skin—not from the cold, but from the eerie sensation of being observed. A slight movement in her periphery caught her attention. Something lurked behind one of the fallen pillars.

Watching her.

Her heart hammered so wildly that it thundered in her ears, but she forced herself to slide out of the water as nonchalantly as possible. Arming herself with Declan's blade, which the archmage had insisted she keep, Evangeline scrambled for her clothing. She fumbled to tug on her slip as her eyes scanned the area where she'd glimpsed movement. A pair of feet, caked with dirt, came into view as the creature stepped around the pillar. Evangeline held her ground, blade poised and ready before she realized the feet were human.

Their owner came into view—a heart-breakingly gaunt woman. Almost emaciated. Her face was smudged with grime and angry bruises, as if someone had gripped her jaw so tightly they left an imprint. Evangeline's throat constricted further as a small face peeked out from behind the woman's threadbare skirt.

"Who are you?" Evangeline raised her voice so she could hear over the thrumming of her own heart. Did they even speak her language?

"Anaiya. My name is Anaiya." The woman's voice sounded hoarse, as if her vocal cords were somehow damaged. "This is my daughter, Surin." The girl, who appeared equally unkempt and malnourished, blinked at her with wide, curious eyes.

"Where did you come from?" Evangeline asked, even as a sickening wave of realization flowed through her. Anaiya opened her mouth to answer, but she shrank back abruptly, shoving her daughter back behind the pillar, her dark eyes fixed on something in the distance. Evangeline didn't need to turn to know what had spooked the woman.

Who are they? A large, reassuring hand at the small of her back. The archmage must have sensed her fear and come to investigate. He'd told her he could sense the mental state of any sentient being even if they didn't try to project at him.

Anaiya tensed like a rabbit ready to bolt down a burrow.

"Wait!" Evangeline stooped and lowered the blade to the ground to appear less threatening. "Please . . . don't go."

Anaiya paused, her eyes darting furtively from Evangeline to Declan and back again. "Is he . . . your master?"

Evangeline's eyes widened. "No, no, of course not." Her incredulous response seemed to bolster the woman's confidence.

"Forgive me, my lady." Anaiya chanced a peek at Declan, who remained stoic. "I apologize, my lord . . . I-I was worried . . . "

While Declan did his impersonation of a stone pillar, Evangeline attempted a reassuring smile. "Please don't worry. Declan won't hurt you. Or your daughter. Now please, tell us, where did you come from?"

Anaiya swallowed, as if mustering the courage to speak. "We c-come from the glider clan just south of here. I am tasked with the washing of the warriors' bedlinens and . . . " She halted, her eyes darted nervously to Declan, and she swallowed again. Evangeline gave her an encouraging nod.

"I heard the guards talking about two landwalkers desecrating the House of Draedyn." Anaiya dropped to her knees in supplication, dragging her silent daughter down with her. "My lady, please forgive me for spying on you, but I am desperate." Anaiya drew in an uneven breath and pressed on in a rush. "Please take Surin with you when you leave this place, my lady. Take her back to where you came from."

When Evangeline failed to respond, Anaiya hastily undid the bundle around her back and drew out two yellow-tinged tubers. "I don't have much, but I . . . " The woman laid the tubers on the ground with trembling hands. "This is all the food I have."

Evangeline's lips parted as she recognized the root. "Where did you get goldenseal?"

Anaiya seemed encouraged by her interest. "They grow freely outside these walls, my lady. But I am not permitted sufficient time to harvest . . . if the warriors knew I hoarded food, they would beat me. Please . . . Surin is still a child, but she's maturing. And to the guards, she will soon be old enough . . . " Another convulsive swallow. "I cannot bear such a future for her." Anaiya's dark eyes lifted, and Evangeline saw in them a mother's desperation.

"The guards you speak of, they are gliders?" Declan asked, sharp and snappish. Anaiya dipped her chin again, seemingly unable to meet his eyes. She nodded meekly, her shoulders slumped.

"They would kill me if they found out, but it doesn't matter what happens to me. I just need to give my daughter a chance to escape." Anaiya shot another beseeching look at Evangeline. "Please, my lady," she implored. Her bony hands fidgeted at the hem of the soiled, damp skirt she'd obviously crawled through the aqueduct in. She went to her knees once more and bowed, forehead kissing the ground as she pleaded. "Help my daughter. She does not belong here, not in this realm. Not to a life like this."

"I am no lady, Anaiya." Evangeline began, throat thick with emotion. "My name is Evangeline. And of course we will help your daughter. And you. Right . . . Declan?" She deliberately used his name and glanced up at him for support.

Her heart sank at the expression on his face.

"No."

Evangeline balked, but his eyes—chips of ice—were fixed on Anaiya and her child. "I made a deal with the gliders from your village. They allow us here so long as we do not impinge on their lands and what is theirs." Declan's expression remained merciless as he studied the child. "Your captors will miss you when you are gone. It wouldn't take them long to realize you sought sanctuary with us." Words of pitiless pragmatism. "And I do not wish to antagonize them."

"You cannot be serious!" Evangeline had seen his ability to care, no matter the frost that encased him. "Please. *Declan*," she entreated, but he merely gave her a look of warning before turning apathetic eyes to Anaiya.

"Return to where you came from."

FOURTEEN

"How could you?" Evangeline dragged fingers through her damp hair.

Anaiya had scurried off with her daughter trailing behind, defeat and desolation written all over the haggard lines of her face. Declan returned Evangeline's glare with enough chill in his gaze to freeze the pool. No hint of tenderness in his eyes. As though the man who had held her with such gentleness had been nothing more than a figment of her imagination. Perhaps he was. Perhaps it had always been wishful thinking on her part, a subconscious need to humanize what was never human to begin with.

Keenly aware she was wearing nothing but her slip and damp undergarments, Evangeline snatched up her clothes. Prior to Anaiya's interruption, she had fully intended to wash them, tired of wearing a dress she was sure smelled rank, but with Declan around, she couldn't quite parade herself in nothing but her slip.

Declan's gaze went to the crumpled dress she clutched to her chest, and the frigidity in his eyes heated. He tracked the rest of her with an intensity that sent fiery tingles down her skin. She gritted her teeth, furious that he could elicit such an involuntary response with a simple glance. More, she was furious at her body's traitorous reaction toward such a heart-less man.

"We cannot help them, Evangeline."

"Horseshit!" She trembled with fury. "You are an *archmage.* I saw what you did with the gliders . . . they were terrified of you! You could have given them safe harbor, just like you're doing for me."

"This is not our realm, Evangeline. I am weak here." His words were quiet, but they were underlaid with steel. "I protect you because you are one of mine. But they are not. If we help them, the gliders will come after us. What then? I may be able to intimidate two paltry soldiers, but I cannot guar-antee to protect you from a horde of them."

She gave a strangled shout of frustration. "Did you actually *see* them?" The scars and bruises on Anaiya's skin. Some fresh. And Surin was pitifully malnourished. "Surin is just a child, Declan. A child!"

He remained unmoved.

She was seized with an urge to hurl a rock at his head. Perhaps that would elicit a reaction. He shrugged out of his coat and held it out to her. "Put this on before you catch a chill."

Glaring at him with open defiance, she batted his offering away and yanked her dress on with as much dignity as she could.

"Put this on," he insisted.

"No."

Perhaps it was her impudent tone, or perhaps he didn't like hearing the word *no*, but his jaw tensed. Even in anger—and she *knew* he was angry—the man hardly showed any emotion. Was it any surprise he lacked compassion?

"They are slaves," he said matter-of-factly. "In her current state, Anaiya won't live long."

Evangeline blanched. His callous words chafed far more than her dress against her damp skin.

"As for the child, it is . . . unfortunate. But it's the way of the world," he added, driving the final nail into the coffin of her self-control.

A steaming haze descended across her vision.

"Unfortunate?" She jabbed a trembling finger in his direction. "You . . . you heartless beast! You think that the poor child who will eventually suffer the same fate as her mother . . . is *unfortunate?*"

The beatings. The rape? With their snakelike lower halves, Evangeline wasn't sure if the gliders were anatomically equipped to violate a human woman in that manner, but from the smutty way the two soldiers had eyed her before, she wouldn't disregard the possibility.

"Do you not feel an ounce of sympathy for those under subjugation?"

Not a flicker of an eyelash. "Return to the altar chamber, Evangeline. It is too cold for you to be in damp clothing." His complete disregard of her fervent outburst only stiffened her spine.

"This isn't Amereen," she said tartly. "You don't get to order me around, Lord Archmage!"

His eyes darkened to the shade of moonlit forests. His fists clenched, and a muscle ticced in his jaw. Her breath hitched. Had she pushed him too much? But her mouth, fueled by fury, seemed to have grown a mind of its own.

"What? Are you going to smite me now? Because I'm not taking orders from a swellheaded monste—"

He lifted her off her feet and tossed her over his shoulder like the butchered slab of meat he'd hauled back days ago.

"Let me down, you cruel, cold-blooded cad!" She thrashed, pounding his back with her fists, but his arms could well be iron manacles over the backs of her thighs.

When her elbow grazed his shoulder where the freshwater demon had stung, she felt the stagger in his footing, though he made no sound. Despite the rage fogging her mind, it occurred to her that the blackhearted brute might not have fully recovered. She stilled her pounding fists, not wanting to inflict more pain to his injury, but it didn't keep her mouth from launching barbs.

"Pitiless, stonehearted swine!"

"Make up your mind." He sounded almost mild. "Am I swellheaded, cold-blooded, or stonehearted?"

She snarled. "If you have a heart, it's blacker than Draedyn's! You're a thoughtless, heavy-handed, emotionally crippled . . . " She sputtered, racking her brain for an insult she hadn't yet hurled his way.

"Pissbucket!"

She was set abruptly on her feet. She scowled. How hateful that the man was so tall she had to crane her neck just to glare at him.

The glint was back in his eye. The one he wore whenever he was displeased. His gaze was fixed on her lips. She flattened them. What manner of reprisal was he devising? Would he burn off her lips? Freeze them shut?

She'd better make her last words count.

"If you want to punish me, then you better make sure I'm dead. Or I'll practice projection until you hear me!"

"You require no practice." He switched to telepathy. *You're already projecting. Loudly.*

She parted her lips. Was she?

"Now calm yourself." He strode off without a backward glance. It was only then she noticed she was back in the altar room, standing beside their makeshift fireplace.

He stalked out, and the pillar barricaded the entry to seal her in. As though she were a tantruming child in need of a breathing spell.

Fuming, she plopped to the ground. She had half a mind to venture out and . . . she gritted out a hiss. And *what?* Take on an entire horde of gliders by herself? Even if she could spirit Anaiya and her daughter away, she didn't have the means to return to Amereen on her own. Without Declan, she was utterly helpless.

Wiping angry tears off her face, she realized the goldenseal root was still clutched in her fist. She found a broken piece of pottery and began smashing the root into pulp. Her shoulders loosened eventually as she allowed the cathartic motion of grinding the herbal tuber into a yellow paste to calm her outrage. His words replayed themselves in her mind.

I protect you because you are one of mine, he'd said. He could easily leave her here. He didn't have to take her back. It wasn't as if her family and friends could do anything if he returned without her. They didn't even know she was still alive. In fact, he could pretty much do anything he wanted to her. She shuddered, furious at the sheer imbalance of power between them. And to think she had hurled profanities at him.

A hysterical bark of laughter escaped her throat.

She'd insulted an archmage to his face . . . and survived.

I am weak here. I may be able to intimidate two paltry soldiers, but I cannot guarantee to protect you from a horde of them.

She had trouble believing he was weak. Then she remembered him drifting face down in the pool, how he'd lain in her arms, feeble and worn after he'd coughed up water from his lungs. He might appear indomitable, but he wasn't invincible.

He felt pain, the way any man did.

The pillar eased to the side, startling her. He marched in, a limp, furry bundle in his arms. Relieved to see him but still seething, she shifted so she wouldn't have to face him and continued to grind at the root that was already fine paste.

He didn't attempt conversation, working in silence to skin and skewer the dead creature. The tension around them intensified. Setting the ceramic pieces aside, Evangeline decided to drop the facade. She hugged her knees close to her chest and shut her eyes. Willing herself to be anywhere but here.

A hand jostled her lightly.

Evangeline's eyes snapped open. The overbearing scent of charred meat that churned her gut once again filled the chamber. She'd somehow fallen asleep. She glanced down and saw a few cubes of cooked meat on a ceramic slab.

He peered at her from the side. "Eat."

Her stomach grumbled, but her throat felt like it was coated with gravel. And the prospect of eating what must be another demonic creature nauseated her.

"I'm not hungry," she lied.

Frowning, he nodded at a sliver of curved ceramic filled with precious sips of water. He'd used the little pieces of cracked pottery like tiny cups. She blinked. When had he collected water?

She drank reluctantly. He pushed forward another sliver, this one slightly smaller. It was just a mouthful, but she drank it nonetheless, thankful she didn't have to venture out into the dark tunnel and pass the grisly torture chambers for it.

He nudged the plate of meat toward her again.

She shook her head, although she was beginning to feel childish. But she refused to take any more gestures of kindness from him than necessary.

"Thank you for the water," she added, not wanting to appear overtly rude.

She went back to staring, this time into the fire. A long moment passed, and then he sidled up beside her. His large frame emanated a warmth that did strange, unwelcome things to her belly.

"Do you sulk often, little mortal?"

She glared. "I am *not* sulking." Bathed in the glow of the fire, he was a bronzed statue of a god. She felt the urge to snarl. He was a callous and compassionless bastard. Inhumane.

"Surin was likely born here," he said quietly. "She knows nothing of freedom. This is her world."

Evangeline gritted her teeth. Did he really want to do this again? "So that's how you justify leaving an innocent child behind in a demon realm?"

He gave a light shrug that was as aggravating as it was rare. "She won't miss what she doesn't know."

She clenched her fists, trying to suppress the inane desire to claw at his beautiful face when he added, "Once I return you to Amereen, I plan to come back to meet the glider chief. I will broker for their freedom then."

She stared at him with equal parts surprise and wariness. "Truly? For *both* Anaiya and her child?"

He nodded once, continuing to pin her with a steady, unwavering gaze. "Would that make you happy, little mortal?"

Make her happy? Was he trying to please her? She sucked in a shaky breath. Despite her fervent nod, she couldn't hide the sudden surge of involuntary tears.

He frowned, dark brows slashing together. "Then why are you crying?"

She shook her head. "I'm not upset. I'm . . . relieved." She scrubbed at her eyes and offered a sincere smile. "Thank you." She wouldn't question the reason behind his sudden benevolence. She would simply accept it on Anaiya and Surin's behalf.

"Thank you . . . Declan. That means a lot to me."

He seemed to relax, sensual lips curving ever so slightly. Her eyes widened.

Was that a *smile*?

"Will you eat something now?" He nodded at the plate of unappetizing meat again.

In an attempt to please him after his concession, she picked up a piece of meat and nibbled. She could probably be persuaded to eat an entire demon *raw* if he promised to rescue any slave he encountered.

"I'm sorry for calling you all those names," she mumbled between bites.

"I've been called worse." Unusual wryness filled his tone. "Although I must admit . . . pissbucket was a first for me."

"I'm glad it was at least novel. It was the best I could come up with at the time."

Mirth danced in his gaze, and the tension that had previously filled the air morphed into companionable quiet.

Eventually, she curled up into the fetal position she usually assumed for sleep. He closed the distance and gave her a gentle tug, cuddling her against his chest.

She stiffened in shock.

Did he think he could touch her now they were back on speaking terms? Railea's tears, did he think she'd somehow bartered herself for Surin and Anaiya's freedom?

He peered down at her, genuine confusion in his eyes.

"What's the matter, little fire?"

She frowned. *Little fire?* Where in Railea's name did that come from? She wriggled away from him. "What do you think you're doing?"

He cocked his head slightly. "I did not think you minded being held," he said, a pointed reminder of *where* she'd slept the previous night.

There had been no nightmares after that.

Evangeline stared at him, heat curdling in her cheeks as the desire to return into the fold of his arms surged. He seemed to sense it, too, because this time a true smile lit his face, turning him from beautiful to utterly devastating.

"Perhaps I shouldn't have assumed." His voice deepened into a beckoning lull. "Would you like me to hold you while you sleep tonight?"

FIFTEEN

Droplets trailed teasingly down his throat as Declan drank from cupped hands.

Determined not to stare, Evangeline wiped her own hands dry on her skirt and settled on the cool stone ledge by the pool. She focused on the steady splash of water and drew in a deep breath. The crisp scent of the river water was refreshing to her befuddled senses. Declan was quiet. Unsurprising, given his natural state. She, however, felt out of sorts. She had succumbed and shamelessly slept in his arms once more, curling into his chest like a cat. There had been no fear. It was as if her body had acclimated to his touch.

"Go back to the altar chamber," he said after he drank his fill. "I'll join you there shortly."

Her nose wrinkled at the idea of returning to the sacrificial chamber alone. "Do you mind if I stay?" At his raised brow, heat bloomed on her cheeks. "I've wanted to wash out my dress since yesterday."

He gave a brisk nod and turned toward the water. Kicking off his boots and socks, he moved to the edge of the pool.

Much to her chagrin, he proceeded to undo the buttons of his shirt.

Oh.

She hadn't realized he intended to wash *again*. Hadn't he just washed himself last night?

Taut muscles corded in his arms and shoulders, rippled across his abs as he stripped off his shirt to reveal the sleek angles of his body—a mouthwatering display of masculine perfection. The clearly defined ridges on his abdomen made her fingers curl and her heart flutter. His hands halted on the waistband of his trousers.

"I-I . . . can wash your shirt for you, if you like," she stuttered, cheeks flaming when it was clear he'd caught her staring. Pure male amusement flickered over his face. But he didn't tease her, not Declan.

"Thank you," he said.

She scurried over to collect his shirt that still bore his warmth and fled to the furthest end of the pool with her head pointedly averted. The rustle of more fabric told her he'd removed the rest of his clothing. A light splash followed.

Evangeline stepped out of her own dress quickly, shivering in her slip before donning his coat again. She slathered goldenseal poultice in place of soap on the garments. It was a waste of the tuber and its antiseptic properties, but it also had a fragrance that would help mask the stench of stale clothes. She was wringing out her dress when she chanced a peek. It was deviant of her, but she couldn't seem to help herself.

His back was to her, which was just as well. She shamelessly drank in the sight of him until she noticed the wound on his shoulder was a dark, festering *hole.*

From the way he'd held himself, she'd assumed his wound was almost healed. Clearly the archmage was a whole lot better at disguising his hurts than she'd thought.

Then he shifted slightly, and her attention was drawn to the way his powerful arms braced against the glistening rock-face. With his head slightly bowed, the muscles on his back gleamed against the heavy torrent of the fall. He was standing in the deepest section, which kept him decent. Just barely.

Heat, dark and rich, suffused her veins and pooled in her belly. The want was so raw, so primal she tore her sight away, appalled at herself. Who was she? She was turning into such a carnal creature that she hardly recognized herself.

She feigned concentration on the laundry, refusing to avert her eyes from the cotton fabric until she felt his presence behind her. He was still glistening from the river, and for the love of Railea, he wore nothing but damp trousers once again. The faint, arcane symbols on his skin teased her gaze, beckoned her touch. Rationally, she knew his markings were like those on poisonous frogs. Nature's way of warning that the creature shouldn't be trifled with. Yet she felt like a witless duck, eager for a bite even though it would spell her doom.

Gathering the wet garments in one hand, he said, "Come, little fire."

"Why are you calling me that?" she asked absently, cheeks still flaming from indecent thoughts. Little mortal she could understand, but *little fire*? It sounded strangely like an endearment. He hesitated long enough to make her frown up at him.

He shrugged. "It fits you."

Suddenly shy, she raised another, more pressing, concern. "The freshwater demon's sting . . . it is not healed."

"No," he agreed. "A part of its stinger must still be buried in my flesh, preventing my body from fully healing itself."

Evangeline gaped. She had checked his wounds, searched for remnants of the stinger . . . Then she realized her folly. "I didn't find any remnants of the barb because your flesh had knitted too quickly." The reason true healers were so rare.

They weren't only trained in the arts of healing the human body, but immortal ones as well.

"There's nothing you can do without carving up another chunk of me."

At her expression, he slowed his pace, and his voice gentled. "It's not your fault. Arthropodal demons usually bury their stingers deep in their prey. Once we are home, one of my healers can easily retrieve it."

It made her feel worse, for she had been on her way to becoming an apprentice to one. "Surely it pains you?" It must, for he paused at her query, brows furrowing as he gave her a peculiar glance.

"No." But his words did not hold his usual confidence.

She raised a brow. Clearly, admitting weaknesses wasn't something the archmage did with ease. "At the very least, let me apply some poultice over it," she said.

The goldenseal from Anaiya wasn't just an edible root with antiseptic properties; it was also a pain-reliever. It helped soothe the wounds on her calves. Perhaps it would soothe the archmage's shoulder.

He remained silent, and she wasn't sure if her insistence had somehow offended him.

Back in the altar chamber, she settled on the ground as he laid the wet garments close to the fire.

A bubble of mirth escaped her throat. At his questioning glance, she grinned up at him. "The god of death," she said, gesturing to Draedyn's glowering stone statue. "Likely has never seen a sight stranger than an archmage airing a woman's dress."

A gleam that looked a lot like amusement lit his eyes, followed by another infinitesimal quirk of his lips. Her pulse ratcheted. Smiles looked good on him.

When he continued to gaze at her, a simmering heat rose

to her cheeks. Tentatively, she patted at the ground beside her in open invitation. He didn't hesitate to settle down.

"Show me," she said, and his brows knitted. "Show me your wound," she clarified. She couldn't get over the beautiful bronze of his skin marred by the gruesome rot of the demon's sting. There was a long pause where he regarded her in silence, and her confidence crumbled. Why did she care? He didn't even act as though the wound bothered him one bit. Perhaps he truly *didn't* feel the pain.

Then he shifted, offering her his back.

Her breath caught in her throat.

Up close, the wound looked worse than it had from her vantage point by the pool. The skin around it was blackening, with purple veins erupting from the core. Almost gangrenous. She would have to trim some of the dying flesh away, but she simply couldn't bring herself to wield the blade on his skin again. Not because she was squeamish, but because the thought of causing him more pain was utterly abhorrent. And perhaps all he needed was something to keep the rot from further festering before his men came for them.

She dipped her fingers into the poultice and went up on her knees so she could better dress his wound. But with the first brush of her fingers on his skin, his entire body tensed in a manner that could only be construed as pain.

"Am I hurting you?"

He shook his head, body tight as a bowstring.

"Lie down," she whispered as she applied a little more.

To her surprise, he obeyed, stretching out on the ground. Only he seemed to think her lap a more comfortable alternative, pillowing his head on her legs with nothing but the cotton of her slip separating their skin. It was extremely indecent. Yet she couldn't bring herself to shove him away, not when it seemed like he was almost seeking . . . comfort.

When she was satisfied his wound was covered by gold-enseal, he didn't pull himself up. She wasn't sure she wanted him to. Haltingly, she ran a gentle hand over the side of his temple, stroking the damp strands shorn short at his nape. His hair was thick and soft like the pelt of a cat. She smiled. Or in his case, a panther.

He made no protest. So she did it again, marveling at the ease she felt with him in such a short period of time. At how his proximity no longer ignited fear, but inspired comfort.

It was when his eyes fluttered shut that she realized he'd been drowsing beneath her ministrations. She'd stroked the archmage like a housecat, and he'd fallen asleep with his head nestled on her lap.

"**S**o why didn't you tell me before that you planned on returning to meet the glider chief?" she asked, needing to fill the silence that was deafening to her ears. While he'd napped, she'd had plenty of time to mull over recent events. Over what he'd said.

"It wasn't information you needed to know."

She bit her lower lip, stung by his words even though she had no right to be. There was no reason for him to disclose his plans. There was no reason for him to tell her anything, really. He was an archmage, and she was but an apothecarist.

"Well . . . ," she began, stretching out her legs to relieve the sensation of pins and needles from holding the same position too long. The archmage had slept for a short while, but even so, her legs had begun to cramp beneath the weight of his head. When he woke, he'd withdrawn from her with a furrow of his brow as though he couldn't believe he'd fallen asleep.

He cut her off, surprising her with an explanation. "The

gliders made it clear that they had an alliance with one of the Unseelie princes of the Winter Court." He picked up a piece of cold, charred meat and offered it to her. She grimaced but accepted his offering.

"I would have liked to meet with the glider chief to discuss the nature of this alliance, but it became apparent that the chief would only take an audience in exchange for some form of payment." He tossed a piece of meat into his mouth. "As I have no such payment available, I intended to return another time."

Understanding dawned on her. "But they would have granted you an audience with the chief . . . with me as payment." She swallowed, but a knot formed in her throat at the possibility of being bartered.

His eyes darkened. "I wouldn't have used you that way."

"I know," she said. The words were almost a whisper as ice trailed its fingers down her spine. Vaguely, she wondered how Anaiya and her daughter had been captured.

The quake that seized her body was as vicious as her nightmare shoved to the forefront of her mind.

"Then why do you seem distraught?" His eyes not leaving hers, he closed the distance between them. A silent man who seemed to see too much with his incisive gaze.

She gave him a listless shake of her head, unwilling to articulate the incomprehensible horror that hounded her dreams and would continue to torment her until she unraveled it. She was rewarded with a disapproving frown.

The forthright display of sentiment was so unlike him that it snapped her from her melancholy. But he didn't give her a chance to regain her voice, tugging her into his arms in the same fashion he had the night before.

Only this time, he wasn't wearing a shirt, and she was wearing nothing but his coat over a diaphanous slip.

There was nothing shuttered about those beautiful eyes now. Not a single trace of ice. Instead, she was gazing into the dark, green depths of a wild sea. Undefinable emotion churned there, and its intensity mirrored the fervent beat of her own heart.

The demons that stalked her nightmares haunted her eyes and dimmed the incandescent flame that was her mind. Reaching out to draw her into his arms, to comfort, had been instinctive. But when she had curled into his hold, her body soft and pliant, to mold herself against him, she became a siren call impossible to ignore.

He ran his fingers against the smooth length of her jaw, tipping her face to his, her skin soft to his touch. Still, she didn't push him away. The darkness that lived deep within him reared up, demanded he claim her. He was an archmage. He had the right to any woman who lived in his province, if he so pleased.

But everything about her was so soft and peaceful. He didn't want to mar her brightness with his depravity, snuff out her innocence. Not this little mortal whose fire burned like pure sunlight.

Then she slid a hand over his chest. Her touch, like a brand, settled to rest just over his heart, shattering his willpower to pieces.

He was just a man.

He would permit himself to steal one kiss. Just a taste. He bridged the distance and pressed his lips against hers. She stilled, a flash of uncertainty skittering across her face. It chastened him. Reining in the almost painful need to push his tongue between her lips, he quelled the urge to plunder.

Instinct told him that though Evangeline had allowed him a kiss, she needed care and consideration.

He continued to rub his lips against hers ever so gently, eliciting a soft hum from the back of her throat . . . until he received a tiny nip on his bottom lip. Pleased, he swept his tongue lightly over the seam of her lips, wanting to know if he was welcome.

She let out a soft sigh, and her nails dug lightly into his skin. That was all the encouragement he needed.

Fisting his hand into the heavy silk of her hair, he tilted her head further and positioned her exactly the way he wanted before delving into her mouth in slow, languorous exploration. The resounding purr she emitted turned him hard as iron. He could barely curb his own groan of pleasure.

She could well be ambrosia.

Her tentative tongue swept forward to meet his. He retracted teasingly, breaking the kiss to suckle on her lower lip, possessed by a sudden urge to *play*. She made a little noise of protest in her throat and cupped the sides of his face. Her actions were a little awkward, motions untrained. Her tongue darted shyly into his mouth in an attempt to reignite the kiss.

That was when he knew he wouldn't stop with just a taste.

She rewarded him with a sigh of approval when he resumed the kiss, further spurring his desire. He slipped a hand beneath the coat that dwarfed her slender frame and gave in to his own need to touch, stroked her gently down the graceful arch of her spine.

When he'd seen her by the pool yesterday in her slip, he had wanted nothing more than to maraud, to run his hands against the sleek and graceful curves. Last night he'd thought of a thousand sinful things he'd do to her, while she'd slept, cuddled up against him.

This morning he'd attempted to douse his arousal in the

pool, where he now felt the chill of the frigid waters, but it had done little to tamp his urges. Now, with her mouth melded against his, her body pliant and open for his touch, all thoughts of self-control spiraled out of his mind.

Indulging in the fantasy that had plagued him in recent days, his hand roamed up to cup the soft mound of her breast. She gasped into his mouth even as she arched into his palm.

Breaking away from her lips only to lave her nape with kisses, he relieved her of his coat. She quivered. Still unsatisfied, he drew the straps of her slip down the delicate arch of her shoulder with the impatience of a man who knew exactly what he wanted.

Another jerk and the soft material exposed her creamy flesh. A rumble of pure male appreciation resounded in his chest. The sound surprised them both. She might be petite, her chest small, but she was exquisitely proportioned.

The most beautiful thing he'd ever seen.

"D-Declan . . . ," she stuttered, eyes still hazy with desire.

He swooped down to take one pert breast into his mouth without warning. Her startled cry of pleasure was a drug to his system. His markings came alive of their own volition, and the glyphs intensified until the golden sheen that spoke of his power illuminated. But it didn't seem to scare her; instead, she writhed and arched against him.

Her movements were artless, without finesse. No display of sexual prowess that was the common denominator for all the women he'd ever bedded.

Somehow, it only made her all the more erotic.

When he released her breast only to lavish the other with the same unscrupulous attention, she shattered his resolve to go slow by weaving her fingers into his hair, tugging at his scalp. Her arousal was a rich, heady musk that perfumed the air. His cock throbbed, threatening to embarrass him. He pushed her down to the ground in one swift motion and tugged the flimsy slip up to her waist, revealing modest cotton underwear. Settling himself above her, he kneed at her thighs, impatient to splay her open.

That was when he felt her stiffen.

Aware that she was no courtesan, he gentled his kisses and stroked her inner thighs with sure, unyielding hands. Another quiver racked her body. But it wasn't borne of the passion-drenched pleasure that had cocooned them at the start. When he met her gaze, it wasn't the shy nervousness of an inexperienced female that he saw, but unadulterated fear. The eyes of a terrified woman.

It doused his arousal far more effectively than any bath in the pool.

He released her, confusion roiling in his gut. "What's wrong?"

She tugged her slip back down to cover herself with jerky movements, her breathing shallow and ragged. The confusion in his gut turned to sickness. Had he completely misread her, forced himself upon her like some savage?

"I thought . . . " Declan swallowed, finding it difficult to speak. "I wouldn't have touched you if I didn't think you wanted me to." He would *never* force himself on a woman. She was pulling his coat back on, and her face reddened.

She appeared distraught, forcing herself to meet his eyes, but her whisper eased some of the tightness in his chest. "I wanted you to touch me." She glanced down to her hands, and her face crumpled. "The problem lies with me. I-I struggle with intimacy." She blew out a tottery breath. "I'm a little impaired that way," she added with a flustered, self-deprecating laugh.

The statement hit him like a pickaxe in the gut. "Has someone hurt you before?"

Silence resounded as she averted her eyes, her luscious lips clamping stubbornly together again.

"Evangeline . . . " He growled in reprimand, unable to leash the sudden, mounting rage that was turning his voice raw. "Tell me." She flinched at his tenor, but when eyes of molten amber snapped up to meet his, he saw the steel in them.

"Is that an order, Archmage?"

She'd transformed from a frightened kitten to a feline flashing her claws in less than a minute. Her fiery reanimation was a balm against a rage that was not directed at her, but at the person who had terrified her so badly that she'd consider herself impaired.

"No." He eased his cool veneer back in place. "A request."

He allowed his gaze to roam, slow and slumberous down her body, and felt the satisfaction of seeing her flush. But he didn't touch her again. And he wouldn't until he found the reason behind her fear.

SIXTEEN

Evangeline worried her lower lip as Declan folded his arms over his chest. A glorious chest she'd petted and all but plastered herself against seconds ago. She turned away only to meet the eyes of the large, stone statue of the stern god staring down at her like a disapproving voyeur.

Heat crawled up her skin again—it might as well take permanent residence on her cheeks. If it hadn't been for the sudden spike of terror that had seized her the moment Declan prowled over her body with the liquid grace of a predator, she would have let him *continue*.

It was utter insanity, the way she'd behaved. Wanton, utterly shameless, and she'd enjoyed every bit of it. But most unnerving was the man she'd glimpsed beneath that carapace of ice.

A man who wanted her as much as she wanted him.

Now he stared at her with unflinching intent, stifling the silence between them.

"I don't actually remember any of it." How could she begin to explain a trauma that ran so deep her brain blanked out the memories? "The earliest thing I recall was my mother spoon-feeding me broth in bed." Memories of Agnes's gentle hands and the hearty smell of beef stew loosened the knot in her chest.

"I was bedridden for a long time. Mother later told me my recovery was a slow process. She'd found me unconscious in a shallow ravine while she was herb gathering."

Declan remained stoic, but she had no doubt he was listening to every word she said.

"Mother couldn't find anything to identify me, and when she filed a report with the village authorities, no one was looking for a missing child." Evangeline had always wondered if her real parents were already dead or if they simply didn't care to look for her.

"So she took me back to Arns, nursed me back to health, and raised me as her own." Idly, Evie picked up what must have once been part of a ceramic bowl and now harbored a portion of leftover poultice. She couldn't help but feel like the broken piece of crockery. Irreparably damaged but still trying to pass as functional. "I don't even know my true age."

Agnes had guessed her to be eleven or twelve at the time. Her current birthday was a random day—the day she'd uttered her first word, months after she'd woken up in the small, charming cottage that had become home.

Ostensibly, she would turn twenty-four come spring this year.

"You have no recollection of how you ended up in the ravine?" His voice was inquisitive and cool, holding not an echo of their passion-drenched kisses. It was as if he had never laid his hands on her, never kissed her with the fervent hunger of a starving man.

"No. My memories of the past before I woke up in my mother's cottage are hazy. I can't even remember when she found me. She said I slipped in and out of consciousness, that weeks passed before I was fully lucid."

His fists clenched.

"But the nightmares . . . " Evangeline blew out a breath. "I've had the nightmares ever since. I only ever dream the same bits and pieces, and sometimes all I remember when I wake is the taste of fear." She looked up. Understanding flashed across his features.

"I think I was once held captive in a cabin . . . where I was tied up." She swallowed convulsively. "So close to a fireplace I can sometimes still feel the singeing heat."

A muscle in his jaw ticced. "Do you remember where?"

She shook her head weakly. All she remembered was terror. Suppression. Anguish. As she tried her best to explain, she continued to fiddle with the broken ceramic, running her fingers over jagged edges that must have once been smooth and free of fractures.

Declan listened to her with preternatural silence, but paradoxically, his remoteness made it easier for her to speak, easier to disclose the fears that made her feel so very fragile, so very vulnerable.

"The oppressors in your nightmares. Can you see their faces?" he asked when she finally finished. Evangeline shook her head. The men in her dreams were nothing more than shadows. Monsters in the dark.

"And when I touched you, I triggered this fear."

She blinked. "It wasn't *you* I was scared of; the fear discriminates no man. It seizes me whenever I . . . and then I just clamp up." She rubbed her arms. "It happens every time I attempt an intimate relationship."

The fact that they'd gone as far as they had was nothing short of a miracle.

He leaned in so he was a hairsbreadth from touching her. "And have you tried being intimate with many men?"

She shook her head. She had courted fewer than she could count on one hand.

He seemed satisfied, and very deliberately, he closed the teasing distance between them and sought her lips, keeping his hands at his sides. When he pulled away, her breathing was ragged and her blood molten in her veins.

"You like kissing me," he murmured, his eyes dark and hazy with pleasure.

She licked her lips but didn't respond. An obvious understatement. Then he placed both hands on her hips in a proprietary hold before drawing her flush to him. Evangeline pressed her palms against his chest in protest as Malcolm's words returned to haunt her. "Declan, I don't want you to think I'm a tease."

"Relax," he coaxed. One hand stroked her back while he tangled the other in her hair. "I enjoy touching you, little fire." Another drugging kiss, his taste intoxicating to her senses. Cathartic. "Let me hold you. I won't ask for what you can't give."

Alone, Evangeline crunched through the ice-encrusted pathway cradled by dark evergreens. Fine tremors badgered her frame, but the trees stood tall and proud, seemingly unaffected by the cold despite their frost-dipped leaves. Her stockings were soaked from sloshing through the canals earlier that morning, and the slate-gray sky gave her plenty of reason to head back into the safety of the temple, but she soldiered on.

Anaiya had said goldenseal grew aplenty beyond the

temple walls. And if there was goldenseal growing in the wild, there would likely be snakewood or jejurine. If she could gather some of those herbs, she would be able to better treat the archmage's shoulder—perhaps even counteract some of the effects of the freshwater demon's venom.

For reasons utterly unfathomable, Declan had insisted on *another* bath this morning. Who in his right mind would be so eager to wade into frigid waters? Evangeline's lips twitched. A being who didn't feel the cold.

When Declan had returned from the pool, she'd insisted on checking his wound again. It had grown worse, the purplish hue around it larger and more prominent. He had endured her ministrations with his usual stoniness and a concerning listlessness. He began to drowse and eventually fell asleep, stretched out beside her.

Evangeline's cheeks heated at the thought of how she'd spent the night wrapped up in the sensuous warmth of his arms, kissing and talking until sleep had crept up on them. He had done most of the kissing, seeming to take pleasure in driving her to a fever pitch, occasionally pausing to pose probing questions about her life in Arns.

In turn, she'd done most of the talking. It was as if he were trying to learn her. But a man with such immense power had no reason to take an interest in a small-town apothecarist and her unremarkable life or care about her lost apprenticeship with the healer of Torgerson Falls. Archmages didn't have anything to do with mortals apart from ruling them. In fact, archmages didn't even take mortal lovers—no one had ever heard of a mortal ayari.

Clearly, he needed a warm body to hold. Hadn't he already said as much himself? *I enjoy touching you, little fire.*

He was the fire. She'd burn if she got too close.

She was lucky he was honorable enough not to push for

more than she could give. And no matter how enthralled she was by him, she couldn't lose sight of the fact that he wasn't just a man, but an archmage. One of the eight supreme rulers of their realm. Incomprehensibly powerful. Indomitable. Immortal.

But even an archmage couldn't help her overcome her past.

Don't overcomplicate things, Evangeline Barre, she chastised herself as she spied the broad green leaves indicative of the root she sought. She bent to unearth the shrub using the bejeweled blade Declan had left with her as a makeshift spade. *The moment you both return to Amereen, you'll never see him again.* And that would likely happen soon. It was already their sixth day in Draedyn's Realm—and Declan was certain his men would soon arrive.

A tiny knot formed in her heart at the thought. An insane part of her now yearned to remain in this frostbitten land just a little longer. Here, she could pretend in the hush of the night, with the crackle of the fire and the steady beat of his heart against her ear, that she was his lover. And he was *hers*.

Evangeline bit the inside of her lip. "Foolish girl," she whispered to herself as she unearthed the yellow root, but it was too small. She would need more. "An archmage belongs to no one."

Even if they did, they most certainly did not belong to peasants.

"Do you have an ayari?" she'd asked him last night.

He had stilled at the question, but his response had been a straightforward and heartening "No." She had been surprised. Every archmage had ayaris . . . or so she'd assumed. Archmages might rule her realm, but little was known about their private lives. But there were plenty of rumors. There was also an entire Keep dedicated to the training of immortal women

—mostly mages, but the occasional halfbreed was said to be accepted—just for the personal use of the Echelon.

And there was a very good reason for the Keep. Something her lust-hazed brain seemed to have conveniently forgotten. Archmages reputedly had such potent powers that should they lose control at any point during sexual intimacy—or at any other point, really—it could be fatal for their bed partners. The ayaris were apparently trained to handle such excess flow of power. Hence, no mortal qualified.

"Why? Have you never found someone to love?" she had prodded after he'd lapsed into silence. It had seemed right to ask, considering he had a hand tangled in her hair and another roving the curve of her spine.

His response had been another flat negative, but then he had added, "The only person I ever loved is long gone."

She'd prodded deeper, compelled by the emotion flickering in the depths of his usually impermeable eyes.

"Her name was Freya." And he'd surprised her by revealing a little piece of himself that she instinctively knew he rarely shared. He spoke of a little girl who had found him with his eyes ruptured in their sockets after he had suffered a near-fatal punishment as a young mage. Evangeline had been too horrified to ask the reason for his punishment.

"She was just a child herself. But she cleaned up my wounds and tried to heal me as much as she could." He smiled, a rare but genuine one that paradoxically caused her heart to ache. "She came back day after day to help me with my bandages. And eventually she took to reading me stories of dragons and other fantastical creatures." His eyes grew distant, and sadness seemed to permeate the ensuing silence. She couldn't bring herself to ask the question burning in her mind.

How did death claim this girl?

Instead, she had lavished him with kisses, hoping to lessen the hurt leaching from him. His story had reverberated in her soul, spoken to her in ways she did not comprehend. It humanized him, perhaps.

"Foolish girl," Evangeline berated herself again. Tightening his coat around her shoulders, she scraped dirt off the sides of Declan's gleaming dagger and dug out another rhizome of goldenseal. A sizeable one. "He is *not* human."

She straightened and braved a few more steps, careful not to wander too far from the entrance of the canal. Declan had said lykosa thrived here, but their howls were only heard after dusk. Dawn gave her a small measure of confidence in venturing out alone.

Evangeline pushed past a row of tightly knitted bushes and grinned when she finally found what she was looking for. The spiny leaves of a snakewood bush. Perfect.

She was harvesting the shrub when a distinct shriek of terror pierced the air. A telltale hiss met her ears, and Evangeline clamped a hand over her mouth to stifle a gasp. She must have unwittingly ventured into dangerous territory. She ducked lower into the safety of the thick underbrush. From between the leafy spindles of her hiding place, she caught a flash of movement. A glider with gray scales backhanded a small dark-haired girl so hard she went sprawling to the ground.

Surin never made a sound.

Anaiya, face blotchy with fresh bruises and stained with tears, scrambled to latch herself onto the glider's arm in silent petition. The demon warrior jerked her loose with a violent shrug before looping the sinuous length of its tail around Surin's torso and lifting her body clear off the ground. Surin convulsed, blood leaking from the corner of her mouth as the glider constricted its tail.

Evangeline shot out of her hiding place. "Stop!"

The warrior reared back, flashing serpentine fangs that threatened pain and poison. Evangeline expelled a sharp breath. Railea's tears, she needed to get the archmage. Could she project her thoughts across such a distance? She'd barely succeeded when she was seated beside him. She brandished the dagger in her hand with deceptive steadiness. "Let go. You're killing her!"

A whimper of warning escaped Anaiya's lips before it was quickly silenced. Evangeline's pounding heart ratcheted up her throat. Another glider with duskier coloring loomed over the other woman, keeping her on her knees.

Archmage, help me! Evangeline projected as loudly as she could. *Declan!*

No response.

Surin's tormentor discarded the child's limp form and darted at Evangeline without warning. She jumped back, but a powerful tail tightened around her midsection before she could run. Evangeline struck out with the blade. At the glider's sibilant slur, she hissed in satisfaction. She'd drawn blood.

The glider snarled another imprecation and slammed her to the ground. The blade flew from her hand while flecks of black danced in her vision. She clawed blindly at the serpentine muscle coiled around her, but her blunt nails were useless against the demon's hard scales. Evangeline's captor heaved her up and knocked her to the ground again, this time with a force that emptied her lungs. The taste of iron coated her tongue.

Evangeline! The archmage's telepathic voice rang in her head, unusually distraught, but she was too dazed to respond.

The demon grabbed a fistful of her hair and yanked her to her feet. Scalp throbbing, Evangeline aimed a sluggish kick at the glider's groin. Her efforts proved futile. So she did the last thing she could. She twisted, ignoring the searing pain at her scalp, and bit down onto her captor's forearm. Hard.

He howled like an enraged bull and hurled Evangeline across the clearing as if she weighed no more than a babe. But she didn't slam into the ledge's rocky surface. It took her a few dizzying moments to realize a protective cushion of air buffeted her body.

Declan.

Despite the blood marring her vision, Evangeline's heart stuttered at the sight of him. His expression was violent, and his eyes burned with such vehemence that the gliders undulated backwards.

Declan spoke in the demon tongue, his voice low and deadly. In response, the warriors advanced, swords drawn. Two against one. There was no contest. No butchery. Just expertly sliced jugulars. Within seconds, the corpses of the two warriors stained the snow dark.

"What," Declan demanded, fury still ripe in his face, "did you think you were doing, Evangeline Barre?" His tone was low and admonishing, but his touch was gentle. So, so gentle as he cupped the side of her face to inspect the stinging gash at her temple.

"They were about to crush her. Surin." Her voice came out a croak.

He shushed her with his gaze pinned on her temple and his hands holding her face. "Be still."

Evangeline blinked but otherwise obeyed. A few breaths later, the wounded skin on the side of her head began to . . . itch.

"What are you doing?"

"Shh…" he murmured without taking his gaze away.

It seemed like a small eternity before Declan released her. Then he narrowed his eyes at the two slaves, as if noticing them for the first time. Anaiya quailed, but she held her daughter in a protective embrace.

"Are there any other guards?" he asked Anaiya.

The woman, fearful though she was, mustered enough courage to speak. "No, my lord." Anaiya shot him a timorous glance before dropping her head. "I snuck away from the village as I was hoping to convince my lady to take Surin with her. But . . . Oarthilin and Yirkwin caught us, and they decided to teach me a lesson. They were going to defile my baby in front of me." Anaiya spat at the bodies.

Repugnance lanced through Evangeline despite her throbbing temple. The gliders weren't even human. Why would they want a human girl?

There is more than one way to violate a woman, little fire. Most demonkind derive pleasure from fear and pain. They can be . . . sadistic. His voice was a soft murmur in her mind, but she could feel the burn of his wrath as he regarded the bodies on the ground.

She stared at him. Her outburst hadn't been verbal. "Are you . . . reading my mind, Archmage?"

He shook his head. "Disgust is written all over your face. Even the deaf can guess your thoughts," he muttered, almost defensively.

"But you heard me? When I called for you?"

"No. I felt your fear." His gaze hardened. "What were you thinking? You should *never* have ventured out on your own."

Her lips parted. Even when she'd called him names, he'd never spoken to her with such censure. She dipped her chin, and her shoulders drooped in accord.

Evangeline turned to the young girl who remained still and silent. "Are you all right, Surin?"

Fearful, dark eyes met hers before quickly darting away.

"We need to leave." Declan lifted Evangeline in his arms

with a tenderness that opposed the rebuke in his tone. "The bodies will eventually be found, and it won't take the gliders long to realize what happened and connect it to us."

"My lord, please. Please take us with you." Anaiya went to her knees, desperation flooding her face. "We will be punished when Chief Ulrik finds his men dead. He will surely kill us."

Evangeline held her breath, imploring eyes of frigid green with her own.

His jaw tensed. "You will need to keep up."

With two slain soldiers abandoned and two missing slaves in tow, Declan forbade any return to the temple. "It will be the first place the gliders think to search," he said.

Evangeline couldn't argue.

"We'll move higher up the mountains. Find new shelter," Declan said as he led them up the rocky highlands, paving the way with Evangeline bundled in his arms. Despite her indignant protests, he insisted on carrying her like an invalid while Anaiya led her daughter through the rugged bends.

Throughout the ascent, both mother and daughter remained as silent as the man who continued to radiate frost. Evangeline kept glancing back, fearful Anaiya and Surin would be left behind and worried her weight would further strain the archmage's wound.

But it was as though he weren't even injured. Declan moved at an unforgiving pace, but the pair was surprisingly nimble footed despite their appearance. They kept up even when their journey took on a precarious path that hugged the mountain's edge. Evangeline snuck a peek over the archmage's shoulder and was overwhelmed by a rush of vertigo. The ledge was a steep fall into a crevasse mired in swirling mist and snow, which did nothing to soften the serrated rocks below.

"Surin!" Anaiya's voice, shrill and fearful, pierced the whipping winds. The girl stumbled out of her mother's reach, arms flailing. Evangeline scored Declan's skin with her nails, certain the child was an instant away from gruesome death. Declan didn't stop; neither did he spare a backward glance.

But Surin didn't fall.

Mother and child seemed to be bolstered by the same buffer of air that had prevented her own collision with the rocky ledge.

Perhaps the archmage wasn't that heartless, after all.

SEVENTEEN

"Are you thirsty, my lady?" Anaiya asked for what seemed like the hundredth time, even though Evangeline had already declined. The woman glanced at her, relentless. "I could fetch you more fresh snow." They were so high up in the mountains that the snowfall reached their knees. Declan had deemed the snow fresh enough to consume, which was just as well, because they had no other sources of water.

Evangeline went to shake her head but winced instead. The action alone caused her facial muscles to protest. She could hardly open her left eye, swollen as it was. Then there was the gash across her temple. It was so deep she suspected Declan had done something supernatural to staunch the wound. A cut that wide could not have stopped bleeding on its own.

Declan appeared at the entrance, hands full of firewood. Anaiya shrank back, resettling herself beside Surin, who remained woefully silent.

Evangeline hadn't thought she would ever miss the grisly

temple and the macabre basin—but she did. This cave, a large bell-like enclosure with a wide, gaping entrance was almost torturously cold in comparison with the altar chamber. Last night, Declan had managed to start a fire easily, but with the limited amount of wood and merciless winds, the flames had flailed and remained pitifully small.

Declan tossed fresh tinder into the feeble fire, his jaw tense as his eyes searched her face. "I'll hunt for some food and look for more of that yellow root. You'll need more poultice." Without another word, he marched out into the cold again.

The altercation with the gliders seemed to have negated whatever had blossomed between them. Declan had reverted to his cool impassiveness, his speech clipped and mannerisms brusque. He barely spoke, but she sensed his fury as much as the chill. The archmage might appear outwardly calm, but he clearly had a temper.

Yet, as they'd settled down for sleep last night, he had tugged her unceremoniously into his arms, though he'd been careful with her bruises. Although awkward in the presence of Anaiya and Surin, Evangeline hadn't protested as he cuddled her to sleep. His nearness had been a comfort.

"His Lordship is displeased." Anaiya whispered even though Declan had long left. Evangeline didn't tell the other woman that he was no mere lord, knowing the truth would only cause the woman more fear, but Anaiya proved more astute than Evangeline had given her credit for. "He is no ordinary mage, is he?" she asked.

Evangeline attempted a faint smile, but her facial muscles groaned, so she grimaced instead. "Declan . . . is a powerful mage," she said at last. Not exactly a lie. "Frostiness is his usual state," she added to put the woman at ease. "But he isn't a bad man."

"Not a bad man, no," Anaiya murmured, gently running

her fingers through her daughter's tangled black tresses. "But he cares for you, and he is clearly displeased at the hurt we have indirectly caused you."

Evangeline blinked. "Of course not."

Declan was annoyed with *her* and her interference, which had forced his hand. She had driven them to their current predicament. Evangeline told the other woman as much.

"Is that what you think, my lady?" A raised brow hinted of the woman Anaiya must have been before her enslavement.

"Please, Anaiya, for the last time. I'm no lady." Evangeline averted her eyes. She didn't want to think about Declan and his feelings. Or his lack of feelings. And because the other woman no longer showed any signs of trepidation around her, Evangeline braved the question. "How did you and Surin end up here?"

For a terrible moment, Evangeline thought she'd driven the woman to tears with her insensitivity, but after a lengthy pause, Anaiya disclosed a heartbreaking tale of a husband with a bad gambling habit that had led to prodigious debts. She had caught the eye of his usurer, and her husband had been all too willing to trade his wife for a clean credit account. The usurer had eventually peddled her into the fae cartel—but not before he impregnated her.

"I'm so sorry," Evangeline whispered, her heart twisting and eyes watering at the woman's hardships. Anaiya reached out and patted her hand, a forlorn smile on her rawboned face. Evangeline swallowed, fighting an internal skirmish to regain composure when a hissing sound broke the silence. For the first time, Surin opened her mouth.

And screamed.

Digging deep into the frozen ground, Declan unearthed a small yellow-tinged root Evangeline had ground into a poultice for their wounds. But this one was barely the size of his thumb. They were too high up. He tugged the tiny root free with a bad-tempered jerk. Impatience gnawed like a gnat beneath his skin, far more persistent than the ache in his shoulder.

To make matters worse, his powers continued to dwindle at an excruciating rate.

He'd exerted so much of his psychic reserve to get Anaiya and Surin safely up the mountain that he couldn't even erect a barrier over the cave's entryway to keep out the winds. And now he didn't dare trek too far to hunt lest the women needed him. *Evangeline* needed him. No. What she needed was to be back in Amereen, to be in the care of his healers.

Where in hellfire was Gabriel?

The vision of Evangeline hurtling across the clearing kept replaying in Declan's mind. If he'd arrived a fraction later, she would have slammed right into the craggy rockface, an impact that would have shattered bones. Why had she wandered out in the open on her own? Why hadn't he thought to reseal the entrance with the pillar when he'd returned from the pool chamber? One night plied with kisses and he'd been reduced to a besotted fool, lulled to sleep by the scent of her alone.

He was culpable for all the bruises that marred her face, the swollen eye, the split lip. The gash across the temple had been so deep he'd had to staunch her wound with telekinesis—a delicate procedure. No easy feat for a being who had never used his powers for anything other than destruction. Too much pressure and he would cause more harm, potentially damaging her cranium.

Evangeline had whimpered in her sleep, not from nightmares but from the pain. The rest of her body must have been mottled with bruises. He'd wanted to rip the ill-fitting garment apart to check the damage done, but he could hardly do more than hold her in the presence of Anaiya and Surin.

His fists clenched harder at the thought of the mother and child. The need to mete out vengeance throbbed in his gut. Once he brought the women back to the safety of his castle, he would return, and Chief Ulrik would find himself face to face with an archmage unhindered by innocents.

As Declan prowled back toward the cave, a mental voice echoed. Far away, but distinct. Relief suffused him. He had never been more glad to hear the Unseelie's voice.

Focusing on the nascent thread of Gabriel's mental signature, Declan deepened the telepathic connection. Wisps of black materialized before him, the smoky tendrils a stark contrast to the snowy backdrop, coalescing into a dark portal. Instead of Gabriel's cocky grin, Declan saw his commander's hard-hewn face.

"Sire, it is so good to see you." Killian's relief was patent as he stepped out of the portal, but after a whole century of service, the commander knew better than to ask after Declan's wellbeing. "All is in order," Killian reported with a reassuring nod.

Declan clasped the commander's hand in silent greeting, grateful for his steadfastness. A chorus of *sires* sounded as five of his battlemages emerged from the depths of the nebulous portal, followed by the fae guildmaster.

Gabriel grinned. "Never thought I'd catch you looking less than pristine, Archmage. Five flaming hells, I wasn't even sure if you needed to shave."

"What took you so long?" Declan couldn't quite keep the snarl in his throat.

The battlemages shifted uneasily at his uncharacteristic

outburst, but Gabriel merely shrugged while the shadows of his portal swirled with the promise of home.

"You warped into an imploding portal, Archmage. Tracking you was like fishing for a siren in the sea." His eyes narrowed at the little root clasped in Declan's hand. "What's that?"

Declan shook his head. Tossed the goldenseal aside. "Doesn't matter. Keep your portal open, and wait for me here." Turning on his heel, Declan motioned for Killian and his battlemages to join him as he marched back toward the cave, eager to get all three of his charges proper medical care.

"Ozenn's blood, where are you going?" Gabriel followed, ignoring Declan's command. After two centuries of alliance, the Unseelie knew when he could get away with defiance.

"I need to retrieve Evangeline and a couple of civilians."

"Evangeline?" Gabriel arched a brow. "She the wench you warped after?" Declan's lack of response did not deter the Unseelie in the slightest. A mischievous gleam lit his eyes. "Is she worth eight days in Draedyn's Realm, Archmage?"

Noto, the gruffest of the battlemages, scowled at the fae. "Don't you ever shut up, Blacksage?"

Gabriel gave another insouciant shrug as they approached the cave. "No one in his right mind would warp into an imploding—"

Declan shot forward, his heart squeezing at the sight of disturbed snow near the entrance. Anaiya lay crumpled on the ground, legs bent at an unnatural angle. Evangeline and Surin were missing.

Killian checked the woman's pulse. "She's still alive, sire."

"Anaiya." Declan cupped the woman's bony face, a lethal calm suffusing his blood. "Anaiya, wake."

It took long, precious seconds for Anaiya to regain consciousness. The woman's eyelids unhinged with obvious effort, the black of her eyes unfocused. "Gliders." A stuttering breath laced with bloody spittle. Anaiya had not only had her legs broken but also a dagger embedded in her gut. The same one he'd left in Evangeline's keeping.

Unadulterated rage, thick and viscous, congealed his blood. Ice in his veins.

It was time the gliders learned the consequences of provoking an archmage.

The rough jostle jarred Evangeline awake. When darkness threatened again, she bit the inside of her mouth to disrupt the catatonic haze.

Declan . . .

Could he even hear her? Her thoughts came slow, her senses sluggish. The glider's darts had to be laced with some form of sedative that rendered her mind a labyrinth of cobwebs. Evangeline blinked. The streaks of red in her vision came from the reopened gash at her temple. She hung upside down, slung over a glider's shoulder like a hunk of meat. Crimson droplets marred the slithering tracks her captors left on the pristine carpet of white.

The air rushed from her lungs as she was dropped to the ground, smooth slabs of stone cleared of snow. Surin followed, discarded in a heap by her side. Relief punched through Evangeline's disoriented state. The child appeared unconscious but otherwise unharmed.

The stench of cadavers cloyed the air, the overripe odor mingling with that of fresh blood. Carcasses of indeterminate creatures piled near a crude oven—a large clay mound on a stone base. Evidence of campfires littered the ground, punctuated by totem poles carved with serpentine heads. Crude thatched huts were decorated with rough textiles and macabre skulls that could belong to no creature from her own realm. Heart sinking into the pit of her gut, Evangeline fumbled to sit upright, but the motion threatened to upend the contents of her belly.

"Declan will come for me," she whispered aloud for reassurance. He'd promised he would bring her home, and Declan wouldn't break his promises. Would he?

But he'd been so angry with her . . .

A heckling laugh assaulted her senses like a lascivious touch. Before she could focus on the source, she was jerked against a bare male torso. The fetid scent of rot filled her nose as another bout of hissing laughter filled her ears. She shoved at her captor, straining to get away. Dough white hands palmed her breasts roughly.

Evangeline yelped. Panic churned in her stomach, and bile rose up her throat. A tail tightened around her midsection much like yesterday, but this time, the scaly tip slid up between her legs with lecherous intent.

Her fear grew talons, shredding her innards.

Thump. Thump. Thump. A woman's breathless sobs. "Come here, little girl." Lewd laughter. Muffled screams she wasn't sure were her own . . .

Every fiber in Evangeline's being recoiled with renewed vigor fueled by terror. Like a mindless animal, she lashed out. Kicking. Clawing. Biting. The glider released her, hissing in pain as her fingers gouged unnatural, chalky flesh.

She was quickly held down by another pair of corpse-cold hands. A fist hammered into her midsection, knocking her breathless. Her vision swam, but she refused to go under. She would not relive this heinous nightmare—death was preferable. She swiped out again and screamed in desperation. Her actions were ineffectual.

Evangeline!

The urgency of the voice broke through her frenzied state. For a moment, she wondered if she'd imagined it, too fearful to hope. Then, craaack! The barbarous sound of crunching bones followed by her captor's tortured shrieks. The glider folded like a house of cards while the rest of its comrades scrambled out of the way. A cacophony of shouts and frantic hisses filled the air.

She blinked rapidly to ensure she wasn't seeing things.

A sob of relief welled in her throat. Railea, goddess of light, she would recognize that profile anywhere. The raven-black hair that was soft to the touch, the broad shoulders and muscled chest she'd come to know so intimately, and the sinewy hands that could be both hard and gentle. The symbols decorating his skin were afire. They flared, as though liquid gold ran through his veins instead of blood. His sword glistened with the same golden blaze as it cleaved through bodies like a scythe shearing hay.

Declan swept through the chaos in a blur of movement, a deadly cyclone dismembering everything in his path. Evangeline stifled a cry as he hacked an adversary in half—the tail still undulating a mad, mindless dance even as the torso hit the ground. No neatly sliced jugulars this time. Declan butchered them like meat.

More gliders swarmed into action, a torrential wave bearing staffs and spears.

Archmage or no, how could he fend off an entire clan of gliders?

That was when she realized he wasn't alone. Other men fought by his side. Men in black armor bearing the distinct sigil of a golden dragon.

Hope rekindled in her chest.

Evangeline mustered the remainder of her strength to turn

to Surin and gather the unconscious girl in her arms before slumping into the metal fixture behind her. Her head was swimming, her consciousness waning in time with the relentless trickle from the reopened gash at her temple.

A whimper registered to her withdrawing senses. She'd backed into a cage.

A cage holding a mutilated occupant impossibly human in form. Haunted blue eyes stared back at her.

"Gods, what have they done to you?" Evangeline gasped, jerking away reflexively, just in time to see a glider drive a spear straight through Declan's shoulder.

The relief of finding Evangeline alive spread through his bones for an instant before the spear punched through his shoulder, right through his festering wound. Declan howled as the lance ripped through muscle and sinew. Pain rippled like a streak of hellfire, but it did nothing to slow the adrenaline racing in his veins.

Nothing to dull the fury churning in his gut.

If anything, it only fueled his frenzy.

Ignoring the worried cries of his battlemages in his mind, Declan jammed his sword through the glider's neck. Severed its head. With a feral snarl, he ripped the spear out of his chest and thrust it through the tail of an approaching glider, pinning the demon to the ground. Another heave of his sword spilled the creature's innards.

In a haze of blood and fury, Declan sliced and slashed his way through the endless horde, fighting to keep Evangeline within his sight.

He didn't need to touch her mind to know her fear. She

had crawled next to a large cage, with Surin cradled in her arms. Her body curved around the child like a human shield.

A glider attempted to haul her into the cage. Declan couldn't remember the last time he'd felt such outrage. When Evangeline did little to fight, he couldn't remember the last time he'd felt such terror.

"Get your filthy hands off her!" His bellow seemed to stun the gliders. A number staggered, tails wriggling wildly as they dropped their weapons to cover their ears with their hands. He'd yelled out on the telepathic plane, too. So loud he'd unwittingly projected the cry into the minds of every living creature within the vicinity.

And it appeared gliders were vulnerable to telepathy.

"Take your whore and leave us." The grated hiss came from an elderly glider wearing a string of miniature skulls around his neck. Intricate tribal tattoos adorned his forehead like a crown. Chief Ulrik, Declan presumed. At their chief's gesture, surviving gliders retreated, leaving Declan and his men in the crimson area riddled with bodies. Without a word, Declan sheathed his bloody sword and hurried toward Evangeline and the child.

He reached for Evangeline, pausing when he noticed his gore-slicked hands. Chest still heaving, Declan wiped his hands on his pants before gathering her into his arms. The wound on the side of her head had reopened. Scarlet trailed down the side of her face while her chest rose and fell with shallow puffs. Declan released a shuddering breath.

He felt her vulnerability as if it were his own.

"Evangeline?" he whispered, even though he knew her to be unconscious. A quick glance at Surin told him the child was equally insensate.

"A portal, Gabriel." His voice came out hoarse, his tone

urgent. Declan glanced up to see Gabriel and his men crowding over him, their faces lined with bewilderment.

A soft whine drew his attention.

A girl, brutalized beyond imagination, cowered within the cage like an animal. Fresh rage swelled in his chest. He stood with Evangeline tucked carefully in his arms and snarled at the glider chief.

"I want every single slave in your possession. Freed. Now."

EIGHTEEN

Brightness seeped through her eyelids, accompanied by the rude trill of cheery birds. The scent of flowering blossoms and freshly cut grass filled her senses. Had she fallen asleep with the windows open again? Evangeline could well be lying on a cloud, her skin kissed by the smoothest silk. Unwilling to leave the hazy folds of sleep, she curled onto her side and was confronted by pinpricks of needling pain. The final remnants of sleep sifted away, replaced by a stinging slap of reality.

Railea's tears, Declan had taken a spear through his shoulder!

She bolted up only to slump back into the soft bedding as a wave of dizziness crashed through her. A moan escaped her throat.

"Whoa," exclaimed an unfamiliar male voice.

"Slow down, sweetness. You're safe." This voice was female, and it sounded kind. Reassuring.

Evangeline blinked rapidly, hands shading her eyes from the searing brightness, trying to make sense of the voices and her surroundings. Two beautiful, high-arched windows were partly open, allowing air and sun into the room. Sedate cream paper covered the walls, trimmed with intricate plasterwork Evangeline had only ever seen in official buildings in larger villages. Where was Declan?

A man sat near her bedside, staring at her with unconcealed curiosity. She squinted up at him, at the egregious scar bisecting one side of his face from eye to cheek. Judging from the subtle aura of power he exuded, he was unmistakably a mage. Evangeline swallowed convulsively. She had never seen a scarred mage before. Their regenerative abilities meant wounds rarely left a scar . . .

"Lie back." He rose from his seat, the breadth of his frame crowding her vision.

Evangeline parted her lips but only managed a small whimper. Her throat worked erratically to find her voice as she stared into his disapproving gaze.

"Sit down. You're scaring the girl." Clad in hues of cream and celadon with jade-green ribbons woven into her straight black hair, the woman appeared no older than Evangeline. In stark contrast to the man, she was small and shapely, with a complexion the shade of fawn and wide eyes slightly tilted at the edges. Evangeline had only ever encountered traveling merchants who passed through Arns with similar coloring and features, and they had all hailed from the province of Jachuana.

The man's frown deepened. "I was only concerned."

The woman peered down at her with a warm smile. "Hello there, I'm Mailin, one of the healers," she said before canting her head at the man. Her lips curved into a mischievous grin. "And I apologize on behalf of Killian. He really isn't as scary as he pretends to be."

"Oh, I can be plenty scary, and you know it," Killian said

with a huff, but the obvious adoration in his eyes as he glanced at the healer loosened the tension in Evangeline's shoulders. Mailin sidled up to him with ease, and Evangeline didn't miss the absent but tender way he caressed her rounded stomach.

Evangeline attempted to sit up again, but the healer tutted. "Take it easy, please. You've taken quite a beating."

"Where am I?" Evangeline scanned the room. "Where's Declan?"

The healer's perfectly manicured brow hiked up. "*Declan?*"

Evangeline's hands tightened on the bedspread. "Yes . . . is he all right?"

Mailin exchanged an indeterminate look with Killian, who chuckled. He straightened in his seat. "My lady, you have no cause for concern. You're in a guest room in the Castle of Amereen. And the sire is well."

Evangeline stared up at him with equal measures of relief and wariness.

Mailin nodded her assurance as she tipped the contents of a flask into a ceramic cup painted with blue petals. "Killian is right. The sire—Declan—is fine. You, on the other hand . . . " She deposited the floral mug into Evangeline's hands. "Drink."

Evangeline took a heady gulp of the water, a soothing balm to her parched throat. Discomforted by their curious scrutiny, Evangeline studied the room.

The rest of the chamber was as luxurious as the bed she lay upon, which was laden with soft furs and plush pillows. A lacquered writing desk was tucked in one corner, adorned with a slim vase of verbena sprigs. On the opposite end stood a gleaming vanity bearing a large, oval mirror in a gilded frame. It reflected a little alcove with a stately fireplace and a plush settee that matched the color of the walls.

The quiet extravagance of her surroundings only amplified

the memory of the taste of iron in her mouth, the sound of clashing steel as Declan hacked his way toward her, and the tiny bundle of warmth she'd been so desperate to protect.

"Surin?" Evangeline tightened her fingers around the mug. "Anaiya?"

"They are in the infirmary, along with the other girl," Killian supplied as he watched her with curious eyes.

"The other girl?"

"The sire ordered every slave be freed. The mother and daughter you asked about, Anaiya and Surin? They are only two of the three slaves we found in the glider village."

Evangeline's hand went to her throat when she recalled the mutilated girl in the cage. Mistaking her reaction for fear, Mailin patted her knee. "You're safe. No one will harm you here. I promise."

Evangeline had guessed as much, so hearing this did little to calm her agitation. "Can I see him? Declan?" She had to see him. Needed to see for herself that the spear hadn't caused as much damage as she'd thought.

Killian's brows arched.

Evangeline's hand flew to her cheek. "I mean . . . the lord archmage. I meant no disrespect."

"I understand, my lady. But the sire is still in the shadow realm."

Evangeline gaped. "But . . . ," she sputtered, worry choking her speech, "the gliders . . . "

Killian shook his head. "The sire all but painted the glider clan in red, slaughtering every demon in his path . . . " He emitted an uneasy laugh. "I've never seen the sire lash out with such feral brutality in all the summers I've served him. The gliders would be fools to challenge him in any way."

At her unconvinced expression, Killian chuckled. "The sire will return soon enough, and I'm sure he'll see you then."

The infirmary was a much larger room than the one Evangeline had woken up in, with several beds lining the walls. Anaiya remained unconscious, her painfully bony form padded with gauze and legs set in a heavy cast. Surin, however, was fully awake, huddled like a tiny mouse beside her mother's bed. A patient in the farthest bed was obscured by a curtain.

"Is that her?" Evangeline asked, remembering haunted blue eyes. Mailin nodded, but the healer's grim expression told her this patient was off-limits. Evangeline turned her attention back to Anaiya and Surin, not wanting to overstep her boundaries. The healer had allowed her a visit to the infirmary, but only because Evangeline had refused to take no for an answer.

"Surin, why are you out of bed?" Mailin raised a brow in reproof but kept her tone light. Evangeline liked the healer even more for it. The child watched Mailin and Killian with open anxiety. She shied away when the healer attempted to usher her back to bed. Evangeline shuffled toward the bedside, her own body still an aching throb, and to her surprise, Surin pressed her little body against hers in silent welcome.

"I'm glad to see you, too," Evangeline said with a soft laugh and hugged the child, not caring of the filth that still clung to her. Surin had refused to be touched—even for a bath.

As Mailin relayed Anaiya's injuries to Evangeline, it became clear the woman should have been dead. But still she clung to life. The woman was a fighter, and clearly, Mailin was no ordinary healer. A quiet hum of energy emanated from the woman as she ran competent hands down Anaiya's torso and legs.

Evangeline frowned. She'd never seen mages heal with magic before. "You're not a mage."

Mailin shook her head with a secretive smile. "No, I'm not."

Sudden realization hit, and Evangeline's lips parted.

"You're a halfbreed," she whispered in fascination. "*Seelie* halfbreed."

Surprise flickered on the other woman's face. "Yes." Then she grinned and tucked her hair back to reveal ears with a subtle point at the tips. "People can't usually guess what I am without looking at my ears."

Evangeline couldn't stem her own delight and wonderment at meeting a halfbreed of any kind. "I could almost feel the healing energy flowing from you. But I thought Seelie halfbreeds were nearly—" She bit down on her lip as she recalled her sense of decorum.

"Extinct?" Mailin finished for her, seemingly unoffended by her line of thought. "We are. There haven't been more descendants from the Seelie. Not since the Winter War."

Evangeline fidgeted with her fingers. "I'm sorry," she said finally. "I didn't mean to raise it."

Mailin's smile was rueful but her tone was pragmatic. "Well, no point skirting facts, especially when they're already history. The Unseelie king may have massacred the entire Seelie race, but he didn't wipe out the halfbreeds. We are dying out because most of us chose to intermarry with humans or mages, diluting our magic with each new generation."

"Pity," Killian mused, running a hand down the healer's back.

"It is, but I wouldn't have chosen differently," Mailin declared, confirming Evangeline's initial suspicion. The pair was mated.

Such tenderness filled Killian's eyes that Evangeline quickly averted her own. Even though the couple did no more than exchange a glance, they exuded an intimacy that made her feel like an accidental voyeur.

Evangeline shifted her attention back to Surin and nudged the girl into bed. "I'll come see you again," she promised with a reassuring smile.

She stroked the girl's hair and cast one last look at the veiled bed in the corner before she allowed Mailin to lead her back to the guest room.

"You're good with Surin," Mailin said after tucking Evangeline up like a child. "She has refused to let any of us touch her since she woke. And what's more, she hasn't uttered a single word."

Heart clenching, Evangeline shook her head. "I haven't heard her speak a word, either." True horror had a way of choking a child to silence. She knew better than anyone. "I need to send word to my mother in Arns. I need her to know I am safe."

Mailin grinned. "The sire has already taken care of that. He had a messenger sent to Arns when it was clear you needed to remain here until you recover."

Evangeline's lips curved in response. Yes, the archmage kept his promises. Sleep whispered like a persistent lullaby, and Evangeline stifled a yawn. She slid under the covers with a little sigh. Her eyelids were heavy, but the need to see him was an ache that ran deeper than her bruises.

"Will he be back soon?"

She never heard Mailin's response as the wings of sleep snared her in their fold.

NINETEEN

I t was already dusk when Declan returned to his castle. Chief Ulrik, he was certain, would never touch a human slave from any realm again. Declan left the glider clan with the chief's head still attached to his shoulders. Whether the demon survived the impairment of his tail was another matter. Regardless, Declan hadn't been able to discern anything useful about the gliders' alliance with the Winter Court.

He clenched his jaw.

The Unseelie would have struck more than one such alliance with the gliders. Ulrik's was likely one of myriad glider clans scattered throughout Draedyn's Realm. How many more humans were trapped in that snow-laden hell-hole? Declan tensed, surprised by the intensity of his rage. When had he begun caring about the fate of slaves?

"Does anyone else know you have been involved in my retrieval?" Declan asked Gabriel, whose violet eyes scoured the dimming skies before fixing upon a soaring eagle.

"Only your own people and my second-in-command were

involved, and my man can keep a secret. But after what you've done to Ulrik's clan . . . " Gabriel trailed off with a pointed shrug.

Declan bared his teeth in a smile saved for when he had death on his mind. "Ulrik and what's left of his warriors will serve as a warning to neighboring clans. They understood that they would only incite my return should they speak of my involvement."

Gabriel grinned. "In that case, I don't think they are liable to speak of it." The eagle dipped and circled low, flying close enough to touch.

"Good."

Gabriel took his leave by way of eagle's wings, his body shifting into a dark, amorphous cloud to possess the wild bird. Another Unseelie would have been enervated by now, with all the portals he'd opened for Declan and his men. But Gabriel Blacksage was no ordinary Unseelie. The guildmaster had magic leaking from his pores.

Declan warped into the hallway outside Evangeline's guest room. Killian, tasked with guarding her, met him by the door.

"She is asleep."

Declan knew as much. He'd unconsciously reached out to her on the mental plane the moment he stepped back into the castle.

Killian proceeded to give him a brief rundown on Evangeline's waking hours. "And she asked to see you, sire," Killian added with a wry smile. "Several times, in fact."

At that, tendrils of warmth curled in Declan's chest to ease the feral edge that had been riding him since his butchery of the glider clan. He gave Killian a brisk nod of dismissal before warping into Evangeline's room, not wanting to risk waking her by using the door.

She was curled up on her usual side, her breathing deep

and even. The bruises on her face remained vivid, but the swelling had receded. Mailin had done well. Evangeline's rich brown hair fanned across the pillow, soft and glossy. Declan fisted his hands in his pockets so he didn't give in to the temptation to touch. He felt like a stalker, stealing into her room in the dark of night, staring at her while she slept, but he *needed* to see her before he returned to his own quarters. Needed to see for himself she was healing, comfortable and safe.

It was some time later before he warped into his bedchamber.

A prickle ran down his spine. He wasn't alone. He was but an instant away from obliterating the unexpected presence when a familiar voice purred.

"My liege, there you are."

She rose from her languid sprawl across his bed to display a sultry dress with too much lace and too little fabric.

"What are you doing here, Vera?" Declan didn't bother hiding his annoyance. He did not permit anyone but the chambermaids —and even then, only a select few—free access to his private quarters. Vera blanched at his tone but recovered swiftly with a deep and graceful curtsy that showed a great deal of cleavage.

"Waiting for you, my liege."

Most men, even archmages, wouldn't mind finding Vera in their bed at night, with her hair of spun gold, smooth caramel skin, and curves in all the right places. But Declan had a peculiarity that distinguished him from most men.

He *never* brought a woman to his bed.

He had a taste for women, had bedded far more than his due, but never here. His bed was a personal sanctuary he didn't want tainted by the scent of anyone else.

He'd lived a mortal lifetime of sexual depravity the first eighty-seven summers in his father's court. He'd experienced everything the act had to offer. On occasion, his father had offered him willing men—a taste he hadn't acquired. Eighty-seven summers mired in constant sex, sweat, and eager women had been enough to put him off sex for a long while. When he'd finally withdrawn from celibacy, he'd sought out women who made no demands of him.

Unlike Vera.

Declan had no wish to bind himself in any way to any woman, not even when he was entitled to as many ayaris as he wished. Freya never had returned the piece of his heart she'd claimed so many summers ago, and his mother had ensured what remained thereafter could never offer anything deeper than affection.

"I don't recall requesting company." He kept his tone cool and clipped, but she was undeterred.

Vera trailed a suggestive finger down his bicep. "My liege, you know you never have to ask for me."

When Declan remained still, she sidled closer, pressing her body against his. "After so many days in the wilderness, I thought you might seek some . . . companionship."

The scent of her was lavish, a bouquet of roses. Seductively feminine and ripe for the taking. The most primal part of him hardened. He could easily tumble her into the bed of the nearest guestroom, get the release his body so patently needed. But it wasn't the scent of lush roses he wanted wrapped around him tonight. What he wanted was a distinct blend of wildflowers with a soft hint of cream.

Frustration flickered across her perfect features. Vera Anastasia Khan was no ordinary courtier. Not only was she a trained ayari, but she was also the only daughter of Sebastian Khan, the archmage of Batuhan. It went without saying that the man who claimed her would indirectly strengthen his ties to Sebastian—an archmage of old, with powers to rival even Declan's father.

"Will you finally take me to bed tonight?" Vera's voice was a husky whisper. She ran her palms down his chest, a bold move from a woman who knew her own worth, even to an archmage. He remained motionless as he considered her offer.

Declan had always been wary of Vera's choice to serve his court. Aside from Sebastian's court, and that of the Echelon's only female archmage, Sonja Tuath, Vera still had the courts of five other archmages to choose from. Although it was unlikely any woman would willingly choose to serve Dakari, a sadistic misogynist, or Alejandro, who already had as many ayaris as the sky had stars. But Vera still had the choice of Orus, who was easily the most benevolent of them all, or Arjun, who was so stunningly handsome it was said the goddess Railea herself had graced his chambers. Then there was also Declan's father, Nathaniel, indisputably the oldest and most powerful of them all.

Vera, a powerful mage in her own right, had chosen to leave her father's court only to serve in Declan's—an overt indication to the world that she wanted to be *his.* Yet Declan had driven his own councilors to the brink of exasperation in his disinclination to lay claim to Vera, or any other ayari for that matter, preferring to seek release in the arms of accommodating courtesans who could give a man every pleasure and no pressure for commitment.

He knew Vera could feel him hardening as triumph laced her smile. She went to the tip of her toes to kiss him. "Make me yours," she whispered, rubbing up against him, further tempting his flesh. "I know you want to."

She was right.

Vera offered something he knew Evangeline could not. He allowed Vera's lips to meet his, but the moment their lips grazed, he tensed. He felt no ardor. Vera tasted wrong. Her fragrance was too potent and her figure too voluptuous. Declan pulled away and extricated himself from her arms. Vera stared at him, confusion morphing into disbelief.

"You should take your allegiance back to your father, Vera. Or if you're intent on being an archmage's ayari, you'd be wise to consider Orus. He likely has more to offer."

Vera drew in an incredulous breath. "Sire, I meant no disrespect but—"

"I don't want to see you in my chambers again."

Her lips clamped shut.

Declan turned without a backward look. "And make no mistake, the next time you venture in uninvited, I *will* punish you."

TWENTY

E vangeline winced as she studied her reflection in the mirror. The woman staring back looked disheveled and brutalized and utterly out of place in the gilded frame. Still, she whispered, "Thank you." A prayer of gratitude to the gods.

She felt like a plant that had survived a drought long enough to finally see blessed rainfall. Her muscles had gone from sore to tender. Even the purple blotches on her face seemed less pronounced, although her temple still ached. Whatever the half-breed healer had done, it had been nothing short of remarkable.

Turning from the mirror, Evangeline padded barefoot toward the two high-arched windows and drew open the drapes to see more of the castle in the morning light.

A happy sigh slipped from her lips.

Her room was high enough that she glimpsed a slice of turquoise glimmering from afar. The Southern Seas. Her view was framed by stately sandstone walls and graceful towers. A glance downward stretched her smile.

A courtyard. It was filled with trees of varying shades, some tall and proud, some gnarled with age. Perennials added unexpected splashes of color. Bursts of hydrangeas waved up at her with wide, round heads, mingling with regal white calla lilies, flanked by taller clusters of foxgloves and hollyhocks. A charming little bird bath stood amid a riot of pink primroses and yellow marigolds, their panned faces basking in the sun. Picturesque.

A place that echoed elegance and beauty, much like the archmage who ruled it.

She wondered if Declan was back. The thought of him still in the shadow realm grated like sandpaper, scraping the smile from her face. With another sigh, she roamed the carpeted room in search of spare clothes. Evangeline had almost swooned when Mailin pointed out the adjoining private bath chamber, which she fully intended to utilize this morning. But when she unearthed a satin bathrobe from the large pecan dresser, a light knock sounded at her door.

"Come in," Evangeline said, fully expecting Mailin. Instead, a sweet-faced chambermaid with a head of dark, bouncy curls bustled in and bobbed a low curtsy that made Evangeline uncomfortable.

The chambermaid, who introduced herself as Tessa, set an exorbitant platter of food on the table by the settee. A dainty pot of tea. Creamed eggs, thinly sliced meats, bread rolls, and an array of mouthwatering pastries. There was even a separate plate just for fruit—perfectly sliced apples, pomegranate halves, and bulbous grapes.

Her stomach rumbled.

Belatedly realizing she was wearing nothing but a chemise, Evangeline hastily donned the bathrobe.

Tessa giggled. "My lady, there is no need for modesty. I all but bathed you while you were unconscious." Tessa gave her a saucy wink. "Nothing I haven't already seen."

Evangeline blushed. She knew someone had washed her while she was unconscious, but she had assumed it to be Mailin. "Thank you, Tessa," she mumbled, but continued to secure the satin sash around her waist. Seeking to diffuse her own awkwardness, Evangeline cast her attention upon the silver tray. "The food looks utterly divine."

Tessa beamed, seemingly pleased by the enthusiasm in her voice. "I had no clue what you'd like for breakfast, so I brought you a little of everything." The maid wandered to the bed and began straightening the sheets.

Evangeline wanted nothing more than to stuff one of the decadent-looking pastries into her mouth, but politeness caused her hesitation. "Um, won't you join me? There's so much food here."

Tessa turned to look at her as if she had grown two heads. Evangeline managed a small smile. No, maids did not join the table of the ladies they waited upon. But Evangeline was no highborn lady. She hailed from the humble village Arns—was as much a commoner as the maid fluffing her pillows.

She was about to explain her social standing when Mailin breezed in wearing a frivolous lilac dress with intricate floral motifs embroidered near the hem of her bell-shaped sleeves. In this outfit, the bump of her belly was even more noticeable. Mailin must have caught her gaze, for she patted her distended belly with a beam.

"Pickle is nearing his second summer now."

"Pickle?" Evangeline's lips quivered as she tried to squelch a laugh.

"It started off as a joke, but the nickname has grown on me, much to Killian's exasperation. But since I'm the one who'll carry him for all three summers, I get to call him whatever I like."

Evangeline smirked, nodding her agreement. Mages gestated for three full years before delivery, a fact Evangeline didn't envy, but the healer made it look easy. Mailin was radiant.

"How do you even know Pickle's a he?"

Mailin shrugged with a good-natured smile. "I don't. But Killian seems to think so." She gave her belly another rub as she eyed Evangeline's breakfast tray. "I am also constantly ravenous. At the rate I'm eating, I'm almost certain Pickle is trying to out-eat his father."

Evangeline chuckled. "Well, you're welcome to share."

"Oh, I intend to. No way you can finish all that on your own."

Evangeline made to pick up one of the trays, but Mailin waggled her finger. "Before we eat, let me do my job."

The healer made approving noises as she checked Evangeline's bruises, lingering at the gash on her temple. "You're recovering much quicker than I expected."

"For a human, you mean?" Evangeline nudged a plate of pastries at the healer in invitation. Mailin grinned and picked up a cherry-covered tart that matched the ribbon in her hair. "Well, yes. I hardly get any human patients around here, so I forget how long it takes for a mortal to recover . . . but you are doing so well. The bruises should fade entirely in a few days."

Unable to resist any longer, Evangeline selected the pastry she'd been eyeing. Crumbly layers of butter and chocolate melted in her mouth in an explosion of ecstasy. She consumed the confection in three greedy bites and swooped up another without hesitation.

"I'll be sure to bring chocolate every morning, my lady."

Tessa's cheeks dimpled as she filled her hands with folded linen. Evangeline swallowed, feeling graceless and ungainly.

"Please call me Evangeline. And I've had nothing but charred demon meat for eight days." Evangeline brushed the back of her hand across her lips to remove stray crumbs.

Seated beside her with soft skirts arranged like lilac petals and her legs demurely crossed, Mailin was a picture of gentility despite her claims of ravenous hunger. The healer took another dainty, birdlike bite of her pastry. But a sheen in the woman's eyes hinted at mischief. "I am probably overstepping my bounds, but everyone is eager to know . . . what exactly happened in Draedyn's Realm?"

Mailin's probing tone brought warmth to Evangeline's cheeks, but she gave the healer and the lingering chambermaid a brief recount of the events, careful to skim over the more intimate details. Then she stuffed another pastry into her mouth to discourage further questions and, when she was done with breakfast, abruptly excused herself in favor of a wash.

To her bemusement, Tessa bustled into the adjoining chamber to draw her bath, paying no heed to her protestations. Resigned, Evangeline left the eager maid to her duties but drew the line when Tessa offered to wash her. When Evangeline finally emerged after stewing pink in a copper tub with sweet-smelling salts, she was surprised to see Mailin still lounging on the settee. Evangeline wrapped arms around herself, self-conscious at meandering before the healer in nothing but a bathrobe.

Mailin didn't bat an eyelash at her state of undress. "Feeling better?"

"Hot water is a luxury I will never again take for granted."

With her muscles lax and her heart complacent, she allowed the maid to help her into a dress with a scoop-necked bodice and a skirt the color of buttercups. As Tessa braided her still-wet hair, Evangeline fingered the silk-soft linen of her flowing sleeves with disbelief. It was likely the finest thing she'd ever worn. She was even given silk slippers to match.

Wondering yet again if the archmage had returned, Evangeline caught the healer's gaze through the mirror. Since she didn't want to sound like a pining puppy, she sought to address the next thing on her mind. "Will you take me to the infirmary? I wish to see Surin and Anaiya again."

To her surprise, Mailin agreed readily. "I'm sure the child will benefit from your presence. She remains incredibly skittish."

They were in the middle of a wide, colonnaded hallway with intricate friezes and marble sculptures when the healer mentioned, "Killian told me the sire returned last night."

Evangeline swallowed, overwhelmed with relief, excitement, and an unwarranted tinge of disappointment.

Declan had returned but had not attempted to see her.

"I see," she managed with an awkward shrug. How did one request to see an archmage? She didn't even know where he resided within the castle, which was far larger than anything she'd ever imagined, the hallways alone longer than the main street of Arns. The Castle of Amereen was originally built as a citadel, Mailin explained as she played the tour guide, occasionally pointing out significant works of art that graced the walls. The infirmary, Evangeline discovered, spanned most of the eastern wing. It boasted twelve wards and even its own dispensary.

All thoughts of Declan dissolved when she arrived in the ward where Anaiya lay, still unconscious. Surin persisted her refusal to be touched or handled by anyone—the girl had not only declined all sustenance except water, but also refused to leave her mother's bedside even to relieve herself, driving the nurses to exasperation.

Surin wrapped spindly arms around Evangeline's waist in greeting, visibly relieved to see her. Evangeline spent the next hour trying to coax food into the girl, and it soon became evident Surin was leery of everything served.

"She's likely never tasted or seen food prepared like this," Evangeline said, recalling the crude clay oven in the glider village. On a hunch, she requested chunks of beef roasted without seasoning or spices. To her relief, Surin snatched up the proffered plate of meat and scampered off to her mother's bedside. She crouched down on her knees like a wary animal before devouring her meal with relish.

Satisfied, Evangeline murmured, "Let's take a bath now. Shall we?" Surin's new surroundings did nothing to mask the odor of urine and grime from her tattered clothes. The child tilted her head from side to side in confusion. It was then Evangeline realized the girl did not actually understand the language they spoke. She had been raised in the glider clan. She must not have picked up her mother's native tongue beyond a few rudimentary words. Evangeline conveyed her suspicions to the healer.

Mailin scrunched her lips, pity written all over her face. "Makes sense. The poor child. That's probably why she doesn't speak."

That and fear.

It was well past midday when Evangeline managed to get Surin adequately cleaned, having coaxed the girl to wipe herself with a washcloth and a basin of lukewarm water in lieu of a proper bath. Surin simply refused to leave her mother's bedside. Only after the girl had been persuaded to trade in her rags for a fresh set of clothes did Evangeline allow Mailin to usher her out of the infirmary.

"You're a patient, too," Mailin grumbled as she led her out of the eastern wing and down the double stairs of the main portico. "I can't have you working half the day the moment you're well enough to get out of bed." They strolled past a perfectly manicured lawn into another grand building.

"And missing lunch," Mailin admonished as if that were a cardinal sin.

"Are you this bossy with all your patients?" Evangeline teased. "With that massive breakfast, I'm not even—"

Evangeline's eyes widened as they came to an immense atrium made almost entirely of multitudinous panes of glass trimmed with gold. The breathtaking chamber was clearly meant for assemblies of sorts. A stately hardwood table with glossy benches filled the front end of the vast rectangular space. More seats lined the posterior in three tiers, arranged in a semicircular fashion.

The current assembly appeared to have just ended. Several men and women were still seated, but some had risen to form smaller clusters, still ensconced in conversation muted by the glass walls. Councilors, judging from their official white robes and gold sashes cinched at the shoulders. At the head of the table, listening to a distinguished-looking member, stood the archmage.

Dressed so distinctly among the sea of white and gold, he was impossible to miss. He wore fitted black trousers and a dark silk shirt with a mandarin collar under a formal coat similar to the one she'd commandeered in the shadow realm.

"Declan," she whispered before she realized she had pressed her palms to the glass, drawing curious gazes from some of the councilors within. She jerked her hands back, but not without leaving a handprint on the otherwise flawless panel. Declan seemed to sense her presence, because his head lifted that instant, and his eyes locked on hers.

Warmth washed over her cheeks.

His gaze alone was more intimate than a kiss.

She had seemingly disrupted the entire atrium, for two gilded panels swung open, and councilors filed out of the room, casting inquisitive glances her way. Unable to tear away from Declan's unwavering stare, she stood awkwardly by the glass wall. Mailin was whisked away by a small group of councilors, who all seemed eager to exchange pleasantries. The healer was obviously well regarded.

A subtle shimmer in the air was the only warning she got before Declan materialized before her. Evangeline backed into the glass panel. The dull thud of her impact reverberated, gaining her reproving stares from passing councilors.

"Be careful. You don't need any more bruises to add to your collection." The deep timbre of his voice was a sound she had grown so accustomed to that she hadn't realized she missed hearing it until now.

"I wouldn't have done that if you'd walked like a normal person." Evangeline fidgeted with her fingers, flustered now he was within touching distance. He was back to being the man she had first met, clean-shaven and pristinely dressed, not a hair out of place. It should civilize him. It didn't. If anything, it only highlighted his deadliness.

No amount of polish could dull the lethal edge of a sword.

"How are you feeling, little fire?" The endearment coupled with the scrutiny of spring-green eyes caused her heart to flutter like the wings of a hummingbird.

"Much better." Her gaze flitted to his shoulder where she'd seen the wicked end of a spear penetrate. Nothing in his stance suggested he was, or had been, hurt. Yet she'd seen the spear pierce his shoulder and protrude from his upper chest. How could he have possibly recovered from such a grave wound in less than forty-eight hours? Having spent solitary days with the archmage, she knew how well he disguised his pain.

"Does it hurt?" she asked, still eyeing his shoulder.

The healer in her wanted to draw off his coat, unbutton his shirt, and stroke the spot to make sure he wasn't still wounded. The woman in her wanted to bury her face in his chest, lay her head in the crook of his neck, and draw in his scent.

But she did neither.

Instead she stood locked in a strange limbo where she did nothing but stare at a man who had, over the course of a few short days, become so achingly familiar yet remained so painfully distant. Now they were back in their home realm, the distance between them seemed amplified, wide as the gulf that separated Amereen from the province of Jachuana.

"What?" he asked, expression as unreadable as ever.

The atrium and the surrounding hallway were empty now, all the councilors gone and Mailin nowhere in sight. He bridged the gulf between them by lifting a hand to brush her hair. His fingers trailed to her cheeks, skimming over the bruises with a gentleness that broke her trance.

She burrowed into his arms.

She should have been mortified by her boldness, but strangely, she wasn't. His arms folded around her like iron bands. It felt like the most natural thing in the world. An errant sob welled up in her throat, and she realized the terror that had gripped her in days past hadn't yet dissipated; it had simply been suppressed.

Being back in Amereen had repressed the raw fear that had coagulated in her veins the moment she saw the spear punch through him in what could have been a fatal wound, even for an immortal. Now that she could finally see, smell, and touch him, it was as though she'd been transported back to that very moment.

"Shh. What's the matter, Evangeline? Are you unwell?" He stroked her hair with one hand and rubbed her back with the other, as he'd done when she'd panicked in Draedyn's altar room. Reining in the urge to bawl, she shook her head and patted the spot on his shoulder to satisfy her need to know if he was truly all right.

"Does it hurt?" she whispered again, hating the telltale tremor in her voice. When he didn't answer and stared at her in confusion, she patted the spot again.

"Here. I saw a spear penetrate here. Does it still hurt?"

Declan stilled, stunned by the realization her anxiety was borne of fear. Yet again, for *him*. A little mortal, her own skin still dappled with bruises, tapped near his wounded spot as if he were made of glass, the worry in her eyes a genuine, unmistakable thing.

In truth, the wound did pain him, the flesh having just knitted back together. But he hadn't allowed anyone to tend to it, not even Mailin, because there was nothing Declan hated more than being a patient. He had spent his entire childhood in and out of infirmaries, under the constant care of healers. If the wound wasn't fatal, it would heal. If it was fatal . . . well then, there was nothing the healers could do about it anyway.

"It does," he heard himself say, an admission of weakness he would never have given another.

Her face crumpled. "Has it scabbed over yet?"

He nodded. It had, sort of. She placed her palm gingerly near the area the spear had protruded, staring at it as if she could penetrate the layers of fabric and absorb his pain. A woman who did not think of him as an archmage with inordinate powers, but as a man who could be hurt.

"I'm fine, little fire. It will soon heal."

Sun winked from the glass, rays of gold dancing over her features, a teasing glimmer in her hair, and a wave of realization hit him like a bludgeon across the head. *She* was what he'd been missing all this time—the piece of sunlight he'd been trying to catch.

He leaned in close enough to feel the warmth of her breath and the pound of her heart. She tipped her face up, incandescent amber pools drawing him deeper.

Footfalls resounded in the hallway followed by a soft, "Oh," shattering the moment to pieces. Evangeline jumped out of his arms like a startled rabbit, cheeks reddening.

Mailin shot them a look of pure amusement even as she genuflected. "My apologies, sire. I only wanted to show my patient"—a pointed look at Evangeline—"to the Dining Hall. She hasn't had anything to eat since this morning."

Declan nodded. "Thank you, Mailin. You may go."

A slight pause before she dipped her head. "As you wish, sire." But Mailin was nothing if not ferociously protective of her patients. The pregnant healer arched a brow at him in warning when Declan's hands remained unmoving on the small of Evangeline's back. "She needs to eat."

When Mailin swiveled to leave, Declan gave Evangeline a little tug, wanting her back in his arms. She complied readily.

"I should take you to the Dining Hall, or I'll risk Mailin's wrath."

She gave him an incredulous look. He shrugged, unable to stop his hand from roving up her spine to stroke the delicate arch of her neck. "Mailin may be small, but she can be fierce. Even an archmage is wise to avoid her ire."

TWENTY-ONE

"**D**o you actually expect me to eat *all* of this?" Evangeline blinked.

Dining Hall turned out to be a gross misnomer, the prosaic term ridiculously misleading as to the nature of the room. The dome ceiling was at least two hundred paces high, detailed with an intricately painted fresco of the five gods. Railea sat in the center in all her glory, holding the sun in her hands. The goddess was flanked by two gods. A slender man with a mischievous smirk, Ozenn, and, a brawny male with tiger eyes, Thurin. Having spent a week in Draedyn's temple, Evangeline identified him easily. Though here, the god of death was not portrayed stoic and austere, but an impassioned lover entwined in the arms of Chonsea, the goddess of life.

Waterfall chandeliers with their crystal droplets glinted in the natural light pouring through wide, aureate doors. Banquet tables spanned the edges of the room while smaller tables filled the middle.

Evangeline sat at one such table across from Declan,

staring in mute fascination as servants filled the table with
one plate after another. His mouth quirked, and her pulse
followed suit, as though he had a direct line to the organ that
beat in her rib cage, every tiny show of expression tugging at
her heartstrings.

"I'll eat with you." The ghost of a smile did not leave his
lips, causing her heart to dance. He nudged a plate of
simmered cod sprinkled with delicate sprigs of watercress
toward her.

"This is one of my favorites. Try."

She rewarded him with a smile as she speared a piece of
the buttered fish. It melted in her mouth, and her taste buds
tingled in ecstasy. When he had all but fed her a bite from
every plate, insisting she sample each decadent dish, Evangeline lifted her hands in mock surrender.

"I can't possibly eat any more."

"Marguerite is particularly good with desserts."

She shook her head and patted her stomach. "Uh-uh.
There's no more space in here."

He persevered. "I happen to know today's dessert features
raspberries and a great deal of chocolate."

Evangeline tried to appear steadfast but couldn't quite help
the giddy smile on her face, a knee-jerk response to the near-
playful look in his eyes.

As it turned out, she did make space.

"You're the one who asked for dessert, and now you're not
having any?" She lifted her brow in mock reproof when she
realized he hadn't taken a single bite of the delectable torte.

"I don't really have a taste for chocolate," he admitted as
she took another indulgent bite. "I ordered this because you
seem to have a weakness for it."

She parted her lips. "And how do you know that?"

"You selected three pastries this morning that all had

chocolate in them."

She stared at him. "Have you been spying on me?"

He shrugged.

Tessa must have told him.

"Well, I can't help it if the chocolate ones look the best." She took another bite. "And this is really, *really* good. Are you sure you won't even try it?" She dug up a forkful and waved it at him. "Just a taste?"

"All right." He leaned toward her, and she brought the fork to his mouth. Ignoring it, he tugged on her braid, tilting her face toward his, and ran his tongue over the seam of her lips. She gasped, and her fork clattered. He took full advantage, delving his tongue deeper.

When he was done, he released her braid and licked his lips.

"You're right," he murmured. "Marguerite has definitely outdone herself."

🔥

They toured the castle grounds, where they eventually came to a garden filled with pruned topiary and flowering shrubs, tastefully arranged around marble creatures suspended in animation. Winged fairies danced in merriment, and solemn mermaids stared at sorrows only they could see, while magnificent dragons reared, poised for flight.

"Such craftsmanship." Evangeline ran a finger down the wing of a cheeky fairy. Every feature was so meticulous that each individual eyelash was visible.

"It's my mother's work," Declan said to Evangeline's surprise. It was the first time he'd ever mentioned his mother.

"She's very talented." Evangeline studied the wicked curve

of a dragon's outstretched talons targeting unseen prey.

Declan nodded.

The relaxed air between them slowly morphed into something cooler. Harder.

"Were you close?" Evangeline asked, scanning his face. History told her that Corvina Alvah had been beloved, an archmage renowned for her benevolence. But instinct told her Corvina's legacy might have taken a darker turn with her son.

His eyes grew opaque. "No."

"Were you very lonely growing up, then?" she prodded, needing the reason behind the sorrow he did nothing to project, but she sensed regardless.

There was a slight pause before he said, "I was raised in an enclave for highly gifted mages for my first hundred and fifty summers. The place was filled with warriors. I was hardly ever alone."

As an immortal at a hundred and fifty, Declan would have been the equivalent of a human boy of fourteen to fifteen years of age.

"Warriors are hardly good company for a child," Evangeline said. "I thought you would have grown up here, in the castle." As Corvina's firstborn, Declan should have been cossetted.

He remained still, his self-possession pristine, yet something flickered in his eyes. A near-imperceptible shadow. Evangeline had spent days studying this man, drowning in the depths of his eyes, and knew this subject made him uneasy.

"My mother did not have the natural inclination for raising children."

Such an innocuous statement, yet a weight settled behind his words.

He placed a palm over the small of her back and ushered her down a meandering walkway crowded with cheerful blooms. He deflected the line of questioning. "Are you close with your adoptive mother, little fire?"

Evangeline smiled. "Yes. She spoiled me, actually." Home-sickness squeezed in her chest as she thought of Agnes, but her heart constricted further at the thought of leaving the castle. She didn't want to leave *him*—a man she had no business lusting after.

In search of a distraction, she stooped to caress the paper-thin petals of a bright orange bloom. "So pretty."

He knelt to pluck a poppy and tucked the stem behind her ear. Pleased by the frivolity of the unexpected gesture, she left it there.

"I've actually never left Mother's side for such a long period of time."

He misread the gloom on her face. "Does she not support your wishes to pursue an apprenticeship in the capital?"

"Oh, no, she's always been supportive. It's just that I've always felt reluctant to leave knowing Mother only has me for company."

"Does she not have other family?"

"They are estranged," Evangeline said with a sad shake of her head. "She chose to mate with a man against her family's wishes . . . and settled in Arns." A village largely populated by humans, free from the disapproval of her family.

Declan remained silent, seeming to sense that there was more.

Evangeline hesitated, wondering if she was betraying her mother's confidence. Then she decided she wasn't. Agnes's story was no clandestine secret—everyone in Arns knew why she remained in the village.

"Her mate left her," Evangeline said. "He walked out one day and never came back. It happened years before she found me in the ravine, and as far as I know, my mother has never left Arns. She still hopes for his return." And because the mating bond linked their lifespan, the fact that Agnes still drew breath meant her mate was still alive.

It meant he had *chosen* to leave.

Agnes had been nursing her own hurts even as she nursed Evangeline back to health.

Evangeline sighed. "I wish she wouldn't." Waiting for someone who had chosen to abandon you seemed too much of a soul-crushing endeavor.

"It is understandable," Declan said, his voice gentler than expected. "Mages mate only once in their lifetime."

She knew that, but still, her shoulders sagged. "For beings who live at least three thousand years, being irrevocably bound to one person seems too cruel a fate."

"I suppose the gods saw the mating bond a fitting way to keep mages from overpopulating the realm," Declan said with uncharacteristic wryness. The mage mating bond didn't merely link their lifespan; it also enabled them to procreate.

An embarrassed laugh leaked from her throat. "I know, but I just wonder why Mother won't take another lover." Mages might be limited to only one mate in their lifetime, but that didn't mean they couldn't take as many lovers as they wished.

The way archmages took ayaris.

Evangeline dipped her head, suddenly discomfited by that line of thought. "Anyway, thank you for informing my mother of my safety." She chewed on her lower lip. "I will leave for Arns in a few more days, if you don't mind. I need to make sure Surin becomes more accustomed to Mailin and the nurses." Evangeline wanted to bridge the girl's trust to the healer, but if she were truly honest, she also craved a few more days with *him*.

"I do mind."

The words were said so quietly that it took her a moment

to realize their implication. Startled, she glanced up at him.

"I have decided you will remain here."

She raised a brow even as her heart began to race. "What are you saying?"

"I have decided to keep you."

She didn't want to leave him, but that didn't mean she wanted to be *kept*. "Keep me? Like . . . some pet?"

His brows furrowed. "No. You will remain here as my guest."

"A guest?" She halted midstride to stare at him. "A guest for how long?"

Another pause. "For as long as I wish you to remain."

"You can't be serious."

Long fingers tilted her chin so she could meet his eyes. "I don't make empty propositions, Evangeline. I want you here." This time, the order in his tone was unmistakable. They were no longer in conversation—he was issuing a command.

Evangeline jerked away from his hold, sparks of anger igniting in her chest. "You may be an archmage, but I am not a house pet. You said you'd take me home. You promised."

"I promised to return you to our realm. I never promised to return you to Arns."

Heart beating wildly, she stared at him in disbelief as she recalled his exact words. *I'll take you back to Amereen.*

Amereen. He'd never said Arns.

"Why?" Her throat was dry as sand. "Why keep me here?"

He took a moment, as if he didn't quite know the answer. "You intrigue me," he said finally. Without warning, he cupped her jaw and claimed her lips in a fierce, demanding kiss. "And I enjoy kissing you."

She raised her hand to strike his cheek, but the jarring impact didn't occur. Her arm stalled midstrike as though enveloped by a cushion of air.

"Striking an archmage is a capital offense, little fire."

She withdrew her hand with an indignant jerk. "You said you'd never ask for more than I can give," she said, struggling to keep her voice steady.

A cocked brow. "I have only ever kissed you, and you've never objected until now."

A heavy flush colored her cheeks at the truth and the sheer arrogance in his tone.

"I will not be held captive." Like a bird in a gilded cage. She gave a bark of acerbic laughter. "Besides, what can I offer that you don't already have? I've seen the way women look at you. Most would eagerly warm your bed . . . and you know I can't."

He wasn't the least deterred by her admission. In fact, he drew closer until his body crowded hers, but she held her ground, refusing to be cowed by his size and stature. His hand reached out to cup her jaw again in a possessive grip. "Sex isn't what I'm keeping you for, although I won't lie; I would very much like to bed you, Evangeline."

Her breath hitched at his words, her blood turning molten in a traitorous, involuntary response even as fury rose in her chest.

She drew in a deep breath. "My mother . . . my friends. I have an entire life in Arns. Please, Declan, be reasonable," she said, consciously using his name, needing him to see the absurdity of his demand.

Something dangerous lurked in his eyes. He backed her into a wall, and the smooth stones chilled her back. "Evangeline, this is not a request. You will do as I command."

She stared at him. "As you *command*?"

He gave an arrogant tilt of his head. Evangeline would have kicked him if he hadn't pinned her to the wall.

"I am your archmage." A pointed reminder he reigned supreme over the very ground she stood upon. A reminder that he could, and *would*, subjugate her to his will if he wanted —and there was nothing she could do about it. Involuntary tears pricked at the corners of her eyes. She shoved at him. When he didn't budge, she battered his chest with her fists.

"Let. Me. Go!"

🔥

Declan allowed her to push past him and watched her flee, knowing he'd made a tactical error. He had been trying to seduce her, impress her, persuade her to stay. Instead he had crossed the fine line into coercion. He clenched his jaw, appalled at his lack of self-control. The darkest, most primal part he kept tightly leashed had recoiled at the thought of her leaving. It had lashed out the only way it knew how.

Mine, it whispered even now. *She is mine.*

He was an archmage, and he could have her if he so chose. No woman would refuse him. No woman could. He had the right to anyone who lived in his territory if he pleased. But he had never used his rank or power to force a woman. Never. Until now. The darkness within him stirred, sinuous and sly, suggesting he could have her.

No matter what, he *would* have her.

But paradoxically, the thought of exercising power to cage her was unacceptable. The darkness within him quieted, chastened. The thought was abhorrent, even. She had trusted him with her secrets, with her scars. Some bastard had once caged her, abused her. He would never do that to his little fire. He understood that though he craved her, she had to come to him, willingly. Anything else, and he would become the tyrant in her dreams, the oppressor who haunted her nightmares.

E vangeline ran through the gardens, not caring where she headed. Declan had allowed her to flee, which told her there was no way she could escape. Tears trickled from her eyes. She blinked furiously, scrubbing them away. The tears did not stem from fear. Not even anger. No, they welled from an ache deep in her heart.

Disappointment.

She had expected more of him. She had come to trust him, believed he was a good, honorable man beneath that cold mask of power. But what was he but another monster who would cage innocents?

She slowed, her breath coming in short pants. She was well and truly lost.

"And where do you think you're going, girl?" A gruff baritone came from behind. Evangeline whirled around to see two men seated on simple wooden stumps by a stone table beneath a large oak tree. A ruddy, weathered face covered with wrinkles told her she was looking at a human. Immortals did not age that way, no matter how deep into their twilight years. Opposite him sat a stunning man, golden in his beauty. A chessboard lay on the table between them.

Evangeline willed herself to swallow the knot in her chest and speak.

"Can you show me the way to the infirmary?"

The younger-looking man relinquished the chess piece in his hand as interest sparked in his eyes. "You're the woman my brother brought home from Draedyn's Realm."

"Your brother?" A slow moment passed before her brain supplied a name. "Lex?"

Tawny-brown eyes widened, and he flashed her a brilliant grin. "The one and only Alexander Alvah." He got off his seat, bowed, and gestured to his elderly companion. "This is Jorge. And you must be . . . " He tapped his chin. "Lady Evangeline Barre."

"How do you know my name?" Apart from Declan and Mailin, her interactions with the people within the castle had been limited. Alexander's eyes raked her from top to toe, not lasciviously, but with overt curiosity.

A crotchety burst of laughter escaped the old man. "The castle may appear large, my lady, but news travels fast around here."

Alexander nodded in agreement. "Yes, by now, everyone has heard about the woman their archmage hoarded like a precious jewel upon his return."

She softened despite the involuntary twinge in her heart. Precious jewel, indeed. So precious he intended to keep her prisoner. Declan's earlier words invaded her mind. *You intrigue me.* Probably because she didn't jump into his bed the first moment he showed interest. She huffed inwardly.

"You flatter me, my lords. I am no jewel, and certainly no lady. I am just an apothecarist from the village of Arns." She forced a smile to soften her biting tone. The old man laughed again and beamed at her, wrinkles stretching.

"Ah, an unassuming one. How refreshing is that, Lex?"

Alexander smirked, and it was only then she saw a whisper of his genetic ties to Declan. It was in the shape of his eyes and the angle of his jaw. Apart from that, Declan could well be a fallen angel, his beauty dark and unearthly, while this man, a golden prince.

"I take after my father," Alexander provided as if he read her thoughts, "while Declan takes after his. No one sees the resemblance, but Jorge reckons we both have our mother's smile."

"Tell me, my lady, what has put such sadness in your eyes?

Surely you've been well cared for?" Jorge asked. Up close, she could see dirt under his nails, as if he had been toiling in the soil. Evangeline plastered another weak smile on her face and made a feeble excuse of fatigue to extricate herself.

"Ah, you're yet unwell. I'm sure the shadow realm must be a harrowing experience for a young and gentle girl such as yourself. Lex here will be happy to walk you back to your room."

Evangeline wasn't in the mood for company, but she could hardly find her own way back. She engaged in vapid conversation until they arrived at the building of her guestroom, but to her exasperation, Alexander did not seem to be in a hurry to leave her side.

"Whoever upset you should be wary of incurring an archmage's wrath," he said after they lapsed into silence.

"You give me too much honor, Lord Councilor, but Declan is unlikely to smite himself," she said bitterly, the words flying out of her mouth before she could think better of it.

A brow winged up. When she made no attempt to explain further, he said, "My brother can be a hard man, my lady, but you will do well to remember that he is an archmage. One of the eight rulers of our realm."

She bit her lip to prevent it from curling with contempt. "Hence he has the right to do whatever he wants with a woman like me?"

A whip of disbelief flashed in his eyes. "My brother has no need to force himself on a woman."

"No," she all but spat. "But he intends to keep me. Like some puppy he's found on the streets."

Disbelief morphed into startled amusement. "Hmm. That is strange. My brother has never shown a penchant for strays."

A biting retort rose in her throat, but a scream derailed her response.

TWENTY-TWO

The screams of distress emanated from the far end of the hallway. A hallway that appeared very much like the one that led to the infirmary wards. Evangeline broke into a sprint, only to be jerked back by a strong hand.

"Let go," she cried.

Alexander gave her a wry, lopsided smile. "Warping is a whole lot faster"—and in the next instant, they were in the ward—"don't you think?"

But his smirk was quickly erased.

The curtain that shrouded the furthest bed was flung open, and its previously inert patient was screaming loud enough to raise the dead. The patient writhed in apparent agony against two restraining nurses while Mailin administered a sedative.

"What in Railea's name . . . ?" Alexander's eyes widened when his gaze landed on the patient's face. Evangeline wasn't sure if he was startled by the tortured screams or her mutilated appearance. It was as if someone had taken a carving knife to her face— cicatrices ran from forehead to chin. Deeper crisscrossing slashes scored both cheeks, severe enough to have formed bumpy, raised scars. The marred skin on her scalp was shiny, a taunting echo of what must have been horrific burns. Tufts of hair grew in patches, adding to her deformed appearance.

The woman finally relaxed, slumping back into the bed. Mailin's usually warm eyes held a tide of sorrow when they met Evangeline's from across the distance. Evangeline made no attempt to speak, having drawn Surin into her arms the moment she'd entered the room. The child had curled up with her hands clamped against her ears. It was the first time she'd ever seen Surin cry.

"**A**re you sure you're all right?" Alexander refused to leave her side, even when Evangeline insisted she knew the way back to her guest chamber. She had only allowed herself to leave when Surin finally fell asleep, spent from tears.

"I could easily warp you there if you like?"

"No, thank you, Lord Councilor. I don't mind the walk. I am human after all." Evangeline feigned a smile, attempting to lighten the mood. He fell silent as he padded by her side, a relentless shadow.

She sighed. "Honestly, Lord Co—"

"My name is Alexander. Lex, if you like."

Evangeline nodded. "Lord Alexander."

His lips quirked. Unlike his older brother, Alexander was proving generous with his smiles. "If you're allowed to address my brother by name, I think you're fine to skip the formalities with me, my lady."

At the thought of Declan, her mood further soured. "Well

then, Alexander," she said, injecting false brightness into her tone, "I suppose it's only fitting you stop calling me a lady."

He nodded, followed by a long, considering gaze. "Many summers ago, a falcon fell out of the sky."

Evangeline raised a brow at the non sequitur, but he carried on, unperturbed.

"It was most likely wounded by poachers. Somehow, it had the good fortune to land on the balcony outside my brother's study. Declan took an interest in the creature. He even hand-fed the bird himself. After several weeks, the falcon recovered well enough to take flight. But Declan wouldn't let it go."

A chill ran down her spine.

"Whenever it was time for the falcon to stretch its wings, Declan would throw a kinetic shield over the creature, never hurting it, but never allowing it too far out of his sight, either."

Bitterness rose in her throat. "The falcon was his amusement."

As she was now.

The corners of his eyes crinkled. "Soon enough, the falcon learned it could never fly into the horizon. Eventually, it learned to return to his hands. Willingly. Tame."

Evangeline halted in her tracks and glared up at him. "I am *not* a bird to be tamed."

"No. But my brother does have . . . " He gesticulated as if looking for the right words. "A possessive streak."

They rounded the hallway that led to the guest quarters. Evangeline waited for him to leave, but Alexander continued to stroll by her side.

"Declan isn't a cruel man," he added.

Evangeline flattened her lips. No, but he was no less ruthless.

"He is just . . . supreme, as all archmages are," Alexander

added when she didn't respond. "But he cares for what he owns."

"I am *not* an object to be owned. Not a falcon to be tamed. I am not a slave." Not a prisoner. Never again. They came up to her room, and Alexander opened his mouth as if to respond. Instead, he paused, staring at her door.

"I should go," he said abruptly. Tossing her a smile full of knavish charm that must have broken countless hearts, he turned on his heel. "A pleasure making your acquaintance . . . Evangeline."

She frowned after him. The man was most certainly not cast from the same mold as his brother. She walked into her room and released a startled shriek. A man leaned by the windows, tall and darkly beautiful, as if he had every right to be there.

He probably did.

"Do you always lurk in the rooms of your guests?"

"I was waiting for you." He moved to sit on the foot of her bed, his movements fluid and graceful. Her heart pounded involuntarily. It wasn't from fear.

He patted the bed beside him. She folded her arms across her chest in open defiance and remained standing. "Have you come to apologize?" she demanded and almost laughed at the absurdity of her own query. Archmages didn't apologize.

He falsified her preconceptions.

"I wouldn't have held you against your will." His unflinching gaze met hers. "I am sorry."

She was still staring when he added, "And I have come to make you a proposition."

"A proposition?"

"I would like to keep you here in my castle, not as a guest, but in my employ. You will help recondition slave-trade survivors so they can re-establish themselves in society."

She blinked. "What?"

"I have reconsidered your argument back in the temple, Evangeline, and I have decided to devote a covert team to infiltrating Draedyn's Realm for the rescue and retrieval of slave-trade victims."

He leaned forward to rest his elbows over his knees and steepled his fingers. "And every one of those victims will be brought back to Amereen and remain here until you deem them fit to return to society."

Conflicting emotions filtered through her. "You're going to start freeing slaves," she managed. "But you said it was a fool-hardy excursion to save the lives of mortals who make no contribution to the realm." Her tone turned caustic as she regurgitated his words. "Incurring unnecessary risks and a waste of resources."

He shrugged. "The days spent in the shadow realm have given me fresh perspective. Also, you make a compelling case for me to expend the resources and take the risks."

Her jaw hung. "You're doing all of this just to keep me here?"

He nodded, unabashed. "You need a reason to stay here. I am giving you that reason."

She continued to gape at him in disbelief. He wasn't rescuing slaves out of the goodness of his heart. He was doing it so he could cage her.

As if he read her mind, he added, "As part of your employment, you will be allowed three days at the end of every month to return to Arns."

He nodded at a piece of paper on the small writing desk by the window. "To make it worth your while, you will also be given an apprenticeship with one of my healers. I highly recommend Mailin. Even without her magic, she is a remark-able healer."

Stunned, Evangeline walked over to the desk and picked up the thick sheet. An employment contract. Written in a strong, neat script. Her primary responsibilities involved tending to and managing the daily welfare of slave-trade survivors, working closely with the healers to facilitate recovery for the victims with the goal of reinstating them in society. On top of that, she was offered an apprenticeship with a healer of her choice.

A sense of wonderment filled her. Slaves would be freed and given a chance. Elation lifted her heart. And an apprenticeship with Mailin? It was a dream come true. *Her* dream. Her eyes trailed to the final lines of the contract and widened at the figure on the bottom line. For her services, she would be paid. Very handsomely. Evangeline blinked at the amount to make sure she wasn't seeing things.

No.

She snapped her head up. "This is ridiculous."

He raised a questioning brow. "How so?"

"There is no need for you to use me over any one of your other healers if you truly want to help assimilate survivors back into society. And even if you did employ me, there is no need to pay me such an extravagant sum of money. This is all just a ploy to keep me here."

He gave a huff of laughter, the sound of it rare but genuine.

"The sum is a standard amount I pay all the nurses. There is nothing extravagant about what I am offering you." He shifted from the bed to stand beside her as she continued to eye him warily.

"I have even deducted a small percentage that will pay for your apprenticeship," he said with an almost devious glint in his eye. "As for the reason for your employment, Mailin has informed me of your connection with Surin. The girl trusts you over the nurses, likely because you have a calming presence, she said. And as you already know, Mailin is immortal. As is every one of the healers in my employ. Since most survivors are likely to be human women, *you* will relate best to them."

She frowned as she considered his words. She did connect well with Surin, but it wasn't because she had a calming presence. It was because she truly understood the fear.

He leaned in close, scattering her thoughts. So close he was a hairsbreadth away from kissing her lips. "But you're right, of course. It is a scheme to keep you here, and if you turn down my offer, I *won't* be freeing slaves."

He closed the distance between them, enslaving her with a smoldering kiss. Lips still brushing hers, he whispered, "Think about all the lives you'll save. All the slaves that will be freed."

She pushed him back, needing a moment to clear her head. She couldn't quite stand firm on her own legs, so she leaned against the writing desk. She had always thought of him as a dark angel, but now she wondered if he was a demon. Seductive and shamelessly conniving, he offered her a contract he knew she couldn't turn down.

"Three days at the end of every *two weeks*." She pushed up from the table to stand at her full height as she met his gaze. "I want to return home for three days at the end of every two weeks. And I want to return home before my contract begins."

Amusement gleamed in his eyes. "Has anyone told you no one bargains with an archmage, Evangeline?" he asked, but there was approval in his tone. His hands went to her hips to draw her toward him again. She resisted.

"Three days at the end of every two weeks," she repeated. "I want it stipulated in the contract."

The sides of his lips curved. "Fine."

Definitely a demon, she decided. An irresistible one. He leaned in to kiss her again, and before her traitorous body could melt, she barred him with every shred of willpower she could muster. "The contract will also state I will *only* be employed for helping the slave victims. Nothing else."

"Yes." His agreement was an erotic murmur in her ears. "Anything else that happens will be consensual."

TWENTY-THREE

Perched high on the grassy embankment at the edge of town, the Barre cottage was built when Evangeline's mother and her mate had first moved into the village. Now, the pale stone walls showed the passage of time through patches of discoloration speckled with moss. But despite its rustic state, the cottage had always appeared welcoming to Evangeline. Charming, even, with its scalloped, thatched roof and slightly crooked chimney of round river stones. The front yard was partially filled with an herb bed of basil, rosemary, thyme, and a comfrey bush laden with purple bell flowers.

"Evie! Oh, thank the gods." Agnes came flying down the cobbled steps of the front lawn, wisps of flame-colored hair streaming loose from the haphazard knot on her head. "I thought you were dead!" Tears swarmed her dark eyes, and her face turned blotchy.

"Mother." Evangeline blubbered at the familiar scent of minty healing balms as her mother drew her into a fierce hug. "I missed you so much." Evangeline returned her mother's embrace with equal fervor, laughing and sobbing at the same time. When they finally drew apart, Agnes gave Killian a startled glance, as if she'd only just noticed his presence. The commander, who had been standing nearby with an amused smile, gave Agnes a brief nod.

"I trust you're in good hands, my lady. I will see you in three days." With that, he left. Agnes's eyes rounded when Killian disappeared.

"Goddess of light, did the man just . . . warp?"

Evangeline bit her lower lip. She'd gotten so used to teleportation she'd forgotten how unusual it was, even for a mage as old as her mother. "Killian is a battlemage, Mother." Never mind the fact that he was actually the commander of Declan's battlemages.

Agnes's eyes widened. "A *battlemage* warped you home?" But she seemed too overwhelmed to be distracted by Killian for too long. "When Stefan told me you were drawn into a fae portal I thought"—a violent spasm shook her mother's slender frame—"I thought I'd lost you forever."

"How is Stefan?" Killian had told her that her childhood friend had survived his injuries but nothing else of his recovery.

"A healer from the capital took care of the wound. The man is as strong as a horse."

The final remnants of tension ebbed, and relief settled into her bones. Agnes clasped her hands tightly and led her into the house. "Come inside, sweetheart, and tell me everything."

So she did. Again, Evangeline recounted her time in the shadow realm, wisely omitting heated details where Declan was involved as they prepared dinner together in the tiny kitchen. The routine lit her soul. She had missed home so, so much.

Agnes kneaded dough absently as she listened, occasionally interjecting with questions. Evangeline knew her mother saw more than she let on. Neither woman had addressed the fact that a battlemage had mentioned he would be back in three days before he'd dematerialized into thin air. Eventually, it seemed Agnes couldn't hold the question in any longer. But her words were unexpected.

"The man who went through the portal with you . . . is he a battlemage, too?"

Evangeline squirmed. She had somehow managed to leave out *that* major detail.

"Not exactly."

Agnes looked somewhat relieved. "A soldier, then?"

Evangeline shook her head and blew out a deep breath. "Declan's an archmage."

The rolling pin clattered onto the pan, sending a puff of flour into the air like fairy dust. Evangeline cringed.

Agnes stood motionless as she stared at the dough, her face freckled with bits of flour. "What did you say? I'm certain I misheard you."

Evangeline attempted a smile, but it came out strained. "Declan is an archmage," she repeated. When her mother continued to blink at her owlishly, she added, "He's our archmage. The one who rules Amereen."

"Good heavens, goddess of light!" Agnes gave the ball of dough a thump. "You spent eight days in Draedyn's Realm . . . with an *archmage*?"

"He's the reason I'm still alive, Mother. He isn't like what people say. Truly."

Agnes only stared at her, knuckles white as she clutched the rolling pin.

"Is it not true he *burns* criminals at the stake during public executions? That he ships people off to"—Agnes seemed to flounder for words—"Prison Island without a care for their survival? Most on that wretched island are said to be so desperate they turn to cannibalism!"

Evangeline blanched. She hadn't forgotten every general fact she'd ever heard about her archmage. But now she knew him, she knew he did everything with purpose. However cold that purpose might be.

"You said it yourself, Mother. Criminals," Evangeline said, crossing her arms. "Murderers. Rapists. Convicts who are found guilty of felonious offenses. He doesn't hurt innocents."

Agnes's lips formed a thin line as she proceeded to fashion flatbread from the unleavened dough. Evangeline directed her focus to chopping the rest of the parsnips and carrots for their vegetable stew. Eventually, she sighed as a sense of guilt and unease crept in from keeping secrets from her mother. Worrying her lower lip, Evangeline mustered courage and gave Agnes the unvarnished version of Declan's employment contract and its terms. She disclosed more of what happened in the shadow realm, driven by a need for her mother to understand Declan for who he was. To see him the way she saw him. Even so, Evangeline skimmed over certain details. Some things were simply private.

Agnes's eyes grew bulbous as the story progressed, and by the time Evangeline finished, her mother was the shade of Marguerite's raspberry chocolate tart with her mouth askew.

"Railea's tears, Evie, you're in serious trouble!"

"It is a legitimate employment contract," Evangeline muttered.

"Has it ever occurred to you that an archmage can *void* any contract he wants to? If an archmage wants you, he will just take you."

"Declan isn't like that. He isn't the archmage of Jachuana," Evangeline said, once again rushing to defend him. Then she sighed. Why was she defending a man she'd known for less than a fortnight?

Agnes blew out a heavy breath from the other side of the table. "If he's setting up this whole operation just to keep you, he's going to want something in return."

Evangeline fidgeted with the ladle she'd been using to stir their boiling stew, discomfiture creeping into her heart. Declan had made it explicit he wanted her in his bed.

He hadn't kept that a secret.

As if reading her thoughts, Agnes powered on. "You cannot . . . ," she faltered. Uttering a low oath, the mage rubbed weary fingers between her eyebrows. "You cannot warm his bed, Evie."

"Mother." Evangeline cast her eyes heavenward, and warmth stung her cheeks.

"He can very literally kill you in the act if he loses control. Do you know that? That's why they have ayaris."

Evangeline folded arms around herself. "You know how I am with men. Even if I wanted to"—her cheeks warmed again —"I couldn't. Fear seizes me every time a man gets too close."

Agnes gave her a grim look. "Evie, he could easily force himself on you."

Evangeline's heart stuttered, but she pantomimed a reassuring smile. "He won't do that." Would he? Declan was many things, but he wasn't dishonorable. Then again, she had once trusted Malcolm to be a good man, too.

The next morning, Evangeline ventured to the village forge.

"Evie." A stuttered gasp escaped Stefan's throat. He dropped his tools, crossed the distance to pluck her up, and crushed her against his burly chest as if he had never been shot. Evangeline cringed inwardly at the physical proximity, heart pounding. Her body might have come to crave the touches of one particular man, but she wasn't entirely free from the shackles of her obscure past.

"Sorry." Stefan grimaced when he noted her expression. He set her down quickly, clenching and unclenching his fists as though he didn't know what to do with his hands. Dark shadows lined his eyes. "I thought you were gone, Evie. I should never have brought you along that day."

The tears glimmering in his eyes caused an ache in her chest. "Stefan, none of it was your fault."

"What happened?" He couldn't seem to let her go, his hand reaching out to brush her temple. His brow knitted as Evangeline provided him with an abridged account of her *adventure*, once again skimming over details where her archmage was concerned. And because Stefan was her best friend, she told him of her contract.

"You're *moving* into the castle? What—"

A facetious knock sounded at the open doorway. A stocky man in a tunic typical of farriers stuck his head in. "Ready, Hanesworth? We need to hurry if we're to deliver our wares on time."

Stefan narrowed his eyes. "Give me a minute."

The man huffed in impatience.

Evangeline shook her head. "Go, Stefan. I'm fine, truly." She gave him a smile intended to dull his reluctance. "Why don't you come by later tonight? For dinner?"

His face crumpled like a child's.

"I won't be back in time. Tomorrow?" he asked hopefully.

Evangeline grimaced. She would be back in Amereen Castle the next day. "I'll see you in a fortnight," she promised. At his crestfallen expression, she bit the inside of her lip, threw her arms around him in a tight hug, and pressed a friendly kiss to his stubbled cheek—something she'd never initiated voluntarily. Brightening considerably, Stefan ambled grudgingly to the doorway. She waved him off.

Satisfied to have seen for herself that Stefan was as fit as a horse, Evangeline made her way down the main street to the apothecary. She should have been elated being home, yet there was a small tightness in her chest.

Two days and she missed *him*.

She missed the whisper of cool silk against her senses. Declan hadn't touched her mind since she'd left the castle. *But that's good,* the little voice in her head said. *You're just an amusement to him. He's an archmage. He isn't meant for the likes of you.*

But he is, another voice insisted. This one buried deep in the crevices of her soul. *He is yours.*

The last was the barest whisper, and it hardly made any sense. Her subconscious trying to convince her she wasn't making a grievous mistake by signing the contract. She was saved from further contemplation when she stepped into the apothecary.

Her reappearance, it seemed, coincided with a sudden surge of villagers suffering from backaches, headaches, and even a few sore ankles. By midday, the entire village had heard of her return and found an excuse for a trip to the Barre Apothecary.

By the time they ushered the last customer out the door, it was near dusk. "I would have disappeared every now and then if I knew my reappearance would draw such a crowd," Evangeline commented laughingly as they closed the shop.

Agnes gave her a terse glare. "Don't you ever say such a thing. All the coin in the world wouldn't make up for my daughter's life."

Evangeline sighed.

"I'm not taking the employment contract because of the money, Mother. You know that."

"But is it truly what you want?" Agnes's gaze scoured her face.

"Yes." Evangeline couldn't explain how she somehow saw pieces of herself in the survivors, especially Surin. If Declan's employ meant saving more slaves, that alone would make everything worthwhile.

Agnes firmed her lips, clearly unconvinced. "Evangeline, I will not have you coerced into such a decision because an archmage has set his sights on you." She narrowed her eyes and crossed her arms, uncharacteristically fierce. "Even if I have to tell him myself."

Evangeline's heart swelled, and a flood of warmth coursed into her eyes. "I am not being forced into anything," she whispered as she drew her mother into a tight embrace. She pulled back, needing her mother to see the truth in her eyes. "Declan isn't a dishonorable man," she added gently, although she knew her mother would never truly believe her. How could she expect Agnes to believe when she wasn't entirely sure of Declan's motivations herself?

He wasn't dishonorable; that, she believed with every fiber of her being. Yet he'd devised a scheme—one that fulfilled every one of her deepest yearnings—all because she intrigued him, because he enjoyed kissing her. She was clearly nothing but an amusement.

Still, she would play his game.

Altruistic reasons aside, he had become an addiction. She craved him the way her lungs craved air. She was drawn to him the way birds were drawn to the sky.

They were on their way home when they came to an unusual crowd of people in the main street. Merchants milled around shopfronts, and pedestrians loitered by the curbside. A playful breeze rustled through the crowd, bringing with it a whiff of springtime blossoms.

Baffled, Evangeline could do nothing but stare.

Flowers lined both sides of the main street. Pots bearing blooms of every imaginable color—coreopsis, buttercups, primroses . . . then she recognized a theme. Every second pot held poppies. She sucked in a breath.

Poppies of the very same shade he'd tucked into her hair.

The pots hadn't been there this morning. And it appeared, as they made their way past the curious crowd, that the ostentatious display led all the way to their little cottage perched on the grassy embankment. An even larger collection crowded the front door.

Yellow daisies, white and pink catmints, and fluffy betonies interspersed with poppies were carefully arranged around the cobbled pathway leading right up to her doorstep. A patchwork of petals blanketed the front yard like a colorful quilt.

"What in Railea's name?" Agnes breathed, equal measures of bewilderment and awe on her face.

What have you done? Evangeline projected the thought almost unconsciously. It wasn't past five seconds when she felt the whisper of a presence beside her. A masculine scent she'd come to associate with both comfort and sensuality.

Clearly, all her practice at projection had paid off.

Agnes gave a startled little scream, but Evangeline calmly pivoted to face the presence. "Did you do this?"

Declan nodded.

Evangeline exhaled and turned to her mother. "Why don't you go inside first?" Agnes opened her mouth, a protest forthcoming. "Everything is fine, Mother," Evangeline added when Agnes remained unmoving. "Please, go inside."

When Agnes reluctantly acquiesced, Evangeline turned her sights to the man responsible. "What is the meaning of this?"

"I am courting you."

"*Courting* me?"

Incredulity winged up her brows, but his knitted together. "Is it not obvious?"

Flabbergasted, she stared at him. "This is your idea of courtship? Burying my house—and half the town—in flowers?"

Genuine uncertainty flickered in his eyes. "I've never had to court a woman before."

Her heart pounded a little quicker at his unadorned admission. His gaze swept the beautiful floral arrangement around her porch. "Lex assured me flowers were a standard requirement in any courtship. Does this not please you?"

She sputtered. "You've covered half the town with flowers to . . . please me? What will the townspeople think?"

His lips curved. "That you belong to me."

Both annoyance and feminine pleasure unfurled within her, warring for dominance. When she finally regained her composure, Evangeline wasn't entirely sure which emotion had won, but she couldn't allow him the misapprehension that she was his.

She folded her arms. "That is not how courtship works, Your Highness."

The curve of his lips did not falter, and a hint of playfulness lit his eyes. As usual, her heart palpitated, enslaved by any crumb of emotion the man displayed. Declan sidled closer, hands moving to her hips in a hold so flagrantly proprietary he might as well hang a collar over her neck with a tag of ownership.

"Would you have preferred different flowers? Chocolates, perhaps?"

Perversely charmed and exasperated, Evangeline emitted a frustrated groan. The sound dimmed the light in his eyes and dampened his smile.

"I did not mean to displease you," he said. "I will have them removed."

His expression remained impenetrable, his tone even. Yet she knew he was hurt.

"Declan . . . " She sighed.

"You left without saying goodbye," he murmured.

When Killian appeared asking if she was ready to return home, she'd agreed readily. Only she hadn't realized he'd warp her right out of the castle, straight home. She hadn't had a chance to say goodbye. But she hadn't thought much of it. After all, it was only three days.

Declan tugged at her elbows, pulling her toward him. Pressing a palm on his chest, she whispered, "Not here." The fingers tugging at kitchen drapes made it patently obvious they were still under surveillance, not including the prying eyes of her neighbors.

Declan didn't even blink, but in the next instant they were standing in the outskirts of Arns. Verdant fields rolled into distant hills dotted with trees. "Why are you doing this, Declan?"

"Because I want you to be mine." Blunt as usual.

"I've already signed the employment contract." She had signed the papers after Declan amended according to her requests. Then he had tumbled her into his lap and kissed her breathless. "Why court me at all?" She was hardly resisting him.

He released her hair from her braid, gently unravelling the strands with his fingers. "The contract merely puts you in my employ. What I want is for you to be mine."

"You can have any other woman you want, Archmage. We both know that. Why are you really doing this?"

He seemed to take a moment to consider his response. "Because you keep me . . . warm."

Keep him warm? For a being who didn't even feel the cold, that did not make very much sense. But then he bent to rest his forehead against hers, laying waste to her thoughts. The sweetness of the simple yet unexpected gesture was far more effective than any gift, for it made it impossible to resist him. With a sigh, she allowed him to pull her into his arms.

He planted soft, fleeting kisses at her temple, slowly making his way down to the side of her jaw. He reached her mouth, and his demeanor changed from sweet to fiery. A hand fisted in her hair, holding her in place as he plundered her lips and ravished her mouth like a man starved.

"Let me court you, Evangeline," he whispered into her ear.

She clung to him, breathless and dumbfounded. It sounded as much a command as it was a plea. Her mother's words replayed in her mind. *You cannot warm his bed, Evie. He could very literally kill you in the act.* She glanced into his eyes, dark pools of desire.

"Yes," she heard herself whisper.

"Yes?"

"Yes, you may court me," she said, nuzzling a soft kiss to the side of his throat. "But only if you promise never to impose on my mother or the village. Promise me you'll always give me a choice. No coercion."

"You have my word," he agreed without pause.

She wanted to kiss and nip at his lips, to sink into him, but Agnes was probably frantic by now. "Take me home, Declan."

His arms tightened around her, and the reluctance was clear in his eyes. He leaned in for another kiss. When their lips parted, they were back on the porch surrounded by flowers and swathed in moonlight. He didn't release her.

"Would you like them removed?"

She pursed her lips. "Yes."

Disappointment clouded his eyes. An emotion she'd never thought she'd see on her archmage's face. She chuckled, her own lips skewing with mischief. "Only the ones lining the main street. And I would like them delivered back to the castle, into the courtyard below my guestroom, if that's not too much trouble."

The little curve that gave her palpitations reappeared at his lips. "You do like them, then?"

"I adore them . . . but who exactly did all of this?"

"I had Killian organize the ones in the village," he said before casting another look at the display around them. The lump on his throat bobbed. "I arranged these myself," he admitted.

Tingles raced over her skin, warmth an explosion in her chest. Evangeline couldn't help the idiotic smile that lit her face, absurdly pleased by the idea of her archmage arranging flowers. Cupping his face, she said, "Thank you. This is the sweetest . . . and most extravagant gift anyone has ever given me."

She was rewarded with a grin, the sight of it so rare she was sure she would crave it for the rest of her life. He leaned in for another kiss.

Right at that moment, her mother appeared at the doorway. "Evie?"

Evangeline jerked back sheepishly.

Agnes's gaze landed on Declan, whose hands remained unmoving around her waist. There was a brief silence, a moment filled with the heady scent of blossoms and the distant cry of a barn owl. "Would you and your *friend* like to come in?"

Awkwardness stifled the air. Evangeline had never noticed how small the cottage was until now. The living and dining spaces occupied the same area, densely crowded with a settee, bookshelf, and a small dining table that only served to amplify his presence. Even the cheerily corbelled fireplace—her favorite spot in the room— now appeared shabby as Declan stood amid scattered memorabilia and knickknacks Agnes had collected over the years.

Evangeline chanced a peek at her mother, who was looking at Declan as if he were a wild animal liable to maim, not a man silently studying his surroundings with impassivity.

"Declan, this is my mother, Agnes Barre."

Agnes paled further at his name, turning the shade of unbaked dough. Perhaps it was too soon for introductions. Declan offered his hand. "Mrs. Barre, thank you for having me in your home."

Agnes stared at his proffered hand as if it were a snake, and for a terrible moment Evangeline wondered if her mother would slap it away. But the mage recovered swiftly.

"Please forgive my nervousness. I've never met a member of the Echelon." Agnes shook Declan's hand with obvious effort and cleared her throat. "My lord archmage, it is an honor to have you in our humble home."

Declan tilted his head, seeming to consider Agnes's formality. "You will address me the way Evangeline has introduced me. You may use my name." Agnes bowed low in response, but Declan shook his head. "Evangeline does not genuflect to me. The woman she calls Mother is not required to do so, either."

Agnes appeared stunned, eyes wide, but very carefully she straightened, smoothing out her dress with her hands. "Very well, then. Would you like to join us at the dinner table . . . Declan?"

Declan glanced at Evangeline in silent question. He'd done so before entering the house, too. Her archmage clearly took his promise of not imposing seriously.

Evangeline couldn't help the upward tilt of her lips. "My mother is no Marguerite, but her meat pies are to die for."

Agnes had set the dining table up as formally as she could, obviously having foreseen the possibility of Evangeline's *friend* joining them for dinner. When Evangeline indicated her seat at the table, Declan slid into the chair beside hers. Stiffly, Agnes took her own seat opposite Evangeline. There was a moment of silence filled with the clinking of cutlery as Evangeline served the food.

Agnes drew in a deep breath, a sign she was mustering courage for a question. Evangeline cringed inwardly and braced herself.

"May I ask you a question, Lord . . . " Agnes cleared her throat again. "Declan?"

Declan nodded, his gaze reserved as usual, but not forbidding. Evangeline took a nervous bite of a roasted carrot.

"What are your intentions with the employment contract?" Agnes asked with the candor that came with almost ten centuries of life.

Evangeline coughed in earnest, food stuck in her throat. Declan nudged her a glass before responding, "I'm offering your daughter a job."

"She already has a job," Agnes contended.

"I can give her access to the best healer in the jurisdiction,"

Declan said without a hint of censure. "Also, I want to keep her close."

Agnes stiffened, and heat warmed Evangeline's cheeks.

"My lord— "

"Declan," he corrected mildly before taking a bite from his fork.

Agnes sputtered for a moment, seeming to flail with her words. Then she squared her shoulders. "With all due respect, my daughter is no courtier."

"I am well aware of that," Declan replied, but he offered no further comment.

Agnes's jaw tensed, but before she could open her mouth, Evangeline blurted, "This is delicious, Mother. Did you add fresh basil?"

Railea's tears, why had she thought inviting Declan to dinner a good idea?

"It's very flavorsome," Declan agreed and took another forkful.

"Thank you," Agnes responded, perfectly civil. "I added thyme and rosemary, too. But no matter the use of herbs, it won't change a meat pie to steak. It's hearty fare, to be sure, but I'm afraid it's too common for one such as yourself, Declan."

Evangeline's fork protested against her plate with a squeak as she stared at her mother. Had she just been compared to a *meat pie*?

Declan, however, didn't seem the least discomposed. He polished off the food on his plate before saying, "Not at all. That was one of the best meals I've had in a while." He turned to face Evangeline. "I fear I may have a taste for . . . hearty fare."

Evangeline gaped at her archmage. She was not the only incredulous one at the table.

"Evie's human," Agnes exclaimed, clearly ruffled by Declan's response. "She will make a terrible ayari. She can't sing or dance or . . . "

Evangeline clasped her cheeks with her hands, mortified by the turn of conversation. "Oh, Mother, *please.*"

Declan leaned forward, a tiny furrow between his brows. "I have no wish for an ayari, Mrs. Barre." Declan turned to Evangeline once more and held her gaze. "It is her presence I enjoy."

This time, the sides of Evangeline's lips lifted grudgingly.

"As do I." Agnes's tone severed their locked gazes like a serrated blade. "She is my daughter . . . " Though Agnes started off indignant, her last words came out a bleak whisper. "My sweet girl."

Evangeline reached over to clasp her mother's hand. "I'll come back frequently, Mother."

"You are welcome in the castle. If you wish, I will have you relocated." Declan's unexpected offer had Agnes knocking a glass off the table. But it didn't shatter. It didn't even hit the ground. It was as though a phantom hand grabbed the glass midair before sliding it neatly back onto the table. Part of its contents, however, sloshed to the floor. Evangeline didn't need to see her mother's openmouthed expression to know who had levitated the glass. A normal mage could never have intercepted it that quickly. Evangeline pushed back from the table, reaching for a dishrag, but Agnes gave her a flustered wave.

"I'll do it. It was terribly clumsy of me."

The interlude proved useful, as by the time Agnes returned to her seat, she had regained her composure. "Declan, if I may be so bold, I've lived in this village since long before you came to reign in Amereen," she said, a startling reminder that

Declan might be an archmage, but Agnes superseded him by age, "and it is here I am needed, and here I wish to remain."

"I understand." Declan's nod was solemn. "But I assure you Evangeline will be well cared for."

Agnes clamped her lips, and her shoulders slumped. Evangeline pushed her peas around her plate. The exchange between her mother and her archmage did more than discomfit, it curdled in her gut with fresh trepidation. She'd never left her mother's side since she'd been found in the ravine all those years ago. Agnes, who'd spent countless days cuddling her by the fire in the early days, trying to get her to speak. A woman who'd held her whenever she'd woken up screaming with sweat-riddled skin.

"Mother, I'm not afraid of monsters in the dark anymore," Evangeline murmured.

Agnes released a weary breath, concern fogging her eyes. "Oh sweetheart, you still wake up from the nightmares . . . "

Declan settled his glass on the table. Whatever it was Evangeline expected, it was not for him to clasp her hand from under the table, his grip strong and reassuring, as he leaned forward to regard her mother with all seriousness.

"I will kill any monster who ever dares scare her again."

TWENTY-FOUR

"Railea's tears, Lily!" Evangeline dashed forward to stop the girl's convulsive thrashing. Lying prone on the bed, Lily lashed out, hands curled like claws, as though fighting an imaginary battle. Wordless cries escaped her lips as she scored Evangeline's forearms. Evangeline didn't release her, not even after the nurses pushed through to administer sedatives and the girl stilled with artificial calm.

"Another episode?" Mailin asked from the doorway with concern etched on her face. Evangeline could only nod, her throat a constricted tunnel as she continued to cradle Lily amid her twisted sheets. Her disfigured face slowly slackened. Evangeline murmured quiet reassurances as the girl's eyes resumed a glassy state.

Like Surin, Lily remained silent. They'd never learned her name, but one day when Evangeline had brought in a bouquet of calla lilies she'd sourced from Jorge—who turned out to be a groundskeeper—the girl had perked up enough to caress the soft, dewy petals. Since then, Evangeline had taken to calling her Lily. The girl didn't seem to mind.

Evangeline lowered Lily back onto the bed and moved aside so Mailin could channel healing energy into the girl. The scratches Lily had given herself knitted back together with preternatural speed. Eyes bright and skin flushed, Mailin reached for Evangeline's arm.

"It's all right. It doesn't hurt," Evangeline said. The half-breed healed by expending inner energy. Every healing process, no matter how small, drained her, and Evangeline wasn't willing to wear out a pregnant woman over a few scratches.

Mailin frowned. "Don't be silly, Evie. It's not going to take much energy, and besides, the sire will not be pleased to see you marked up yet again."

Evangeline sighed. Mailin was right. She had been back for less than two weeks, and she'd already been kicked in the gut, scratched, and bitten. Every evening she met Declan for dinner, and he was already making a habit of examining her for evidence of Lily's violent tendencies, expressing quiet displeasure with every new mark he discovered.

"Perhaps this wasn't such a good idea after all," Declan had muttered darkly the previous night as he traced faint scratch marks on her forearms that had escaped Mailin's notice.

Mailin's healing energy flowed into her bloodstream, and Evangeline shut her eyes with a sigh as her body tingled from the warmth. Mailin, the only halfbreed in Declan's employ, had healing energies distinct from the other healers in the castle. Perhaps it was the burgeoning friendship they had, but the healer's magic somehow resonated with her.

They were walking out of the main ward into Mailin's office when the healer blurted abruptly, "You've been hurt before, haven't you?"

Evangeline blinked. "Huh?"

"You've been traumatized in the past. So badly your psyche bears scars."

Startled by the unexpected remark, Evangeline stumbled into a stack of carelessly placed books, toppling the pile. Mailin caught her deftly by her forearm and winced. "I really should tidy up. And . . . I'm sorry, Evie. I shouldn't have mentioned anything. It was intrusive of me."

Evangeline brushed off her skirt before crouching to help Mailin with the books. "You saw . . . my past?"

"No, but whenever I heal, I momentarily connect with the patient, and I can see"—Mailin frowned as though searching for the right word—"no, I can *feel* their essence. Their psyche. And yours . . . "

Mailin's lips fashioned a thin line. "I don't know how to explain it, but I can taste your scars. They run so deep . . . " She shivered and then shook her head. "You don't need to tell me anything, Evie. I should never have raised it. It is not my place to ask."

Evangeline fidgeted with the end of her braid, flummoxed that she was scarred on a psychic level she couldn't see. "I couldn't tell you even if I wanted to. I don't remember anything from before my twelfth birthday."

Except for the distorted nightmares that periodically haunted her.

Mailin didn't look at her with pity. The healer's eyes brimmed with sadness. "The mind works in wondrous ways, Evie. Sometimes memories get embedded so deeply they can never be forgotten. And sometimes memories are so traumatic, the brain needs to forget in order to survive."

Evangeline stared down at her feet, encased in soft pastel slippers that matched her muslin dress. A nurse rushed up to them, suspending her response.

"Healer Mailin. Lady Evangeline." The nurse bobbed a

curtsy despite her flustered demeanor. Evangeline returned the curtsy. She'd learned that nothing deterred Declan's people from treating her like anything less than a dignitary.

Mailin merely nodded. "What happened?"

"Guildmaster Blacksage has returned from Draedyn's Realm with three new survivors."

Blood and grime swirled to form a murky shade as Evangeline scrubbed her fingers under the flow of tepid water. But she couldn't scrub the ache from her chest. One of the rescued slaves hadn't survived. So badly battered, the woman had taken a final stuttering breath in Evangeline's arms before death glazed her eyes.

"Are you all right, Evie?" Mailin peered at her from the doorway. Even her magic had been unable to heal someone who'd lost the will to live.

Evangeline nodded, unable to give voice to the myriad conflicting emotions churning in her chest. Anger. Grief. Fear. And a sickening inkling that this wasn't the first time she'd held death in her arms.

Not the first time she'd seen eyes go flat. Unseeing.

Mailin's voice was gentle. "Why don't you take the rest of the day off, hmm?"

Evangeline opened her mouth to decline, but a question she'd wanted to ask since Mailin had agreed to take on her apprenticeship slid from her throat, barely a whisper. "Do you think you can help me remember?"

The healer did not misunderstand. "Are you sure you really want to?"

Evangeline's response rolled off her tongue easily. "Yes."

Meandering through rows of primly cut hedges, Evangeline was startled by the distant clash of steel and raucous male laughter.

Mailin had released her for the day. "The new survivors will be fine. Go. Get some fresh air," the healer had insisted before shooing her out of the infirmary. So she'd done exactly that, taking to the courtyard that led her into the gardens.

Now, curiosity propelled her past the row of red-leafed shrubs leading deeper into the grounds that were shaded by large oak trees.

A wide clearing came into view, the dirt devoid of the usual carpet of green.

Evangeline blinked, and faint heat warmed her cheeks. Men, or likely soldiers, milled the area, wearing nothing but buckskin leathers, muscled torsos on full display. Most sparred with swords while some engaged in a lethal dance of curved blades, and a number wrestled with their bare hands.

Despite the boisterous crowd, Evangeline singled out a man whose sweat-slicked torso gleamed under the sun, his god-gifted glyphs glistening. The heat on her cheeks intensified. She had seen him shirtless countless times during their time in the shadow realm, yet the sinuous way he moved ignited her blood.

He was on the far side of the clearing, where the dirt seemed a shade darker than the rest of the ground, facing a blond man. The contrast between the two could not be more apparent. Alexander's wiry frame still bore the hints of youth, his skin smooth and unmarked, while his brother was all rigid planes and hard angles decorated with the symbols of his ascension. Alexander also wore his hair the same way he wore a smile, longer and easier, where his elder brother's was cropped short like his amicability.

They had both chosen curved swords but used them in markedly dissimilar styles. Alexander, bold and brash, delivered each blow with more brute force than finesse. Declan's movements were sparse in comparison. Economical, but graceful. Every motion he made appeared not for attack but defense, as though he was testing Alexander's caliber.

Kinetic energy exploded from Alexander in a crescent wave. Evangeline gasped aloud. Declan deflected it neatly, and the energy rippled into the ground. He paused, seeming to sense her presence. Declan angled to meet her gaze across the sea of sparring men, and a subtle curve lifted his lips.

Little fire.

A torrent of flames erupted from Alexander's outstretched hands, wrenching a scream from her throat. Evangeline sprinted headfirst into the clearing without rational thought. Flames engulfed her archmage as though he were slicked with oil.

Strong hands enfolded her from behind. "My lady!"

Evangeline bucked against her captor. Another scream tore from her throat. "Declan!"

"My lady, calm down." It took her a few moments to recognize Killian's gravelly voice. She turned to meet dark eyes filled with concern. "My lady," he repeated, "Archmages are impervious to the elements they control."

Evangeline stiffened, and her mouth fell open of its own volition. Killian's eyes crinkled with amusement as he took in the heat spreading like a rash across her cheeks. Keenly aware she'd unwittingly drawn the attention of every soldier in the vicinity, Evangeline resisted the urge to cover her face with her hands.

"I didn't know that," she mumbled.

Killian waved curious soldiers aside, clearing a path for them toward her archmage and his opponent.

Declan leaped out of the flames, utterly unscathed, to meet Alexander head on, blades clashing. The councilor dematerialized midair, reappearing to deliver a roundhouse kick to his opponent's back. Her archmage must have expected the move because he pivoted out of the way and continued to deflect Alexander's onslaught without retaliating.

"How can Alexander wield fire?" Evangeline couldn't hide her confusion. Control of the elements was an archability, or so she'd believed.

"The children of archmages often develop minor archabilities without ascension, my lady."

Evangeline saw nothing minor as Alexander rounded on his brother with another whiplash of fire that Declan warped to evade. The fire charred the ground black.

"It is no surprise the councilor inherited the ability, my lady. The sire himself mastered fire prior to his ascension. After all, Corvina was a fabled pyrokinetic who once set the seas on fire."

Evangeline shook her head. "I've never heard of mages who control the elements."

Killian's eyes were trained on the sparring match, but he issued a grunt of acknowledgement. "That's because they are rare, and most archmages slay younger mages who develop the ability. They do not like competition."

Evangeline's eyes widened, but before she could query further, Declan struck out abruptly, as though he'd decided the match was over. Within seconds, Alexander was disarmed and flipped deftly onto the ground. Alexander groaned, sprawling with such exaggeration that even her archmage's lips twitched.

Declan pulled his brother up by the forearm. "You've

gotten faster." His tone was filled with unmistakable pride, which had onlookers hooting with approval. Alexander rubbed the back of his neck with a beam.

Declan turned to meet her gaze. But Alexander sauntered over first, his expression complete with a cocky grin. "Ah, Evangeline. Have you come to admire some male finery?" Alexander flexed his biceps for emphasis, coaxing an embarrassed laugh from her throat.

Declan's brows furrowed as he retrieved his shirt from the edge of the clearing, and Evangeline watched with regret as he shrugged it on.

Killian snorted. "Perhaps she came to admire you with your ass planted on the ground."

Seemingly unperturbed, Alexander chuckled, his beauty a glorious, golden thing. "Come anytime you wish, Evangeline. This is the first time I've ever lambasted my brother in flames." Alexander wagged his brows wolfishly. "You're clearly my lucky charm."

Declan's frown deepened. Instead of walking, her archmage materialized right in front of her. Used to his abrupt appearances by now, Evangeline smiled up at him. Though Killian had been standing a respectful distance from her, he increased that distance by taking a subtle step away. Alexander however, remained unrepentant, seemingly intent on baiting his brother as he shot her a flirtatious grin.

"You'll need more than luck if you're to survive ascension," Declan muttered, not a hint of amusement on his face. "Get back to sparring."

Killian snickered. "A match, Councilor?"

In response, Alexander dematerialized and reappeared in the area of charred dirt and beckoned the commander.

As Killian strode off, Declan studied her. His mind brushed hers, a lick of fire across her senses before his hand lifted to her cheek. "Never rush into the sparring field, little fire. You could get hurt."

Evangeline toyed with her fingers. She wanted to lean into his arms, but she was acutely aware they were still on public display. "I didn't expect Alexander to set you aflame."

His lips twitched, and her pulse rollicked. "I'm an arch-mage, Evangeline. Very little can hurt me." He continued the mesmerizing stroke of his hand across her cheek as he canted his head, studying her intently. "What saddens you, little fire?"

Evangeline sucked in a breath. "Am I projecting uncon-sciously?"

If you were, I wouldn't have to ask you the question. Declan stepped even closer so that their bodies almost touched, his gaze unwavering. "Tell me."

Evangeline cast a cagey look at the sparring field and the milling soldiers. "Can we go somewhere else?"

The barest flicker of his eyelashes and they were standing before a small pond with flowering lily pads and a charming wooden bridge across the middle. A large weeping willow shaded the picturesque pond, its tendrils falling to skim the water.

"Where are we?" Delight lightened her steps as she made her way onto the bridge. Colorful carp swam in lazy circles around the pond.

"Just another part of the castle grounds," Declan murmured by her side. "Jorge spends much of his time creating spaces like these. Little pieces of perfection, he calls them." Glancing at his profile as he studied the fish, Evange-line nearly sighed her appreciation. Perfection, indeed.

Declan sidled closer, his arm skimming down her back to wrap around her waist in a hold both gentle and possessive. Releasing a soft breath, Evangeline shut her eyes and leaned into him. She drew in his heady, masculine scent laced with sweat and smoke, left over from the sparring session. He peppered her temple with slow kisses before running an errant tongue into the shell of her ear, creating an explosion of sensation across her skin. A soft hum escaped her lips as he continued to explore her earlobe with his tongue and teeth. She was so addled by his ministrations that she didn't realize he'd lifted her off her feet until the wooden bridge creaked in protest.

He walked them down to the other side of the pond and positioned her with her back braced against the willow tree, his tongue carousing in her mouth in the most hypnotic manner. Evangeline purred and ran her hands into the thick silk of his hair. He tasted like man, salt and spice. Absolutely divine. His hands roved to hike up her skirts before nudging her legs apart. In one fluid motion, he draped them over his hips and pushed himself close so she could feel his hardened length against her.

Evangeline stiffened, her heart drumming in her throat. Declan didn't release her, his hands still supporting her thighs, his eyes hazy with desire. But he tensed.

Do you wish for us to stop, little fire?

Evangeline swallowed hard, battling the urge to shove him away. She nodded.

Declan released her with obvious reluctance, smoothing down her skirts as he settled her on the ground. Shaken, she let out a trembling breath.

"I'm sorry. I—"

He hushed her. Stooping to rest his forehead against hers so that their breaths mingled, he brushed a chaste kiss over her lips without touching her anywhere else. "You have no cause to apologize, Evangeline."

She chewed her lower lip, once again mystified by his reaction. This had become an almost daily routine. Declan had been sequestering her in the evenings, starting with dinner and then taking her on a stroll around the castle. His strolls usually ended with their mouths fused until her fear reared up and demanded they stop. By now, the men she'd been with in the past would have shown signs of impatience. Annoyance at having their pleasure stifled.

But her archmage was always ready to release her. And never did he once make her feel at fault. Perhaps patience came easily for a being with such age. He was, after all, over six centuries her senior.

He swapped their positions so his back rested against the tree. He seemed to understand, too, the need to wait until her fear subsided before she'd welcome his arms again. When her breathing regulated itself, he drew her into his embrace and she settled against his chest—the position a familiar one she'd assumed since the shadow realm.

"Will you tell me now, little fire?"

It took her a moment to realize he was still waiting to learn the cause of her sadness. She smiled despite herself. Declan listened with his usual impassiveness as she recounted her morning, starting with Lily, followed by the heart-wrenching demise of the newly recovered slave. But this time, his words were not so affectless.

"If it will alleviate the sadness that plagues you, I will do everything I can to free those enslaved by the Unseelie trade, little fire. Even if I have to scour the five realms myself, I will have them freed."

Her breath hitched at the enormity of those words from a man who made no idle promises. Declan had only ever mentioned freeing slaves from Draedyn's Realm—and even that had been part of his ploy to keep her here.

"You'll free every slave, from every realm . . . just to make me happy?"

A resolute nod.

Evangeline stared. "Why?"

"Because I can."

A man who saw nothing unconquerable.

There was a moment filled with the gentle lapping of the pond before he bridged their foreheads together again. A sensation of silk slid against her mind.

Because it upsets me to see you sad.

A man who could indeed conquer everything—even the heart of a woman who'd once thought she could never truly love a man.

TWENTY-FIVE

"House," Evangeline said, flipping the card over the bedspread to show the image of a cheerful cottage. Surin's brows knitted, and she reached for another card, one with the image of a brown rodent. "Mouse," Evangeline said with a grin, putting emphasis on the initial consonant.

Surin parroted the words before glancing up at her mother as if seeking approval. Anaiya, face thin but no longer gaunt, beamed at her daughter. She had finally woken from unconsciousness, and although still bedridden, appeared to be adapting well to her new life of freedom. Evangeline shuffled the deck and laid out three new cards with random images. "Which one shows a flower?"

Anaiya spoke the equivalent in the demon tongue. Surin's finger moved slowly but surely to land on the image of a sunflower. Evangeline exchanged proud glances with Anaiya. "Well done, Surin."

Glancing at the bronze clock at Anaiya's bedside, Evangeline slid off her perch at the edge of the bed. It was almost time for her next session with Mailin. Anticipation tingled in her chest. Over the last three weeks, she'd had private sessions with the healer where she would meditate, bathed in the warmth of Mailin's healing energies.

Though she hadn't found any answers to her nightmares, she'd left every session feeling a little closer to her lost memories. Once, she'd even caught a glimpse of her past. A fraction of a memory of verdant fields, heard a woman's husky laugh, and smelled jasmine. The vision came as quickly as it went, but it was free from the fear that usually accompanied her dreams. Instead, it brought a lingering sense of happiness.

It gave her hope.

Perhaps one day, she would uncover the past that had made her. A past that wasn't a complete nightmare.

Just as she was about to venture out, Mailin swept into the room, bearing a smorgasbord of sweet treats. "I knew I'd find you here." She grinned. "I was down in the kitchens and thought I'd bring us some treats."

Surin tucked her small body against her mother and slid her legs under the bedspread as she watched Mailin with cautious eyes. It was a vast improvement. Evangeline clasped her hands together with delight and scooped up a teacake delicately lined with slices of strawberries.

Mailin scowled at her. "You missed lunch again, didn't you?"

Evangeline widened her eyes, trying her best to appear innocent. "I wasn't hungry until now."

"Lady Evangeline has been running to and fro between the two new slaves the whole morning." Anaiya, still insistent on formalities, selected a pastry. "My lady hasn't stopped for breakfast *or* the lunch trolley," the woman further reported as she bit into a buttery scone with an audible sigh. Evangeline made a face, causing the convalescent woman to chuckle between bites.

"It's just been a busy day." Evangeline plied her mentor with a smile.

Mailin crossed her arms and tapped her feet. "Well, a teacake isn't good enough. Just because the sire is away doesn't mean you get to neglect your own wellbeing."

Evangeline pursed her lips lightly. It had been five days since she'd seen Declan. The three days she'd spent in Arns, she found herself missing his touch, his kisses. It was maddening. When she finally returned, all too eagerly, it was to find a note on the writing desk in her room beside a vase of artfully arranged wildflowers.

L*ittle fire,*
     A matter of urgency will keep me in Salindras for a few days.
I will see you upon my return.
Declan

There had been no words of love, but it was enough to put a dreamy smile on her face. An archmage did not answer to anyone. That he'd thought to leave her a note informing her of his whereabouts spoke louder than the flowers or jewelry he'd taken to sneaking into her drawers. Each night, she would trace the looping lines of the written script with her finger before tucking the note back under her pillow.

Mailin's impatient sniff jarred her back to reality.

"I promise I'm not neglecting myself," Evangeline said with

a little laugh. "After our session, I'll head straight to the Dining Hall."

"Fabulous timing." A man filled the doorway, leaning casually against the doorjamb, wearing his usual cocksure grin. "I was just seeking your company."

"Alexander." Though Evangeline had taken to calling the councilor by name, she still made a habit of genuflecting to him. She rose from the bed and curtsied even as Anaiya greeted him. Surin disappeared entirely beneath the bedspread, and Mailin inclined her head.

"What brings you to the infirmary, Lord Councilor?" Mailin asked.

"To entice your new apprentice into having a drink. Now I reckon dinner is in order."

Mailin's lips parted. "You would take Evie to dinner in the sire's absence?"

A gleam of mischief lit the councilor's eyes. "I like to live dangerously."

Evangeline raised a brow. "And what makes you think I'd have dinner with you?"

Mailin let out a burst of laughter at Alexander's look of exaggerated affront. "Well, I've certainly never had a lady turn me down before." He cocked his head and pinned her with a cajoling gaze. "Come on, Evie. You need to eat, and I want company."

Evangeline tilted her head at the cavalier use of her name.

"What?" His lips molded into a jaunty curve. "You can call me Lex if you want. Lexander. Alex. Whatever, I don't mind."

Evangeline folded her arms, but despite her best intentions to appear stern, a smile escaped her.

"Well, missing one session won't make a difference." Mailin conceded, clearly reading Evangeline's expression. "We'll do it tomorrow."

Expectant eyes landed on Evangeline, who dawdled by sneaking another teacake from the platter. It wasn't the councilor's winsome grin or his perpetually sunny demeanor that she found difficult to turn down. It was the sincere warmth in his eyes that spurred her grudging nod. "All right, *Lex*."

Evangeline followed Alexander into the Dining Hall, but he beckoned her down the steps to the kitchens. Frowning, Evangeline trailed after him, but the bustling hallway eased her wariness. He continued to tug her down the corridor, stopping to exchange a few flirtatious comments with the kitchen maids.

"You're really shameless, you know that?" Evangeline said wryly after he'd winked at another bypassing servant, causing the poor girl to blush so hard she nearly dropped the colander of vegetables in her hands.

He snorted. "I'm not the one teasing an archmage here, so I wouldn't throw stones if I were you."

Ignoring the flush scoring her cheeks, Evangeline crossed her arms and served him a hard glare. "How do you know we're not already . . . " Her throat constricted with embarrassment.

Alexander shot her a sly look. "Ah, Evie, chambermaids know everything that happens in this castle, and I happen to know some of the chambermaids *very* well."

Evangeline flattened her lips. "Well, Declan knows exactly what to expect from me."

Alexander appeared incredulous, but he didn't attempt to challenge her as they came to an unembellished doorway. He shoved the heavy wrought iron door ajar with one shoulder and led her into a room she hadn't known existed.

"There's a taphouse down here?" Evangeline gaped at the crowd. Men loitered around high tables. Women in slinky dresses deviant enough to raise heat in her cheeks arranged themselves over cushioned settees, and some, over the men. Crystal decanters of all shapes and sizes lined the shelves of the curved bar. A woman dressed in provocative red swayed on the stage at the far end of the dimly lit chamber, crooning lyrics Evangeline didn't understand but recognized as the old magerian tongue.

"I figured Declan wouldn't have brought you here." Alexander chuckled at her wide-eyed gaze. He waved, and Evangeline recognized the bronze-haired battlemage, Noto, who gave them a nod of acknowledgement from across the room before returning his attention to a woman wearing a chemise masquerading as a dress.

Evangeline was relieved when Alexander led her to the stools by the bar counter instead of a settee. The brewmaster introduced himself as Frederick and took Alexander's oblique order of "some food for the lady and two of the usual" while giving Evangeline a curious once over.

"Do you come here often?" she asked, trying hard to focus on Alexander instead of the woman in her direct line of sight who was crawling over Noto to straddle him on one of the burgundy settees. Alexander was chuckling again, this time at her. She narrowed her eyes in reply, inwardly berating herself for living up to the stereotype of a classic village girl. The brewmaster settled a glass before her, and she immediately lifted it to her lips.

Liquid fire seared her throat.

She sputtered and coughed, blinking hard to hold back the sting of tears. Alexander's guffaw rang in her ears. Even Frederick seemed amused, a blithe smile on his bearded face.

"What *is* this?" She eyed the contents of her glass with disdain.

Shoulders still shaking, Alexander smirked. "I gather you don't drink much, either?"

Evangeline glared daggers at him.

"Mujarin, my lady. The finest in the realm," Frederick said before he returned to industriously polishing glasses.

"Well, it tastes horrible."

Alexander shook his head. "Evie, Mujarin is the most—"

He halted, distracted by a particularly well-endowed woman with flame-colored hair who sidled over to run her hand down his arm.

"Councilor," she purred. "You haven't been here in a while." She peered at Evangeline with a frown. "Who is she?"

Alexander patted the redhead's hips in a gesture that suggested they were intimate. Or had been. "Not today, Mischa. I'm with a friend."

Mischa sidled off, but not without a scowl aimed at Evangeline.

"I don't think Mischa likes me very much."

Alexander took a hearty swig from his glass. "She gets jealous."

Evangeline swallowed another gulp of Mujarin, this time welcoming the burn down her throat. "Is this the castle equivalent of a brothel?"

"Well, I'm glad my brother didn't go for entirely innocent and naive."

"I may be sheltered, but I'm not naive."

"What tipped you off? Was it Noto over there with Yvette crawling all over him, or the fact that half the women in here are wearing less than you'd wear as a nightgown?"

She cast another cursory glance around the thriving

taphouse. "I didn't expect a place like this in the castle. Why did you bring me here?"

He regarded her a little more closely, mouth building into a slow smile. When Yvette released a very audible moan and Evangeline's cheeks darkened, he chuckled. "I just wanted to see if you were truly as innocent as you appear to be."

Evangeline scowled. "And here I thought you were trying to be friends."

Alexander propped one elbow on the counter and gave her a smile that could have charmed the stars right out of the sky. "Oh, but I am. Is it so strange that I'm interested to know the woman who has my brother so enthralled?"

She traced the curve of her glass with her fingertips, determined to keep her eyes averted from the settee, where a second buxom blonde had joined the amalgamation of Noto and Yvette.

"And you decided this was a good place to get to know me?" Abruptly her finger halted on the rim. A bitter taste that had nothing to do with Mujarin rose at the back of her throat. "Does Declan come here often?"

Alexander shrugged. "Not as often as most." A devious arch of his brows. "He can be a cold bastard, but he's still a man, you know."

She bristled. "A man who keeps a brothel in his castle."

"Ah, Evie, I was jesting before. This isn't a brothel."

She narrowed her eyes in a silent demand for an explanation.

"My brother wouldn't be so low as to keep a whorehouse in his castle. He is not the archmage Dakari, nor is he his father. This is where men come to seek female company, yes." He gestured around the room. "And the women here are light-skirts, yes, but not whores. They're courtesans."

Evangeline scoffed. "What's the difference?"

He shook his head and took another swig. "They are here of their own free will. They're not even paid to do what they do. They are given rooms, yes, but also treated like guests. They are free to come and go as they please, and they are never required to take a man to bed if they have no desire to do so."

Her bile receded slightly and she traced the rim of her glass. "And I suppose a certain type of woman isn't drawn here? The ones who are too vulnerable to be out on their own might have no choice but to remain and . . . and . . . serve. Or they might feel pressured to leave the safety proffered by the castle."

Alexander shrugged. "Yes. It does attract a certain type of woman, but usually the more . . . genteel types end up next door, working in the kitchens for an honest wage. Marguerite keeps a keen eye out for any new girls who show up. There is no coercion here."

Evangeline relaxed in her seat, then wrinkled her brows. "If not, what are these women doing here?"

He stared at her, mouth agape. "Pleasure, Evie! They are here for pleasure. This is the easiest place to get acquainted with elite soldiers, battlemages, councilors, and if they are lucky, perhaps even an archmage." Evangeline scowled, but Alexander merely waggled his brows. "For some, that is reason enough."

She bit her lips. A question grated between her teeth, one she wasn't sure if she even had the right to ask. But the contents of her glass seemed to have loosened her tongue.

"Does Declan keep any regular company here?"

Alexander took a long swill from his own glass, drawing out her impatience with obvious enjoyment before responding with a flat "No."

At her dubious appraisal, his gaze turned earnest. "Evie, he doesn't even have an ayari. My brother prefers uncommitted uh . . . meetings. He picks one, and when he is done he doesn't see her again." Another swig. "That's why you're so interesting. You don't fit the pattern of his usual behavior."

Evangeline wet her lips, unsure if she should feel heartened or frightened by Alexander's remark. "Well, I'm not about to be used and discarded like a toy."

Her head was starting to spin when Frederick reappeared to settle a basket of assorted fritters in front of her. She picked up a piece and bit into the crumbly texture of perfectly battered fish.

Alexander leaned closer. "He doesn't look at you like a toy. He looks at you like—" He broke off midsentence with a shake of his head. "Anyway, I think I rather like you, Evangeline Barre. Prude as you are."

"Mm, thanks," she said through a mouthful of fish. "Although I must say your preferences in women are quite disturbing." She could almost feel the burn of Mischa's glare from across the room.

Alexander rubbed a hand over the back of his neck but made no attempt to wave the redhead over. In fact, he leaned in closer still. "Mischa can be possessive." A sheepish laugh. "She's been here for a long time and uh . . . all but led me through puberty."

Evangeline tilted her head. "You were raised here, in the castle?"

But why had his elder brother been raised in an enclave?

"Born and bred." He gave an absent wave to Noto, who was now leading a merry band of *three* women through the door. "I was also spoiled rotten, and I knew it," he said wryly. "My mother would let me get away with almost anything."

That was exactly what she'd expected of a child of an archmage, yet it was incongruent with everything she'd managed to garner about Declan's past. When she voiced her query, Alexander sobered. He downed the rest of his drink and motioned for Frederick to refill his glass before he explained.

"Nathaniel Strom was . . . " Alexander shook his head in disgust. "*Is* arguably the strongest archmage. Strong enough to force himself on my mother . . . and impregnate her without the mating bond. And for reasons I don't entirely comprehend, my mother chose to keep the pregnancy."

Evangeline's palm flattened against her breastbone. It shattered her understanding of the world. Archmages were supposed to be so powerful that no one could hurt them. But clearly, a pecking order existed even within the Echelon.

"But why didn't Nathaniel claim his own son?" Perhaps it was nature's way of compensating for such long-lived creatures, but even with the mating bond, mages had low birth rates. And as far as she knew, they treasured their young.

Alexander drummed his fingers over the countertop with a sneer curling his lips. "There was no mating bond, so the swiving bastard had no inkling his rape yielded anything. At least not until rumors started to spread about a boy hidden in an enclave who looked exactly like him. It was then, I guess, he started paying attention."

Evangeline shook her head. "What happened when he realized Declan was his son?"

"When Nathaniel finally learned the truth"—the hardness in Lex's eyes was a creeping chill down her spine, the first time she'd ever felt fear in his presence—"he murdered my mother for her apparent deceit."

"I'm so sorry, Lex." Heart lodged in her throat, she could only stare as he swirled the amber contents of his glass.

"When he killed her, my father, linked by their mating bond, fell, too. Then Nathaniel massacred all her battlemages and soldiers who dared revolt." A dry laugh. "Nathaniel would have slaughtered me as well, but Declan appeared out of nowhere, grabbed me by the scruff of my neck, and warped me out of the castle. He dumped me by some pond in a glade near the enclave. When I finally returned, Nathaniel was gone. And Declan with him."

"What happened after that?" she asked softly, heartbroken for the boy Alexander must have been.

"Nothing." He shrugged. "Amereen lost its archmage and its battlemages. No one was going to provoke Nathaniel into a fight. The Echelon assumed control over our province until Declan's ascension." The grit faded away to be replaced by a sheepish grin. "When Declan was named the archmage of Amereen, I tried to kill him."

She gawped.

He nodded grimly. "But all I ended up with was a few broken ribs. Bastard even told me where my errors were and how I could improve if I were to reattempt his assassination with a higher probability of success."

He stole a fritter from her basket. "I did try again, by the way. Seven more attempts, in fact."

Evangeline blinked at him. "How are you still alive?"

He chewed and held out his glass as Frederick moved to refill it. "I was young, belligerent, driven by the need for vengeance. But the bastard never did do anything more than thwart my attempts. Initially, I thought he was playing some kind of sick game."

He snorted. "It took me a long time to realize my brother *doesn't* play games. I don't think he actually knows how. And then even longer for me to finally see that my parents' death had nothing to do with him—if anything, he'd lost his mother, too."

Evangeline swallowed, both disturbed and heartened by the revelation. She could tell they shared a brotherly bond.

Heard the hint of pride in Declan's tone whenever he spoke of his younger brother, even though his expression showed no affection.

"My brother," Alexander said abruptly, "isn't heartless, even if he thinks he is. He can be cold and ruthless, but he is capable of loyalty." Tawny-brown eyes met hers solemnly. "But take care how you handle him, Evie. I have been the only exception to the fact that the people who cross him always end up dead."

TWENTY-SIX

Impatience was a dagger in his chest, but indifference was all Declan exhibited as he viewed the troupe of dancers before him. Tradition dictated members of the Echelon be entertained for a day before they could discuss matters of importance. But it was already the second day, and Alejandro had yet to broach the reason for his invitation.

A briny breeze ruffled the banderols bearing the crest of a blue serpent that lined the walls of the sea-facing pavilion. His little fire would likely enjoy Alejandro's palace, cradled in turquoise seas and filled with tropical flowers. But he would never introduce her to any member of the Echelon. It would draw unwarranted attention to her, a mortal woman as easily crushed as a hothouse bloom. Evangeline should be back in his castle by now, but the distance was too vast for him to reach her mind. Declan drained his mug in a single swig to rein in the restless need to return to his lands.

Archmages never extended invitations for the sake of pleasure alone, and custom gave Declan no alternative but to accept. His refusal would have been taken as an indication of hostility. A pretext for war.

Alejandro Castano, archmage of Salindras, sat surrounded by his many ayaris. One stood behind, massaging his shoulders as he watched the performance with rapt attention. His prized ayari, Sariel, lounged on his lap, stroking his chest as if he were a cat and not a grown man, while two more lay by his feet. The rest of Alejandro's forty-three ayaris gathered around the filigreed dais inlaid with sapphires, attentive to the barest flick of their archmage's finger.

When the dancers finally reached their coda, Declan shifted in his seat to meet the other archmage's gaze before another performance could commence. "Alejandro."

The other archmage nodded and waved away his women. They flounced off to melt into the bevy of varying shades and sizes, but Sariel remained. Alejandro made a habit of collecting ayaris from every race and culture—including women from other realms. And Sariel, an Unseelie with enough magic to create portals, made it possible for Alejandro to do so.

But Declan wasn't one to judge. They all had their vices. Where Alejandro collected women, Declan amassed lands. As a result, Salindras was a mere fraction of Amereen, even though Alejandro had been an archmage far longer.

A woman emerged from the crowd to approach the dais. Tall and regal, with hair of flowing bronze and intricate patterns inked into her forearm, she was unmistakably animati. She curtsied low before Declan. "Lord Archmage Thorne." Turning to Alejandro, she dipped with far more sensuality. "Sire."

Alejandro smiled and crooked a finger. The ayari dipped again before stepping up onto the dais to arrange herself over his armrest.

Declan inclined his head to the bronze-haired beauty. "Nikah. It's been a while."

Nikah beamed, clearly pleased he'd remembered her name. "It has, indeed, Archmage Thorne. Indulge me, Lord Archmage. How is my brother faring?" A searching gaze paired with a small smile. "He hasn't given you any trouble, has he?"

"Noto makes a fine battlemage. One any archmage would be pleased to have in his command."

Alejandro snorted, still sore that though Nikah remained his ayari, her twin had chosen to serve Declan's court. Sensitive to her archmage's emotions, Nikah's smile strained. "It eases my heart to hear such high praise from your lips, Lord Archmage."

Declan nodded but offered no further commentary on Nikah's twin. Nikah and Noto had been a gift from the ruling family of Thurin's Realm to the Echelon centuries ago. Slated to Alejandro's care and raised in his palace, Noto's eventual desertion for Declan's court had been a point of contention between the archmages for many summers.

Alejandro slunk an arm over Nikah's waist and gave Sariel's hip a gentle pat. "My loves, why don't you tell Thorne what you've learned in your recent travels?"

Sariel, who had been silent the whole time, ceased her petting and straightened. "Archmage Thorne," she said with a nod of deference, "I have caught wind of troubling whisperings of late. Of drakghis flying over the Winter Court Palace."

Declan permitted a slight purse of his brow.

Alejandro raised his high enough to kiss his hairline. "You don't appear nearly as surprised as I expected, Thorne."

Declan had gathered enough from his own network of spies to know the Unseelie king had been supplying glider chiefs a steady stream of human slaves in exchange for demonic *favors*. From Gabriel, he also knew of the cage erected near King Zephyr's palace, large enough to house an entire village. The presence of drakghis, the limbed cousins of arrowtails, did not come as a surprise, though Declan had no inkling how any man—fae king or not—could master such brutish creatures.

At Declan's continued silence, Sariel nodded. "If that comes as no shock, Archmage Thorne, then perhaps you'll also find Sister Nikah's findings less disturbing than the rest of us." Sariel nodded at the animati woman.

Nikah, unlike her twin, who wholly abhorred the animati realm, had chosen to remain in contact with her family with the help of Sariel. The animati woman inclined her head. "Archmage Thorne, I, too, have heard of disturbing whisperings from *my* realm—rumors of human slaves being exchanged for the *mahalwei*—the shieldmakers."

This information sent a ripple of disquiet down his spine. Animati were a unique people, born with the ability to shift between two forms—man and beast. But a rare minority lacked the ability to alter their forms. And perhaps Thurin saw fit to compensate for their lack of bestial forms, for they were blessed with a far more unique gift, likened to the camouflaging abilities of a chameleon. Only the shieldmakers had enough magic to cloak and conceal entire armies.

Declan frowned. "I find it hard to believe your people would willingly trade shieldmakers for something as prosaic as human slaves."

Nikah colored and dipped her head. "They are only whisperings. It is true that the *mahalwei* are rare, but my father believes some of his enemies may have already struck an alliance with the Unseelie king."

Alejandro leaned forward, his arm tightening around Nikah's waist as if to bolster the woman's claims. "Rumors alone are unsettling enough, Thorne. Have you forgotten Zephyr has always held a grudge against your father?"

Declan shifted in his seat. It was true Nathaniel Strom had many enemies—and none as deadly as the Unseelie king. Formidable even without the aid of drakghis and shieldmakers. Declan pinned Alejandro with a steely gaze. "If you believe Zephyr to be rising against us, why did you not call for a meeting of the Echelon?"

Alejandro curled his lips. "You know how they are, Thorne. Too old and arrogant to listen to my ayaris." He huffed. "I will not call for a meeting until I have tangible proof."

Declan conceded with a nod. Alejandro might be three centuries his senior, but they were both below the mark of a thousand summers—young, by the standards of the rest of the Echelon.

Alejandro regarded him with a questioning brow. "Now, will you use your resources to help me, my friend? Sariel is my only key to the realms, and Nikah far too precious for me to allow in Thurin's Realm for too long."

Despite Alejandro's hedonistic appearances, the archmage doted on every one of his ayaris, which was likely why they were so devoted to him.

Declan inclined his head. "I will have Blacksage and his men investigate."

Declan materialized into the main office of the infirmary the moment he took his leave from Salindras. But she wasn't there.

"Evangeline?" he asked the only woman around.

Mailin blinked, her surprise as plain as the potions and paperwork around her.

"In the Dining Hall, sire."

With a nod, he warped, only to find a sea of councilors, courtiers, and soldiers milling in the large hall. But his little fire was nowhere to be seen. He dismissed the greetings with a brisk wave and reached out on the mental plane until he found the warm glow of her mind. Homing into it, he warped.

To his shock, he found himself in the nondescript taphouse beneath the kitchens, the last place he'd have thought to search.

His little fire was perched on a high stool, playing cards with his brother. Evangeline gave a happy squeal as Lex revealed his hand. Lex responded with a mock growl, eliciting another infectious giggle. She clasped her hands together with glee. "Again!"

A foreign emotion coated the back of Declan's throat. Darkness coiled tight in his chest. He prowled over, the patrons in the lounge parting like a sea for him. "What is going on here?"

Alexander's eyes widened. "Brother, I didn't expect you home so soon."

Evangeline swiveled on her high stool, legs thumping lightly against the wooden frame. "Declan?" Delight lit her face. "Killian told me you wouldn't be back for another day yet." She stretched out her arms as if to hug him. The darkness in his chest eased. Her amber eyes were incandescent, accented by a pretty sheen of rose on her cheeks.

Declan moved close enough so Evangeline could wrap her arms around his waist. She beamed up at him, thoroughly silencing the strange emotion in his gut. Sighing, he leaned forward to touch his forehead to hers. "How much have you had to drink, little fire?"

Evangeline giggled impishly and held up two fingers. Then another. And another.

"They were watered down," Alexander muttered.

Declan shot a barbed look at his brother. "I see. And do I want to know what you're doing down here?"

Evangeline obviously had no idea she had Alexander's neck wrapped in a hangman's noose. "Lex thought we should get to know each other better."

Declan's arms flexed inadvertently. "Did he, now?"

Brother, I merely wanted to be friends with a woman you clearly hold in such high regard. Alexander was wearing the same expression he'd worn as a child when Declan had found him stealing into the stables in the dead of night to ride the geldings without a saddle.

Evangeline settled a hand on Declan's chest. "Yes." She nodded gaily. "He's trying to educate me." Alexander coughed pointedly, but Evangeline seemed oblivious. "We're playing drinking games," she added, waving the deck of cards at Declan like an eager child. "Do you want to join us?"

Declan felt his lips twitch despite himself. "I have work to tend to later, little fire."

"Oh." Her shoulders fell. "In that case, you shouldn't. It's pretty heady."

Knitting his brows at her glass on the counter, he brought it to his nose for a whiff and then widened his eyes at Alexander. *You gave her Mujarin?*

The blackguard feigned innocence. *I only thought to give her a taste of your favorite drink.* Only, Declan thought darkly, the most potent liquor of magekind. Declan considered reaching over to crack a bone on his brother's person.

Evangeline rested her cheek against his chest and sighed. "I missed you." It was a tipsy whisper, but one that completely vanquished his macabre thoughts. "I'm actually really sleepy. Will you take me back to my room?"

Declan drew her up readily.

She craned her neck toward Alexander to give a parting smile. "Thanks for the night, Lex . . . I had fun."

Alexander grinned, seeming to have recovered from his bout of guilt. "It was my pleasure, Evie." *Mortal she may be, but your lady is special, brother.*

Declan fixed Alexander with a glare that would have had lesser men quaking, but his younger brother merely ducked his head, hiding a smirk. *She's pure sunlight . . . and you, brother, have been living in winter for far too long.*

🔥

Declan warped them straight into her room, marveling at how well she fit in his arms. Like a missing puzzle piece. Evangeline nuzzled against his chest, her body curved in a familiar way, reminding him of their time in Draedyn's Realm. He settled them both on the settee, but he didn't release her. Neither did she push away from his hold.

"Will you hold me tonight?" she murmured.

Declan stiffened. Evangeline had never invited him to hold her to sleep. He eyed the four-poster bed with unscrupulous intent. Declan had always prided himself on self-control, but now he doubted he could last the night doing nothing but holding her.

"No," he finally managed, finding perverse satisfaction in the disappointment dancing across her face. Since she'd signed his employment contract, he'd been trying to seduce her, but he'd failed. Spectacularly. Every time she made the little whimper indicating he'd gone too far, he would freeze like an errant child caught red-handed.

He'd also lost *all* interest in women, bar her. It was as though Evangeline had dulled his senses to every other woman. He'd taken to relieving himself when he fantasized of her sharing his bath. He was an archmage, for Railea's sake, and he was palming himself in the tub, envisioning her supple legs wrapped around him the way they had when he'd awoken in Draedyn's temple to her straddling him. With her sodden dress clinging to her skin. Only his fantasy renditions featured her wearing nothing but the hot slick of steam and water.

"No," he heard himself say again. "I do not think that would be a good idea."

Her eyes rounded with understanding, then she pushed out of his hold sheepishly. "You're right. You should go."

His arms felt bereft. "I want to kiss you."

Her lips parted, and the desire in her eyes told him he wasn't the only one with a yen. She returned into the fold of his arms so eagerly it took every ounce of self-control not to toss her onto the bed and have his way.

Seduce, not pillage, he reminded himself.

He gave her a chaste kiss and ran his hands lightly down her spine. She closed her eyes and sighed. There was nothing carnal about the sound, yet it sent fire rippling through his veins. Kissing her had become an exercise in self-restraint.

He continued to ply her with featherlight kisses until he received an impatient nip at his lower lip. Smiling, he delved between her lips, relishing the taste of her—an intoxicating blend of Evangeline and Mujarin.

"Don't you need to change into your nightgown?" he asked, his voice dropping an octave. Her response was a soft whimper, one of pleasure. She reached for the laces at her back. He swept her fingers away.

He pressed kisses anywhere he found skin, circling her

step by slow step until he stood at her back. She shivered as if in anticipation. Declan took his time undoing the laces, stippling little kisses along her spine, and felt satisfaction at hearing her breath hitch. He allowed the pale lilac fabric to pool at her feet before he turned her to face him.

It stupefied him how modest undergarments could be so erotic on her.

He nudged her toward the mattress, where her nightgown lay draped over the edge. Instead of helping her into it, he folded them both into the bed. When he rose over her, he caught the first hint of fear darting in her eyes. Carefully, he rolled onto his back so she could settle over him.

When the fear receded from her gaze, Declan felt victorious. He drew her down toward him and proceeded to court her with more kisses until she relaxed into a bundle of quivering flesh, straddling his hips. Inadvertently he bucked, rubbing his desire against her. A startled gasp escaped her throat and her fingers curled. Pliant to panicked.

He groaned and eased her off.

He'd gone too far again.

He pushed off the bed, needing a moment to regain control. No surprise he'd frightened her. He was stiff as iron. When he met her gaze, it was to see embitterment.

"I'm sorry," she whispered. She scrubbed her face with her hands. "I'm sorry."

"Evangeline." He tugged her back into his arms. "It's all right."

"No, it's not. I want to give you what any other woman can," she said, dejection chief in her tone. "But I can't."

She pushed out of his arms and crawled away from him to the other end of the bed. "We need to stop. We can't keep doing this. I don't want you to think you can ease me into this . . . I just can't, Declan. This isn't a game for me."

He hauled her back into his arms. "I don't play games, Evangeline. I promise I won't kiss you unless you want me to, but I don't like you pulling away from me."

Her lips firmed. "Don't you see what you're doing to me? I *want* you to kiss me, but . . . " She sputtered, cheeks flushing. "But I always feel so frustrated afterwards."

Declan heaved out a breath. He was such a fool. If he had been reduced to palming himself, he should have realized she was equally unsatisfied. Before he could plead his case, she launched another volley. "Even if I did overcome the fear and sleep with you, what then? I'm not an amusement, Declan."

He frowned. What had he done to lead her to such thoughts?

"I am mortal. My hair will turn gray and wrinkles will line my face while you'll remain ageless. What then?"

His heart ached—a sensation he hadn't felt in a long time—but he refused to think about her mortality. Not yet. "You may not give me carnal pleasures now, and you may never do so. But haven't I already promised not to ask for more than you can give?" He forced himself to release her, shifted back on the bed to give her space. He needed her to see his sincerity, to understand that all he wanted was to be in her presence.

"I enjoy touching you, kissing you, holding you. I enjoy being close to you. I enjoy your *mind*." Her psyche was a warmth that drew every part of him. Especially the coldest, darkest part.

He reached out to take her hand. In the end, that was all he needed, just to hold her hand. For a painful moment, he was transported to a time when he'd been a boy. When all he'd wanted was to hold a girl's hand and listen to her read by the pond. Centuries had passed, yet Evangeline had reduced him to the boy he'd once been. He hadn't had the power to keep Freya then, but now he was an archmage. And, he realized with a start, he would do just about anything to keep Evangeline.

But all the power in the world couldn't earn him her trust.

"Believe me, little fire." Declan swallowed, then uttered a word he hadn't used since the day he was forced to make his first kill. "Please."

Her beautiful eyes took on a wet sheen. Her lips trembled as she regarded him for a long moment, and he felt like a prisoner awaiting judgment. Her sentence was a benediction as she curled back into his chest and whispered two words that punched the air right out of his lungs. "Kiss me."

So he did.

By the time he released her lips, the musk of her desire saturated the air. She was flushed, but he knew it wasn't from his kisses alone. Was he taking advantage of her inebriated state? But he wouldn't leave her frustrated this time. Not when he could give her release.

Very deliberately, he moved back so their bodies no longer touched.

Confusion clouded her eyes, and she moved as if to crawl back into his embrace. He held her firmly by the hips. "If you want me to stop, all you need to do is say so."

She frowned up at him.

"Let me give you pleasure." Slowly, his hands roamed over her thighs to delve under her undergarment and cup the hottest part of her. Her slickness almost derailed him. Clenching his jaw, Declan searched her face, seeking her reaction. She appeared more scandalized than fearful.

His name came as a startled gasp on her lips.

Giving her a reassuring smile, he dipped a finger into her and drew another sensual cry from her throat. Very gently, he searched for the sensitive nub of her sex.

She squirmed and scored his arms with her nails. "Declan . . . "

She arched in the bed, eyes hazy with lust as she writhed under his ministrations, seeking a release she didn't seem to understand, but he did.

"Come for me, little fire," he whispered. Another stroke and her body spasmed, the wave of her orgasm threatening to undo him.

"There you are," he murmured as she went limp. Her hands still clutched his arms, seemingly unable to release him. Willing his own thundering heart to slow, Declan withdrew his fingers and bridged the space between them to lay beside her.

He waited until her eyelids fluttered shut and her breathing deepened before tucking her beneath the covers. He warped back to his own room and blew out a low sigh of resignation. Stripping off his clothes, he headed into the bath chamber.

TWENTY-SEVEN

Thump. Thump. Thump. Felicie's breathless sobs.

Evangeline jerked at her binds until the skin at her wrists burned. She rattled the chains linked to the manacles, causing her skin to chafe further. She didn't mind it. The stinging pain helped distract from the heinous nightmare in the adjoining room.

Thump. Thump . . .

She stared blankly at the darkened hearth. The chains kept her close to the metal grille of the fireplace. So close that when the hearth was lit, the fire caused her manacles to heat up to an unbearable temperature. Sometimes she prayed for her hands to be scorched off her wrists and done with. Yet they never were.

It never got hot enough to do more than blister her skin.

Felicie let out a muffled cry. Evangeline strained against her binds until the metal cut into her flesh. The thumping resumed. Blood coated her mangled wrists. Evangeline lowered her head to her hands, trying to plug her ears with her fingers.

It was cold tonight. The fire had dwindled to smoky embers, but the monsters were so deep in their cups they hadn't bothered to stoke it this time when they'd returned. Their breaths were rancid with liquor, and their laughs reeked of malice as they proceeded to entertain themselves.

Thump. Thump . . .

Sickness perforated her gut.

Another spasm racked her frame as Felicie's smothered sobs rose in volume, paired with animal grunts and lewd laughter from the other room. They would be done soon. Evangeline kept her eyes tightly sealed and pretended she knew nothing of the horrors taking place in the other room. Things she should not know.

But sometimes they made her watch.

Her chains rattled the grille.

The thumping had fallen into a rhythm now. Felicie's cries hardly audible.

Evangeline jerked her wrist harder, until blood lubricated her manacles, but still she could not free herself.

The door creaked, and a man with soot-colored hair emerged wearing a smile of vile contentment, face flushed and chest heaving. *Monster.*

"Stop it, you little brat!" He stomped two steps toward her, hand raised in warning. "All this rattling is giving me a headache."

She stilled instantly. She hadn't realized she'd continued to shake and strain against her chains. He was heavy-handed, this one, and was always willing to raise them. She kept her head lowered. Her fear was so palpable it could well be a person in the room.

Another man with ash-white hair sauntered out of the room, his lingering gaze raising every hair on her skin. This monster was as pale as the other was dark, his voice soft as the other's was harsh. This one had cold, dead eyes, and he hid malevolence well beneath the quiet. He never raised his voice or his hands in warning. But strike he would. Only he did it when no one saw it coming.

Now he fixed those deadened eyes on her. "Want to play, sweet angel?"

Soot sauntered to the single chair in the room, sat down, and lifted his boots to the table. Laughed. "Haven't got your fill?"

Ash smirked. "I'm in the mood for seconds." Then he clucked his tongue disapprovingly at Evangeline as though reprimanding an animal. "Besides, it's time she got an education."

The floorboards groaned beneath his bare feet, every creak compounding the contractions of her heart. He went to his haunches, and she caught a whiff of the musty odor of Felicie's fear and perspiration.

He stroked her cheek.

Her insides shriveled. She shrank as far into the corner as her chains would allow and shook her head mutely, pleadingly. His face contorted with displeasure. Suddenly he was upon her, freeing her chains from the grille. The wizened floorboards creaked as he hurled her onto her back.

"Be a good girl," he rasped into her ear, his breath fetid.

"Leave her alone!" Felicie lurched through the doorway wearing her tattered dress and patchwork of fresh bruises.

Soot sneered from his seat across the room. "Go back into the room, whore, unless you want to watch."

"She's just a *child!*" Felicie launched herself across the room. But before she could take more than two steps, Soot grabbed her and hurled her roughly against the wall. She crumpled to the ground.

Evangeline grabbed hold of Ash's arm and bit down as

hard as she could. He swore. Drawing up the chains still attached to her manacles, he gave her a violent jerk that snapped her head back. Then he seized her throat with both hands, severing her air supply. Evangeline stared into his death-filled eyes, struggling to breathe as her vision wavered.

She was screaming inside, but fear had long since rendered her mute.

Finally, the pressure receded and air filled her lungs. Before she could scamper away, rough hands hiked up her skirt. She finally found her voice when he shoved at the softest part of her. She screamed, high and shrill until it mellowed into gasping rasps. Tears streamed down her cheeks.

The invasion halted as quickly as it started. Above her, Ash froze. Then he howled. Curling shadows erupted seemingly out of nowhere to creep over his hands, jerking him off her, and he went staggering to the ground.

Evangeline scrambled up, but shock kept her frozen.

The cabin door was *open.*

And there was a third man in the room. A man with long, silver hair and cold, flat eyes shrouded in foggy black. Dark shadows discharged from his core, sinewy black limbs slinking across the wooden floorboards, sliding up the walls. They curled around Soot, constricting him the way a snake might its prey.

Soot's eyes bulged while blood frothed in his mouth. Ash was the picture of horror as he stared at the silver-haired man and his comrade in death throes.

"Plea-se . . . !" Ash's usually composed voice was shrill.

"How *dare* you betray me?" The silver-haired man raised a hand, and a surge of black shadows erupted like a webbed snare. It engulfed Ash completely. Red welts erupted where the tendrils touched bare skin, along with the smell of seared meat. The shadows were slowly charring off the monster's skin.

Ash's cries heightened to screams that matched the crescendo of Evangeline's heartbeat.

Hands gripped her forearms.

Felicie.

"Come!" Her sister jerked her up and yanked her toward the cabin door. It was now open but blockaded by the darkness still seeping from the silver-haired man. Felicie plunged headfirst into the gloom, dragging Evangeline behind her.

Darkness nettled at her skin like the prick of a thousand pins, but Felicie hauled her out. Out of the fog of darkness. Out of the cabin of horrors.

"Run!" Felicie urged, and they fled into the moonlit forest. Pain assaulted her from every angle. Her skin was raw from plunging through the shadows, the tender spot between her legs ached, and her bare feet chafed as she ran across the uneven forest path.

Evangeline ignored it all and pounded across the unforgiving ground as fast as her feet could carry her.

Freedom. They were finally free to go *home*.

With a yelp, Felicie stumbled. Evangeline skidded to a halt. Fresh terror clotted in her chest. The moonlight illuminated black veins roiling beneath Felicie's bruised skin. Blood dark as ink leaked from her sister's nose. More dribbled from the corners of her mouth. Evangeline caught the crook of Felicie's arm and tugged, willing her to stand. But Felicie shook her head, chest straining as her breaths turned into shallow gasps.

Evangeline whimpered, tears clouding her vision, but she couldn't summon her voice. Once again, locked inside her. Felicie lay in a crumpled heap over the dead leaves and bracken covering the ground. "Run," she gurgled. More blood trickled from her lips before her grip slackened.

Her eyes remained open, but unseeing.

E vangeline gasped, chest heaving as if she'd run a hundred miles, body steeped in sweat. The memory, dark and slick, replayed itself in her mind. Things she'd always known but could never fully see finally shoved their way out of the depths of her mind.

Raw, anguished sobs clawed at her throat, as if a beast were trying to tear out of her to consume her whole. Felicie. Her *sister*. A sister who had saved her. A sister she'd forgotten.

She screamed into her pillow, trying to suffocate the agony that threatened to rip from her chest. She kept keening until someone wrapped their arms around her. Dimly, she heard the chambermaid drop the breakfast tray. Tessa's terrified voice rang in her ears, but Evangeline couldn't stop the anguish pouring out of the battered hole that was her heart. Couldn't rein in the avalanche of grief or stem the tide of sorrow and salt that flowed from her eyes.

Declan materialized into the room, his usual mask of reserve displaced by undisguised shock. But when he drew her into his arms, she only shook harder. He was so large. So quintessentially *male*. And the very feel of a man sickened her. Reminded her of the monster pinning her to the wooden floorboards, the stench of ale-laced breath and of sweat-slicked bodies. Roused the echoing screams of a forgotten sister who had haunted her dreams for years.

It was only when she felt a flood of warmth—the unmistakable brand of Mailin's magic—that her tremors waned and her sobs ebbed. Evangeline curled into the healer's embrace, allowing the other woman to whisper reassurances into her ear as she pumped healing energy into her body.

The morning passed in a blur. She lay curled in the bed, vaguely aware of people moving in and out of her room. Her mind was rooted in the past, replaying the horror with startling clarity, as though it had happened yesterday. When she finally stirred, the sun at the apex of the sky indicated half the day had passed.

Evangeline examined her wrists, half expecting to see bloodied and chafed skin. But her flesh was deceptively smooth. Unmarked from the horror that had ruined her life and stolen her innocence. Killed her sister.

"Evie?" It took her a moment to realize Mailin was still in the room. The healer had been sitting in the corner the whole time.

"I want to go home, Mailin." Evangeline said, her voice husky. "I want to see my mother."

Mailin nodded obligingly, studying her with concern as she sat carefully on the bed beside her. "Of course. The sire said to provide you with whatever you need."

Evangeline blinked, suddenly remembering how she'd struggled against his arms.

"Where's Declan?"

"The sire . . . removed himself from the room when it was evident his presence upset you." For the first time, Mailin appeared uncertain. Her voice was quiet as she said, "Did the sire hurt you, Evie?"

"No." She managed a weak laugh. "No, he didn't."

The healer seemed to relax, but concern didn't leave her eyes. "Do you want to talk about what happened?"

Evangeline stared at the woman who had become a friend. A woman whose healing sessions had loosened the knots of her memories and eventually unlocked them.

Evangeline told her everything. The words sounded hollow to her own ears. As if someone else were narrating the most traumatic moment of her life. "The worst is that I don't remember everything." She'd just been given a glimpse of her life before she became Evangeline Barre of Arns.

Confiding in Mailin helped anchor her to the present, and a soak in the tub further distanced her from the past. The healer remained in her chamber, trying to coax some food into her, but her appetite remained nonexistent, and there was something she needed to set right.

The moment the request left her lips, Declan materialized into her room. Clearly the healer had passed on her wishes telepathically. Mailin shot her a final look of concern and bowed to her archmage before padding out of the room.

He appeared impassible once again, and she could almost be fooled, except his eyes burned bright. Almost feverish. He remained at the foot of her bed, tall, imposing, and motionless. Uncertain if he was welcome. Evangeline pushed off the covers to go to him, but he warped so he appeared by her bedside before she could get up.

But he didn't touch her.

"Declan—"

He shushed her. "I shouldn't have . . . I won't touch you like that again." His voice was gruff. Suddenly it occurred to her that *he* took the blame for the sudden onslaught of her memories.

"Did you think what happened today was because of . . . last night?"

A grim set of his jaw. "What else could it be? You were intoxicated, and I . . . "

She shook her head. "The sessions I had with Mailin," she

explained, reaching out to draw him down to her side, "unraveled a memory."

After a moment of hesitation, the mattress dipped with his weight. He took her hand experimentally, as though expecting her to flinch away. Evangeline sighed and curled into him, drawing a deep breath. He smelled of the crisp, spring air, cedar, and something intrinsically Declan. Nothing like the monsters. His arms wrapped around her. Strong, muscled arms she knew would never hurt her.

"I didn't mean to push you away this morning. I know you're not them."

He stilled, his arms tightening around her. "Who?" he growled. Then he grimaced. "You don't need to speak of it, not unless you want to."

She could hear the rapid pound of his heart in his chest.

Safe. She was safe with this man.

"I was raped as a child." The words came easily this time, her voice surprisingly steady. The admission made her feel less a victim. More in control.

Declan's eyes hardened, but there was no surprise in them. He regarded her silently, willing her to go on. With Mailin, she'd shared her anguish, but she gave her archmage the facts. She spoke quickly, not trusting herself to linger on the finer details of the cabin and her captors lest she broke down again. She didn't speak of her desperation and despondency, or the miasma of terror, but from the tempest raging in his eyes, she didn't need to. He understood.

"The man who stopped your captors. Can you remember his face?" His expression hard, his tone crisp. She was dealing with the archmage of Amereen.

Evangeline shook her head. "Silver hair and purple eyes. That's all I remember."

"Fae. There is no doubt you were a part of the slave trade. Your captors . . ."

A tremor rippled through her, and that was all it took to shred his composure.

"I will find them," he vowed, and the glyphs on his skin took on an eerie sheen. His eyes shone with green effulgence and radiated violence so patent it siphoned warmth from the air, the temperature dipping despite the crackling fireplace. "If they still breathe, I will make them rue the day they were born."

"I want justice, not vengeance." She did not want to see him go cold with fury like that. It frightened her. When the violence in his eyes receded, she sidled closer, tugging him down so their foreheads touched and their breath mingled.

"I want the entirety of my past. I want to find the man who . . . saved me." A man who had overcome her monsters and claimed betrayal. Who was he?

"I want to find my family." Her shoulders curled the moment the words left her lips. It felt disloyal to Agnes to say that, but she *needed* to find her biological family. Somehow, she knew deep in her bones that she hadn't been merely a sister. She'd once been a cherished daughter. She was loved.

"Anything," Declan murmured. "I will do everything within my power to help you find them." She remained nestled in his embrace, drawing comfort from the unyielding strength of his arms while he threaded his fingers through her hair, massaging her scalp until she fell into dreamless sleep.

TWENTY-EIGHT

E vangeline left the castle, wanting her mother and the normalcy of Arns. Back in the comfort of the little cottage, she purged more grief wrapped in her mother's embrace. Agnes doted and fussed, her concern fierce and her love more effective than any balm against the trauma of the memory.

Weeks passed. No battlemage appeared to escort her back to the castle, but Evangeline felt the occasional weight of a gaze or caught a watchful presence. Her archmage might not enforce his contract, but she was certain his men remained close.

Instead of annoyance or fear, she felt yearning. She missed him. Despite her emotional turmoil, she found herself longing for his embrace. The days were easier as Agnes kept her well occupied in the apothecary. But the nights were hard, and she often woke in the tangle of her own sweat-soaked sheets. Her nightmares had grown less distorted and more vivid. As though she was destined to relive the horror every night.

Her heart still pounding from the dream and her ears still

ringing from Felicie's screams, Evangeline swung her feet out of bed, donned her night-robe, and crept out of her room, careful to avoid the steps that creaked for fear of waking her mother. She slipped out to the backyard with nothing but chirruping crickets and the waxen moon for company.

She drew in a deep breath of the brisk night air laced with fragrant honeysuckle. But it did little but make her shiver.

"I miss you, Declan," she whispered into the starless night.

The air beside her shimmered. "Do you?"

She jumped to her feet, startled by the shadowy figure at her side. When she realized who it was, her heart only raced faster. "What are you doing here?"

"You said you missed me," he said, as though it explained his sudden appearance.

She stared hard at him. Despite his telepathic abilities, she doubted he could hear telepathically over the distance between Arns and the capital. He must have been close enough to hear her. "Have you been spying on me, Archmage?" she asked incredulously.

His lips flattened. "Of course not. I was only checking in on you."

She arched her brows. "In the middle of the night?"

She received no response. Instead, he sat down beside her, stretching out his long legs as he removed his coat and draped it over her shoulders. "Why are you outside on such a cold night, little fire?"

She fingered the lapels of his coat and hid a smirk. She supposed she should feel disturbed by his stalkerish behavior, yet she didn't. It was evidence he missed her as much as she did him.

Overwhelmed by longing and a sudden surge of tenderness, she leaned close and wrapped her arms around him. He didn't hesitate to pull her closer. His lips found hers, and soon she found herself on his lap, curled in his embrace. He watched her, riveted as though entranced by the sight of her toying with the short strands of his hair.

"Go back to bed, Evangeline. You'll catch a chill," he murmured, running a finger over the seam of her lips. She sucked it into her mouth, and his breath caught.

"Do you remember the last time you took me to bed, Archmage?" she asked when she released his finger.

He swallowed hard, and his breathing grew harsh. His usual reserve seemed to be missing, and somehow, his lack of composure only fueled her desire.

"What you gave me that night . . . it was pleasure, Declan. It was wonderful."

"You were intoxicated. I shouldn't have touched you."

"I wasn't entirely sober, but I wanted it," she whispered. "I wanted you." She had always wanted him. "I *want* you."

His arms flexed in response. But she wasn't done. She cupped his face and pressed a tender kiss to his lips. "I want . . . to give you the same pleasure."

He stiffened again, and she caught the blatant yearning before his gaze mellowed into inscrutability. "You don't owe me anything, little fire."

"No," she agreed. "But I want to do it."

His lips parted. She chuckled. It was the closest thing to shock she'd ever seen on him. She curled her arms around his neck, drawing him closer, and repeated it again, knowing he needed the words as much as she wanted to say them.

"I want to, Declan."

His voice was a tangle of thickets in his throat. Declan parted his lips, but the words wouldn't come, snagged by an undefinable emotion that swelled in his chest. He held her tight and rubbed his cheek against her hair. Drew in the heady scent of wildflowers and cream and willed his heart to slow.

Cupping his face, she drew him down for a full kiss. Her tongue licked between his lips, teasing a reflexive shiver down his spine. Declan drew her closer, held her tighter. He couldn't seem to hold her tight enough. Couldn't seem to find his voice to tell her what her words meant to him. He could only show her.

Before he knew it, he had her legs wrapped around his hips, his hands running the length of her thighs under her nightgown.

Gritting his teeth, he forced himself to release her. He would not lose control here, in her backyard. Not knowing of the demons that plagued her dreams. But she surprised him by raking her fingers through his hair, tugging him down for another hungry kiss. "Now that I remember," she whispered, "I know you're nothing like them."

He fisted his hands at the thought of the whoresons who had hurt her. Promised himself to find the perpetrators and mete out a slow, torturous death. He would flay them, salt their wounds, scorch their—

She caught his cheeks with her hands, mild reproof in her gaze. "Do not bring darkness between us."

He complied, consciously unclenching his fists. His reward was a husky whisper that threatened to shatter his control and set her cottage on fire.

"Take me to bed, Declan."

Cradling the face that had become so dear to her between her palms, Evangeline caressed his chiseled cheeks with her thumbs. His eyes darkened, glittering gems of green, but he remained adamant.

"No," he murmured again. "You need sleep, Evangeline. A clear head is the best weapon against the past that haunts you."

In that instant, she was absolutely certain she wanted him. So much that she was sure to expire if she didn't have him. All of him.

"What I need is you." It was as though a deeply buried part of her, a part that had been dormant, had somehow awakened alongside the long-buried memory. A part that wanted him so badly it ached.

That he was a being who had lived centuries to her own paltry years—and one who would go on living for centuries long after she was dust—no longer mattered to her. The fact that he was one of the eight supreme rulers of the realm, a being who could crush her without so much as a blink of an eye, no longer mattered. At that very moment, he was just a man and she a woman. A woman who needed him more than the blood in her veins.

She layered the side of his jaw with soft kisses and watched his facade crumble. Driven by a primal need to feel his bare skin against hers, she tugged at his shirt. The lump on his throat bobbed, eyes darkening further. She had never attempted to remove his clothes before. All the times they'd kissed, he'd made the moves. But tonight would be different.

Tonight, she would love him.

She gestured to the open window of the cottage. "That's my room. Take us inside."

Her surroundings blurred. She blinked. They were not

standing in her bedroom in the cottage but the bedchamber she used in his castle.

"Not with your mother sleeping in the next room," he muttered.

She blushed. She hadn't been thinking at all. She eyed the darkened room and the much larger bed. He was right. This room was much better equipped for her intent.

"Take off your clothes," she whispered. Her skin tingled at her own boldness.

He remained unmoving for a heartbeat before he obeyed, unbuttoning and shrugging out of his shirt, displaying the perfectly sculpted torso that had made her fingers itch since she had first seen him shirtless beneath the waterfall. The arcane symbols played over the hard canvas of his chest, flaring an unearthly gold where she touched. An abrupt jolt of power caused her to jerk back reflexively.

Her mother's words replayed in her mind. *He can quite literally kill you in the act.*

He seemed to read her mind. "I won't hurt you, little fire." He encircled her wrists and dipped his head to brush his lips over her knuckles. "I will never hurt you."

She broke into an unsteady smile. He hadn't broken a promise yet.

Trembling slightly, she splayed her fingers over his chest, acclimating herself to the soft bite of his powers like static on fabric. Only, the sensation was tenfold. He remained still, watching her with rapt eyes.

She traced the markings with her fingertips. Whenever she moved along the line, more symbols shimmered to life, hot to the touch. As though she was stoking a fire beneath his skin. Fascinated, she trailed the illuminating swirls from his biceps to his broad shoulders, curled over the planes of his pectorals, dipped down to the spectacular ridges of his torso.

"Why hasn't this happened before?" She'd touched him skin to skin in the shadow realm, and they'd never lit up this way.

"I wasn't this . . . stimulated then." His words were gravelly.

The tendons at the side of his neck stood stark, his jaw a stiff line. She'd had no idea her curious exploration affected him this much. Before, she would have been embarrassed, but now it only emboldened her. *Excited* her.

She had never felt more powerful.

She placed both palms on his chest and gave him a little shove. To her delight, he complied, lying back on the bed. She clambered over him with more eagerness than grace, but he didn't seem to mind. His arms curved around her hips, shifting her so she straddled his waist, but he did little else to interfere. He seemed to understand her need to explore.

To touch and not be touched.

She had never had the chance to study a man's body, particularly not at her own pace. Delighted with the free rein, she roamed over him, marveling at the tensile strength beneath the satin of his skin. She peppered him with kisses, reveling in the sensual sounds he made as her fingers played over planes, occasionally running her tongue over the hard ridges. Eventually she reached the dusting of dark hair below his navel and was quickly distracted by the bulge straining his trousers. After a moment of uncertainty, she reached to undo his pants.

His hands gripped her wrists abruptly. "Evangeline," he said, voice deliciously low and husky. "I don't think it's a good idea for you to touch me there." The muscles at his neck looked so taut, she worried they might snap.

An ache formed in her chest. She would have him. She looked straight into his eyes and whispered, "I want this. I want you."

He didn't need further encouragement. He undid his pants himself. He was fascinatingly stiff and a whole lot larger than expected. Evangeline had seen the village boys nude on occasion when they stripped and threw themselves into the creek in the warmer months. But Declan's throbbing readiness was nothing like the anatomy of a child.

"I should hope not." It was almost a growl. "I haven't been a child for over four hundred summers."

She hadn't realized she'd uttered her thoughts aloud.

Hotly embarrassed but undeniably aroused, she gripped him with both hands. The solid circumference left her light-headed. Unable to help herself, she ran her thumb experimentally up and down the shaft. An unwitting image crept around the edges of her mind—being pinned on the hard cabin floor. . . and the pain that followed.

She shivered.

"Little fire?" Concern wrinkled between his brows.

She fed him a reassuring smile and thought instead of the women serving in the taphouse. Lex had claimed the women were there voluntarily. Pleasure seekers. But how could the act of copulation be pleasurable for females when the male anatomy was so hard and rigid? Yet, despite her growing apprehension, she couldn't deny the desire thrumming in her chest. The inexplicable *want.* She ran a finger over a thick vein and was appalled by her perverted urge.

Would he mind if she . . . licked him there?

She leaned down, certain the warmth rising to her cheeks would result in heatstroke, but she couldn't seem to stop herself. She placed a hesitant kiss against the hardened length. His skin was hot, almost feverish to her lips. A rumble resounded from his chest, alarming her slightly. He remained unmoving, so she leaned forward again and gave him a little lick. She sighed her appreciation. He tasted like the ocean.

Giving herself to instinct, she took him fully into her lips. She had barely begun to suckle when his self-control snapped.

Without warning, he reared up and flipped her onto her back. She yelped at his sudden animation, her apprehension replaced by a stirring anticipation. He crowded her with his body, securing her on the silken sheets to plant molten kisses over her neck, grazing her skin lightly with teeth. Her breath hitched, and a mixture of emotions coursed through her—arousal, excitement, desire. And not a single hint of fear.

He loosened the ties of her bodice with the efficiency of a man who knew exactly what he was doing and drew her dress over her head to reveal her sheer linen chemise. A low growl came from his throat, as though her undergarment were an offense. With a few deft rips, he tore the seams at the sides of her chemise and peeled it from her body like a man unwrapping a priceless gift.

Self-consciousness crashed through her. The first time they'd tangled in the temple, he'd seen her bare, yet now she squirmed under his scrutiny. After seeing how well-endowed most of the courtesans were, for the first time in her life, she wished she were more voluptuously formed. But her thoughts proved irrelevant.

"Perfect," he breathed. "You are perfect."

Eyes bright and fervid, he caressed the hardened peaks of her breasts with the slow deliberation of a potter molding clay. Her flesh, already hypersensitive, tingled with his every touch. She writhed, wanting him to do more, touch more, but his gaze returned to lock on hers. Searching her reaction, searching for fear.

He must have been satisfied, for he finally dipped his head to take her breast into his mouth, as though he were a connoisseur and she a sampling dish. Her breath ratcheted, every fiber of her being yearning for his touch. Another deep male rumble resounded from his throat, and warmth pooled between her legs. Without leaving her breasts, his hand snaked down to tug at her underwear. She squirmed, a mewl of excitement escaping her throat.

He must have mistaken her reaction for fear, because he stilled instantly, mouth still clamped on tender flesh. With a frustrated moan, she arched, fingers digging into his scalp, urging him on.

He relaxed and released one breast only to ravish the next. Her undergarment soon met the same fate as her chemise, and she quivered beneath him, bare as the day she was born. He lifted his head once more, viridian eyes studying her face, seeking her reaction. She waited for the usual panic to rise in her chest, but felt nothing but a pulsing need that had her panting.

His eyes hooded, and his lips took on a roguish curve she had never seen him wear. A heart-poundingly wicked grin. He dipped his head again and roamed downward, pressing feverish kisses down her abdomen to trail between her thighs.

She gasped. "Declan!"

He chuckled, a mystifyingly sensual and mischievous sound that caused more wetness between her legs. To her extreme mortification, he burrowed his face and kissed the most secret part of her.

"What are you doing?" She gasped, wiggling in protest, but he gripped her hips and held her firmly in place.

Let me taste you, Evangeline. A command.

Until he added, *Please.*

Her heart raced, not from fear but sheer embarrassment, as he did unspeakable things with his tongue and wrenched moans from her throat. A pressure built within her, as if she were a wind-up toy, and his tongue were the key. She threaded her fingers into his hair, bewildered by her own building need and mortified by the indecency of what her archmage was doing between her legs. All rational thought spiraled from her mind when he wound her up to a peak and sensation splintered in her core. A visceral scream tore from her throat, echoing the pleasure ricocheting through every fiber of her being.

She was still aquiver when he nudged her legs apart to position himself at the juncture of her thighs. He rubbed against her, a low groan in his throat. But he stilled, visibly restraining himself. He rubbed against her again but did nothing else.

Evangeline parted her lips, dumbfounded. Despite the urgency riding him, he was still awaiting consent. Strangely relaxed, she curled her arms around him, purring her acquiescence. A shudder rippled through him, and he began nudging into her, hot and hard and unyielding. She sucked in a gasping breath at the invasion.

His girth stretched her muscles, and the sensation propelled her back into the nightmare of her past. He stilled instantly, eyes darting up to meet hers. Whatever he saw on her face had him withdrawing.

"No." She wrapped her arms around him, holding him close. "Give me a moment."

His brows furrowed, but he obeyed, burying his face against the crook of her neck. When the tension ebbed from her body, he nuzzled at her ear.

"I'll stop whenever you need." Hopeful eyes searched her face. "Yes?"

"Yes," she whispered.

Relief written clearly on his face, he reclaimed her mouth and kissed her senseless. He parted her thighs and nudged into her again, drawing another involuntary gasp from her. As he inched himself in, he covered her mouth with his, drinking in her whimpers, soothing her with soft kisses. When he was fully sheathed, he held himself blessedly still as she adjusted to his size.

She was torn between the wild heat of desire burning in her chest and the dark knot of panic rising from her gut. She was trapped. Quite literally impaled beneath him. Snippets of her nightmares bounded through her mind, as merciless and relentless as hounds on a hunt. She shuddered and stiffened as the memory of agonizing pain and soul-stealing terror seized her.

Evangeline slapped it aside. And forced her eyes open.

Staring down at her was not a monster's leering face, but a man whose usually imperturbable countenance was filled with nervousness as he studied her expression. A man who was patient and gentle and infinitely tender. A man who would never hurt her.

She smiled. "I'm all right."

The brackets around his mouth deepened, but he continued to hold himself still, as though he didn't quite believe her. She gave an experimental roll of her hips, wrenching a strangled groan from his lips as twin jolts of pain and pleasure shot through her. She did it again, relishing the rousing sensations and his barely contained reaction.

It struck her then, the disparity between this act and the one that had imprisoned her subconscious in shackles. She wasn't an enslaved object being used. She was a woman, a *lover*, with the power to give—and receive—pleasure.

A sudden, primitive need to take more of him over-whelmed her.

She wrapped her legs around his hips, drawing him deep into herself, and released a trembling sigh. He seemed to understand, for he began rocking his hips, thrusting into her with slow but sure movements, building a tension only he could satisfy.

He groaned her name. The sound of his voice, raw and discomposed, was almost enough to shatter the storm building within her.

Then she realized something was burning. Literally.

"What is that?" she asked in alarm. The smell of ash penetrated the haze of their primal act. "Nothing," he groaned as he thrust into her. "Nothing you need to worry about."

Another thrust.

Just as abruptly, the scent was gone. A sensation far magnified from what he'd done with his tongue began to build within her, a gathering maelstrom. She lost the ability to think. She clamped her legs around his hips and her arms around his shoulders, fingers raking down the hard muscles of his back. He modulated his movements based on her moans, skillfully working her into a fever pitch, but the sounds she made seemed to undo him.

His motions grew less and less measured until he was thrusting deeper and slamming harder with each maddening stroke. Merciless in his quest for release. She was screaming his name when she shattered in an explosion of ecstasy. Her blood was molten pleasure in her veins and her limbs liquid wax when he finally spilled into her in shuddering silence.

Still panting, she stared up at him. Every single symbol of his ascension was illuminated. The gods had written lightning into his skin. He was the most glorious being she'd ever seen, and for this one indelible moment, he was *hers*.

"Goddess of light . . . " Evangeline was unable to find the words to describe her emotions. She buried her face in his chest. She didn't even feel the jolt from his powers anymore. He let out a low laugh of pure male satisfaction. Gently, he withdrew, only to curve his body around hers. He was still tracing lazy circles on her hip when her lids drooped and fatigue claimed her in his stead.

E vangeline's body was humming. It was almost dawn, judging from the muted rays teasing from behind the heavy drapes. Euphoria and guilt consumed her. Declan would have to warp her back before Agnes discovered her missing and panicked. But he was still asleep, his breathing deep and even, rumpled sheets all around them. She smiled and took the opportunity to study his slumbering form.

Even in sleep he was indomitable. He had one arm wound around her waist and the other tucked under her, boldly cupping her bottom. Unable to help herself, she nuzzled into him. His lids lifted, and in that one instant, eyes still mired with sleep, he appeared utterly transparent. Almost vulnerable. But his eyes sharpened, and a wicked smile crested on his lips. A smile that stole her inhibitions and rendered her wanton.

"Good morning," she murmured.

He'd roused her twice more in the middle of the night, insatiable, to take her at a slow and languorous pace. Declan stretched beside her, a self-satisfied cat, and her skin heated. She all but purred, damp for him again. He must have read her mind because he shot her another heartrending grin full of wolfish intent and rolled onto her.

"You need to take me home," she protested with a breathless giggle.

Agnes would be worried sick if she found her missing.

"I'll send someone to inform your mother and fetch your things."

She opened her mouth to demur, but a glint from the floor caught her attention. Frowning, she patted at his chest to push him off so she could sit up and take a better look.

What was she looking at?

The lush carpet that had spread across the center of her room seemed to have disappeared overnight. The hardwood floor was now several shades darker. And *what* in Railea's name was that translucent, glimmering layer over the darkened wood?

Her jaw dropped like an anvil plunging into the ocean.

"You charred the ground *and* iced the floor?"

TWENTY-NINE

Charred floorboards. Burnt so uniformly the entire ground appeared blackened. And then coated with ice as thick as the width of Evangeline's palm. Declan's gaze roamed the ruined ground. He swallowed, sheepish for the first time she had ever seen.

"I may have lost control several times last night."

Her eyes snagged on the cracks in the rock wall at the furthest corner of the room. It was as though someone had bludgeoned the wall with an iron-studded mace.

Stupefied, she stared at the man beside her who was taking in the rest of the damage around the room with a clinical eye. The pecan dresser closest to the bed had suffered the most. It was no longer standing on its legs, its lower half burnt to a crisp, the contents spilled to the ground, some pieces almost comically encased in ice. The little writing desk and the cushioned chair she'd become quite fond of were frozen in place with blackened legs. The settee was still standing, but Evangeline wouldn't be sitting on it, as it appeared ready to collapse under any added weight. Then she realized why sunlight was filtering through the room to glint off the ice despite her drawn curtains. The hem of the weighty drapes was a jagged crisp several inches from the ground.

How was the bed still standing?

"Does this happen every time you . . . ?" She sputtered, dazed. She had been so consumed by what he was doing to *her* that she had been oblivious to what he was doing to her room. Gingerly lowering one foot to the ground, she tapped the surface with her toes. Hard, solid ice.

"No." He peered down as she tapped her feet experimentally. "Not like this."

Shivering, she retracted her foot from the floor.

"You were never in any danger, Evangeline," he said. He'd mistaken her reaction for fear.

She knew he would never hurt her, yet . . . "You set my room on fire and put a crack in a rock wall," she said dryly. "And let's not start on the ice."

Despite the impassiveness of his expression, she knew the archmage of Amereen was chastised as he swallowed again. "I set the ground on fire by mistake. But I banked it before it could do any real damage . . . and channeled my powers to ice." A slightly less destructive outlet. His eyes tracked the fracture in the wall, and his lips firmed. "That happened when you put your lips on my cock."

Her cheeks burned, yet she found it difficult to keep a straight face. He appeared adorably abashed. Then she frowned. "Is this because I'm human?" She was no ayari. Nor was she an immortal courtesan with psychic abilities.

There was a dark chuckle, and she was hauled back onto the bed.

"It is because you are *Evangeline*." His mouth descended on hers once more, and her mind fizzled. It was much later when he warped them both into the bath chamber, after which the ice on the ground grew by a couple more layers.

Evangeline was adding another dash of minnowseeds into the mortar when the wooden scoop slipped out of her fingers, scattering a spray of ground herbs across the workbench. She groaned, scrubbing her face with her hands. So far, she'd managed to bungle nearly every single task she'd been given.

Clearly, her faculties hadn't quite recovered from the previous night.

Evangeline crouched down, wincing as she searched the cupboards for a rag. It seemed her body hadn't quite recovered, either. She was tender in areas she hadn't known *could* be sore.

Mailin ambled by and surveyed the mess with a furrow in her brow. "Are you sure you're ready for this, Evie?"

After Evangeline had persuaded Declan to warp her home to reassure her mother and pack her things, they'd returned to the castle and she'd headed straight to the infirmary. She was done wallowing in the past.

"I'm fine, Mailin, honestly." *More* than fine. She'd fortuitously vaulted over a memory that had haunted her ever since she could remember.

Mailin's frown deepened, and Evangeline found herself on the sharp end of a penetrating gaze. Color crept up her cheeks. Could the healer tell? Agnes had taken one look at her this morning and shot impeaching brows into her hairline. Declan's presence had not helped. But her mother must have sensed the shift between them, for with a resigned hug and a reluctant sigh, she had murmured, "do have a care" into Evangeline's ear, though her eyes had been pinned squarely on Declan as she spoke.

Her archmage had nodded.

Evangeline tore her sight away from Mailin's assessing eyes to lean deeper into the cupboard and continue fishing for a cleaning rag.

"The sire said you might be needing rest today—"

Evangeline bumped her crown on the ledge of the cupboard. "Ouch!"

Mailin tutted and immediately reached out to channel healing energy into the throbbing spot.

"Thanks," Evangeline muttered with a wince. "But four weeks is rest enough. Work is good for the soul." So was having an archmage warm your bed and ice your floors. Evangeline pinched the bridge of her nose as though it would banish her unruly thoughts.

Mailin gave an agreeable nod as she continued to fuss, even though the hurt had dwindled to a slight sting.

"I would like to resume our meditation sessions," Evangeline blurted. She wanted to regain *all* her memories. No matter how painful. She needed to know.

Mailin retracted her hand but continued to study her. "Of course. I'll be here for you whenever you're ready. But perhaps when you're more rested. Did you get any sleep last night?"

Evangeline's cheeks mirrored the jar of saffron before her.

"Um . . . sort of," she mumbled and began mopping up the mess, hoping to discourage the healer's scrutiny. The muddle of powdered seeds on the workbench reflected her emotions. Chaotic.

Her newly acquired memory was a paper cut, seemingly shallow in the breadth of recollection but stinging in its clarity. She had a lost sister. A lost family. A lost identity. But now, all she could think about was how she'd spent her first night with her body fused to Declan's. Her cheeks heated at the thought of her archmage's wild loving. Burned at the recollection of her own wanton responses. It was as though they had been different people last night, fueled by passion and lust.

Even now, she ached to return to his arms. To voice the fears that had crept into her heart since they'd parted ways that morning. Yearned for him to allay those fears. Yet she knew it to be a childish need, for no one could ease her qualms. Not even an archmage. No one could change their incompatibility. An immortal archmage and his *human* lover. That discrepancy would hang over her like a dark shroud for as long as their relationship lasted.

But *new* fears, ones she had never before considered, chewed at the corners of her heart like vermin gnawing through the cellar door. Agnes had always said men were fickle creatures. Now he'd finally *had* her, would he tire of her? Alexander's words resounded like a taunt. *Once he's done, he doesn't see them again.*

Her heart thudded wildly, fear a chill creeping down her back.

Firming her lips, she swept up the remaining minnowseeds and envisioned them as her insecurity. She emptied them into the bin. Declan might be her first lover, but she was certain last night hadn't been *just* sex for him. He had taken her fervently, but he had done so with conscious tenderness. He'd touched her, kissed her with reverence, as if her body were a temple and he were in worship. He had made love to her.

The erratic beat of her heart regulated.

And hadn't he been curiously affectionate in the aftermath?

By the time they'd left her battered room, Declan had relegated his passion and warped her back to the Barre cottage every inch the unflappable archmage of Amereen. The ease with which he had switched back to his usual reserve had been unsettling, but then again, she wasn't sure what to expect from a man like him after an intimate night together.

And back at the castle, just before they'd parted ways, she had been unable to resist rubbing her nose against his. It had been an inane moment, her own affections running rampant. Standing in the hallway just outside the Dining Hall, in full view of the breakfast crowd within, her archmage had not only cracked a smile. He had rubbed his nose back—assuaging all sense of disturbance in her heart.

"Evie? Hello?" Mailin waved at her, snapping her out of her reverie.

"Hmm?"

Mailin crossed her arms.

Evangeline feigned ignorance. "What?"

Mailin's eyes took on an incriminatory glint, but she relented, her next words nonchalant. "So, I'm thinking of taking Surin and Anaiya out to the capital today. I think it would be good for you to join us."

Sunlight streamed through the balcony doors, caressing the study with the brightness of dawn. Declan reclined deeper in his seat as he considered his battlemage and fae ally.

"The animati would never trade *mahalwei* for human slaves, sire." Noto punctuated his statement with a sharp shake of his head. "Why would the animati share their *mahalwei* with the Unseelie? Shieldmakers are their best form of defense."

Before Declan could respond, Gabriel snorted from the

cushioned seat opposite Declan's desk. "Perhaps Zephyr has made them an offer they cannot refuse."

Noto narrowed his eyes. "Wars were fought and won on the backs of shieldmakers. There is nothing you and your insidious kind have to offer that could tempt the animati into trading their greatest asset."

Gabriel's violet eyes rolled upward, and his lips fashioned the sardonic curve he often wore for Noto's benefit. "And there it is. That animati arrogance that keeps you blind to possibilities."

Noto peeled back his lips in a snarl. "I am no animati, Blacksage. I have no allegiance to a realm that chose to cast me and my twin out like strays."

Declan lifted a hand to stifle Gabriel's comeback. "If you are both done acting like children, perhaps you could be of some use to me."

The battlemage clamped his mouth shut, while the guild-master folded his arms. Declan suppressed the urge to sigh and shook his head instead. Archmage or not, he could never get them to get along. "Regardless of what we believe to be truth, Nikah's claims will need to be investigated." At the mention of his twin, Noto's expression softened visibly. Understanding what the battlemage sought to know but refused to ask, Declan switched to the privacy of telepathy. *Your sister appears well cared for. There is no cause for worry.* Aloud, he added, "Return to your home realm, Noto, and get me some answers." Noto's shoulders stiffened, but he dipped his head. "Yes, sire."

Gabriel smirked. "I'll have one of my men cast you a portal. Do you have to pack before you leave or—"

In response, Noto lifted his hand and made an obscene gesture at the fae. Gabriel only laughed. "I forgot. You don't need clothes where you're going, do you?"

Pointedly ignoring the Unseelie, Noto prowled toward the balcony railing and shed his clothes. Shifting into his other form, the animati leaped over the railing in a flash of bronze, leaving his clothes in a heap on the ground.

Gabriel snorted. "Heathen."

Declan ignored the comment. Beneath the Unseelie's banter was true respect for him and his battlemages. "The human operators," Declan said, changing the subject. "Have you found any new leads?"

Gabriel retrieved a folded piece of parchment from his coat pocket. "I have seven names of those who preyed on your lands twenty-five seasons ago." Gabriel unfolded the sheet and handed it to Declan.

"And the ones who sold children?"

The Unseelie shook his head. "I couldn't find any proof they'd taken children."

Declan nodded as he studied the names. "Find them. If they still live, bring them to me." If these traders had never come across Evangeline, Declan would grant them a swift death. But if any of these men did turn out to be Evangeline's kidnapper . . .

The fae looked pensive. "It isn't a profitable use of an archmage's time and resources to track down these traders. They are merely pawns."

Once, Declan would have agreed. An archmage should focus his attention on toppling the kingpin, not the traders who did the grunt work.

Gabriel studied him with scrunched brows. "What do you intend to do, exactly?"

Once, Declan would have held his silence and left Gabriel to draw his own conclusions. But today Declan gave the guildmaster a measured smile.

"Introduce myself."

THIRTY

U pon Gabriel's departure, this time by way of a snowy barn owl, Declan warped straight into another session with Killian. As lord commander of Amereen's battlemages, Killian acted as an intermediary with Declan's army.

Each battlemage controlled a faction of high mages, and each high mage oversaw a battalion of elite soldiers. As he'd ascended only two centuries ago, Declan's army was nascent compared to that of other archmages, but he took pride in his men. He'd done his best to select only the ones who offered the most skill—and loyalty.

The loyalty he'd never received from his mother, he would get from his people.

When he had first assumed control of Amereen, only a handful of Corvina's soldiers had submitted to his rule. Some had revolted, which he had slain without mercy, but most dispersed upon her death, choosing to serve in the territories of stronger, more experienced archmages. Declan had no dispute with their choices. He had no wish to inherit loyalty from his mother's men—most, if not all—who saw him as nothing more than a bastard.

Alexander alone saw him beyond the circumstances of his birth.

But that was not the reason his half brother had been spared. Declan had not been above fratricide. Railea knew Alexander had given him reason enough to end him with the repeated attempts on his life. He hadn't spared Alexander out of respect for Corvina's memory, either, nor did he do it out of the goodness of his heart. Snuffing out lives with categorical violence had come far too easily after the time spent in Nathaniel's court.

No, it was because Alexander, a boy barely grown, had been filled with such righteous fury and fueled by the need for vengeance that he had reminded Declan of himself, wrought with grief over Freya's death.

Declan understood the agony of lost love. He understood Alexander had lost the mother *Declan* had always yearned for. Understood his half brother had lost a love Declan had never received from the woman who had carried them both in her womb.

Declan had even allowed Corvina's marble statues to remain in the gardens, knowing Alexander often sought solace there. The same way Declan sometimes sought solace by a small, marshy dip in the ground that was once a duck pond in Lindenbough Forest.

When he was done with Killian, Declan spent the next couple of hours reviewing his councilors' reports and realized how little attention had been afforded humankind, even though they made up close to half the population of his lands. Marking up some changes, he delegated the implementation to select members of his council—and knew he would be met with more than one raised brow. No matter. There would be a law in place. One he hoped would encourage humankind to be more forthright with their grievances.

If there were any more missing women and children, Declan didn't want them buried beneath the common laws implemented by his vicegerents.

He wanted to know about it.

Satisfied his lands were in order, Declan went in search of his favorite quarry, but she was nowhere to be found.

"They're in the capital, sire," a nurse said with a little bob. Apparently, Mailin had organized an outing for Surin and her mother today.

Declan returned to his own quarters, which felt strangely hollow. Never once since his ascension had he yearned for company in his personal chambers. After Corvina had fallen, Nathaniel had insisted on Declan's fealty. He had submitted, possessed by the need to know the man who was his true sire.

But his father had deemed him too innocent. At two hundred summers of age, Declan had been nearly an adult, who'd never had a woman. Perhaps it was the only way Nathaniel knew to make up for the monstrosities done to his son, but the archmage had ordered a new woman into Declan's bedchamber each night, insisting his bastard learn to be a *real* man. Declan had been baptized into manhood in a harem of sweat-slicked bodies. A lust-hazed experience he was not eager to replicate in his own castle.

Now he glanced around his quarters, a private sanctuary he'd built for himself since the start of his reign. He'd lived here for near two hundred summers, but the space held no paraphernalia apart from the little bookshelf in his study with his sacred collection. A familiar knot in his chest tightened whenever he contemplated the time-weathered novels. He hardly dared open them now. They were so frail that the pages crumbled at the slightest touch. But he knew every word of each story by heart. He'd read them all until the words were etched into memory.

Declan regarded the rest of his room with a frown.

It felt empty. Cold, even.

He lit the fireplace, something he hadn't done in a long time, but the crackling heat did nothing to warm him. If anything, the dancing shadows only amplified the size of the sparse space.

Running his hand through his hair, he expelled a breath.

He was missing a woman with sunlight eyes and sweet-smelling skin. One who gazed at him with such adoration and touched him with such tenderness, he felt almost . . . precious.

He wanted her in his bed. Her scent in his sheets.

He considered reaching out for her mind. He frowned again and decided against it. He was an archmage, not some needy mageling.

A knock resounded on his door, and his steward stuck his head in. "I brought you your dinner, sire." Declan waved the man away after he set the tray down. He contemplated the meal for a moment, then decided he wasn't hungry.

He warped out of his room and paced the grounds, meandering with no true purpose. He was at the main entrance of the hallway when he heard the chime of feminine chatter.

Anaiya, still painfully thin but far more robust, clasped her daughter's fingers in one hand and a crutch in the other. With her free hand, the rosy-cheeked child clung to the woman who was the reason for and the antidote to his disquiet.

Evangeline's lips flirted with a shy curve, and Declan felt his own tug up in response. "Did you have a good time?" he asked after Mailin left to escort mother and daughter back to the guest quarters.

Her smile deepened, like the sun peeking out from behind a cloud. To his delight, not only did she move to twine her fingers around his, but she began regaling him with her day, her motions lively and lighthearted as she spoke of the markets and dining houses.

"Surin's eyes were so wide when she saw the performing parrot that I was certain she was about to speak if the matron hadn't been so loud and brash." She jiggled his hand in a way that reminded him all too much of the way a little girl once had.

He led her down the private corridor.

" . . . when the matron recognized Mailin, she actually stuttered and apologized for—" Evangeline stopped midsentence to frown, staring at the polished oak doors that led to his quarters. "Where are we?"

He opened the doors and nudged her inside. Lips parted, she took in the stately antechamber, but he didn't give her time to linger. Eager to show her his private sanctuary, he led her into his study. Her gaze darted to his lacquered desk adorned by nothing but a neat stack of reports and ledgers that still required his attention. She began to wander, her fingers skimming the barren walls to pause at the only decor. The painting of a little pond in a stunning glade, crowded by waterfowl and sprinkled with wildflowers.

"This is not the sort of painting I expect to see in an archmage's study," she murmured, studying the painted ducks, and his heart twinged involuntarily. He led her through another set of doors, and her eyes widened when they landed on his bed.

She blushed. "That is a very large bed, Declan."

Pleased at the direction of her thoughts, he bent to nuzzle her neck. "It's also very comfortable."

"Have you not eaten?" she asked, eyeing the untouched platter by the settee.

Declan ran his hands greedily down her back, fingers

undoing the teal ribbon in her braid to free her hair. Tossing the silken fabric aside, he burrowed his face in the fragrant fall and luxuriated in the feel of her soft strands between his fingers. "Hmm. I'm hungry for something else."

With a little sigh of pleasure, she leaned into him. Then she pushed back with a frown. "Will you lose control again?" She glanced around with obvious concern. "I don't want you destroying this room, too."

He shook his head. Last night had resulted in a momentary breach of self-control. Likely a result of the tension built up over the weeks. Now that she was finally *his,* and willing, there was no reason for another breach.

Relaxing, she allowed him to pull her back into his arms. He dropped kisses at the delectable arch of her neck, and his hand roamed down to stroke the most feminine part of her. She let out a sexy little moan, and like a well-trained animal, his male member came to attention instantly.

"Are you feeling sore, little fire?" A reminder to himself that she was new to this. But she turned, cheeks a pretty shade of pink, to give him a secret smile.

"Yes." She buried her face in his chest as though she couldn't bring herself to meet his eyes. "But I . . . like it," she added, voice muffled.

He hardened even more.

Control, he ordered himself. *Control yourself.*

She chose that moment to rise to the tip of her toes, cup his cheeks, and rub her nose against his. The sweetness of the gesture turned his blood to honey even as it stoked a fire in his gut. He gritted his teeth. *Control.*

She started undressing him, and he lost all ability for coherent thought.

Much later, she was snuggled against him on the settee, warm and sated. She wanted his dinner reheated, but Declan was happy eating it cold. He could be eating ice chips and they would have tasted divine.

"I may have lost a little control," he admitted finally. He wasn't entirely sure how it had happened. Again.

She tensed, her hand stilling midair with a half-eaten grape between her fingers.

"Where?" She surveyed the room. Nothing was out of place.

"Outside." He inclined his head at the balcony doors. She drew the heavy drapes apart, opened the glass doors, and padded barefoot out onto the moonlit balcony overseeing the lush green of his grounds. Her gasp was a thunderclap in the hush of the night.

The alder tree beside his balcony had been ripped from the ground, the thickest part of the trunk snapped in two.

"A *little* loss of control?" She stared at the unfortunate remains of the tree that had shaded his balcony for decades. He firmed his jaw. She chose that moment to bend over the metal railing as if to take a closer look at the tree. The hem of the shirt she'd donned—his shirt—rode up to hint at the mouthwatering curve of her behind. She appeared genuinely aggrieved. Debauched as he was, he found it all the more arousing.

"Perhaps I've not satiated myself with you quite yet," he murmured, sliding up behind her to glide his hands beneath the shirt.

"You spent the night in the *sire's* chambers?" Shock was written all over Mailin's face.

Evangeline cringed and cast a quick, furtive glance around the dispensary to see if anyone had overheard the healer. No one paid them any attention. Just as her shoulders relaxed, Mailin snorted in laughter loud enough to draw curious gazes from all around.

"Can you keep it down?" Evangeline whispered testily. The rising heat in her cheeks alone was admitting to all and sundry her carnal sins.

"It's hardly a secret now, is it?" Mailin's grin was wide enough to match the circumference of her rounded belly.

Evangeline narrowed her eyes at the pregnant healer with enough frost to give Declan a run for his money. The concoction bubbled abruptly, threatening to spill over onto the stove.

Evangeline hastily doused the fire and stirred the boiling mixture. "Could you hand me the liverwort berries?" she asked, attempting a nonchalant tone.

Mailin snickered knowingly at her request, and Evangeline squirmed. It was barely noon, but the day was already cringe-worthy. The moment she'd parted ways with Declan after breakfast, she had been on the receiving end of surreptitious glances ranging from undisguised shock to sly amusement. As though the entire castle was privy to what had transpired between her and their archmage last night. Although she could hardly blame people for noticing. It was far simpler the previous morning, when all her archmage needed to do was command a couple of discreet chambermaids to clear the ice from her room and instruct custodians to repair and replace the furniture.

Evangeline added a bad-tempered sprinkle of ground balfur root into her infusion. To her absolute mortification, it had become clear come dawn that her archmage hadn't just upheaved the poor alder tree, which incidentally, had been further maimed over the course of the night and reduced to a shocking pile of tinder. The man had somehow blistered and *exhumed* parts of the earth. The grounds in the immediate vicinity of his balcony now looked like toiled farmland.

"Seems we're out of liverwort," Mailin informed her after checking the stock cabinet. Evangeline stilled.

"But I do have a personal ration stashed up. . . for emergencies."

Evangeline clutched it with unconcealed relief while Mailin cleared her throat in a poor attempt to disguise a chortle.

"This isn't necessary, you know." Mailin shook her head as she watched Evangeline grind the berries to a pulp before stirring them into the pungent infusion. "Mages are near-infertile without a mating bond. You know that, don't you?"

"Well, yes, but I figured . . . "

"That it's better to be safe than sorry?"

Evangeline could only nod.

"Well, I empathize." The healer rubbed a loving hand over her belly, but her chuckle was wry. "I downed this terrible concoction for years until Killian and I finally decided we were ready for a child."

Logically, Evangeline knew lovemaking with her archmage was unlikely to result in a child—the chances of a mage siring children without the mating bond was miniscule. But humans were naturally more fertile, and halfbreeds resulting from such unions were not completely unheard of. And after last night . . . Heat suffused her cheeks again.

"Mailin . . . " Evangeline bit into her lip.

"Hmm?"

"Has he . . . " She lowered her voice and licked her lips sheepishly. "Has he done this much damage with . . . with other women?"

Mailin guffawed.

At Evangeline's death stare, the healer held up her hands in mock surrender, shoulders still shaking. "Railea's light, I'm sorry." Mailin pinched her nose as though in valiant effort to stifle her giggles. "I'm sorry, but I have never seen or heard of such damage inflicted due to . . . " She wagged her brows.

Evangeline furrowed hers nervously. "Could I be doing something wrong?"

Mailin canted her head. "Has the sire expressed dissatisfaction in any way?"

Unable to hold Mailin's gaze, Evangeline stared down at the murky depths of her now complete contraceptive infusion. Not if insatiability was any indication.

Mailin snorted. "I didn't think so."

A couple of nurses strolled by. Mailin held a hand up in greeting while the women waved, tittered, and tossed sly, feline grins in Evangeline's direction.

Railea's tears! How was she ever going to live this down?

Mailin must have caught her grimace, for her tone gentled. "Oh, Evie, the . . . attention you're receiving today isn't really due to the damage done on the grounds." She pressed her lips together to smother another snort. "Although it will likely be conversation fodder among the servants for a while yet . . . "

Evangeline squirmed.

"As far as anyone knows, the sire has never brought a woman back to his private chambers before." Mailin clasped her hands together with unconcealed glee. "Ever."

Evangeline's brows creeped up. "Ever?"

"It's one of his idiosyncrasies many courtesans have been vying to break."

Elation flooded her, humiliation momentarily forgotten. She *was* more than just a conquest to him. More than simple affection and lust.

Bolstered by the sudden rush of pleasure, Evangeline

downed the now lukewarm concoction in a single gulp. At the look of Evangeline's scrunched face, Mailin dissolved into laughter once again but quickly proffered a glass of water like a peace offering. Evangeline had barely emptied the glass when one of the nurses came rushing up to the table, face flushed.

"Healer Mailin! Lady Evangeline!" She panted. "Lily is threatening to kill herself!"

L   ily had somehow acquired a little scalpel and now pressed the sharp end of it to the side of her neck. One of the healers on duty was trying unsuccessfully to coax the hysterical girl from damaging herself.

"Get the sedatives," Mailin ordered a nurse at the doorway before charging into the room.

Evangeline pulled the healer back with a firm shake of her head. The thought of the pregnant halfbreed anywhere near the sharp end of a scalpel sent her heart palpitating. She pushed herself ahead of Mailin and murmured, "Lily, what are you doing?"

The girl blinked, tears rolling down misshapen flesh when she saw Evangeline—the only person she ever seemed to converse with.

Evangeline took a step closer. "Put that down before you hurt yourself."

"I saw myself in the mirror." A tremulous whisper. The scalpel moved against her skin, producing a bead of red among the scars.

"We'll find a way to take the scars away," Evangeline said softly.

Words that could well be a lie.

Lily wavered and closed her eyes for a moment, and Evangeline considered lunging for the weapon.

"I've become a monster." Lily sobbed. "They have turned me into a monster."

A thousand pinpricks stuck the underside of Evangeline's skin, but she ignored the painful sensation. Slowly, very slowly, she edged herself to Lily's bedside.

"They are the monsters," she whispered, loud enough to be heard but soft enough not to startle. "Not you. You're free now."

Lily's face crumpled, a look of utter desolation that splintered Evangeline's heart like the alder tree beside Declan's balcony. Evangeline extended a hand, and when Lily didn't react, she quickly closed it around Lily's wrist.

"I can never be free." Lily whimpered.

Evangeline tugged the scalpel from Lily's grasp and tossed it aside before drawing the trembling girl into her arms.

"You will be free," Evangeline whispered fiercely. Fury boiled in tandem with the painful prickling under her skin. "You *are* free."

Warmth bloomed over her skin; the underside prickled with pain as though her veins held needles instead of blood. The sensation lasted for a fleeting heartbeat, but Lily relaxed in her arms, as though she'd been administered a sedative. Evangeline lowered the girl back onto the bed and continued to cradle her until her eyes fluttered shut.

When Evangeline lifted her head, it was to meet Mailin's wide eyes. "This is the first time Lily has ever fallen asleep without calming tonics or a healer's touch." Unmistakable awe filled her tone. "And I could have sworn I felt a surge of healing warmth from *you*."

Mailin's latter comment was so outlandish that Evangeline's lips lifted in a wry curve. "If I were a halfbreed, then I'd be immortal."

And if she were, she would be a lot less fertile and wouldn't have bothered with consumable contraceptives that tasted like a glassful of bitterberries.

THIRTY-ONE

That evening, Evangeline met Declan by the glass atrium. He had touched her mind intermittently throughout the day. His mental presence was warm velvet, like a cat rubbing its pelt against her calves. He didn't give her any words, yet the fleeting caresses felt so intimate that they could well be stolen kisses.

He was still engaged in conversation when she arrived, a little earlier than he'd requested, impatient to see him again. The lord commander had his back to her, but Declan saw her the moment she walked into the hallway.

Evangeline. Another intimate brush. *I'll be a moment.*

She nodded and sidled away, careful not to touch the glass this time as she admired the full length of the atrium. In the waning light, the panels splintered the setting sun, causing the entire hallway to shimmer with an orange glow.

Little fire.

She turned to see the two men by the glass entryway, so silent she hadn't realized they had exited. Unlike his half-breed mate, Killian gave her a warm smile of acknowledgement before warping off. No sly looks in her archmage's presence.

Declan held out a hand, and she went to him eagerly. He folded her into his arms, head cocked with a contemplative gaze. "Something saddens you."

She buried her face in his chest, drawing in his comforting scent, and held on for a moment before she told him of Lily.

Declan's expression remained unchanged, but his words were entirely unexpected. "The scars can be removed if she wishes. It will be an arduous and painful process, but it can be done."

Evangeline's eyes rounded. "How?" Even Mailin hadn't been able to promise to remove the scars. The skin was too brutalized, the marks etched too deep.

"It's a primitive method." His hand crept back up to the base of her neck, fingers threading into her hair, massaging her scalp. "She will have to be made unconscious so I can scald off the top layers of her damaged skin."

That snapped her out of the mesmerizing stupor. Visions of her evenly charred floorboards flashed in her mind. She blinked.

"It will have to be done in sections, and in concert with the healers. The skin that re-forms under the guidance of healing energy will be new. Free from scars."

The thought of Declan searing Lily's skin off had Evangeline swallowing bile, but she considered his offer. "She won't feel it while you're burning off her skin?"

He shrugged. "I will stop if I sense her consciousness. But I imagine the pain will be considerable during the *healing* process, which will be lengthy. And since she is human . . . " Lily would heal at a far slower rate compared to that of a mage. Still, it was an option, albeit a grisly one. But it was a choice Lily could make to regain control of her life.

Regain freedom.

Evangeline rose onto her toes to kiss him. "Thank you."

When she pulled back, he studied her closely. "Are you having more nightmares, little fire?" She hardly had time to sleep, much less for nightmares. She told him exactly that, which resulted in a slow, satisfied smile that had her toes curling.

"Have you received any pointed looks from anyone today, Archmage?"

A dark brow lifted. "What do you mean?"

"No sly smiles, no recriminating gazes?"

Confusion smudged his eyes, the color of springtime leaves. Evangeline pinched her lips together. Of course, he would have suffered no recrimination. No one would have dared look at him sideways, much less waggle an errant brow his way.

She huffed. "That is so unfair."

When she explained herself, his expression darkened. "I'll take care of it."

She frowned, taken aback by the grim set of his lips. "Don't go around punishing people on my account, Archmage."

"I will not have my people judge you for being mine."

Heart skipping at the blatant possessiveness, she gave a little laugh in an attempt to dispel the gathering storm clouds in his eyes. "Apparently, Archmage, the surprise is at *your* behavior."

He merely stroked a knuckle over her cheek, awaiting her explanation.

"Am I truly the first woman to have spent the night in your bedchamber?" she asked, unable to keep the giddy smile from her face.

His knuckle wandered down her throat and back up again to tip up her chin until she met the solemn earnestness in his gaze. "It seems you're a first of many things for me. The first woman I've attempted to court." He lowered his forehead to hers. "The first woman I've massacred a tree for."

She was still grinning like a fool when they warped.

Back in his room, he nudged her onto his bed and settled beside her. Their mouths fused, and she had difficulty discerning where her limbs ended and where his began. Declan evoked her most carnal instincts, turned her into a primal creature. Kissing him was an addiction. Touching him, a benediction. Tasting him . . . was madness.

He was wearing nothing but his trousers and had her skirt scrunched up to her waist when he finally allowed her to breathe. Instead of resuming the erotic melding of tongues, he rolled over to straddle her.

And you will be the only woman I've ever taken here.

Suddenly she was staring up at the star-studded sky, the clean lines of his profile illuminated by the moon and the glowing symbols of his ascension. She was still lying on the coverlet, but from the uneven hardness, she knew they were no longer on the bed.

Blood still molten, she reached up for him. He shucked off the remainder of his clothing and removed hers. When he kneed her thighs, she parted them readily.

Little fire. His eyes were dark pools of slumberous heat. *Mine.*

He delved into her with a single, devastating thrust that had her back arching to accommodate him. Dimly, she heard herself crying out in pleasure, but her voice was muted by the sound of crashing waves.

When she regained enough of her faculties, she lay tucked up against him, head pillowed on one muscular arm. With their legs still tangled, he traced the dip of her navel with hooded eyes and a languorous hand. Her breath hitched when she caught sight of the luminous horizon separating the star-kissed sky from the moon-licked ocean.

"Where are we?" she murmured. Pine and fir trees crowded them from behind, while the ocean buffeted them from below.

He pressed a languid kiss against her nape. *The peak of Torgerson Falls.*

Intrigued, she shifted out of his arms to brave the edge. She felt no fear peering down the precipice. Her archmage wouldn't let her fall.

Her lips parted.

A series of waterfalls cascaded down the cliff face over a series of rocky steps adorned with tiny shrubs and stunted trees. Mist plumed from the river far below, wending through the estuary like a glistening serpent gliding into the sea in a procession of froth and foam. The sight was wild and dangerous and breathtaking, just like the man enveloping her from behind.

Declan's arms coiled around her as he burrowed his face into her nape. Though they were atop a cliff facing the vast ocean, she wasn't cold. Not even a gust of briny sea breeze touched her skin, though the grass around them blew back as if by a phantom wind, and the leaves of the trees behind them billowed.

Her archmage had apparently erected a shield to keep out the winds.

She smiled. "Did you destroy anything?"

His lips curved against her neck. "I punched my powers into the ocean." *I may have also dislodged some rocks.* A shrug of indifference. *There is no visible damage.*

Even if there were, there was no one to tell.

She shifted back into him. His markings were still faintly

illuminated, electric currents of power rippling under her fingertips.

"Do you come here often?"

"Yes." He tugged her away from the ledge, rolling onto his back so she could lay over his chest. "I come here whenever I wish to escape my duties. Or to forget I exist."

Her fingers stilled midtrace. "Why?"

Pain had edged into his voice. Almost imperceptible as there was no change in his inflection, but somehow, she could tell. It was a wound she could almost feel.

His fingers wound into her hair, while his telepathic voice weaved into her mind.

I thought I was finally free to live and rule the way I saw fit when I ascended. But I was wrong. Amereen had been my mother's. Ruling what was once hers will always remind me of what I lost.

She wanted to lavish him with kisses and remove the hurt in his eyes . . . but she'd bared her own soul to him. She couldn't pretend she didn't want him to do the same.

"What did you lose, Declan?" she asked quietly, pushing up to sit.

He gazed at her for a long moment before responding, "A piece of my heart."

Evangeline stroked his cheek, her own heart weighing heavy. She'd seen this shade of sadness in his eyes before. In the derelict temple, the first night they'd explored each other's bodies when he'd spoken of the one person he'd ever loved. She hadn't been brave enough to ask then. But now . . .

"What happened to Freya?"

"Look what you've made me do!" His mother paced. Declan could hear her stomping steps and ragged breaths, feel the rage rolling off her in waves. He tried to push himself up, crawl away, but he couldn't move. Thick, stringy fluid coated the back of his mouth, the taste of iron overwhelming even over the searing pain. He gurgled and wheezed, struggling to breathe through the viscous liquid filling his lungs.

He was drowning in his own blood and vomit.

"Shhh . . . you'll be all right," she whispered. Hands stroked the back of his head, making him flinch. "Perhaps a night out in the glade will teach you to never embarrass me again." As unconsciousness beckoned, he felt her leave his side, relief and a soft breeze taking her place.

The temperature in the air dipped as he faded in and out of awareness. Chirruping insects replaced birdsong, telling him dusk had fallen. Still he couldn't muster the strength to move a single muscle. Every inch of him felt like raw meat. He heard a slight rustle. The sound of footsteps. Had one of his guardians come looking for him? The lightness of the footsteps dashed his hopes. His guardians wouldn't bother with his whereabouts. No one cared as long as he completed his tasks.

A hand prodded his back, causing a fresh ripple of pain. Fear dug into his chest like a burrowing rat. Was *she* back? He gurgled pathetically, trying to push himself up. He heard a soft gasp, and his panic abated. It wasn't his mother.

"Oh, goddess of mercy, you're still alive!"

A girl's voice. The last thing he felt was a pair of small hands tilting his head up, a cloth wiping the sick and blood off his face before he blacked out from jarring pain.

When he regained consciousness, she was still there.

"I'm sorry." A soft voice in his ear. She'd somehow shifted him so he lay on his back, but his broken flesh no longer burned as badly. Tender hands patted his forehead. "I've tried healing you as much as I can, but . . . I can't heal your eyes." An odd, almost singsong lilt to her speech. A heavy pause.

"It will get me in a lot of trouble, but I can get you help. Quentin will do a much better job than me."

He attempted to speak through the pain.

"Don't," she said sharply. "You'll hurt yourself." She scolded him, but she continued to apply soft touches to his face, every one channeling warmth across his skin.

Why did it matter to her if he hurt? No one had ever cared.

Can you speak with your mind? The barest brush against his mind before her musical voice tinkled, but it made him flinch. He'd never felt anyone's mind against his own apart from his mother's.

Hello? Can you hear me? Another tiny, hesitant prod. He relaxed, feeling the difference of her lighthearted psyche from Corvina's. This girl was ethereal. Gentle. Warm.

Oh heavens, Freya, he needs help. Stop being such a coward!

He heard her thoughts. Clearly too young to stop projecting her thoughts after she'd made initial contact on the mental plane. He could hear her talking herself into getting help from a male called Quentin. Abruptly, she stood, and the slight warmth she exuded left his side.

Wait. He reached out with his mind, not wanting her to leave. *Who are you?*

She gasped. Then her musical voice filled his mind once more like a wash of sunlight.

Freya. My name is Freya.

Declan forced the painful memory back into the depths of his mind while Evangeline tugged on her chemise to cover herself. Modest, even after all they'd done together. She watched him with expectant eyes, her hair a glorious cascade around her shoulders, framed by the glimmering ocean at her back. She looked like a pagan princess.

One he'd just sullied.

It didn't feel right telling her about another female who had a claim on his heart. Not even when Freya was long gone. It made him feel selfish. Then again, he'd been selfish all his life. He'd taken from Freya her friendship, basked in her healing magic, soaked in her presence when he'd had no right to. Now he was taking everything he could from Evangeline—her body, her mind. He'd claim her soul for himself if he could.

"I was her death," he said and watched her eyes widen. He might not be able to give Evangeline his full heart, but he could give her the past that made him. "Freya's family fled Ozenn's Realm during the Winter War to seek refuge in our world."

Evangeline remained still, her eyes laced with wariness, but still filled with adoration. Would they soon be tinged with disgust?

"They settled in the outskirts of Lindenbough, a small town south of the Thorne Enclave."

Evangeline's lips parted. She had noted the significance of the name. But that was no secret. He'd refused to take Nathaniel's name—had chosen the one name that had shaped him.

"My mother was displeased with me that day." Declan gave a hollow laugh. Everything he'd done displeased her. "She'd wanted me to execute a prisoner. Back then the thought of killing made me queasy." He had been young then, no older than a human of fourteen summers.

"Like a coward, I warped away from the execution site." He had disgraced himself and his mother. Corvina hadn't been merciful when she'd caught up with him in the glade in the Lindenbough forest.

"She flayed my back. Dislocated my jaw and ruptured my eyes." Evangeline emitted a small sound that made him pause. She was trembling. Mentally, he checked the barrier he'd constructed to shield her from the winds. Still erect. He blinked. Her physical response was wrought by his story. "Don't fret," he murmured, tugging her into his arms. "It didn't kill me."

Though some days, he wished it had.

"Freya found me. She was young. A child, really, but she poured every ounce of healing magic she had into me."

Evangeline drew in a breath. "Freya was Seelie."

Declan nodded. Dark fae, the Unseelie, couldn't heal. Their magic was manipulative and destructive by nature. Their light counterparts, the Seelie, had more nurturing abilities. "Her compassion was my luck." Freya loathed to see a living being hurt. "And her downfall." In the end, it had led her through death's door.

"I'd never met anyone like her." No one had ever showed him an ounce of tenderness before Freya. He'd soaked in every bit of her attention, lapped up every ounce of care.

He'd just wanted more.

"I asked to meet her again." And she'd innocently returned, day after day. "She came back to help me with my wounds." Freya had also come with treats and books. Spent hours by his side, talking to him, reading to him. She made him feel like a regular boy, not an unwanted son locked away in an enclave.

"Is that how you fell in love?" Evangeline's question was soft as she fidgeted with the coverlet he'd brought along so he didn't rut her into the ground.

"I didn't know what it was I felt then." By the time he realized, she'd been ashes. "She was just a child. Whatever she must have felt for me was innocent."

Declan swallowed the bile that came with the next memory.

"Because my eyes were so badly damaged, I claimed I was resting in my room. But in truth, I snuck out to see her." He'd met her every day for the months he remained sightless. But like all things held in secret, they eventually came to light. "My mother was furious when she found out."

He swallowed. "Corvina torched the entire Lindenbough village, with Freya in it." Declan kept his eyes on Evangeline's fingers that had gone still. He couldn't bring himself to glance at her face. The shame and guilt of Freya's death and the death of all the innocents in the little village weighed heavier than any responsibility, any duty. A burden he'd carried and would continue to carry for the rest of his existence.

"I wasn't there to stop my mother," he whispered, giving voice to his iniquity. A rusted nail lodged deep in his heart. "Freya was crying for me telepathically. Screaming my name . . . " A cry he could sometimes still hear in his dreams. "But I wasn't there." His body had been a sack of shattered bones; he'd been useless. Unable to protect the only person who mattered.

Her hands gripped his wrists, her knuckles white.

He lifted his eyes to meet hers. They weren't filled with condemnation but mired with tears. She surprised him even more when she wrapped her arms around him and held him like a child, hands stroking the back of his head.

"It was not your fault."

The darkness threatened to claw out of his chest. "If I had been less of a coward and done as I was told, Freya would never have had the misfortune of meeting me. If I had been less selfish, I wouldn't have asked for her return. If I hadn't been so weak, I could have protected her."

Her grasp around him tightened. "You were a *boy*, Declan. The only one to blame was your mother." Evangeline stared up at him, amber eyes swirling with sadness.

"*Why* did Corvina treat you that way? Lex said she cosseted him."

"I was a result of—"

"A rape." Gritted words. "I know."

Alexander had told her quite a bit, it seemed.

"But she was still your mother. How could she hurt you like that?" Her words were laced with vehemence. As a child, he'd often asked himself that same question. The answer was straightforward, of course. He just couldn't see then.

"Sometimes she got angry just looking at me," he said. As an adult, he'd finally understood. He couldn't bring himself to voice the truth, so he spoke with his mind. *I was the living, breathing reminder of her rape. I never should have been born.*

Evangeline cupped his face, forcing him to meet her eyes. "But she was still your *mother.*"

He blinked. How could he explain Corvina'd had no choice in the matter? A child of not one but two archmages, he was a pregnancy she could not terminate. An anomaly borne without the mating bond. A *parasite* that could not be aborted. Corvina hadn't kept his attempted abortion a secret. She'd reminded him with every opportunity.

"I would have torn out my own womb to be rid of you." She'd once hissed into his ears, her voice filled with loathing. "But I had yet to give my mate an heir."

Her words had been more vicious than any abuse.

How could he explain the shame he'd felt when he'd learned the true nature of his father? The shame of bearing the face of a man with such depraved tendencies that he would rape a child if the mood struck him.

"None of it was your fault. Not—" Evangeline pressed a soft kiss to his left eye. A subtle recompense for the violence of his past. "—your—" She kissed his other eye with equal tenderness. "—fault." She pressed the third kiss against his lips.

Tears continued to trickle down her face.

"Evangeline," he whispered, running a finger across the wet trails on her cheeks. A woman who would cry for his past. He wiped the moisture from her face, humbled.

"I'm sorry, Declan." She started raining kisses all over his face as she stroked his chest. "So sorry."

"It all happened a very long time ago," he said, throat thick.

She gave him a tremulous smile. "It doesn't make it any less real."

Declan averted his gaze. He didn't deserve her compassion. He didn't deserve half the things she was giving him. "It made me who I am."

"A man who would bury his emotions in ice?" She shook her head. "You are a person, Declan." She caressed his cheeks, spreading warmth over his skin, into his heart. "A flesh and blood man who feels pain and love, with wants and needs."

His pulse quickened. He laid his forehead against hers. "And I want more."

She didn't mistake his meaning. She rolled onto her back readily.

"Come," she urged, and he wondered what he'd ever done to deserve such a gift. "Come into me."

He rolled down beside her, buried his face in the crook of her neck, drawing in her intoxicating scent. "No," he forced himself to say. "Just now was once too many." She arched her brows in question.

"Your body is not ready." He cupped her gently. She might still be innocent, but he had no excuse. "I am misusing you." He frowned at the unexpected laughter that bubbled up in her throat. She didn't give him a chance to speak before she wrapped herself sinuously around him.

"Not if I want you to." Her voice was a coaxing murmur. "And I want you, Declan. So badly." Her fingers trailed down below his navel to take him in her hands. She tightened her grip in demand. "Once more," she whispered into his ear. A shudder rippled through his body, and Declan knew he was lost. Or perhaps he was found.

When he finally sank into her, it felt like going home.

THIRTY-TWO

B irdsong filled the air, complementing the first rays of dawn seeping in beneath the drapes of his bedchamber. Declan burrowed his face into Evangeline's hair and breathed deep. She was like opium to his senses. A drug he willingly lost himself in. The first time he'd ever felt this way had been holding Freya's hand. Ever since Freya had been wrenched from his life, he'd forgotten this sense of . . . contentment? He felt lighter somehow. At peace.

He glanced down at the woman in his arms, still in deep sleep, and a wash of tenderness flowed through him. She was something he'd never known was missing but was everything he wanted. He adored the kindness in her soul, luxuriated in the sweet guilelessness of her nature, craved the brightness of her mind. More, he was addicted to the scent and taste of her, the sounds she made every time he pushed her over the edge. She was a living fantasy he'd never dared to dream.

Sex had always been but an act of release. Yet now she made him feel like an inexperienced and randy youth. All he wanted was to bury himself in her and take her again and again. But no matter how many times he claimed her, it only seemed to further fuel his desire.

He had always left as soon as he'd sated both himself and his bedmate, but now it seemed he had nowhere more important to be than here in her arms. Leaving while she remained asleep was near impossible.

He enjoyed watching her eyes fan open each morning to reveal mesmerizing pools of amber, still hazy with sleep, and watch them sharpen into focus on his face. He enjoyed being the first person she saw, the first thing she smiled at.

Sweeping out with his mind, he found his steward and rescheduled his appointments for the day. He couldn't remember the last time he'd taken a day off. Then he sought his lead healer's mind. *Evangeline will not be going into the infirmary today.*

Mailin was no telepath, but her psychic voice was strong. Undoubtedly the healer had had ample practice in projection with her mate. *Is she unwell, sire?*

She is fine.

The healer's concern ebbed into surprise. *I will find a replacement for her duties this morning,* Mailin said readily, but a mischievous chuckle accompanied her telepathic words.

Retracting from the psychic plane, Declan nuzzled the reason for his truancy. She let out a soft little moan and stretched languorously against him. He hardened again. Determined not to overuse her, he contented himself by stroking the dip of her waist and the delectable curve of her slender hips. "Good morning," he murmured, soaking up the lazy smile that stirred his heart in ways he didn't quite understand.

"Mmm." Her slumberous gaze shifted to the bronze clock on the bedside table, eyes half-mast. Abruptly she reared up, nearly gouging his eye with her elbow. "Railea's tears, why didn't you wake me sooner?"

He looped an arm around her waist, reluctant to move from the cozy bed. "It's all right."

She squirmed out of his hold. "I'm on shift for Lily's room this morning."

"Mailin has been informed of your absence today."

She shot him a suspicious glance. "What? Why?"

He tugged her back to his chest. "I wish to spend the day with you." They hadn't spent an entire day together since they'd returned from Draedyn's Realm. And if he got his fill of her, perhaps he wouldn't turn into an insatiable rutting beast come nightfall.

Her eyes softened. "What about your duties?"

"I rescheduled."

"Well, what do you want to do?" Her cheeks reddened as she stared at the rumpled sheets around them. He gave her a suggestive look, one he knew would draw more heat to her cheeks. A faint wave of rose bloomed down her neck to trail tantalizingly over her chest.

"I thought you might enjoy the capital with me."

Surprise and pleasure suffused her face, but she gave him a mock pout, slapping him lightly on the chest. He laughed, and the sound surprised them both.

"I like the sound of your laughter, Archmage," she purred and rewarded him with a sensual kiss.

"If you keep this up, maybe we'll spend the day in bed after all." He growled lightly.

Her giggle filled the room, causing his heart to swell with a foreign sense of giddiness. Unable to stop grinning, he warped them both into his bath chamber. Before they headed out to the capital, there was a certain fantasy he'd been meaning to fulfill.

H umming a happy tune, Evangeline smiled at her mother. "Do you like it?"

"Any more gifts and this house will be buried in them," Agnes said wryly even as she repositioned the glass vase Evangeline had bought her for the umpteenth time.

"The vase looks fine exactly where it is, Mother."

"Look who's back," drawled a masculine voice by the door that had been left ajar. Evangeline swiveled with a delighted cry and bounded into his arms, surprising them both with her forwardness. She grinned when Stefan enfolded her in a bear hug, and she felt nothing but the joy of embracing a friend. She might not have regained all her memories, but it seemed she was well and truly over the trauma.

"You look happy." Stefan released her.

"Happy as a lark, she is," Agnes confirmed with another wry smile. "Join us for some tea, won't you, Stefan?" she asked, but she was already pouring an additional cup.

"Enjoy working at the castle, Evie?" Stefan said, picking up his tea.

Evangeline grinned again. She probably appeared a loon. "Yes."

It was the truth. Despite the shroud of darkness that was a deep yearning for a sister she had lost and a buried past clinging to the periphery of her every waking moment, Evangeline was happy. Though she missed home, her apprenticeship with Mailin coupled with every sign of the slave-trade survivors' progress in their newfound freedom far outweighed the sense of satisfaction she'd derived from working at the apothecary.

Most of all, she was happiest with the man who held her

close each night, as if she was the most precious thing in the world.

Despite the scalding heat of the tea, Stefan downed it in one gulp. "Heard you're seeing someone. That true?"

Taken aback by the abrupt question, but unwilling to lie, she nodded.

"Yes," she said for the second time, allowing the depth of emotion to filter through that simple word. But she didn't linger on the point. She divulged pieces of her new life by giving Stefan an overview of the castle, of her tasks, and of her patients. Stefan's face grew bleak as she explained about Lily, who remained the most painfully traumatized.

"Evie, the girl is beyond help," Stefan said.

Evangeline frowned at the unexpected judgment. "Lily will make it." Eventually.

Stefan shook his head. "She's been scarred too badly. A woman like that will never make a full recovery."

Evie firmed her lips. "We can help her. Declan has promised to remove her scars if necessary. It will be a painful process but—"

"Nothing is going to help the girl." The bite in Stefan's tone startled her. "You're just too tenderhearted to see it. She is too badly brutalized. Too broken. And if the archmage says otherwise, he's just using that to keep you in line. Can't you see that?"

"Lily *was* a victim, but no longer." It was as much a statement for Lily as it was for herself. Evangeline hadn't had a single nightmare since she had been sleeping through each night snug in Declan's arms.

"The archmage." Stefan spat the words out as though they were poison. "Whatever it is you think, it won't last. He's playing you."

"He is not!"

Stefan jammed both hands into his hair, ruffling the brown strands. "He is an archmage, for the love of Railea! Do you think he would forego the dozens upon dozens of women who are more than ready to take your place? You can't be anything more than a toy to him. One day you'll grow too old, then it'll be all too simple for him to toss you aside."

"Stefan!" Agnes interjected with a dangerous flash in her eyes, but Evangeline flinched, for he'd hit the nerve of one of her deepest fears.

Under her mother's rebuke, Stefan softened his tone. "I don't want to see her hurt, Mrs. Barre. Surely you understand."

Agnes exhaled a weary breath. Even she had no ammunition against simple fact: archmages had never taken mortal lovers. Not seriously.

"Declan will never do that to me," Evangeline said, wishing her words came out with more conviction.

"Sweet lies, empty promises," Stefan snapped, blue eyes flashing with derision. "Don't be foolish, Evie! Lining the street with flowers, *buying* you like . . . like a . . . " He trailed off when Agnes pinned him with a glare. Growing up without his own mother, Stefan had spent many days in the Barre cottage, and Agnes had mothered him like her own. Stefan looked to his boots, as though shamed, but he wasn't done. "A man like that isn't going to give more than he takes from you."

"You may well be right, Stefan Hanesworth, but you know what?" Evangeline crossed her arms. "It's my life." Yes, she was well aware every night spent in Declan's arms came with a price. A payment that would shatter her the day her archmage decided to walk away. He might be enamored with her now, but she had never been disillusioned enough to believe he would remain that way. Still, she would take as many days as she could get, for Declan had become as vital to her as the air in her lungs.

Stefan blew out a snarly breath and took two steps back. "Think about what I said . . . When he's done with you, you'll be no more than a used-up toy." He turned on his heels and stalked out the door. "And sometimes, certain things are just too broken to be fixed." He gave Agnes a curt nod and then the door slammed shut.

Evangeline turned, throat thick, into her mother's arms.

Agnes sighed. "Stefan has overstepped his boundaries today," she murmured. "But his concerns are not . . . unfounded."

"I love him, Mother." Evangeline heaved a sob, knowing Agnes wouldn't misunderstand. Declan had torn through even the miasma of her trauma, broken down all her barriers, and laid her heart bare. And he'd claimed it. The thought of life without him was simply anathema. Yet, it was also a fool's dream to think he would hold her in his arms throughout her days as she aged and he remained ageless.

Stefan's words hurt because he *was* right.

Declan was not hers to claim.

THIRTY-THREE

Declan propped himself on one elbow on the bed and ran his other hand down Evangeline's back, knowing she was still awake. Since she'd returned from Arns, a pervasive sadness plagued her eyes that she didn't seem to realize was there. When queried, she evaded his concern or feigned fatigue.

He bent over the graceful curve of her shoulder and grazed the delicate skin with his lips and teeth. She sighed in pleasure, rolling onto her back in invitation. "I want you, Declan." His little fire was proving as insatiable as he was.

He smiled against her skin. "You just had me."

He had warped them back from the clifftop that had become their love nest. The grass-stained coverlet on the floor was evidence of their passionate coupling beneath the stars. She tugged him into her embrace. He complied, crawling over her and bracing his weight on his forearms to lavish her collarbone with the same attention. But the sorrow in her eyes gave him pause. "Tell me what upsets you, little fire."

She shook her head, fingers toying with his hair. "It's nothing."

He nearly sighed. Why did she always insist it was nothing when there was clearly something lurking in the depths of her eyes? Instead of pushing her, he stole a few more kisses before pulling back. "My men have found twelve families who have reported missing children in the last twenty-five years."

Her eyes widened.

"Of the twelve families, four reported missing girls younger than twelve summers at the time."

"Declan," she whispered, voice quaking from a wealth of emotion.

He brushed a kiss over the tip of her nose. "The families are all located in small towns within my province. I will have Killian take you to them, if you wish." He hadn't planned on telling her until he'd done more to ascertain if she was from one of those four families, but he couldn't bear the bleakness in her eyes any longer.

Her lips trembled.

"They may not be your family," he cautioned, not wanting to give her what could well be false hope. "You could have been born to a family in another province entirely, but it is unlikely for Agnes to have found you in the ravine. You can't have been held captive too far from Arns. It would have been near impossible for a human child to have traversed from a neighboring jurisdiction into my own."

She pressed her forehead against his with tender emotion, and a loud sob escaped her lips. Alarmed, he drew back. "You don't need to do anything if you're not ready."

A droplet spilled down her cheek.

"I'll check the families, ensure if one of them is yours before you decide." He wiped the offending moisture from her cheeks. *Don't cry, my little fire.*

Blubbering, she tugged at his shoulders. He shifted to cover her trembling body with his. He was careful to keep his touches tender, his kisses sweet, lest he inadvertently tear out a chunk of the room. But she clearly had other ideas.

"I love you." The whispered words struck him like a rapier through the heart.

He could only stare. Emotion was an iron chain wrapped around his throat, choking him, rendering him mute. He dipped his head to take her lips, needing to fill every crevice that separated their bodies, desperate to show her what her words meant to him.

What *she* meant to him.

"Love me, Declan," she whispered, when they finally broke apart. He obeyed, unable to do anything else. He wrapped her up with the sheet from his bed and warped them to the isolated beach just beyond their cliff. She gasped as he lowered them to the warm sand, careful to spread out the sheet under her.

"Declan, someone could be here," she protested. He kept her pinned beneath him, still trying to calm the fervent beat of his heart.

No one will see us. I would never let them.

As she relaxed, he fused their bodies together and made her cry out his name. Her moans of pleasure were barely audible as the placid waves turned violent and crashed against the beach.

Nathaniel Strom was a force of nature, his presence akin to a maelstrom rippling on the psychic plane. Responding to the potential threat of that presence, Declan warped to the far end of the Torgerson range. At the very edge of the mountain, a lone man faced the horizon with his hands clasped at his back, his stance casual as though he were a wandering woodsman pausing to admire the setting sun. But no woodsman would be dressed in a surcoat threaded with gold filaments and a bejeweled girdle that winked in the sun.

Nathaniel had always fancied himself a god.

Declan gave no preamble as he joined the man at the ledge to overlook the rocky canyon that melded into the windswept grasses of the lowlands. "What do you want, Nathaniel?"

"My son." Still insistent on using familial references no matter the lines Declan had drawn. "I see you are well."

At Declan's curt nod, Nathaniel's lips thinned. "I've heard whisperings of an archmage who warped headfirst into an imploding portal into Draedyn's Realm and left a clan of gliders butchered in his wake."

Declan merely turned to regard him, unsurprised by the other archmage's knowledge. His father had the most extensive network of spies in the realm. What did surprise him was the man's personal appearance. Nathaniel, like all members of the Echelon, rarely journeyed into the lands of other archmages without an invitation.

Nathaniel sighed. "I am merely concerned."

"If so, you can leave. As you've already noted, I am well."

The corners of the man's eyes crinkled. "I also heard rumors that you've set up an operation to rescue slaves sold to other realms."

Declan didn't see any reason for secrecy. "Yes."

Nathaniel's brows rose at his stark admission. "A sudden development of human scruples?"

Declan shrugged. "The days spent in the shadow realm have given me new perspective."

It was the truth.

Nathaniel frowned and pinned a steely-eyed stare on him. "Does this have anything to do with the woman who was pulled through the portal with you?"

Everything in Declan stiffened, but he manufactured a smile. "She is but mortal," he said with enough flippancy in his tone to suggest Evangeline amounted to nothing more than a plaything. "What is it that you truly want, Nathaniel? Do not waste my time."

Ire tensed Nathaniel's jaw. "Is it so hard to believe a father's concern?"

Declan met the man's gaze. It was almost like looking at himself in the mirror. He'd spent an entire century of his life serving Nathaniel's court in Flen before his own ascension. An entire century learning Nathaniel was as cunning as he was capricious, capable of care for as long as it served his interests.

"There is no cause for concern. I am an archmage."

"You are still my son." The vehemence in the other archmage's tone gave Declan pause. Since Nathaniel learned of his existence, the archmage *had* shown him care, distorted as it was. "How long will it take for you to forgive me for not being there to shield you from Corvina's vindictiveness?"

Declan offered no response, because Nathaniel had never understood the transgression he'd committed was not Declan's to forgive. Nathaniel heaved another sigh. Unwilling to linger in the past, Declan said, "My sources believe Zephyr to be amassing an army in the fae realm. He has drakghis."

Declan didn't mention Alejandro's suspicion of shield-makers in the mix. He wouldn't implicate Nikah. Not until Noto returned with concrete evidence.

Twin furrows knitted Nathaniel's brows together, but Declan gave no pause. "If Zephyr rises against us, Flen will likely be the first place he'll strike."

Nathaniel folded his arms and curled his lips. "And why would you believe that?"

"Maybe because you made a cuckold of him all those years ago?"

Nathaniel scoffed, arrogance etched into every line of his face. "Zephyr's *queen* was nothing but a whore begging to be swived. Seraphina was no more fit to be queen of the Unseelie than your mother an archmage."

Declan firmed his jaw. Considering the other man fore-warned, he stepped back from the ledge. "Leave my lands, Nathaniel. I have no desire to play host."

The archmage of Flen folded his arms and arched his brows to complete a picture of lofty derision. "Fools are men who give a woman more than the seed he sows into her. Women are meant for pleasure. Nothing more. You'd be wise to remember that the next time you take your little mortal to bed."

Tamping down the urge to strike out and risk a war, Declan gave no indication of the violence churning in his gut. Taking offense would only serve to heighten Nathaniel's interest in his *little mortal*. Instead, Declan forced a mild smile. "And fools are men who offer unsolicited advice. Remember that the next time you step into my lands uninvited."

THIRTY-FOUR

There was no light, yet she was not in darkness.

She floated, formless and featherlight, no more substantial than a mote of dust swirling in the breeze. She drifted with the current, but she wasn't wet. She was insensate. Immaterial. Yet she existed. She knew. She felt. And if the gods allowed it, one day she would find her way home . . .

Evangeline awoke with a start.

It took several blinks before she realized she was in her small bed in the Barre Cottage. She sighed and shifted to curl onto her side, seeking sleep. Her dreams were distorted snippets of murky gray. Not her usual nightmares. Those had stopped since she spent her nights bundled in Declan's arms, only to be replaced by odd dreams of flowing in the depths of insubstantial matter that—

A telling creak of one of the floorboards sent every hair on her skin to attention. Her pulse spiked. A dark silhouette stood by the door.

Someone was *in* the room.

Evangeline groped for the oil lamp beside the bed. Screamed.

A man loomed before her, garbed in black with a hood obscuring his face. He lunged.

She darted from the bed, but a large hand clamped over her mouth to stifle her cries and subdue her efforts to escape. She bit down on the flesh until she tasted iron. Her assailant released her, swearing inarticulately in a terrifyingly familiar voice. She stumbled out of bed and shoved her way toward the door. "Mother!"

A fist connected with her temple. She crumpled. Dazed. Projected a cry to an archmage, and prayed he heard her despite the distance before everything went black.

Evangeline's eyes snapped open.

Her lips tasted of dry chaff, and the overpowering stench of musty earth and manure crowded the air. She winced. Her temple throbbed. Rubbing the sore spot, Evangeline blinked, trying to make sense of her surroundings under the feeble light. Where was she? Disorientation ebbed, quickly replaced by a surge of adrenaline. She'd been abducted! Breaths shortening, she fumbled, groping in the dark. Straw. The ground was covered in straw.

Hooves stamped nervously. A horse whinnied.

Something shuffled close by.

Evangeline edged away from the source of the movement. Prickly stalks abraded her skin, and squinting in the muted light, she noted rough wooden walls and a dirt ground strewn with hay. Bales of hay stacked on one corner opposite lined enclosures. An animal bleated. Goats shuffled in the pen at her back. A lone mule circled nervously in the next.

A woman lurked beside her.

Evangeline muffled a shriek. Dark, bruised eyes set in a face etched with wariness and concern stared at her.

"Shh!" the woman whispered, motioning for Evangeline to be quiet. Following the woman's gaze to the far corner, she sucked in a breath. Women gathered by a metal feed trough flanked by oat sacks and neatly stacked buckets. The tall double doors that fed feeble light into the room were *ajar*. Open farmland bathed in moonlight stretched beyond.

Yet no one made any move to leave.

"Shhh . . . ," the lurker whispered again. Her hair was a wild tangle of curls. Though she appeared a woman, her cheeks still bore the softness of youth. A well-endowed girl.

"Who are you? Where are we?" Evangeline asked when she found her voice.

"I'm Tanika. We're at the Dwyer Farm." Her voice was a threadbare whisper Evangeline had to strain to hear. Relief had Evangeline emptying her lungs. Still in Arns, then. Her gaze darted again, this time taking in the neatly arranged tools tacked to the walls—broom, shovels, a pitchfork, curry combs, bridles, halters, and leads. A chill slithered down her spine. "Where is Mrs. Dwyer?"

Evangeline knew the widow who tended the farm, a lonely old woman who had ventured into the village on occasion to purchase healing balms from the Barre Apothecary.

"I don't know." Tanika trembled and threw a furtive glance around the barn. "They keep us here, the traders."

Despite the fear growing in her veins like thorny vines, Tanika's revelation no longer came as a surprise. Evangeline nodded at the only thing that didn't make sense for a slave smuggler's den. "Why are the doors open?"

Another woman broke from the crowd of women to introduce herself as Azalea. Like Tanika, her movements were skittish. Unlike Tanika, Azalea's clothing bore no rips and her warm beige skin lacked grime and bruises. "I've tried, but I can't go through it," Azalea said. Her accent, like the wrap-around grenadi she wore, spoke of her Jachuanan roots. "It's sealed up with magic."

Magic? Evangeline walked up to the double doors. The girl was right. An invisible wall blockaded the entrance.

"No one outside can see or hear us." Azalea's whisper was a trembling breath behind her. "There were workmen here a few days ago, and they looked right through as though they saw nothing." Evangeline swallowed her fear and projected her thoughts as loudly as she could. *Declan!*

No answer. No velvet brush against her mind to indicate he heard her.

"Where are they?" Evangeline demanded. "These traders?"

"Curious little thing, aren't you?" A masculine voice at her back.

The animals shuffled, the mule releasing a nervous bray. The way Azalea and Tanika scurried back to join the other women huddling like terrified sheep told her she'd found the answer to her question.

Evangeline steeled herself and turned. He appeared utterly human, with his rounded ears and coal-black eyes, but somehow, she knew it to be a ruse. Declan had told her faekind could veil themselves to hide quintessential fae traits and appear human if they wished.

"Who are you?"

"Jericho," he responded without hesitation. He dipped his head in a low, theatrical bow and dread trailed icy fingers over her skin, raising every hair on her flesh. The fact he did not bother wearing a mask and kept all his captives unbound suggested he was either very arrogant or confident there was no escape.

"My mother will realize I'm missing at dawn," Evangeline blurted when Jericho continued to grin, eyeing her with unconcealed malice. "People will be searching for me," she added even as she realized the frivolity of her threats. Traders didn't abduct people from their homes. Her abduction was *planned*. A new sickness curdled in her gut. What had happened to her mother?

Jericho chuckled, soft and sinister. "And search they will, but they will find nothing. No one will bat an eye at your disappearance. They will assume the archmage has you tied up somewhere."

He gave her another once over, and this time lascivious intent was clear. Then he snapped his fingers, a fluid motion that invoked a shadowy portal in the middle of the room. The mule brayed and kicked, scattering grain from a feed trough.

Two men emerged from the tenebrous portal. The first was unmistakably Unseelie—pointed ears and violet eyes, skin shrouded by a dim shadow. The second, an inordinately large man with unremarkable features counteracted by a tattoo of a howling wolf on one side of his face, was not so easily identifiable.

The men acknowledged Jericho with silent nods and eyed Evangeline with such vulgar intent that she stumbled back, her fear as palpable as the cobwebs clinging on the rafters. Tanika whimpered audibly, drawing everyone's attention.

Jericho laughed. "Don't worry, Tansy. This time it won't be you."

The man with the wolf tattoo licked his lips. "I wouldn't say that, Jer. Tansy gave us quite a ride last time, didn't she?" He shifted his gaze to rake Evangeline from head to toe and his leisurely perusal ratcheted her pulse. "Pretty. But too skinny to give a man true pleasure," he said with a snide curl of his lips.

Evangeline couldn't help the shudder of relief that racked her frame, suddenly grateful for the slightness of her figure. The fae with silvery-white hair shot Evangeline a licentious look. "Aren't you curious though, shield-maker? The archmage braved an imploding portal to retrieve her."

"And you'd be fools if you think he's not going to notice me missing," Evangeline snapped, feigning bravado. Her outburst only elicited a bout of raucous laughter.

"Even an archmage won't be able to find you." Jericho smirked and gestured to the shieldmaker, whose gaze wandered to linger on a petrified-looking Tanika. "Gaius's shields are as impenetrable as they are undetectable. Your archmage may search for you, but he'll find nothing. And eventually he'll forget you. Men like him have more women than they know what to do with."

"Declan painted an entire clan of gliders in red because they tried to take me." Evangeline flashed her teeth, and watched with satisfaction as his cocky grin faltered. "What do you think he will do to you when he finds this place?"

Jericho darted close. Rough hands clamped over her throat, a constricting vise causing her to choke and sputter. "He won't find us. Not even an archmage can see through a shieldmaker's shields." He jerked his chin at the entrance. "And no one thinks to look here. Even if they do, they *see* nothing, *hear* nothing beyond an empty barn."

He fondled her breast, igniting a fear so primitive she lashed out like an animal in a trap. Jericho pinned her arms effortlessly with a single hand and smirked, showing a row of perfectly white teeth with not a single hint of fang. "And you can spend the rest of the night showing us what makes you so special."

It took every shred of willpower she had not to surrender

to the raw panic skittering in her pulse. She thought of Declan and willed herself to calm.

Jericho grinned. "That's a smart girl. No need to make this harder for yourself than it needs to be." He released her arms, and his hands roved down her hips to paw at her thighs.

Evangeline clawed at his face and scrabbled for his jugular. If he thought she was going to make it easy, he was mistaken. Jabbing her thumbs into his windpipe, she shoved him off and lunged for the shovel hanging on the wall. Before she could unhinge her weapon, he tackled her to the ground and barreled a fist into her gut, emptying her lungs.

"Stupid whore!" With one hand fisted in her hair, Jericho slammed her into the prickly hay. Fear was a battering ram in her chest when he clambered over her, restraining her with his weight.

Somehow, she found enough strength to dislodge her arms and cause more damage with her nails. *"Get. Off. Me!"*

The other fae laughed. "Need any help, Jer? She's marked you up pretty good."

"Shut up, Blyrin!" Jericho peeled back his lips with a snarl, displaying lengthening canines. He raised a hand and delivered an ear-ringing slap to her cheek. His dark eyes grew pale as his irises lightened to a shade of violet. "Clearly the archmage hasn't taught you how to lie *still*." He pinned her arms again and jerked them above her head.

"Get the fuck off her, Jericho!" Worn leather boots, scuffed at the edges, appeared in her periphery. Evangeline's breath stuttered.

"Want a taste of her first then, human?" Jericho snarled.

Stefan stood tall, fists clenched. He appeared furious but didn't look the least surprised to see her. Evangeline recalled the inarticulate cry of pain when she'd bit into her abductor's hand, and her heart dipped in tandem with her jaw.

"Stefan?" She couldn't keep the incredulity from her voice as her gaze landed on the bandage wrapped over his forearm like an incriminating red flag.

He ignored her. "You'd do well to keep your hands off this one. She's slated for your king!" Stefan said, curdling her blood with his words.

"King Zephyr requested her person but made no indication of the state of her delivery," Jericho said with a thin smirk.

"And you think he'll be pleased to find her used up by his lackeys upon delivery?" Stefan rolled his eyes. "Are you that much of a fool, Jericho? Or do you just have trouble keeping your pants up? Use one of the other girls if you must, but keep your hands off this one."

Jericho's lips twisted to a scowl. "Watch your mouth, mortal, or you might find your innards in it." Nevertheless, Jericho eased off and straightened. Evangeline scrambled onto her knees, but Jericho caught another handful of her hair before she could escape and leaned in with an insidious whisper. "I hope my king keeps you alive for a long time, whore. When he's done with you, I'll be there waiting to finish what I started."

When Jericho released her, Evangeline scrambled back only to stumble into the legs of another man. Gaius loomed over her, taking a lock of her hair between his thumb and forefinger, as if she were an animal for sale. "Curious. I still see nothing so special in this one that warrants an archmage's devotion or your king's interest."

A scoff came from another man in the room she hadn't sensed until now. "Oh, she's plenty special, I assure you."

A man wearing an obnoxious expression with perfectly styled copper hair she'd recognize from a mile away.

THIRTY-FIVE

S hock assailed Evangeline again, slackening her jaw, stealing her words. Impeccably dressed as always, Malcolm leaned casually against a bannister obscured by shadows, a bottle of ale in one hand. "So special she believes herself too good for the likes of mere mortals," he said, voice slurred.

Jericho narrowed his eyes. "You'd be wise to slow your drinking, Fairsworn. You need to be sober on the job."

Malcolm merely lifted his bottle in a mock toast and grinned. "Whatever you say, boss."

Gaius, who had continued to toy with Evangeline's hair, now ran a finger down her cheek. Evangeline slapped it away, but it only fueled the man's interest.

Gaius smiled with approval, contorting the wolf on the side of his face. "I do enjoy a woman with some fight."

Evangeline gulped, trying to swallow the clot of dread in her throat. Stefan stepped up as if to distract the shieldmaker, but the words that came out of his mouth were like a badly written script. "Why waste your time sampling an archmage's whore when you're welcome to as many innocents as you'd like?"

Gaius threw his head back and guffawed. He stepped up to slap Stefan on the back, and Evangeline realized with a start that the shieldmaker was truly a mountain of a man—his thighs alone were the size of tree trunks. He made even Stefan appear small.

"You make a fine point, human." The shieldmaker grinned wide and shifted his attention to the group of women huddled in the far corner, trying to hide behind the rusted water trough. His lips curved as his gaze latched on one.

Azalea screamed when the shieldmaker stalked in her direction. Her terror incited a wave of frenzied bleats from the goat pen, and like hapless sheep, the other women scurried out of the way, leaving Azalea to fend for herself.

"No, no, no, please no!" Azalea cried, shrinking back into the group of women, trying unsuccessfully to evade capture.

Evangeline rounded on Stefan and gripped his forearm as if her life depended on it. "Help her." She shook him. "Stefan, please, stop him!"

Stefan shrugged her off. "Be quiet!"

Who was this stranger? A man who wore Stefan's face, his clothes, and shared his voice. But he was *not* the man she knew, not the boy she'd grown up with.

Jericho snapped his fingers, and a chasm cleaved the air. Evangeline watched helplessly as Gaius hauled Azalea—screaming and kicking—into the dark and nebulous portal. Blyrin strolled through after them with a leisurely gait.

Jericho nodded at Stefan and Malcolm. "Find us one more tonight." He leered at Evangeline. "We need a dozen for the next shipment, and she doesn't count." Without another word, he slipped into his own portal.

Azalea's screams reverberated, growing distant as the

portal shriveled until there was nothing left but haunting silence.

Breathing hard, Evangeline stared at Stefan. "How could you?"

He remained silent, but the hardness left his face, and his gaze fell to his boots.

"*How could you?*" Her voice rose perilously close to a shriek. When he didn't move, Evangeline hurled herself onto the pads of her feet and pounded his chest. "Stefan Hanesworth, answer me!"

But it was Malcolm who spoke. "You'd be wise to show some respect, Evie. He's the only thing standing between you and Jericho and his merry band. Or worse, the animati shieldmaker."

Evangeline stared at the two men she'd once trusted. Her voice splintered. "What have you done to my mother?"

"Nothing. All it took was a forged letter from her mate requesting to see her and she left the house so Hanesworth could break in." Malcolm's lips lifted in a snide smile. "Though I wouldn't call it a break-in, since he knew exactly where the spare keys were."

Disbelief threatened to buckle her knees as she stared at Stefan. A man she'd trusted with her keys, her friendship, her secrets.

Malcolm tossed the empty bottle of ale, and it hit the wooden planks of the mule pen with a dull thud. He folded his arms. "I must admit, the order for your abduction was unexpected." He grinned. "But serendipitous. You'll make us a hefty profit."

"Why?" Evangeline croaked.

Stefan mistook her meaning. "Why? You drew the interest of the fae king with your dalliance with that archmage, that's why!" His nostrils flared. "I told you to stay away from him, Evie! Why wouldn't you listen to me?"

The world spun in dizzying circles, and her breath came up short. But it wasn't the fae king's interest that threatened her balance. "How long have you been involved in this, Stefan?" she cried. "This is . . . It's treason! Declan issued an edict against all involvement with the cartel. You'll be hanged for this." Evangeline gripped his arms, desperate for answers. *"Why?"*

Stefan's shoulders slumped, and he seemed to cave in on himself. His words were barely a whisper. "My father and I have been working for the cartel ever since I can remember."

Malcolm chuckled. "Admirable family business, is it not?"

Evangeline shook her head vehemently, unable to shake the denial clawing in her chest. She *knew* this man. Stefan was no slave trader. But when he reached for her hand, she recoiled instinctively. Stefan's lips trembled. The same way they had when he'd fallen out of a tree and skinned his knee. A tree he'd scaled because *she'd* wanted an apple.

"No," Evangeline whispered, clasping a hand over her mouth. Something clicked in place. Repugnant and sly, but it clicked. She paled. "All along, you've been helping Mrs. Dwyer on the farm . . . for this?" Animals shuffled nervously in their pens, as if they, too, felt the tension stifling the air.

"I had no choice." Stefan sounded as though he'd inhaled sand. "My father had no choice. They have my mother. Do you understand?"

Evangeline could only stare. "Your mother is dead."

Stefan's gaze lowered to his boots again—the well-worn pair she'd gifted him for his birthday three years ago. "My mother isn't dead," he said quietly. "She was taken by the Unseelie after my birth."

His gaze continued to track the dirt, and his voice

quavered. "When Jericho ordered your capture, I refused. Then . . . then, they took my father, too. If I hadn't delivered you tonight, they would have killed him, Evie. Then my mother." Stefan's blue eyes shimmered with unshed tears. "I'm sorry."

Moisture filled her own eyes. "Why didn't you *tell* me?"

Stefan only hung his head.

Evangeline parted her lips, overwrought with despair. "I would have helped you, Stefan . . . I—"

"Even an archmage can't help the poor sod. Jericho took his father into the fae realm," Malcolm supplied.

Evangeline shut her mouth with a snap. She'd momentarily forgotten Malcolm's presence. "How are you involved in this, Malcolm? You're the village *constable.*"

Unlike Stefan, who seemed to have shrunk in on himself, Malcolm stood with his chest puffed and his legs apart. "Makes it easier for the cartel to get access to runaways, don't you think?"

Nausea brought bile up her throat. "You sick, repulsive monster! What will your father think?" At Malcolm's hardened eyes, Evangeline barked out a laugh. He'd always sought his father's approval. "He doesn't know. Does he? I can't imagine Governor Fairsworn would be proud."

Malcolm stalked forward and backhanded her without warning. He aimed a kick at her, but Stefan gripped him by the forearms and jerked him back.

"Touch her again, and I'll level you to the ground!"

Malcolm bared his teeth but retreated. "Play the hero if you want, Hanesworth. But we all know what's going to happen the moment she lands at the fae king's feet." With a spiteful smirk, Malcolm strolled toward the entrance. "I'll grab us another chit. I have just the one in mind." He sauntered out, whistling a lighthearted tune, utterly impervious to the shield.

Rubbing her stinging cheek, Evangeline expelled a trembling breath. "Stefan."

He flinched, the rims of his eyes reddening. "Don't make this any harder than it has to be. Why did you have to cozy up to that archmage? This is your fault!"

"My fault?" Evangeline gaped. When he failed to respond, she voiced the question that churned the contents in her belly. "How many women have you abducted, Stefan?"

His gaze remained plastered to the dirt.

"All these years, why didn't you tell me?" she asked again.

Stefan glanced up, eyes damp, jaw set. "And what could you have done, huh? The Unseelie have my mother locked up somewhere in their realm. Ozenn's Realm! There is no saving her. If my father and I don't do as they bid, they torture her."

Tears returned to distort her vision. "And that makes it right for you to abduct and sell innocent women?" A harsh sob escaped her throat. "Sell . . . *me*?"

Stefan kept his head bowed as he ruffled his wheat-colored hair with a rough hand. When he finally met her gaze, his eyes were bloodshot and bleak. "I'm sorry, Evie . . . but I had to make a *choice*." An angry shake of his head. "Malcolm made his easily. The swine unearthed my father's operations, and instead of reporting us, he wanted to get in on it." He clenched and unclenched his fists. "He's in it for the thrill. For the chance to abuse and debase women. I never wanted to do this. I never wanted a part in any of this."

His voice broke. "But I had to make a choice."

E vangeline joined Tanika on the ground and wrapped her arms around her knees. She kept her gaze trained on the open doors, waiting for sunrise when she was certain her archmage would seek her presence on the mental plane. But the skies remained dismally dark, a night that seemed to drag on forever.

Stefan had retreated toward the far end of the room, eyes hard and unyielding. He'd refused to engage in further conversation and had all but turned to stone.

Malcolm returned with an unconscious girl slung over his shoulders like a sack of grain. With a grunt, he heaved his senseless cargo onto the hay before ambling to the back of the barn to empty his bladder into a makeshift latrine—a wooden bucket—which explained the cloying stench alongside the scent of barn animals and manure. When he was done, he returned to inspect the girl with the same triviality of a dock master checking his manifest.

Stefan remained stoic and unmoving.

"She's just a child, Malcolm," Evangeline said quietly. The girl appeared no older than fourteen, dressed in the dirty and tattered garb of a street urchin. A runaway, perhaps. The sort who might sometimes seek refuge from the constables at Marshall Hall.

Malcolm shrugged. "If she's old enough to steal, she's old enough to bear the consequences." He strode closer, hands in his pockets with his hips thrust forward. "Just like you. Didn't I say you'd pay?"

Evangeline grimaced. "This isn't you, Malcolm." No matter his profligate debauchery, she refused to believe him capable of such monstrous acts. "Your father will—"

He cut her words short with a vicious glare. "No one sees me as anything but my father's shadow. No one believes I'll amount to anything more than the governor's son." His laughter soured the air with bitterness. "Even my own father believes me inept. Incompetent, he called me, despite all the slavers I've seized."

Malcolm's eyes hardened and his lips lifted in a sneer as he viewed the unconscious girl. "Why should I toil where my efforts aren't appreciated? With Jericho and his men, I'm an irreplaceable asset."

I t was barely dawn, the sky touched by the slightest hint of blush when Evangeline caught the telltale ripple in the barren field. Her heart soared. The silhouette of an imposing man materialized against the horizon in her direct line of sight. With hair as black as a starless night and his dark clothes, he appeared woven into the very fabric of the predawn sky.

"Declan!" Evangeline hurtled forward to pound her fists on the invisible barrier that could well be steel. "I'm in here!"

Declan's gaze swept past her.

"Don't waste your breath. He can't see or hear you," Malcolm said from the other end of the barn. Evangeline only yelled harder, pounding on the unyielding barricade till her fists throbbed. To her dismay, Declan stalked off, striding out of her line of sight. At her sob of exasperation, Malcolm gave a self-satisfied chuckle. "What did I tell you? No one sees or senses what's in here, not unless Gaius allows it."

Evangeline ignored him and attempted to arrow her thoughts.

Archmage, please come back!

Nothing to indicate she was heard.

Declan, she pleaded into the void, *why can't you hear me?*

&

Declan rapped his knuckles against the worn-out wood, fighting the urge to kick open the flimsy door. The farmhouse was derelict—decaying wood, walls in need of fresh paint capped with a sagging roof. The fatigued building was the only structure in the vast farmland, save the ramshackle stable and the empty barn that screamed neglect.

Declan clenched his fist and rapped again, impatience simmering. He'd been asleep, but Evangeline's cry had roused him. It had been almost imperceptible, but he'd caught it. More, he'd somehow *felt* her terror. The overwhelming sense of panic had been louder than any scream. Just as quickly, it had dissipated. He'd thought she was having one of her nightmares. But when he'd reached for her mind, he'd found nothing. So he'd warped straight to the Barre cottage and found it empty of both Evangeline and Agnes. But it wasn't until he entered her small bedroom and saw the rumpled bed and a broken oil lamp on the ground that panic reared. He'd felt this way before—when he'd found Evangeline missing from the cave in the shadow realm.

The door creaked open, and a wizened mortal woman pinned him with rheumy eyes. "Young man, what can ye possibly be needin' at this ungodly hour?"

Declan didn't bother telling her he'd outlived her six times over. "I am looking for a young woman. Have you seen anyone pass through this area? Given anyone shelter?"

She squinted at him as though he were daft. "Do you *see* anyone out here?" Her voice held the telltale tremble of age, but it was counteracted by a sharp edge in her tone.

He peered over her shoulder into the dim hallway. An oil

lamp cast flickering shadows on the walls. "Do you live here alone?"

The tiny old woman wiped her liver-spotted hands on a frilly pink apron and folded her arms. Either she didn't notice the symbols on his skin, or she didn't care. "My husband passed years ago." Crinkly eyes narrowed defensively.

Frustration consumed him from the inside. What *was* he doing out here? He'd warped on instinct, materializing on one of the many farms in Arns, surrounded by untouched lands stretching as far as the eye could see. He should be helping his men scour the village, but his gut had led him here. The same irrational impulse that had sent him warping into the imploding portal after Evangeline.

Whoever had abducted her couldn't have gone far—unless they were mages strong enough to warp. Or fae slavers with the power to open portals. The darkness that lived within him reared up violently at the thought. It couldn't be. Slave traders targeted stragglers, picked on the ones no one would miss— they didn't abduct women from their homes. Only Evangeline was no ordinary woman.

She was *his*.

Ice flowed through his veins, so thick it chilled him down to the marrow.

Evangeline had laughingly dissuaded his attempts to appoint her dedicated guards. *I don't need guards accompanying me home, to a village within your domain,* she'd protested. When he'd insisted, it had only driven her to exasperation. *I'm your lover, not a puppy in need of a leash.* Her statement had caused him to reconsider, and he'd eventually succumbed to her wishes. He'd taken to warping her himself but had done little else to ensure her safety.

Could he have been any more of a fool?

Many would prey on what belonged to an archmage—for

vengeance, political reasons, or simple glory. He'd all but painted a target on her back and sent her to the wolves.

"If there's nothin' yer needin', then I bid you a good day." The door slammed shut.

Nothing wrong with a widow living out here alone. A deceased husband explained the ill-tended place. Yet he couldn't ignore the niggling feeling in his gut that told him something was amiss. Firming his jaw, Declan prowled back to the spot he'd warped to. He could almost feel his Evangeline here—her presence a lingering perfume. He closed his eyes and drew in a deep breath.

Where are you, my little fire?

As if in response, light blossomed on the psychic plane. Bright and incandescent and achingly familiar. His head snapped up, but there was nothing but the empty barn sitting innocuously on acres of fallow farmland. His eye caught a gleam on the ground, nestled amongst the several water barrels set out to catch rainfall. Just an empty bottle of ale.

His heart thudded.

An empty bottle of ale.

THIRTY-SIX

Jericho and his men reappeared like a creeping nightmare. Gaius appeared last, with a glassy-eyed Azalea in tow. The girl's expression was reminiscent of the one Lily often wore. Blank. As if she'd retreated somewhere deep into her own mind.

Jericho gave Gaius a reproachful look. "Fuck's sake, shield-maker, if you break her, she'll be worth nothing."

Gaius merely shrugged. "She's still alive, isn't she?" He gave Azalea a shove and sent the girl stumbling to join the huddled group of women. He snickered. "Although I won't be using her again. She's about as lively as a corpse."

Evangeline couldn't help the revulsion clawing up the back of her throat, bold and reckless. "Repugnant leech!"

Stefan hushed her immediately, but even the malice in Jericho's eyes did nothing to tamp down her anger. Evangeline clamped her lips shut and grated her teeth. She'd not be doing herself any favors further inciting Jericho's attention.

Blyrin scratched the back of his neck. "Who the fuck is that?"

Declan still circled the dirt road within sight of the entry like a prowling wolf on a scent.

Jericho swore. "What is the archmage doing here?"

As though in response, Declan went preternaturally still, head tilted slightly. Could he sense her? Was he trying to reach her? Evangeline screwed her eyes shut and receded into her mind, projecting everything she had to the man who was her lover. Her heart.

Heat washed over her in a feverish ripple. Her skin, stretched taut, felt as if it would tear, and phantom pins needled beneath her skin. A strange, near-painful sensation—but whatever it was, it'd worked. Her archmage whipped up his head at that very moment and turned to look her direction.

Her heart hammered. "Declan!"

Malcolm kicked her right in her gut, and she doubled over, the contents of her stomach rising. "Shut your mouth!"

Anger emboldened her. "He'll find me. When he does—"

"Evie, enough!" Stefan hissed as Malcolm's hands unclenched, ready to throttle her.

Would Stefan stop him?

She never got the chance to find out.

"Ozenn's blood!" Eyes wide, Blyrin backed into a wooden pillar.

A ripple of energy slammed against the invisible barrier like a golden tidal wave. The barn groaned, timber slats straining beneath compounding energy. Another wave struck, and another. The walls creaked under the relentless assault.

Jericho paled. "Shieldmaker!"

Gaius hurried to the entrance, drawing a dagger from his coat. With a slash, he spilled his blood to the ground. His lips moved, but Evangeline couldn't make out the words.

"I told you he would find me," Evangeline murmured, but

her vindictiveness only lasted for an instant before the view of her prowling archmage stole her breath.

Her archmage wasn't merely angry; he was furious. He wore a chilling expression she'd only seen once before—just before he cleaved a glider in two.

Another torrent of energy surged and slammed. The barn quaked, and the walls quivered. Translucent lines fractured the otherwise invisible shield. Evangeline knew the moment the shieldmaker's barrier faltered because Declan's eyes tracked the barn. Found her. And his expression turned downright murderous.

"A portal, Jericho!" Gaius bellowed. The blood trickling from his forearms no longer served to augment his crumbling shield. "I can't keep him out much longer!"

A portal flourished in the center of the room, a chasm of eddying shadows. Jericho barked orders. But a dozen unwilling women were a hard pack to herd. Evangeline scrambled up, trying to stay out of the clutches of the traders. Someone knocked her to the ground.

Malcolm.

"Your delivery will prove my worth to the Unseelie king." Malcolm wasn't a large man by any means, but he was still bigger than her. Stronger. He grabbed hold of her ankles and dragged her across the dirt floor. Evangeline bucked and raked her nails into the ground, fingers sifting through straw. Stefan caught her forearms. It was impossible to tell if he was trying to help her or subdue her.

An earsplitting crack resounded, the sound of a dozen mirrors shattering before the shieldmaker went sprawling to his knees. Gaius's shield was no longer invisible but splintered with lines of shimmering blue. There was a moment of suspended animation while everyone stared as Declan stepped through the fractured barrier. The scent of burning hay pervaded the air.

Declan was ablaze.

Unearthly fire clung to him like flames to a pyre, leaching from the marks on his skin as though he were made of molten metal and not flesh. The dirt at his boots was a ring of smoldering ash, framed by an unholy circle of burning straw and crackling hay. His eyes, pools of eerie green, were fixed on her. He warped, but instead of materializing to her, he reappeared exactly where he stood.

Crimson stained the ground just before his boots. Blood.

Declan's gaze snapped to Gaius, who bared his teeth with a smile of a man who knew he was already dead. "You can break my walls, Archmage, but I can make new ones just as easily."

The fool might as well have marched into a lion's den.

Declan narrowed his eyes, and the shieldmaker lit like a struck match. Agonized screams proliferated the air as flesh melted in a nauseating parody of a liquefying wax candle.

As the animati shieldmaker burned, the Unseelie proved their arrogance and drew their arms. They didn't even get a chance to charge. Jericho hurtled back. His bones cracked as he collided with the wall. The rafters shrieked, and a wooden beam came unhinged. Its jagged edge speared Jericho to the ground.

Blyrin looked ready to flee, but Jericho's portal had already dwindled to wisps of black as the fallen leader spasmed in a puddle of his own blood. Not all fae could create portals, and it seemed Jericho had been the only one.

Declan advanced, lethal intent vibrating with every step.

Trepidation coursed through Evangeline.

"Run, Stefan," Evangeline whispered. But Stefan didn't seem to hear. He seemed transfixed by the gruesome scene unfolding before them. "Stefan, get out before—"

Rough hands grabbed her from behind. A cool blade pressed against her neck. Evangeline strained her eyes enough to glimpse the perpetrator.

"Don't be a fool!" She seethed.

Malcolm bared his teeth, eyes manic. "He wants you, doesn't he?"

"Do you think a knife is going to stop him?"

"Shut up!" The blade pressed harder. "He can't hurt me, not if he wants you alive."

There was another audible crack, a part of the roof tearing off completely. The light of early dawn spilled through as Declan skewered Blyrin in the same fashion he had Jericho.

In the midst of it, a tiny old woman came rushing in. With a start, Evangeline recognized her. And she'd never seen Mrs. Dwyer so distraught. The woman made a keening sound when she saw the bloody mess on the ground. "Jerry, oh gods, Jerry!"

Declan didn't even spare her a look. He turned, searching for Evangeline. When he found her, his gaze locked onto the knife on her throat, and he snarled like a feral animal. Despite his trembling hands, Malcolm was desperate in his bravado.

"Stay back, or I'll slit her throat!"

Declan stilled like a predator might just before attacking its prey, eyes fixed on the blade. Flames receded from his body, seeping back into his ascension symbols. His skin smoldered but his clothes remained pristine.

"If you release her now"—Declan's voice was vaguely guttural—"I will grant you a swift and merciful death."

Malcolm whimpered. He forced the blade deeper into her throat, drawing a trickle of warmth against her skin—inadvertently signing himself up for a torturous end. But he was spared for another moment as Killian and three other men materialized outside the barn. Gaius was nothing but a blackened stump on the ground, yet the shieldmaker's wall remained, barring Killian's entry. The commander yelled his displeasure as he palmed the barrier, discernible due to its blue cracks.

Declan ignored his men, his gaze unmoving from the blade at her throat. Malcolm's body jittered as he dragged her backwards. His fear was so tangible Evangeline could smell it in the musk of his perspiration.

"Release me," she whispered. "Let me go, and I'll ask him to spare your life."

Malcolm ignored her.

"M-make me a deal," he said, choosing to bargain with death. "If you want her alive, you'll let me li-live."

Eyes of soulless green narrowed. "Granted."

Malcolm didn't release her. Seemed to think better of it. "No imprisonment. N-no torture. Not from you or your men." He was covering his bases. A slow smile crept over Declan's face. "Granted. Any more requests, human?"

Her captor shook like a leaf in the wind. "You'll honor your word?"

Declan prowled closer. "My word is my honor."

Malcolm relaxed for a single breath. Then he screamed. Chill lapped at her neck, a gust of frost shrouding the hand that threatened her throat. A hand that was solidifying into ice.

"You p-proooomiiised!" Malcolm's shriek was shrill enough to rupture her eardrums.

"Consider this the price for threatening what is *mine*." Declan closed his fingers over Malcolm's hand. Twisted. The limb splintered into shards like frosted glass.

Not a single shard touched her as the knife clattered harmlessly to the ground, still attached to four frozen fingers.

Evangeline stumbled to the ground in shock, her knees seemingly unable to support her weight.

Declan hauled Malcolm up by the collar and waited until the bloodcurdling screams abated. "We wouldn't want you to bleed out, would we?" A dark and sinuous whisper. "After all, I promised to let you live."

Fire blazed on Declan's hand, and the nauseating scent of burnt flesh assailed Evangeline's nostrils as he cauterized the stump that was Malcolm's arm. When he was done, Malcolm no longer screamed. He seemed to have lost his voice, his breath whistling as he writhed on the ground in silent agony.

Declan crossed the room in three strides to Jericho—pinned like an insect in a glass case with Mrs. Dwyer hovering beside him. Grabbing the fae by the lapels of his coat, Declan snarled but made no move to harm him. Or so it seemed. A tense moment passed before Jericho's eyes suddenly rolled backward in his skull, and his limbs twitched violently as though an unseen current coursed through him. Mrs. Dwyer keened, but Declan's onslaught continued until an expanse of darkness shimmered to life in the middle of the room.

Evangeline's jaw fell. Her archmage had somehow created a portal through Jericho's barely conscious body. Her disbelief heightened when Declan returned to grab hold of Malcolm's ankle and haul the pitiful man toward the churning depths of the portal. Malcolm's inarticulate sobs became whines that turned to wheezing pleas. "I wouldn't have killed her! I wouldn't have hurt her! I am of use to you, my liege! P-please, you gave your word!"

"If I wanted to kill you, you'd already be ash. If I wanted to torture you, I could have made it hurt a lot more, for far longer."

Declan hauled Malcolm up by the scruff of his neck. "But I promised to let you live. Though you didn't stipulate where." A dark smile. "The lykosa can be vicious in these parts, so I'd seek shelter if I were you." He threw Malcolm into the portal.

Declan's gaze lifted, and Stefan chose that moment to run.

But Declan's men already crowded the entrance. Stefan seemed to recall belatedly, and his steps faltered before he turned to face an archmage wearing an expression of fatal intent. Declan might be taller, but Stefan was no lightweight. It was impossible for her archmage to be holding Stefan's entire body up with a single arm—yet Stefan was choking, thrashing in Declan's grip as though he weighed no more than a child.

Evangeline's tongue untangled. "No!" She lunged toward her archmage. "Stop, Declan! Please!"

Not releasing Stefan, whose face was turning blue, Declan turned to face her. "Who is *he* to you?" Low, furious words.

"A friend," she whispered. Declan didn't loosen his hold. "He's a friend, Declan!"

He continued to stare at her, eyes empty of compassion, and Stefan started to go limp.

"Please," she cried. "Please, I can't bear his death."

Declan loosened his hold, and Stefan slumped to the ground, drawing in ragged gasps. A sob of relief worked its way from her throat. Her knees were on the verge of buckling again. Then she was in his arms, pressed against the thundering beat of his heart. Declan held her so fiercely it was as though he were trying to fuse their bodies together. Evangeline reined in a sob as she burrowed into his chest, overcome by both fear and relief.

When she looked up, it was to see patches of dirt near the entrance go up in bouts of flames until the ground blackened. It took her a slow moment to realize Declan was burning the area where Gaius had spilled his own blood to fortify his shield. The telltale shimmer of blue splinters that barred Declan's men from entry eddied and faded.

Killian and his men darted in to survey the skewered slave traders and fearful women with grim eyes.

Evangeline twisted and craned her neck to check on Stefan, but Declan tightened his grip around her. "Clean this up." A command to his men before the barn and its occupants melted away and Evangeline found herself back in his bedchamber.

THIRTY-SEVEN

D eclan settled her on the edge of the bed and started peeling off her clothes.

Evangeline slapped his hands aside. "Declan!"

He bared his teeth, the expression so fierce, so foreign, it stunned her momentarily. "I need to *see*," he said. With that, her dress was ripped off, his hands skimming over every vestige of her skin. But not in lust. His touches were light. Clinical.

Inspecting her for injuries.

His jaw was set in such a hard line she was certain it would crack if he wasn't careful. She squirmed. "Declan, I need to see Stefan. I—"

Feral eyes snapped up. "No." He gripped her shoulders. It didn't hurt, but it wasn't gentle, either. "No." He repeated. "You are *never* leaving the castle."

She stared at him. Blinked. "But my contract—"

"Is void." He glared, almost daring her to challenge him. "You will not leave the castle. I am never letting you out of my sight again."

Evangeline flattened her lips but held her tongue, knowing better than to contest his illogical sanction. At her silence, he expelled a breath and resumed his inspection. Tension thrummed off him in waves, but his touches soon gentled. He inspected every part of her skin with a tender caress of his fingers, followed by the softest stamp of his lips, as though she were spun of gossamer. Kiss by methodical kiss, he moved from the crown of her head down her neck to linger at the gash from Malcolm's blade. With downturned lips, he continued his thorough examination until he was kneeling between her legs with his head bowed like a supplicant as he studied the bruises on her abdomen.

Evangeline swallowed past the lump in her throat.

Her archmage was frightened.

His pupils were dilated, and his chest heaved while he took a thorough account of her injuries, behaving the way a wild animal might as it licked its wounds. When he was finally satisfied, he heaved a sigh. Still on his knees, he braced his arms on the edge of the bed, trapping her in between. "I'll run you a bath. Then we'll have Mailin tend to all the bruises."

Not allowing him to stand, Evangeline looped her arms around his shoulders and wrapped her legs around him. He remained still for a moment before he leaned forward to wrap his arms around her back and bury his face in the slope of her neck.

"I'm fine, Archmage." she whispered, as she ran soothing fingers through his hair. "I'm fine."

"You could have been completely lost to me." Muffled words against her skin. "If I had been just a minute later . . . " He didn't finish his sentence. Didn't need to. If Malcolm had taken her through the portal, the chances of him finding her would have been close to none. So she stroked him, murmuring soft reassurances as he nuzzled her. They would never be equals, not in this life. The disparity between them was as vast as the ocean separating the continents.

But at that very moment, she knew she was the stronger one.

Evangeline sat propped up against Declan's headboard with plush cushions at her back. Her archmage lay sprawled beside her with his head nestled on her lap as she massaged the muscles between his shoulder blades. A false sense of peace seemed to settle over them, wrought by the warmth and the soft crackle of the fireplace.

"What will you do to Stefan?" Evangeline asked finally, unable to ignore the undercurrent of apprehension simmering in her blood any longer. The warmth from the fireplace seemed to recede. Declan, whose eyes had been closed in apparent serenity, glanced up to meet her gaze with his lids half-mast.

He had eventually, albeit very reluctantly, warped her back to Arns, where she'd assured her near-hysterical mother that she was fine. But only after he deemed her suitably taken care of. He had insisted she take a warm bath and a hot meal, followed by a visit to the infirmary with Mailin's healing hands. In turn, Evangeline had insisted on a surreptitious visit to their usual spot on the clifftop, driven by an overwhelming need to love him. To remove the tinge of vulnerability that continued to cloud his eyes.

Instead of responding to her query, he drew a lazy hand down the length of her thigh, igniting a frisson of heat across her skin. Determined not to be waylaid, Evangeline halted his unruly hand. "Declan . . . " She sighed.

A purposeful rap interrupted.

He drew himself up on his forearms and tilted his head, brows slightly furrowed—communicating telepathically to whoever it was behind the door. "Killian is here to give me a report," he murmured.

Evangeline sighed and slid out of the bed to pull on a robe. When she was decent, Declan opened the door to a grim-looking Killian. Though she was beside herself with worry, Evangeline forced herself to curtsy. "I'll wait for you here," she said, assuming the men would warp into the adjoining study Declan sometimes used for his private meetings.

Declan gripped her wrist. "No." He tugged her toward the settee and drew her down with him. So she remained, curled up at his side. He took in Killian's recount while stroking her knuckles in absent circles with his thumb.

The fact that her archmage was so profoundly impacted at the thought of losing her caused her heart to flutter, but it also crushed her on the most fundamental level. Surely the gods have never meant for such love to bloom between an immortal and a woman who would eventually succumb to the inexorable march of time? What would become of him when death claimed her? Would he slowly grow demented, like Jericho?

According to the stoic commander, Mrs. Dwyer was Jericho's human lover. Or at least, she had been. Harriett Dwyer had admitted to surrendering the use of her barn to support her lover's perverse vocation. What sort of sick, twisted love would motivate a woman to willingly harbor such acts of abhorrence? To subject her own kind to slavery?

"The Dwyer widow attacked one of our guards like a woman possessed," Killian muttered, eyes rolling. "He reacted by throwing her off, and frail as she was, he broke her spine by mistake."

At Evangeline's involuntary gasp, the commander released

a penitent sigh. "My lady, she attempted to gut the guard with his own knife when he tried to remove the wooden stake from Jericho's person." Killian gave her a slight, regretful bow as if it were the most natural thing in the world for the lord commander of Amereen's battlemages to genuflect to her.

She fidgeted in Declan's grasp, but he seemed not to notice her discomfiture.

Instead, he trivialized the widow's death with a wave. "Unfortunate, but she would not have survived her punishment regardless." Just like that, Harriett Dwyer's tragic life was dismissed.

Evangeline listened to the rest of Killian's report in silence and was pleased to hear that the battlemages had begun returning the women to their families. Some, like Azalea, had come from distant jurisdictions. When Killian looked ready to take his leave, Evangeline interjected quickly. "What will happen to Stefan?"

The temperature of the air plummeted again. When Killian didn't respond, she turned to face his liege. Eyes of adamantine green met hers, and dread knotted in her heart.

"He will face punishment," Declan said, voice soft but unyielding.

"What sort of punishment?"

A pause. "He can live out the rest of his life on the Isle of Groydon."

Evangeline paled. *"Prison Island?"* Swallowing the lump in her throat, she pleaded his case. "The Unseelie captured his parents, Declan. They've held his mother captive for years. He wouldn't have done this—"

"I don't care for his excuses."

"He didn't hurt me."

"He *took* you."

"But he protected me," she insisted. Her archmage's eyes

flashed dangerously, and the air turned frigid. Killian shifted in place, obviously uneasy, but Declan didn't scare her.

"Jericho and his men would have raped me." She paused for emphasis, and her archmage blanched. "But Stefan stopped them." She held his gaze, unwilling to back down. She was Stefan's last hope. Whatever atrocities he might have committed, he was still *Stefan.* Her best friend.

"He abducted you. For that alone I would have ended his life," Declan said, his voice a cutting blade. "I spared him for you. I will not gift him another smidge of mercy."

"What difference is there if you send him off to Groydon? You might as well sign his death warrant!" Agnes had told her the Isle of Groydon was filled with souls so depraved they were rumored to cannibalize each other.

Declan remained unrelenting, his expression stony. In utter desperation, she reached out with her mind. He was most susceptible to her when she projected her thoughts. *Please, my love, reconsider. For me?*

"He works for the cartel, Evangeline. He stole you right out of bed in the dead of the night. What would you have me do? Send him home with a thank-you note?" His tone remained even, but his expression was hard. Dangerous.

"He does deserve punishment," she said carefully, knowing she was treading thin ice. What Stefan had done was unforgivable, but worth his life? "Just not banishment to Groydon. Please, Declan, I know he's done bad things. Terrible things . . . but it's not out of free will."

Declan remained silent while Killian appeared riveted by the wainscoting. "I'll think on it," her archmage said gruffly. The finality in his tone brooked no further discussion. He dismissed his commander, who looked all too eager to leave.

Evangeline pressed herself against Declan in silent supplication, knowing that she might have only bought Stefan one additional day. Declan might sometimes bend to her will, but he was still the archmage of Amereen.

W
hen they lay in bed that night, Declan drew out a velvet-lined box from the nightstand. He sidled close and propped himself on one arm while he breathed the words softly into her ear. "Will you be my elorin de ana, little fire?"

Evangeline blinked. She had just heard those words moments ago; he'd whispered them into her ear as their bodies fused passionately under the starlight. She understood what the word elorin meant in the old mage tongue. Cherished. Or precious. Since working at the castle, she had heard mage lovers use the endearment. Hearing the words slip from his lips had been a wondrous moment, but . . .

"I wish for us to mate. Will you wear my mark?"

Those words were so unexpected she simply stared at him.

He uncovered the box to reveal contents that glittered in the flickering glow of the fireplace. Her heart jumped to her throat. At her prolonged silence, he nudged the box closer.

"Evangeline?" He swallowed, eyes tracking her face.

With a trembling finger, Evangeline traced the delicately sculpted pendant. The jewels glinted with a sheen she had only ever seen in his eyes. She had never seen such fine jewelry or felt such covetousness.

"I cannot accept this."

For the third time that day, the temperature plunged in the room.

"I am human, Declan," she whispered, voice shattering alongside her heart.

"Do you think I would ask this of you lightly? I have

considered your mortality and its implications. The gods have gifted me a mortal de ana, but I am not so much a fool as to let her slip away."

When she didn't answer, he reached out to grasp her hands. "I know I'm a hard man to love, but whatever remains in my chest, what still beats, belongs to you."

Evangeline flattened her lips against the despair rioting in her throat. "As my heart belongs to you. But there is no need for us to mate." She would willingly live the rest of her life by his side, but never once had she expected to be anything more than his lover. Not when mages only mated once in their lifetime. How could she knowingly subject him to an eon without a mate upon her death?

"You *are* my de ana, and I want to claim you as such." His eyes lingered on her chest where her heart beat beneath. "I want you to bear my mark."

Despite the yearning in her own heart, Evangeline steeled her spine. "If you feel the need to stake your claim in some way, then issue an edict. I'll be your honorary ayari."

He looked as if she'd just slapped him.

"You are *not* an ayari." Words so cold they could have banked the fire.

"Declan, my heart," she whispered, fingers tracing his cheeks to soften her rebuff. "In time"—when she was nothing but ashes and dust—"you will find someone else worthy to be your elorin de ana."

For how could a woman not love a man like him?

For the second time of the day, Declan snarled. "I don't want anyone else. Only you." He pulled her close and plundered her lips until she whimpered. "Will you deny me?" A husky, ragged whisper. "Deny your archmage?"

"And will you break your promise to me?" she asked. "You promised to always give me a choice."

Freya had once touched his heart, then her death had shattered it to pieces. Evangeline had somehow taken the mangled remains and put them back together. Freya had been a child who never had the chance to become a woman, a fleeting sliver of light he had failed to protect. Evangeline was a woman who had become the fulcrum of his world, a woman who could shatter his world if she so chose.

A woman who, even now, slowly shredded his heart as she stared at him with tearstained eyes, fingers clenching and unclenching the crumpled sheets around them.

Could she not see how much they had both changed since the shadow realm?

Months ago, she would never have sat before him, hair a wild tumble over her shoulders, wearing nothing but her skin. Months ago, he would never consider a woman in his bed, much less yearn to be anyone's elorin de han. She might not believe that she was made for him, but he knew otherwise.

He had been born for her.

"You're my de ana. Mine." It was clear to him now, what had possessed him to warp after her into that imploding portal. It was the primal recognition of his mate. A recognition he'd only ever felt once before and thought he would never feel again. Now he had a second chance, he wouldn't waste it. Not for a thousand immortal lifetimes.

He ran his fingers lightly at her collarbone, trailing down to the soft swell of her breast where he yearned to place his mark. And more than anything, he wanted to wear *hers*. The need to mate with her had become a compulsion. A primal demand.

"Yes," she murmured. "I am yours. I will never willingly

walk away from you, Declan, but archmages do not mate with mere mortals."

He despised her self-deprecating tone, but it was a truth he could not dispute. Archmages rarely mated, and when they did, court machinations were usually at play. Foreign dignitaries brokered peace between precarious cultures—the offspring of archmages who failed to ascend still held ample political sway, and wealthy vicegerents enhanced commercial and trade alliances. In the rare instance an archmage was known to mate out of affection, like his mother, they had chosen warriors. Corvina's mate had been the commander of her battlemages, second to none in her army. A man strong enough to lead.

His little fire, however, was neither of noble blood nor warrior borne. She had no mind for the subtle maneuverings of court and a tender heart that would add nothing to his rule, but everything to his *reason* for being.

Through her eyes, he saw beyond shades of black and white to his own inadequacies and failings. All the things he lacked, she had in abundance. Empathy and compassion. Benevolence and kindness. And as far as he was concerned, his little fire was more regal than any queen and stronger than any warrior.

Her presence alone commanded his every attention, and her eyes . . . they were enough to bring him to his knees.

But before he could make his riposte, she charged on. "My mortality aside, what happens when I grow old? When my hair turns gray and wrinkles line my face? When I can no longer warm your bed, what happens then? I will willingly stay with you until I die, but . . . " Her voice broke with a tremor. "I do not want us to become like Harriett and Jericho."

He clenched his teeth and brushed the upsetting moisture from her cheeks and met her gaze, needing her to see the truth in his words. "I've told you once before that there are many ways to enjoy a woman, Evangeline. When you no longer want my body, I will still want you. When wrinkles line your face and when your hair turns gray, you will still be beautiful in my eyes. I will still enjoy your mind, your soul, your spirit. It is your essence I crave more than anything else in this world, and I will enjoy you, I will have you, until you draw your last breath."

Her tears fell, droplets of grief that pooled resolve in his heart. "I can't age with you, but mating will lengthen your life by another hundred summers or so."

Her eyes widened. "A hundred more years of life? How is that possible?"

"Mating with a mage is more than a human marriage, little fire. It is an exchange of psychic energy, and your human body will draw its lifeforce from mine. But even an immortal lifeforce can't do more than double a mortal's lifespan." He paused, wondering if it was wise to tell her the rest. But he hadn't lied to her before. He wasn't about to start now. "A psychic bond between humans and a mage has existed in the past, but . . . when one dies, the other follows."

Her breath hitched, an outraged hiss escaping her throat. "You're going to give up thousands of years of life to buy me an extra hundred?"

"Not just for you, Evangeline. For *us*."

Declan had never been a lovesick fool, and this wasn't a romantic proposal. It was a selfish one. It mattered little to him what happened after she was gone. One way or another he would follow her into the grave when the time came. Until she'd entered his life, he'd been pitifully unaware how numb he'd become since Freya's death. And now that he had a taste of what life could be, he had no wish to return to his prosaic existence when his little fire was snuffed out.

But before it happened, he would ensure Alexander had the necessary knowledge to rule once he was gone—the most logical solution ensuring the continuity of his lands at his untimely death. At the rate Alexander was going, his brother would likely be ready for ascension in a matter of centuries. Mating might just buy them enough time for Alexander to take the throne from him. He told her as much.

"No." Evangeline said the word with such vehemence her body trembled. "You will do no such thing, Declan Thorne." She jabbed his chest with a finger. She must have realized from his expression that, with or without her consent, he was intent on his plans. He could almost see the wheels turning in her head, trying to outmaneuver him.

"What if you're wrong?" she demanded. "What if Alexander chooses not to ascend?"

There was a reason why there were only eight archmages in the world. Ascension almost always killed the mage, regardless of the maturity of their powers. Only the truly brave, or the ones who sought to taunt death, attempted ascension. Declan had been courting the latter when he'd thrown himself into the pit of *Arksana*. Ironically, the goddess had deemed him worthy.

"And since I am human, it is unlikely I will bear you an heir even if we are mated," she added, regret darkening the shade of her eyes. Though halfbreed offspring between an immortal and mortal being were not completely unheard of, they were rare enough to be a novelty. "I know now that there are many shades of cruelty, Declan," she said without giving him a chance to speak. "Would you subject Amereen to the Echelon if Alexander fails? Render your lands vulnerable without an archmage?" she asked, tearing at his sense of responsibility.

"It is a risk I am willing to take." He grasped her shoulders, willing her to see into his heart. "You once told me that every life, mortal and immortal alike, is equally important," he whispered. "That every suffering, every joy, matters."

She broke out in a fresh wave of sobs, but he wouldn't stop. He needed her to understand how much he wanted this. "Evangeline, look at me. Don't I deserve happiness, too?"

"You're asking me to end your life prematurely." Her voice wavered, her amber eyes whirlpools of disbelief. "How can you even ask that of me?"

He rested his forehead against hers so their faces were inches apart. "I would rather live one mortal lifetime as your elorin de han than to see a thousand meaningless sunrises incomplete." Declan drew her closer, tracing her blotchy cheeks with his thumbs. He kissed them, tasting salt and sorrow. "I want to be yours, little fire. As much as you are mine."

More than anything he'd ever wanted in his life.

THIRTY-EIGHT

Evangeline's heart ached. When Declan had woken, he'd wreathed her with featherlight kisses before readying himself to interrogate Jericho and his men. She had pretended to be asleep. She simply couldn't bring herself to face him.

Declan was hers. The knowledge burned through her soul. She'd always known. *Hers.* But how could she claim him?

Don't I deserve happiness, too? His words rang in her mind, causing torment to knot in her chest. A dark, reckless part of her wanted to say yes. They would have approximately two hundred years to look forward to together. Double what she could ever hope for without him. Precious years that belonged to them *both.* Years where she could lighten the darkness in his eyes. Make him laugh. Love him.

But how could she selfishly tie his immortal life to her own? The very thought of condemning him to premature death, of depriving Amereen of its archmage shriveled her soul. "We have time yet," he'd whispered amid kissing away her tears last night. "Promise me you'll consider it, little fire."

She shuffled to the side of the bed, picked up the velvet box, and gingerly removed the contents to admire their beauty. A startled laugh escaped her lips. It was the symbol of their first night in his room. She had lamented his destruction of the alder tree, and he'd solemnly promised it would receive a tribute for its sacrifice. Tears glimmered in her eyes even as she chuckled, delighted with his *tribute*.

She fingered the gold branches tipped by jeweled leaves the shade of his eyes. Emeralds, he'd called them. The tree hung, perfectly balanced, by a gold clasp strung on a fine gold chain. How she wanted it. How she wanted him. She forced herself to place it back into the velvet lining, heart curling like her fingers.

He was not hers to claim.

Evangeline's mind fought a skirmish of quandaries: Declan's surreal proposal, Stefan's impending punishment, and the Unseelie king's sudden interest in her. She'd wanted to bury herself in work, but Mailin had insisted she take the day off.

With no true purpose, Evangeline had wandered the castle grounds until she found herself back at the courtyard of Corvina's statues. She stared at the majestic beast, marble wings forever locked in flight, and her heart clenched.

"Freya loved reading," Declan had once said when she'd questioned the novels she'd found by his bedside. It was small of her, but Evangeline couldn't quite help the twinge of jealousy whenever Declan spoke of the girl. Freya, no matter the years that passed, would always have first claim on his heart. A claim that could well be etched in stone.

When her archmage loved, it was forever.

"What saddens you, my lady?" The unexpected weathered voice came close from behind, raising the hairs on her neck.

Evangeline spun around to find the smiling face of a craggy old man. She gave a startled laugh. "Jorge! You surprised me."

His eyes, cloudy with age, twinkled. "I shouldn't have snuck up on you like that, my lady. My deepest apologies." He executed a deep bow that flustered her. Jorge was always respectful, but he'd never bowed to her before. In fact, she had never even seen him genuflect to Declan.

"That's alright, Jorge. I was too deep in thought. That's all."

Jorge glanced at the statues, an almost whimsical smile plastered across ruddy cheeks and weathered skin. "Grand, aren't they?" He didn't wait for her response. "Did you know they live in Draedyn's Realm?"

Evangeline shuddered. "I don't find it surprising that they exist. I encountered a horrifying flying serpent in the shadow realm with wings wide enough to shade this garden and a tail sharp as an arrow."

Jorge's gray eyes turned to hers, his gaze almost sinister in the pale sunlight. "Ah, you refer to the arrowtail?" He shook his head as though amused. "I can assure you, my lady, drakghis are far more . . . deadly. But they are really just animals. Much like wild horses." A lascivious chuckle. "Or women. They become tame if you know how to ride them."

Evangeline took two instinctive steps back.

"Have I offended your sensibilities then?" He shook his head with a grace she had never associated with one as old as Jorge. "How very rude of me," he said, but he didn't sound the least repentant. A telling tinge of violet crept over his gray eyes.

Her innards turned to ice.

Her pulse spiked, her heart screaming for her to flee, but her legs seemed rooted to the ground. A sudden weightiness descended over her mind, dulling her senses. It was as if he reached into her mind and deftly shut the door to her rising panic.

She managed a whisper. "Who are you?"

"Zephyr, king of all faekind," he said as he gesticulated in the air with flourish before bowing low once more.

"How did you get through the shields?" Her voice sounded faraway to her own ears. Distant, as though she were hearing herself speak through a glass wall. The castle barriers were strengthened by her archmage, himself. *No one* could penetrate them without his knowledge. Declan had told her so. Slowly, as though in a dream, she reached out to brush Jorge's arm. Her fingers ran through as if he was nothing but air.

An illusion.

Jorge's face split with a wide grin. "You're a clever one, aren't you?"

"What have you done with Jorge?"

"Ah, my little Jilintree. Have you any idea how long I've searched for you?" He clucked his tongue. "I thought you were dead, like the rest of your kind."

Jilintree? He took a step toward her, and she swayed back.

"Relax. I am nothing but a manifestation in your mind's eye," Zephyr said with another disturbing chuckle. With an exaggerated wave of his hand, Jorge's crotchety form morphed into the figure of a woman with sky-blue eyes and straw-colored hair. Breath escaped Evangeline in a rush that had her almost crumbling to her knees.

The resemblance was uncanny.

"*You're* the one holding Stefan's mother captive?"

The woman threw her head back and laughed. The display

was so convincing. The only thing wrong about her was her voice—an oddly lyrical one no human woman should possess.

"Diana Hanesworth is far too beautiful to belong to a mere blacksmith, don't you think?"

"What do you want from me?" He might be an illusion, but he seemed to have seized her mind. She felt sluggish. Slow. As though she'd drunk undiluted Mujarin straight from a bottle. Evangeline willed her legs to move, but her limbs remained heavy.

"If you reach out to your lover, know this." The illusion lifted a hand as if to slit her own throat with an imaginary knife before she giggled, the sound both girlish and garish. "Stefan will never see his mother again."

"Why are you doing this?" Evangeline couldn't make sense of it all.

"I want you to leave the castle walls, my little Jilintree. If I knew you'd grow to be even more beautiful than Felicie, I would have searched much harder."

"You knew my sister?"

As if in response, the illusion of Stefan's mother distorted, morphing from Diana Hanesworth's lush figure into a slenderer frame. A younger face that could well be her own stared back at her.

"*Felicie?*" Evangeline whispered.

"Come with me, Evangeline," the illusion pleaded, beckoning with her hands. "I need to show you something."

Unbearable yearning caused Evangeline to reach out to touch, only to sift right through the mirage. Grief churned in her chest like a storm, yet she couldn't even release a sob. A lone tear leaked down her cheek—the sole expression of her turmoil.

"What are you doing to me?"

The illusion that was Felicie laughed. "You want to know,

Jilintree? Meet me outside the castle walls." Felicie executed a graceful pirouette, dancing to a phantom tune. "I won't hurt you, Evangeline. If you come, I'll tell you *all* your secrets."

Waves cavorted into the beach. The briny sea breeze lifted strands of her hair to tickle her face like a mischievous imp. Evangeline padded onto the warm golden dunes, a peaceful place of untouched solitude. Felicie, or the illusion of her, swayed barefoot on the sand, her moves strange, yet familiar at the same time. An intricate dance that compelled Evangeline to toe off her own slippers and join her sister.

The illusion beckoned her again. "Come on, little Jilintree! Join me!"

Evangeline took a tentative step forward, propelled by a primitive longing that was almost impossible to ignore. *Declan will never forgive me.* The thought of Declan had her digging her toes deeper into the warm sand. She couldn't do this to him. He would be furious when he returned to find her missing. More, he'd be hurt. Her own words echoed in her ears. *I will never willingly walk away from you, Declan.*

Yet . . .

"Evangeline!" Felicie's laughing face caused a painful compulsion to obey, yet she held herself back. Deep inside her chest, her heart revolted. She should alert her archmage. Turn back. Run. But her body refused to conform. So she stood, strained and still, a silent spectator to the internal skirmish waging between her mind and heart.

Felicie's laughter faded into haunting sorrow. "Don't you want to remember?"

More tears trickled from the corners of Evangeline's eyes.

"I do," she whispered, feeling as if her heart were being torn in two.

"Then come with me." Felicie reached out with both hands. "Come *home*, and I'll tell you everything you want to know."

Evangeline shook her head. "I don't want to leave Declan."

Felicie furrowed her brows in reprimand and walked, her feet leaving no footprints in the sand, to stand before her. "The archmage isn't right for you. You're not meant to be together. You know that." Ghostly fingers reached out as if to stroke her face. "You don't even belong in this realm. That's why you can't remember. You belong with *me*, Jilintree."

Felicie's mirage wavered and distorted, stretching into that of a tall, slender man. A man with white-blond hair that hung long and straight past lean shoulders. The air rushed out of Evangeline's lungs when recognition slammed into her despite the fogginess of her thoughts.

"You . . . ," she breathed, staring into his violet eyes.

The man who had saved her from the monsters in the cabin.

A slow smile spread across his face. "Yes. You remember me, don't you?"

Evangeline stared, trying to shake off the cotton clogging her senses. He shook his head with a chuckle. "How very willful you are." He sighed. "All right, I'll make you a deal, sweet Jilintree. If you come with me, I'll leave Diana Hanesworth and her husband in your stead. Stefan can have his family back, and you'll have *all* your memories." He snapped his fingers, clearly more for show than purpose, and a dark portal coalesced in the sand.

Evangeline hesitated.

"You know I never break promises," the man murmured.

Yes, faekind never broke their promises. How did she even

know that? Yet the knowledge ran marrow deep. An irrefutable truth. Evangeline shut her eyes and stepped into the eddying darkness.

Forgive me, Declan.

THIRTY-NINE

The silver-haired slave trader sucked in whistling, ragged breaths. Blood so dark it was almost black dribbled from the corners of his mouth. Killian had inadvertently ruptured his lungs. Declan gestured for his commander to stop.

He still needed information, and it wouldn't do to gift the bastard premature death. As he gave the man a few moments to heal before his next interrogation, Declan shifted his attention to the one called Jericho, who lay slumped against a broken bannister. The one Evangeline seemed to loathe above the others. So he'd left Jericho relatively unscathed, allowing fear to build as he witnessed Blyrin's torture.

Anticipation was sometimes more effective than actual pain. And given the abhorrence in Evangeline's eyes when she looked at the fae, Declan would ensure Jericho experienced both in equal measures.

"Ready to talk?" Declan went down to his haunches before Jericho.

The fae hissed. Fear had reduced him to a near-mindless

animal. Impatient, Declan thrust his fist into the Unseelie's ribcage, tearing through sinew and bone to lace his fingers around the man's sternum, an action guaranteed to elicit agony, before repeating his query. Declan was operating from the most primal part of himself. He'd always unleashed the deepest, darkest part when he deemed torture necessary. And that part of him was in no mood for games. Leaving Evangeline's side this morning was hard—her refusal to accept his proposal still smarted.

"Why was the shieldmaker involved?" Declan asked. The fae was inarticulate, gurgling between splutters of bloody spittle. Such weakness.

Declan loosened his grip.

"King Zephyr made a deal . . . ," Jericho managed between heaving gasps. Declan applied more pressure around the breastbone, eliciting another agonized scream. "An alliance with the animati."

"What kind of alliance?" But Jericho went out like a doused flame, eyes rolling to the back of his head. Pathetic. Careful not to inadvertently rupture the heart, Declan removed his hand from the bloody crevice and wiped his bloodstained hands over the fae's tunic. He wouldn't permit death to claim Jericho quite so quickly. He had plans for this one.

Perhaps he did like games, after all.

Resuming his full height, Declan surveyed the barn. It was nearly falling apart where he'd torn the railings from the roof, but he had no intention of allowing the place to remain. Once he was done with the slavers, he'd raze it to the ground.

The fae were either unconscious or near death. That left the one mortal he was forbidden to touch. Declan half-heartedly leashed the darkness within as he prowled up to the terrified human, aware he would probably never be forgiven should he inadvertently kill the mortal.

"Sire," Killian spoke quietly. "Lady Evangeline . . . cares for this one." His battlemage's verbal warning only served to simmer Declan's blood. His other battlemages chimed their telepathic agreement with the lord commander.

Blackguards.

Declan shot his battlemages—men who had served him for over a hundred summers with unerring loyalty—a reproachful glare. They wisely averted their gazes. Satisfied, Declan hoisted the brawny human onto his legs so he could look him in the eye.

"I've promised to spare your life, but it doesn't mean I can't hurt you," he whispered, fingers itching to throttle the life out of the man who'd thought to betray his little fire. Stefan shuddered, but to Declan's surprise, met his gaze with unflinching eyes.

Stefan's lips trembled. "I'll tell you everything I know if it means keeping Evie safe."

A bitter emotion he'd never tasted crested at the back of his throat. How dare this man refer to his little fire with such familiarity?

"A little too late to play the role of a true friend now, isn't it?" Declan was unable to keep the venom from his tone.

"I would never have betrayed her if I'd had the choice." Stefan's voice was earnest with remorse. "They would have tortured my mother and taken my father's life if I'd chosen not to. I—" His words faltered abruptly, then his shoulders sagged. "Kill me, Archmage. It will be a mercy after all the sins I've committed."

Seeing the genuine self-loathing in Stefan's eyes, Declan released him. "Killing you is the one thing I've promised not to do." He would have said more, but that was when he heard it. Soft. Barely a whisper in his mind.

Forgive me, Declan.

"**W**elcome home, my sweet Jilintree!"

Slowly, Evangeline turned to face him. No longer an illusion. For the first time, she noticed the simple laurel crown that encircled his head, resting over sharp-tipped ears. Evangeline tilted her own head, the motion causing her vision to whirl, but she couldn't stop herself from staring. Much like her archmage, this man had a coldness to him. But there was also a layer of cruelty beneath the cold. His cheekbones were almost cutting, his lips a touch too thin. And when he smiled, every hair on Evangeline's skin came to attention.

Her befuddled mind clawed at long-forgotten memories for a lengthy beat before she grasped the echo of an answer.

Zephyr, the Unseelie ruler.

King of the Winter Court.

The knowledge invoked nothing but mild surprise. A rational part of her knew he'd done something to her. That she *should* be scared. Yet, standing before him now, she felt no fear. No dread. Only a strange fogginess as she studied her surroundings.

The cavernous room reminded her of the Receiving Hall in Declan's castle, although this was easily double in size, and a lot more ornate. The walls were a milky white, but the marbled steps leading up to the benches lining either side of the room were limned with gold.

Bejeweled thrones gleamed from the end of the room, one larger than the other, perched side by side upon a lofty dais overlooking the red processional carpet that stretched endlessly across the chamber. Tall gilded windows framed both sides of the dais, obscured by heavy drapes shielding the outside world from her view.

Her gaze swept upward, and like in the Dining Hall in Amereen Castle, an intricate mural decorated the curved ceiling. The dome was split in two halves. One half was painted in stark monochrome, the unmistakable rendition of Zephyr upon his throne, his hand clasping that of a black-haired beauty who could only be his queen. Both overlooked a fair race with hair of white, black, and silver. A variety of animals, mostly nocturnal, were painted with intricate detail—owls, snakes, bats, mice, and even a few wolves.

In the other half of the dome, the mural grew warmer, taking on a sepia hue to feature a less elaborate wooden throne bedecked with intertwining vines and a myriad of blooms. A stunning woman graced the seat wearing nothing but a crown and glorious hair long enough to keep her covered.

"Queen Katerina of the Summer Court," Zephyr provided, as though he could decipher her thoughts. Evangeline couldn't bring herself to look away from that section of the dome, a sudden, inexplicable ache filling her heart.

"Seelie," she whispered.

The painting depicted the queen surrounded by reverent subjects with hair of varying shades of gold, brown, and red. A variety of flora, flowering shrubs and thorny vines, completed this end of the fresco.

"Have you any idea how I grieved for you? How long I've searched for you?" Zephyr asked, his indulgent tone drawing her attention from the ceiling. "Imagine my surprise when I found you in Railea's Realm, and in an archmage's possession, no less." He gave a dark chuckle, like it was a joke she should understand. "Which is all just as well, I suppose. It fits perfectly into my plans."

Evangeline frowned at his words, trying to make sense of them. A twinge of fear sprouted in her chest, but it withered as quickly as it came. The fog that had shrouded her senses at the castle seemed to thicken, completely suppressing the fear scurrying beneath her skin. It also seemed to impair her faculties. Her tongue seemed thick, her throat constricted.

"Where are ... we?" she managed at last.

"You're standing within the walls of the Winter Palace, my sweet Jilintree," he said in a doting tone.

"Why ... call me ... that?"

Zephyr's eyes gleamed. "Where have you been all these centuries that you'd fail to recognize your master?"

That wrought a sharp tang of emotion, wavering her trance. "I don't belong to you."

Zephyr chuckled. A dark, familiar sound. "Oh? And I suppose you think yourself Thorne's?"

Evangeline frowned. She belonged to Declan, but not in that way. He was her lover, not her master.

Before she found the words to articulate her thoughts, Zephyr laughed again. "You'll remember me soon enough, Jilintree." He seized her chin with possessive fingers, tilting her face up to meet his. His eyes were such a vivid shade of violet, so beautiful they were uncanny.

She twisted sluggishly to free herself from his grip. "Where is my sister?"

His expression sobered, and he shook his head with genuine regret. "Dead. I found her body in the woods. Weakened as she was, she made a fatal choice when she plunged through the cabin door that night. The cabin was shrouded in shieldmaker's magic—one that prevented her, or you for that matter, from creating a portal for escape.

"I always suspected you were alive, little Jilintree. I never did find your body. And now Ozenn smiles upon me." He beamed at her. "After all these winters, you're finally back where you *truly* belong. Here, with me. This is my home, and now it is yours."

She stared at him in equal parts confusion and captivation. Wordlessly, he drew her toward the dais, his footsteps silent against the lush red carpet. Instead of making his way up the steps to the jewel-studded thrones, he veered to the side, toward the windows.

With a dramatic flourish, he drew the heavy curtains wide.

Light poured through pristine glass, and her breath hitched. How could this possibly be the Court of *Winter*? The barrenness of the landscape reminded her of Draedyn's Realm, but where the shadow realm had been a blanket of white, this land was a bloodstained desert. The soil appeared cracked and craggy, as though it had suffered a long drought. Dehydrated and desolate, the grounds stretched wide and contrasted sharply with trees bearing leaves of startling crimson.

"Once, I could draw apart these drapes to admire the beauty of the Soul Trees," he said, gesturing at the copse of red-leafed trees. Graves. A shudder snaked through her at the sudden, inexplicable knowledge.

Soul Trees marked the passing of every fae.

"But no longer," Zephyr said. There was regret in his voice. Almost sadness. "Ever since the Seelie was purged from the realm, my lands remain as dry as dust, no matter the season. Over time, our crops have slowly withered, and our livestock perished along with them." His lips twisted. "Even the Soul Trees seemed to lose their luster."

Against the pale, colorless sky, the deep red of the Soul Tree leaves appeared almost menacing—soot-colored branches raised to the heavens, like the arms of devoted priests offering bloody sacrifices to the gods.

A glimmering, winged shadow soared through the sky,

wrenching her captivation from the graves. It swooped in close enough that her breath rattled in her throat.

Arrowtail? But this creature had forelimbs as well as wings. Wicked spikes protruded from tail to spine, and even from the distance, she made out sharp talons. The dragons depicted by Corvina's statues. A slow moment provided a name. Drakghi. Yet, she felt more fascination than fear.

"Who am I?" she whispered.

Zephyr smiled down at her, an almost tender expression on his face as he drew her closer. Something fluttered in her heart, but there was not a single hint of fear. He even smelled nice. Sandalwood with a hint of citrus. He leaned down so their foreheads touched, the coolness of his crown pressing against her skin. It echoed a move so like Declan's that her heart thudded abruptly. Rebelled. She tried to push him away, but all she managed was a sluggish palm against his chest.

"You are a survivor," he said. "And my *salvation*."

Then she felt his mind, dark and slick, shoving against hers, seeking entry. A mind she'd tasted before.

Seated at the edge of the pond, she paddled the water with her feet and stared at the warbling ducks. She ran absent fingers across the grass and took joy in the way the wildflowers sprang up at her fingertips. Egrets stalked the other end of the pond cordoned by reeds and long grasses. Beside her, a couple of frogs lounged on lily pads, surreptitiously eyeing dragonflies in erratic flight that occasionally dipped in and out to break the surface of the water.

The air shimmered, and there he was—a tall, lanky boy with hair the color of raven feathers and golden skin, eyes still obscured by bandages. She couldn't wait for the day she could finally see his eyes.

Somehow, she fancied them to be green.

"Hi!" she chirped. "I almost thought you weren't coming today."

His head snapped in her direction, a smile gracing his lips. He bent, groping for the ground, and she reached out to guide him. Settling beside her on the soft, moss-covered edge, he removed his shoes and rolled up his trousers. She grinned. It had taken weeks of coaxing before he'd joined her in dipping his feet into the water. Now it had become a habit.

"I'm sorry to be late," he said, reaching out for her hand. He always did this—sought her touch as if it were critical to his existence. She slipped her hand into his readily, enjoying the warmth of his skin.

Then she spotted the fresh bruises mottling his forearms.

"Do you want to ascend one day?" she asked abruptly, trying to swallow the bile rising in her throat. "When you are fully grown?"

He seemed to consider her question, absently running his thumb over her knuckles.

"No," he said. "It scares me." He sat with his back ramrod straight, gazing at the pond he couldn't see. She frowned. She couldn't imagine anything scaring him, this beautiful boy who had endured grievous injuries without a single tear.

"Well, I hope you do," she said.

"Why?"

"Then you'll be strong enough to stop whoever it is that keeps hurting you," she said bitterly, scowling at the bruises on his collarbone that peeked from beneath his brown tunic. He wouldn't talk about what went on in the enclave, but she could guess.

His head dipped, shoulders drooping.

"It won't change anything," he murmured. The defeat in his posture and his tone caused her heart and the tiny dandelions around her to wither.

"Of course it will. No one hurts an archmage," she said, unable to stop her pout or the widening patch of withering grass around her. "And then maybe we won't have to meet in secret."

He raised his head and brightened slightly with a smile. "If I ascend, I'll use my power to end the war in your realm. Then you can go home whenever you wish." Warmth unfurled in her chest, and the withered grass began perking up. But heaviness descended swiftly at the thought of leaving him.

The flowers didn't bloom.

"I want the war to end but . . . " She swallowed and stared at their interlinked fingers. "I don't want to leave you." Just that morning Quentin had said he'd found Unseelie scouts close to their camp—close enough that it meant King Zephyr suspected their presence. Close enough that they might have to move again.

"But you'll come back to me. Won't you?" he asked softly, and her heart ached. Papa had always said he'd known the moment he met Mama. A kind of recognition, he'd said. The strange feeling of missing someone even though they were right beside you.

Was this what he meant?

"Always," she whispered. She would *always* return to him.

"If I ascend, I will rule a kingdom. Then I'll make you a princess," he declared. "You'll have a crown and everything."

At the playful grin that curved his lips, a giggle worked its way up her throat. He was smiling a whole lot more lately. Once, she'd even made him laugh aloud when she'd confessed how she'd dyed her hands—and most of Quentin's clothes— red when she mistakenly used Felicie's ochre paste in place of detergent. It was the last time she'd ever been given laundry duty.

"Truly?" she asked.

He nodded, and she wondered if Papa would allow her to remain in this realm after the war ended. Her heart shriveled like the deadened flowers around her.

Papa would never allow it.

Her family wasn't royalty, but they were no less revered than Queen Katerina herself. As the Summer Court's most venerated general and Queen Katerina's most trusted advisor, Papa was blessed with the ability to magnify or allay magic. And unlike Felicie, who could only magnify, *she* had inherited both of Papa's abilities, which made her a much-sought-after weapon in a warring realm.

Their birthright was the very reason King Zephyr actively hunted them.

And when the war was over, she and Felicie would be expected to return home and serve Queen Katerina's court. With no sons, Papa would expect nothing less of his daughters.

Swallowing the lump at the back of her throat, she reached for the book with her free hand, leafing through the pages until she came to the earmarked section. It was difficult to read and turn the pages with one hand, but she didn't mind. Reading and holding Declan's hand soothed her as much as it did him.

As she read, tension drained from her while he became utterly absorbed—both engrossed in the story of a swash-buckling pirate and seafaring sailor warring for the love of a beautiful mermaid.

Ducks and egrets squawked and burst into abrupt flight, shattering the tranquility. A woman with a waterfall of dark hair materialized in the glade, standing like a regal queen amid the soft carpet of green.

Startled by the interruption, her book slid off her lap to fall into the water with a wet plop. There was no mistaking the swirling marks inked into the woman's porcelain skin. The archmage of Amereen.

Declan scrambled out of the water, and she followed, fingers curling tight around his.

"*This* is who you've been sneaking out to see? She's nothing but a child!" the woman scoffed, arms crossing over a simple white dress, cinched at the waist with a silver band. But despite her simple attire, Corvina Alvah was easily the most beautiful woman she'd ever seen.

And the most terrifying.

"I'm sorry." Dread was thick in his voice, yet he nudged her back so he shielded her body with his. The archmage's derisive laugh and Declan's obvious fear heckled her.

"We are friends!" Her canines sharpened with belligerence.

"Friends?" Corvina curled her lips and released another caustic laugh. "Child, magekind will never be friends with you and your devious ilk."

Invisible barriers smoldered in the air to constrict her movements, choke her throat. Frantically, she lashed out, calling upon the earth. Thorny brambles snaked out to wrap themselves against her aggressor. But her magic was laughable compared to the woman's powers. The branches were wilted silage before they could cause any real damage.

"Mother, no!" Declan's pleas sounded garbled as the invisible bonds tightened around her throat.

She projected her thoughts in desperation. *Help! Declan, help me!*

"Please, stop! Let her go, and I will never leave the enclave again. I swear it."

Black dots danced in her vision. A sudden blaze of fire billowed at her feet, scorching her skin like a brand. *Help . . .*

A flurry of ice stamped out the heat, and the invisible manacles around her throat loosened enough that she crumpled to the ground. The woman looked shocked. But apparently, it wasn't at her son's open defiance. "You can wield ice?"

Declan curled his shoulders as if ashamed. "Let Freya go. Please, Mother."

Freya clung to his arm, instinctively using her birthright. If they were back in her homeland, she could amplify his powers to give him a fighting chance. But here, in this foreign realm, all she could do was augment his powers a little.

"You would defy me for a fae child?" Corvina's expression darkened with murderous intent. Another flurry of ice clouded the air, Declan's defiance a frozen wall shrouding them from his mother's wrath.

"Run, Freya!" Declan cried, his voice hoarse. "Go!"

A torrent of flames shattered the ice wall, hot vapor rising to fog the air.

"Go, Freya, please!"

She sobbed in panic. *I'm scared, Declan! She's going to hurt you!*

I'll be fine, he responded, more ice surging to sustain his crumbling wall.

Don't be scared. Go, and don't look back. He paused, head angling in her direction as if he could see her. *Be brave, Freya.*

Freya whirled and fled, but not without projecting a final thought into his mind.

I'll come back. I'll come back to you, Declan.

A fae's promise. One that could only be broken upon her death. But she didn't know if he heard her. As she fled the glade, she felt a gut-wrenching pain—a phantom knife severing the psychic connection that seemed to have formed over the last months. She held a hand over her mouth to stifle the sobs. Prayed to Ozenn to keep him safe.

But fear kept her running.

A fresh wave of dread seized her as she came upon the familiar footpath to the campsite on the outskirts of Lindenbough village. Overzealous hoofprints muddied the trail and muddled the green carpeting the ground. Her heart sank when she saw the clearing—Felicie's carefully babied blooms were trampled, delicate petals crushed into the dirt. Smoke billowed where tents had once stood, now nothing but charred black stumps. A man's body, broken and discarded amid the bloodied soil, caught her gaze. Grief wrenched her out of her stupor, catapulting her to Quentin's side.

"Quentin," she keened, praying to the gods that he wasn't dead. What had happened to everyone else? What had happened to her sister?

"Felicie!" She blubbered, searching for her sister through the haze of tears even as she shoved whatever magic she had left into Quentin's unresponsive frame. Her magic was far too weak in this realm. "Felicie, where are you?"

She didn't see the dark, ominous shadow lurking by the side. Didn't see it until it coalesced into a man and caught her by the scruff of her neck. She screamed, both mentally and verbally, for a boy who no longer responded.

"Ah, another Jilintree." A dark chuckle. "How much do you think the animati will pay for a pair of the Summer Court's greatest treasures?"

FORTY

Evangeline wrenched out of Zephyr's hold with a violent jerk, silent tears streaming down her face. Uncontrollable shudders slapped her frame as raw and painful scenes continued to unravel, the long-buried memories of her dormant mind slowly coming to life. She clenched her fists, trying in vain to slow the visions of the past uncurling like morning glory petals at the break of dawn.

How had she forgotten?

"Do you remember now, Jilintree?" Zephyr asked, lips drawing into a soft smile. Snippets of her captivity in the cabin flickered to life. The first semblance of fear took root, a thorny vise curling around the edges of her heart, but still she remained sluggish. Memories battered her mind, but Zephyr's touch was a drug that lulled.

"Do you remember how I saved you from your captors?" His gaze roamed over her, incisive and inquisitive. Evangeline blinked, trying to clear the tears blurring her vision.

"You . . . " She flailed for words, trying to speak past the thickness of her tongue. "It was you." Despite the vehemence in her chest, her words were barely a gasp.

He nodded with a beatific smile. "I killed your captors. The men who defiled you and your sister."

She trembled. Not from fear, nor gratitude. But from all-consuming rage in her chest, fueled by a hatred so ancient, it relieved her of the trance.

"The monsters." She choked at the knowledge afforded by long-lost memories. Angry tears streamed down her face to obscure her vision from the sight of a true monster.

"They were *your* men."

Declan gripped the rail of the infirmary bed until the steel frame began to liquefy from the inadvertent use of his powers. He loosened his grip, physically and psychically, but he couldn't quite keep the threat from his tone. "If you betray me, mortal, I will flay the flesh from your bones."

Stefan's gaze snapped up from the beds where Diana and Patrick Hanesworth lay, side by side, unconscious. "Reap my mind, Archmage." Stefan lifted his chin as though in challenge. "If you don't believe me, see the truth for yourself."

Mailin, who had been by Diana's bedside, widened her eyes at Stefan. "Foolish human. Psychosis is a common effect of a psychic reaping."

Stefan flattened his lips. "So be it. All my life, I did what I had to to keep my mother alive." His eyes held a wealth of emotion as he studied the comatose woman. "Even at the expense of innocent women. If it will help Evie now, I will gladly embrace death." Stefan pushed from the bed to face him. "Insanity is a small price to pay."

Declan regarded the man for a moment before he unclenched his fist, sensing truth. Turning, he nodded to the Unseelie hovering by the doorway of the ward. "Do it."

Gabriel grimaced, unmistakable censure coloring his eyes. "With all due respect, Archmage, Ozenn's Realm is Zephyr's domain." Stating the obvious. "You will lose your ability to wield the elements."

Declan gritted his teeth.

Before he could voice his displeasure at Gabriel's reticence, Killian interjected from his side. "Sire, let me assemble our men. An army—"

"Will immediately put Zephyr on defense," Declan interjected tersely. Vengeance was a blade in his gut, and he certainly had no qualms retrieving Evangeline through bloodshed. Indeed, Zephyr had asked for nothing less with his audacity. But Declan wouldn't risk bringing his own people to war if he could avoid it.

Killian nodded, understanding without the need for further explanation, but Cassius, one of his battlemages, remained doubtful. "Sire, an army of our elite and a brute show of strength will ensure Zephyr never impinges on what is yours again."

Declan shook his head. "That may work with a clan of gliders, but the Winter Court is vast. Zephyr's men too many. War would be inevitable if I brought an army." He waved an impatient hand at Gabriel. "An army of mages is also much too large to traverse Gabriel's portal." A fae portal could only ferry a small number of beings at a time. The stronger the fae, the more they could transport. Gabriel might be inordinately strong, but even his portal couldn't take more than a small group of men at a time.

But for the first time, Gabriel appeared in complete agreement with his battlemages. "Give me some time, Archmage. I'll rally my own men, the ones strong enough to cast portals."

"No," Declan said, making it clear with his tone that if the Unseelie refused him, he wouldn't be above wrenching a portal from Gabriel's being.

Declan didn't *have* time.

Evangeline was at the mercy of the Unseelie king. A bloodthirsty dictator responsible for the destruction of the entire Seelie race in the span of mere decades. A king rumored to be teetering on the brink of insanity, who possibly saw reason to strike at Declan for the simple fact that he was the son of a man who had once made a cuckold out of him.

"A portal, Gabriel." Declan growled. "Into the heart of the Winter Court. Do it, and I will release you from your debts."

Shock lit the Unseelie's face. Gabriel held his gaze for a long moment before he nodded.

"The moment we have Evangeline, you are to bring her back here, straight to Mailin. Do not wait on anything else."

Should an altercation erupt between him and the Unseelie king, Declan needed to assure his little fire's safety. And unlike in the shadow realm, there would be no shortage of Unseelie soldiers within the Winter Court. Vessels Declan could use to wrench a portal through psychic force to return himself and his men to his own realm.

Gabriel nodded, revealing deadly fangs through the curve of his lips. "I've waited centuries for a chance to rain chaos on Zephyr's rule, Archmage. Today is as good a day as any."

FORTY-ONE

W hatever it was Declan expected, it was not to see his little fire mauling Zephyr's throat like a wild animal in the empty Winter Court throne room. Bathed in sunlight streaming from the windows and bent on all fours, Evangeline had her fingers curved like talons, clawing at the Unseelie king, who lay prostrate on the marbled ground. Her face was buried in the side of Zephyr's neck, as if she was attempting to rip out his jugular.

"Ozenn's blood . . . ," Gabriel sputtered, giving voice to the silent shock Declan and his battlemages felt.

Zephyr let out a low moan, not borne of pain, but ecstasy. Declan's incredulity morphed to outrage. Zephyr's face held a rapture that echoed the bulge in his trousers—one Evangeline was nearly riding. Swearing with enough vehemence to breathe fire, Declan moved to wrench Evangeline onto her feet.

But she didn't recognize him.

A feral, half-crazed gleam lit her eyes. Eyes now ringed with a faint, telling sphere of violet. Her ears had lengthened too, taking on the distinct shape of a delicate leaf. Like an enraged feline, her ears flattened to the sides of her head as she hissed, flashing tiny but sharp-looking canines.

Shocked, he released her.

She lunged and snapped fangs at his neck. His men surged forward.

"Don't you dare touch her!" Declan snarled even as Evangeline raked her nails over his neck. "Evangeline!" he cried. "It's me. *Declan.*"

At the sound of his name, she halted almost immediately. She blinked up at him, recognition flitted over her irises, ears angling as if chastened.

"Declan?" She sounded astonished. "You came for me."

Of course he did. "I'll always come for you."

He stared at the violet rim around her irises, dazed. "What has Zephyr done to you?" But she didn't answer him. Tears welled in her eyes.

You came for me. Her mental voice was no longer a faint projection. It was clear. Strong. She began chanting the words repeatedly.

You came for me. You came for me . . .

In his periphery, Zephyr straightened to his full height as his battlemages reached for the fae king. But with a flick of his wrist, darkness bloomed, oily and slick, to repel Declan's men.

Stand back, Declan commanded.

A smirk formed on Zephyr's lips, violet eyes trained on them as though viewing an amusing play, but Declan could not tear himself away from his little fire.

"Evangeline," he whispered again. "What's happened to you?" He wiped the blood from her mouth with his sleeves. She burst into sobs, burrowing her face into his chest, fingers clenching the fabric of his shirt. Stupefied, he could only hold her.

Fae? How could she be fae?

Dark laughter drew his focus.

"She really means something to you, doesn't she?" Zephyr continued to eye him with unbidden delight. "So much you'd venture out of your own realm." Fresh blood still dripping down his neck to stain his unbuttoned shirt, Zephyr ran his hands through his hair, seemingly unperturbed by the presence of Gabriel and the battlemages.

"What have you done to her, Zephyr?" Declan growled. Every sob from Evangeline savaged his heart and shredded his composure. Every tremble heightened his confusion and threatened his civility.

"What have *I* done?" Zephyr let out a bark of laughter. "Surely you witnessed what the little minx was doing to me?" The king sauntered across the dais, taking his seat upon the throne of heavy oak that glimmered with gems matching his eyes.

Declan hissed a breath between his teeth. *Gabriel, take Evangeline home now.*

Beside him, Gabriel shifted. *Something is suppressing my magic, Archmage. I can't summon a portal.*

Zephyr gave a knowing smirk, as though privy to their psychic conversation. He clapped his hands, and at their back, the burnished doors of the entrance flowed wide. Three hooded men in animati ceremonial robes strode into the room followed by a procession of Unseelie guards.

"My friends," Zephyr crowed, gesturing at the hooded shieldmakers. "Ensure that all intruders have no means of escape."

Gabriel released a low hiss, and Declan's battlemages bristled by his side, drawing their arms and taking a defensive stance. The Unseelie guards took on a line formation behind the shieldmakers, forming a sea of silvered armor and scythes.

Declan gathered Evangeline tighter into his embrace and shifted so he had a view of the formation of the Unseelie brigade and the dais where the king lounged. Gabriel and the battlemages shifted in accordance.

Killian and Cassius moved to flank Declan, facing the shieldmakers and the procession of guards. Gabriel and the rest of the battlemages guarded his back in a combative herringbone formation.

"I hope there is no one waiting on your return," Declan said to the shieldmakers with a calmness that belied his churning emotions, "because you'll never see them again."

The shieldmakers kept their gazes shrouded beneath their hoods, but one shifted perceptibly to Declan's threat.

"Pay the archmage no heed, Tijin," Zephyr said mildly from his throne. "I am the true master here. An archmage isn't worth half his weight outside his own realm . . . and only those who seek to betray me have true reason to fear." A pointed look in Gabriel's direction.

Gabriel hissed again, pointed ears flattening—a disturbing congruence to Evangeline's physical traits. In Declan's arms, Evangeline's sobs ebbed. But she was still trancelike, specific strings of words playing over and over in her mind.

I never wanted to leave you . . . I never wanted to leave you . . . I never wanted to leave you . . .

"It's all right, little fire. I'm here," Declan murmured into her hair, stroking her back to soothe her trembling thoughts and his own turmoil. "I'm here."

Zephyr chuckled. "Such tenderness! I would never have thought Nathaniel Strom's mageling capable if I weren't seeing this for myself." The first and last time they'd met, Zephyr had recently toppled the Summer Court and become the *only* monarch in the fae realm.

Declan fought the urge to lash out, but Zephyr wasn't

wrong. His elemental powers were once again seeping from his veins. Dwindling. He couldn't afford to antagonize Zephyr without ensuring Evangeline's safety, not in the presence of an army of Unseelie and three shieldmakers. Noto had not returned from his foray into the animati realm, but clearly, the Unseelie and animati alliance ran deeper than he'd believed.

Zephyr gave a little chuckle. "Seeing my Jilintree has developed an attachment for you, Thorne, I am open to extending a proposition."

Zephyr might as well have bludgeoned Declan with an iron fist. Air rushed out of his lungs. "*What* did you just call her?"

"Spare me the pretenses." Zephyr curled his lips. "Why else would you keep her sequestered in your castle?"

Declan's throat constricted further. "Evangeline hails from the Summer Court?"

Zephyr snorted. "You truly had no idea? I've always thought you sharper than this, but clearly I gave you too much credit."

Declan looked down at Evangeline. Her eyes were still glazed, her mind still affixed on disjointed thoughts that didn't seem to make any sense.

I'll come back to you . . . I'll come back to you . . . I'll come back to you . . .

Declan wrapped his arms around her still-quivering frame, tucking her close to assuage his own mounting fears at her current state. How could it be possible? The Summer Court and all that descended from it had been wiped out of existence for centuries. He'd always hoped Freya had somehow survived the massacre of Lindenbough village. Since his ascension, Declan had allied himself with Gabriel and scoured the realms but found *nothing* to suggest any of Seeliekind had survived the Winter War.

Yet the truth of Zephyr's words resonated in his bones. Evangeline had always seemed more than human to him—her psyche too bright. But how could she even be fae to begin with?

"Evangeline is human," Declan heard himself say. His little fire was mortal in a way Freya, even as a child, never had been.

Zephyr chuckled. "Does she *look* human to you now, Thorne? She is fae, and very much one of *mine*."

"The fuck she is," Declan gritted out with a snarl. "If what you say is true, Evangeline belongs to the Summer Court."

"The Summer Court is no more. Every fae, Seelie or Unseelie, bows to me."

Gabriel interjected with a bark of acerbic laughter. "In your dreams, perhaps. You are no king of mine, Zephyr."

Zephyr curled his lips at the guildmaster's retort. "I'll see you on your knees, Blacksage, before this day is over." The Unseelie king stood abruptly, giving up his throne to make his way down the dais steps with a boldness that echoed his confidence in his defenses.

"It has taken me hundreds of slaves, but the alliances I've cultivated will ensure I'm a true power to be reckoned with, Thorne. And that woman in your arms? She's a *weapon* you don't even know how to use. A weapon that completes my army. One even your father will need to bow to. He'll be sorry he ever touched my Seraphina."

"Evangeline is *no* weapon. She is . . . " Declan stared at the woman burrowed in his arms as if seeking succor. Could she truly be one of the fabled Jilintrees? Related to *Freya*?

"You've had her for months and still don't know?" Zephyr shook his head in disgust. "You're just like your father, bloated with power and blind from it. Open your eyes and do your world a favor, mageling—put an end to Nathaniel Strom. If

I'm not mistaken, you have every cause to despise him as much as I do."

Declan narrowed his eyes. "Fool. The Echelon stands together. No amount of alliances will help you bring him down."

Zephyr broke into exaggerated laughter, as though Declan had just made a joke. "Ah, mageling. So young. So naive. I do not only have support from the animati and shadow realms." A conniving glint lit Zephyr's eyes. "*One* of the Echelon already stands with me."

Declan's lips parted. "Impossible." The Echelon might not be amiable with each other, but they had no cause to betray their own kind.

Zephyr laughed again. "Some are eager to rid the universe of the destructive force that is Nathaniel Strom. Your alliance will tip the scale of power in my favor."

Declan sneered. Alliance? "You won't be alive to face him if I crush you."

Zephyr tutted as though Declan was a misbehaving child. "Come, now. Let's not be rash. We can be of use to each other. In the old days, the fae ruled alongside your kind. We were true allies then! A force beyond any the universe had ever seen."

Declan curled his lips. "Until *you* decided to wipe out half of your own kind in favor of despotism."

"Ah, Thorne, you were green when it happened, but surely now you see the need for the Winter War? The Summer Court was a hindrance. Queen Katerina never really understood what it was to rule."

"Katerina maintained the fragile balance in your lands for centuries during her reign. The fae realm was never meant to be ruled by a solitary race. You needed the Summer Court as much as your lands need rain."

Zephyr gave him a chastened nod and sighed deeply. "Yes. Yes, you're right. I may have been overly brash when I massacred Seeliekind, but you see, I've spent decades trying to redeem myself!" He gestured at Evangeline with a flourish. "The Jilintree will not only be an asset to my army. She will be *my* new queen. Bear me heirs with Seelie blood that will replenish my lands."

Declan swallowed bile. "Evangeline is no broodmare." He struck out abruptly with his mind and sent the king hurtling into the air. But Zephyr hadn't ruled for two thousand summers to be so easily castigated. Deflecting Declan's psychic assault with a web of black magic, he landed with catlike grace on the ground before calmly waving his antagonized guards back.

Zephyr beamed as though the entire affair invigorated him. "Well, now, if the Seelie wench means so much to you, I'm not averse to sharing."

Windows shattered in an explosion of crystalline shards. The ground rumbled. Hairline fractures rippled through the surface of the polished marble steps, and concrete dust fell from the overarching buttresses. As Zephyr teetered on the quaking steps, Declan lashed out with another telekinetic punch. The Unseelie king dematerialized into an insubstantial cloud of shadows before coalescing into solid form to stand between his own soldiers.

"Enough!" Zephyr roared. "Cease this childish display, or my men will attack."

Zephyr's front line wielded scythes, but nightcasters armed with shadowbows lurked in the back. Declan drew deep into his marrow and erected an all-encompassing kinetic shield over his own men—an impenetrable dome.

Declan smiled silkily. "I'd like to see you try."

Zephyr's eyes darkened. Volleys of dark magic slammed

into Declan's protective barrier. Arrows of blackfire rent the air, and Zephyr's dark magic crawled over Declan's shield like a ravening beast, shadows licking and lapping for the slightest crack.

"We need to defend ourselves, sire," Killian said, his voice a low growl and his grip white against his sword. "Let me out."

Declan nodded and turned to his Unseelie ally. "The moment I bring down the shieldmakers, I want you to summon a portal and return her to Amereen."

Gabriel bristled, showcasing fangs much larger than Evangeline's. "I'll send your woman through the portal, but I'll not be leaving you and your men to battle Zephyr alone."

"If Zephyr's claims are true, he will never stop hunting her. If I do not return, I need you alive to protect her." None of his men could shelter Evangeline from a fae king. Declan arrowed the thought at Gabriel. *She is my mate. Give me your word, my friend.*

Gabriel's throat worked. He nodded, curt but resolute.

Satisfied, Declan stroked the black gauntlets on his wrists —magerian bands he'd donned in anticipation of battle. The bands protracted, metal plates extending in response to his kinetic energy. The armor covered his torso, spreading fluidly to encompass his entire body, curving up to cover his head in a helm tipped with a crown of curved horns.

The glassiness of Evangeline's eyes seemed to dissipate that moment.

Perhaps his armor shocked her out of her stupor.

"Declan," she gasped.

Declan touched her mind with his, knowing that she could now *see* him as he could see her on the psychic plane. "Everything will be all right, little fire," he murmured even as the first shards of Zephyr's magic crept through his shields, a scalding undercurrent of blackfire. "You'll be home soon."

Declan pressed a fierce kiss to her temple. Unable to leave her utterly defenseless, he summoned the *draga sul.* The talisman pulsed as though it sensed an impending battle and thirsted for blood. He clasped her fingers over the rubied hilt before thrusting her into Gabriel's hold.

"Keep her safe."

Gabriel dipped his head with a somberness he rarely displayed. "With my life."

Declan retracted his shields and released all residue of elemental energy left within his veins. A roar of fire swept out in a radial wave, devouring everything in its wake.

FORTY-TWO

She had never seen his psyche before. Not as Evangeline Barre.

Her archmage's mind reflected the very elements he commanded. Fire and ice. Darkness and light. His mind was a glacier, filled with crisp planes and cutting edges tempered by the smooth silk of flame. Everything about him warred between two extremes. How he'd changed from the boy he'd once been.

The years had hardened him.

The screams drew her back to the present, to the scent of smoke, the brutal tang of seared flesh and scorched armor. The frontline soldiers bore the brunt of Declan's flames, writhing in agony as fire heated their armor to unbearable temperatures. Some rolled on the marbled ground; some scattered like frenzied animals.

Declan and his battlemages gave their enemy no time to regroup as they tore through like black wraiths. Declan went straight for the shieldmakers. He slashed and severed, but no fire fueled his attacks. He warped to deflect blows and defend his men, but no ice came to his aid. His ability to use the elements was gone.

She wasn't the only one who noticed.

Stealthy shadows seeped from Zephyr's skin, pooling on the ground like a creeping fog. The amorphous cloud slithered to lash at the golden energy that surrounded her like a dome— looking for ways to get *in*.

"Stay inside!" Gabriel ordered, pivoting to avoid an errant scythe. "Don't let the shadows touch you!" With a sword in each hand, the guildmaster was a whirlwind of blades who never strayed far from her translucent gold sanctuary.

Evangeline's knuckles were white, her fingers wrapped around Declan's dagger. The same one she'd used to carve the stinger from his shoulder. She peeled her lips back in a hiss as another soldier lunged for Gabriel's throat. "I want to help!"

"The point is to keep you alive!" The guildmaster spun in a deadly blur, slaughtering two soldiers before Evangeline could blink.

"I have no wish to end your life, Thorne!" Zephyr's holler and the cacophony of clashing blades and bloodcurdling screams drowned Evangeline's response.

The Unseelie king peeled back his lips, canines elongated, his sword drawn for attack.

Declan twirled his own sword, the gesture both mocking and menacing as he gave a bark of laughter. "You are so certain I would fall?"

Zephyr sneered, and Evangeline curled her fingers, itching to scratch the smugness off his face. "You're in *my* realm, Thorne, with nothing but a handful of battlemages, facing an army you cannot hope to defeat."

Declan's markings flared. Gold illuminated beneath his armor just as he pivoted sharply to behead a soldier charging at his back. Evangeline could hear his grin despite the metal helm. "We'll see about that, won't we?"

A fearsome crack resounded, loud as thunder. The entire length of a buttress crashed down over Zephyr's head. A heartbeat before the concrete slab met its mark, the Unseelie king discharged a pulse of dark magic. Blackfire. The fatal piece of rubble ruptured into gravel, accompanied by a harmless hail of dust and debris.

Evangeline stumbled to her feet as a nearby pillar toppled like a chess piece to smash over the dais and cause the ground to quake. She snarled her frustration. She was nothing but a butterfly in a glass jar amid a cyclone. No amount of fluttering helped anyone. Evangeline stared at her hands. She was fae. A being born to command magic.

"Gabriel, I can help!"

"You stay where you are!" A slash, and an arc of blood underscored his gritted command. "One more shieldmaker—"

Craaaack! Another chunk of the domed ceiling crumbled as though smashed by a phantom giant. Shafts of light streamed through the now topless throne room to illuminate the battle.

The Unseelie king jumped out of a sudden portal in a deadly rush of shadow and sword, but Declan had anticipated the attack. He warped just before Zephyr struck.

More Unseelie soldiers swarmed into the room, filing through the entryway and pouring through the glass windows. It was a dismal sight—Declan and his men were grossly outnumbered. Yet the battlemages fought with a confidence and ferocity that seemed to unnerve the Unseelie soldiers. They had the element of surprise. Their ability to warp made them hard to pin and their attacks hard to predict. Limbs were hacked and necks severed because the Unseelie had no idea when to expect a fatal blow.

And their archmage provided unwavering support.

In between clashing swords, Declan wrenched apart the remnants of the domed ceiling, destroying the beautiful rendition of the Winter and Summer Courts to annihilate and scatter clusters of Unseelie soldiers. Zephyr, however, seemed solely focused on his personal battle with Declan, leaving his men to fend for themselves, allowing the marble slabs to crush those who couldn't disperse in time.

To avoid the lethal edge of Declan's sword, the fae king *evaporated*, his body seemingly liquefying into shadow form. Evangeline gasped. An ancient part of her slowly awakening mind understood what she was seeing. Vaporization. The formless king shot across the hall like a black comet to coalesce upon a fallen column. Discharged a sly streak of blackfire.

"Watch out!" Evangeline cried.

Gabriel, inundated by Unseelie soldiers, moved a moment too slow. He dropped to his knees with a howl.

"I told you that you would bow to me, Blacksage!" Zephyr cackled, narrowly avoiding the thrust of Declan's blade as he danced upon a recumbent column like a drunken sailor.

"Gabriel!" Evangeline punched her arms through Declan's shimmering shield—avoiding the still-slithering shadows—to wrench the fae into the protective bubble. She was trying to help the guildmaster to his feet when the roar reverberated.

The shafts of light streaming through the now-open dome were suddenly masked by a cloud of concrete debris. Evangeline slapped her hands over her ears at another deafening bellow. She glanced up, and her heart plunged.

A gargantuan creature perched upon the edges of the broken walls.

Corvina's statues had depicted them as regal creatures, but up close? It was just another monster. Skeletal ribs and bat-like wings. Rapacious red eyes. And brawny limbs that were eerily human in musculature. A true demon. The drakghi extended its leathery wings, blocking the sun to bare a ridged underbelly armored with obsidian scales. Another thunderous rumble dislodged a storm of debris.

Amid the plumes of smoke and swirling dust, Zephyr wore a maniacal grin, and his long hair flew wildly as he stretched his arms wide as if to embrace the demon.

Declan lunged. Missed.

The fae king vaporized again. Disembodied darkness shifted into sinuous strands to coil around the winged demon. The drakghi released an earsplitting wail, flapping frenetically to create a billowing storm in the battered hall. It did nothing to deter the dark tendrils that stretched into thin wisps and prodded at the demon like sly fingers. The shadow seeped into the corners of the drakghi's eyes and nostrils and flowed freely into the demon's gaping maw.

Possession. Like vaporization, this was an Unseelie ability. Knowledge continued to flow from the ancient parts of Evangeline's kindling mind, but it did nothing to calm her. Even the strongest of Unseeliekind couldn't possess anything larger than a wolf, yet . . .

A hellacious roar.

The drakghi released a breath of *blackfire*. Volatile fumes blasted, so close the air around her thinned and sweat beaded on her forehead. Declan—locked in a battle with fae soldiers—hurled a piece of concrete at the creature. The possessed demon merely pumped its strong wings and soared into the air with a derisive screech.

Coughing from the ash and smoke, Evangeline propped up the Unseelie rebel.

"Are you all right?"

"I am fine." His hand clutched at his throat, wheezing as

though he had trouble breathing. His skin was pale and his movements jerky as he battled unseen hurts. He lifted his arm but groaned as though the effort to reclaim his blades was too great. As the battle raged around her, Evangeline hissed with helpless frustration. She had to do *something*. She was *Seelie*, wasn't she?

Born with the ability to heal.

Evangeline placed a tentative palm over Gabriel's heaving chest, exactly where his heart beat. She shut her eyes and opened her sixth sense, willing threads of magic to her fingers. Her head throbbed. The effort of pushing a long-unused muscle caused her to pant. Pinpricks of pressure stabbed at her temples as if something were trying to compress her brain. Her breath gushed in and out of her lungs before she finally felt it.

Gabriel's pain. It was almost all-consuming.

He shoved her hand away. "Don't! You're not strong enough yet . . . Jilintree." The latter he uttered with undisguised awe. Then it finally struck her—what the name meant. Her birthright.

One she hadn't accessed in eons.

She whipped her head up, seeking her archmage, but Declan was no longer there. In fact, the battle had dispersed, scattering from the ravaged throne room into the dry, craggy lands beyond the broken walls. Into the Orchard of Soul Trees.

From a distance, she made out her archmage—a dark figure in black armor, distinctive with his horned helmet. He warped ceaselessly, hurling bursts of kinetic punches, stoking the drakghi's ire and warping just before it breathed blackfire.

"Sire!" Killian's cry was hoarse as he warped midfight.

It wasn't a cry for help, but one of warning.

Zephyr struck out with both fire and claws. Killian rematerialized beside Declan, but it was too late. Declan deflected the flames into arid land, but the drakghi's claws—each talon the length of a sledgehammer—caught him in the flank, shredding armor. With another swipe of its paw, Killian hurtled through the field.

Evangeline's scream was just another note in the symphony of chaos.

Her archmage warped seconds before the drakghi descended upon him. The creature sent a scorching wave of blackfire rippling across the plains, consuming everything in its path, including the fae king's own men.

"Where are you, you coward?" Zephyr's furious voice—distorted and discordant—blared from the drakghi's form. "Show yourself!"

Declan rematerialized beside his fallen commander. He was nothing more than a silhouette in the distance, but he limped as he attempted to haul Killian up from his knees. The commander seemed unable to stand. The drakghi spotted them, too, for it dove, descending with claws outstretched.

A pulse of telekinesis threw the demon off course. Then Declan warped again, this time reappearing upon the drakghi's back. He plunged his sword down, but the demon bucked before his sword met its mark, throwing its rider off midair. Declan's fall would have been lethal if he hadn't warped a hairsbreadth from the ground.

When he rematerialized, he staggered, slow and sluggish, and Evangeline knew the man she loved more than life itself was faltering. The girl that was Freya felt a crushing wave of despair and quailed in fear. War was not in her nature. But the woman that was Evangeline felt a surge of wild rage. Adrenaline filled her veins.

She did *not* spend an eon fighting to return to Declan only to lose him now.

Gabriel's face appeared in her vision.

The fae rebel was bleeding from every orifice on his head, bloody trickles distorting the violet in his eyes. He jerked her forearm roughly and nudged her toward a dark swirling portal. "Go, now! My portal will take you back to Declan's stronghold."

Evangeline bared her fangs. Lengthened canines she hadn't felt in centuries. There was so much pain prickling beneath her skin it was as if something was trying to claw itself out of her flesh.

"No." No more running.

If her mate was fated for death on this day, she would die here with him. She gave into the pain coursing through her. Screamed as the strain beneath her skin snapped, like a cork released from pressure. Blazing light of purest white erupted around her being.

A portal.

Allowing it to engulf her, she arrowed her will toward the man that was the other part of her soul—and appeared on the dirt right beside him.

Emerald eyes filled with disbelief bored into hers.

Evangeline! Get out of here! There was terror in his voice, the same brand of manic fear she'd heard all those years ago.

She would not run this time.

Gathering everything that made her the single surviving daughter of the Summer Court's fiercest general, everything that was her namesake, she brought it to her fingertips and bestowed it all to her archmage with a simple touch to his gauntleted arm. Light flared beneath his armor. She slumped to her knees, limbs quaking. White spots danced in her vision, but she grinned deliriously. Declan's markings flared brighter than she'd ever seen—gold leaching through the plates of his armor.

Use the elements, Archmage.

The soaring drakghi snapped its wings shut and dove, jaw wide to emit another deadly bellow of flames. Declan must have been in shock, for he wasn't warping himself out of the way. Evangeline's legs were numb. She couldn't run.

The blackfire would incinerate them both.

She flinched, but all that met her was a wash of scalding steam, allayed by prickling frost. Another wave of frost surged into the air, freezing the tips of the creature's tail before the drakghi flew out of the way.

The winged demon howled murderously, seeming to rally all the Unseelie soldiers within the vicinity. As the soldiers swarmed her archmage, the drakghi pivoted midair and careened toward her with talons outstretched, jaw opening as if to swallow her whole.

Run, Evangeline! Declan's voice rang in her mind, equal parts panic and command. But there was no point trying to run. Her legs remained numb. Useless. Zephyr had annihilated her people. Massacred her family. Destroyed her life. But he wouldn't destroy the man that was her heart.

In a final act of defiance, she picked up a discarded scythe from the rubble. Hurled it into the drakghi's eye. Her aim was true, but it blinked, and its eyelid threw off the blade before it could even scratch the glowing orb.

But she had infuriated the demon enough that instead of snapping, it swiped out with its paw. Pain seared as talons tore through her flesh.

FORTY-THREE

H is little fire hit the ground with a dull thud that would forever haunt his dreams.

"Evangeline!" Declan no longer knew if he screamed verbally or telepathically or both, only that it was barely audible through the roar of blood in his ears. She had abruptly filled him with so much *power* it scorched his veins and left him stunned. Declan reclaimed his faculties in time to thwart the drakghi's trajectory. Freeze the Unseelie soldiers charging at him. Yet he was one second too late where he was most needed. A moment of inertia he would never forgive himself.

With a howl of rage, Declan released a pulse of telekinesis before the drakghi could further damage Evangeline's battered body, tumbling the creature to the dirt.

It roared, its frenzied wings caught between the black branches of twisted trees. Drakghi scales were impervious to flames, so Declan would not use fire.

Frost crawled over the drakghi in an unforgiving wave. The demon's flailing ceased, frozen with one wing taut and the other folded in midanimation. The ice crackled up its throat and the last of its furious screeches ebbed. Declan warped close. Thrust his sword into the demon's neck. His staverek barely penetrated ice-encrusted flesh. A punch of telekinesis, and he nailed the sword into the demon's throat until it was buried to the hilt. Another burst of power and his sword exited, severing the creature's head from its body. The head rolled to the ground in a heap, black gore oozing sluggishly from a body still encased in ice.

Darkness amassed, and inky tendrils flitted out of the beheaded creature to coalesce into a semisolid man with a faceless visage and shadowy limbs.

Declan snarled. Before the fae king could fully solidify, flames erupted to consume the man of flesh and shadows. Agonized screams ruptured the air. Swirling specks of cinder lifted to the sky in accompaniment to the scent of gore, yet the shadowy manifestation of a malformed man remained. A semisolid phantom oozing spurts of scarlet and spewing hair-raising screams. The mutilated specter retracted, folding in on itself before retreating into a chasm of darkness. A portal.

Declan didn't try to stop it.

His men still fought a ceaseless battle. And his heart was shattered, lying motionless in the dirt. Power was potent in his blood, thick and heady from the surge Evangeline had shoved into his body. Declan used it to amplify his telepathic reach, projecting the Unseelie king's defeat to every soldier still unaware of his cowardly escape.

Your king is defeated. Lay down your arms, and you will be granted amnesty. Refuse, and you will be executed.

Ignoring the telepathic cheers of triumph from his battlemages, Declan warped toward the Soul Tree, where Evangeline lay like a child's discarded toy, sheltered beneath blackened branches.

The drakghi had scored her flesh. But unlike him, she wore no armor. Bloodied gashes ran the side of her body. Her dress was in tatters, stained with crimson. Declan slumped to his knees, scooping her up despite the searing pain of his own injuries. An incessant ringing in his ears canceled all noise except the pounding beat of his pulse.

He laid his forehead against hers. *Little fire.*

No response.

Declan lifted trembling fingers to caress her cheeks. When she remained motionless, he nudged her telepathically again. Usually a bright shimmering blaze even in sleep, Evangeline's mind was now an empty shell. Hollow.

"Little fire," he whispered, rocking her gently. "Evangeline, wake up." Her head lolled to the side like a broken doll. A low moan escaped his lips. A wave of despair threatened to claw its way out of his chest, swallow him whole. She couldn't possibly be gone. She was *Seelie.* Immortal wounds healed quickly. Her flesh would soon knit together.

Wouldn't it?

He injected command into his tone, voice brittle to his own ears. "Don't play games with me, Evangeline. Wake *now.*"

But she refused to obey him. Continued to lay limp in his arms like a marionette with cut strings. Desperation had him begging. *Please don't leave me. Please. . .*

A tentative hand clasped his shoulder.

"Sire," a solemn voice murmured. Cassius had warped to his side, his face grim and streaked with the grime of battle, but otherwise unharmed.

"Even immortals do not survive fatal wounds." The battlemage's mild whisper sent a violent tremor down his frame. The full weight of despair descended. Crushing him. *No, no, no, no . . .*

He couldn't breathe.

A whimper escaped his lips.

Somewhere, an animal howled with an intensity that mirrored his anguish. A sound of utter desolation that rang as deep as the drought that plagued the lands around them.

A sound that came from his throat.

Was she back in the Abyss?

Immaterial and weightless matter shrouded her—as if she was standing amid a dense fog. Yet it wasn't completely dark. No, this wasn't the Abyss. She had never been here before. Fear ignited in her chest, quickly parried by a deep sense of sorrow. She'd lost something. Something very important. What had she lost?

"What are you doing here, Freya?"

Evangeline whirled around and found herself face to face with a woman with a creamy complexion and wide, violet eyes.

"Felicie?" she whispered, sorrow morphing into joy. "I missed you."

"I missed you too, Frey . . ." Felicie drew her close. The familiar scent of jasmine curled around her with welcome. "But you shouldn't be here."

Evangeline furrowed her brows and burrowed deeper into Felicie's arms. She was smaller than Evangeline remembered. But her sister's embrace felt warm. Safe.

"Whyever not? You're here, so I can be, too."

Felicie gave her a slightly patronizing smile. "You have a different fate, little sister. There is more to your life. You have choices to make. Roads to travel. My sweet Frey, you don't belong here."

"Don't I?" All fear and anguish seemed to have dissipated

within the safe circle of Felicie's arms. There was no pain.

A howl reverberated in the fog. The sound of it haunting, like a wolf mourning the moon.

"What is that?" she asked, confused by the sudden pang in her heart. Her sister smiled and ran tender fingers down her cheeks.

"That's where you belong. With him."

"Him?" Evangeline wrinkled her nose. "I'm not leaving you for a *man*." But despite her words, the grievous cadence was a desperate tug in her chest. The man sounded in pain, and somehow, his sorrow caused her heart to ache.

Felicie grew cold to the touch. "Oh Frey, you spent centuries in the Abyss fighting to return to him. Remember?"

Felicie pressed a kiss to her forehead, and the fog slowly faded away. She could still feel her sister's lips, cold against her skin, when a meld of scorching fire and glacial ice coursed through her, chasing away the remnants of the fog, and with it, Felicie.

"Felicie, don't go! Please!"

"Don't forget me again, Frey. Don't forget who you are . . ."

The echo of her sister's voice was the only thing she heard as she shut her eyes against the near-blinding flash of light. Her veins burned with raw energy. Painful. Powerful. Poignant. With a ragged gasp, she jerked up.

And stared into eyes of misty green.

"Evangeline." Her name spoken like a prayer from the lips of a desolate man. She blinked until the rest of her vision came into focus.

"Declan?" she whispered. A powerful shudder racked his body, still clad in obsidian plates. The armor covering his head had receded, leaving his hair disheveled. Burying his face into the side of her neck, he moaned her name over and over.

Dazed, she realized she lay beneath a Soul Tree, shaded by

branches bearing bloodred leaves. Zephyr's stronghold. A kaleidoscope of memories straightened in her mind, shimmering over her senses like the variegated scales on a glider's tail.

"I thought I'd lost you," he said, still shuddering. She had never seen Declan so discomposed. His face was wan and utterly transparent. Too overwhelmed for words, she lifted her hands to his face and marveled at the dampness on her fingers.

Her indomitable archmage was crying.

"I love you," he whispered, voice ragged.

She stroked his tearstained cheek. "I know." She'd never needed the words. She'd already known.

He swallowed hard and clasped her hand before carefully placing it over the breastplate of his armor, over his heart. "I love you so much it aches."

"I know," she repeated, because she felt exactly the same way. She flattened her palm against his armor only to feel the abrasive edges of sharp metal, cool against her skin. "Oh gods, Declan, you're bleeding!" Badly. The side of his armor scored by the drakghi's talons was a gory sight of twisted metal and gouged flesh that seeped claret, further soaking her dress.

She tried to squirm out of his hold, struggled to sit upright. Pain streaked up her spine like a strike of lightning. She gasped. She couldn't move her legs.

"Don't," he said. "Zephyr fractured some of your bones." He continued to cradle her, eyes widely dilated, slight tremors running down his frame. Fear curdled in her veins when she attempted to move her toes but failed. Her growing fear was amplified by her archmage's ashen pallor, by the raw scent of iron saturating the air.

Desperate, she reached for his wounds. He gripped her wrist and firmly tucked it back against his chest.

"I am fae, Declan. Seelie. I can heal you."

He shook his head at the latter part of her sentence and gave her a pained smile. "You . . . have given me so much power that my wounds are healing as we speak."

She craned her neck, needing to see if it was true.

"If you're healing, why are you still bleeding so badly?"

He hesitated. "I think my body is compensating for your wounds."

"*What?*"

"I couldn't get you to wake up, so I . . . initiated the mating bond." He gave a plaintive smile. "I wanted to go where you went."

Evangeline parted her lips. He'd bound his life to hers. "What have you *done?*"

"Everything will be all right. Gabriel is barely alive, but the bastard still draws breath. My men are working on contacting members of Gabriel's guild. The moment his men arrive, we can go home."

"Declan—"

"Mailin will heal your legs. Everything will be fine."

Her legs weren't her priority. *He* was getting paler by the minute.

"How could you have initiated a mating bond? I thought it needed to work both ways."

"It doesn't matter. All that matters is that you're alive."

"But I'm . . . " She faltered, suddenly nervous. She licked her lips. "Declan, I'm—"

He didn't let her finish. "It doesn't matter to me what you are, little fire. I love you."

Exasperation had her blurting, "I am Freya."

That got his attention. He stared, lips apart.

Evangeline drew in a deep, steadying breath. "My name is Freya Katerina Jilintree."

FORTY-FOUR

Declan remained motionless as he reeled at the significance of the name. Freya. A name belonging to a girl who would always have the first claim to his heart.

A girl who should have been long dead.

"I am Freya." She paused with a faint smile. "Don't you recognize me?"

His heart clenched as though she squeezed it in her fist. A girl who had spent secret days tending to his wounds and reading him fantastical stories by an idyllic duck pond. A girl who allowed him to hold her hand because she knew he craved the sensation of a kind touch. A girl who had burrowed her way into his heart even though she was just a child, and he an older boy.

A girl whose face he'd never even glimpsed.

"Declan?" Tears pooled in amber eyes now ringed with violet, a meld of the girl who'd first claimed his heart and the woman who had pieced the mangled remains back together.

"Freya," he finally managed, scarcely daring to breathe lest he woke and found this all a dream. "My Freya?"

She nodded, seemingly unable to speak now that he had. She traced his cheekbone with a tender hand. Her thumbs lifted to trace the corners of his eyes. A tinkling laugh, faintly mischievous. The barest echo of a girl's voice he'd missed for centuries, matured with a woman's softness.

"I always fancied your eyes to be green."

"How?" he whispered. "My mother killed you." When he'd finally recovered from his mother's brutal punishment, he'd seen the remains of white ash scattered across the ruined fae camp in Lindenbough. "I searched and searched for you." He had spent decades searching for her. It wasn't until he'd scoured the realms to find no trace of Seeliekind left that he'd bitterly accepted the pile of ash as all that was left of his Freya.

Comprehension hit him like a hard slap across the face. "Corvina destroyed the camp, but you weren't there."

Evangeline gave a little nod. "Zephyr's men infiltrated the camp while I was fleeing from the glade." She paused, her face contorting with pain that had nothing to do with the memory. Tapping into the nascent thread of their incomplete bond, Declan directed more of his powers into her body and watched with satisfaction as the pain ebbed from her face.

Fresh blood trickled from his wounds.

She wet her lips. "They captured me and my sister. Brought us back to Ozenn's Realm. But instead of turning us over to Zephyr"—a shiver seized her frame—"they kept us caged in a cabin warded by shieldmakers that prevented us from casting portals," she trembled again from the memories, and her voice cracked. "The first thing I tried to do the moment I escaped was cast a portal to return to this realm. To Amereen. To you." Her eyes turned bleak. "But I'd never cast such a far-flung portal before."

His heart was a stampeding rampage of a hundred horses, attempting to break free from his chest as he pieced together what must have happened to her. "Your portal imploded, and you ended up in the Abyss?" The one place in the universe where time and space ceased to exist.

She nodded.

He stared at her. He knew she was ostensibly turning twenty-four soon. Knew she'd lived for twenty-four *human* summers. Freya had been an immortal child before her abduction. His jaw hung when he did the arithmetic in his head.

Four centuries in the Abyss.

Where she would have existed outside the impact of time.

"I had no real inclination of time or place. The only thing I held onto was my promise of returning to you. And one day, I must have regained enough energy. I willed a new portal to take me back to Amereen . . . where my mother found me."

Declan swallowed and breathed through the stinging pain in his side. It did not explain her humanity. "But how did you lose your immortality? Your memories?"

She frowned, eyes focused on the distance, as if in recollection. "I . . . I'm not entirely certain." She shook her head. "I suspect it was stripped in the Abyss. I felt . . . " Her brows furrowed as though trying to find the right word. "Weightless. Insubstantial. As though my body had become nothing more than a cloud. I had no real awareness of space or gravity . . . just a mass of gray."

Declan shuddered. There should have been no escape. How had she survived? How was she in his arms?

"In a way, Zephyr saved me." Her lips quivered. "His men stole me from the camp before Corvina destroyed it . . . and by bringing me back here, he somehow awakened my memories."

And judging from the tinge of violet rimming her irises, Zephyr had reawakened her immortality, too.

Emotion coursed through him like a rising tide, releasing a deluge he could not control. "I'm sorry." His shoulders shook, and tears trickled from his eyes to mimic the wounds on his side. "I'm so sorry." His voice cracked, so he spoke with his mind, needing to express the guilt that had battered his soul and the condemnation that had hardened his heart for centuries. *I should have protected you, but I failed.*

She did not misunderstand him. "You were unconscious, Declan. I felt it when your mother . . . " She swallowed. "What did she do to you?"

Declan shook his head, disgusted at himself. "Why does it matter? I was useless."

Evangeline reached up to cup his face, expression fierce despite the pain in her eyes. "Declan Thorne, you stood up against your own mother for me. She was an archmage and you a boy." He hung his head, still overwrought with shame.

"Don't you ever think it to be your fault," she asserted, as though reading his mind. Perhaps she was. He'd erected no barriers since linking himself to her.

"Everything you suffered was because of *me*," he said. Because of him, she'd used vast quantities of healing magic, which had likely led Zephyr's men to her camp. Because of his selfish need to be near her, she'd stoked Corvina's ire. Because of him, she was saved from Corvina's wrath only to suffer at the hands of Zephyr's men.

Declan stared at her unmoving legs. "Even now, I have failed to protect you."

"Don't you dare." She hissed, flashing tiny fangs. "Don't you dare think that way. You defied your mother to protect me. I was dying, and *you* brought me back. I came back for you, Declan. While I was trapped in the cabin, all I wanted was to come back to you. While I was trapped in the Abyss, I conserved all my energy so I could eventually come back to you." Tears stained her cheeks to mirror his own. "I will *always* come back to you."

Light-headedness caused his vision to sway in dizzying circles. He tightened his arms and stared into her eyes. But the amber in her eyes was no longer clear. The color had deepened to a near-golden sheen, rimmed by varying shades of violet. It was like drowning in an endless sunrise. Speechless, all he could do was lower his head to hers and hold her as the world spun around him.

Freya.

Evangeline.

His little fire.

FORTY-FIVE

E vangeline was nestled beneath the covers, enjoying a cup of steaming rosehip tea and the solitude of the crackling fireplace when Mailin waddled in unannounced. The healer's belly had grown well beyond an inconspicuous bump to a glaring protrusion, and much to Mailin's mortification, she had developed a gait to match.

Barely dressed, Evangeline arched a brow at the healer.

"I saw the sire talking to Lex in the Great Hall," Mailin said. "He told me you were awake."

Evangeline huffed her response before setting her mug on the bedside table and reaching for her robe. "Oh, don't bother," Mailin said with a wry smile. "I'm here to examine your ribs anyway."

Evangeline sighed. "Surely you have more important things to do than check on me each morning?" Since her return from Zephyr's palace nearly a month ago, the pregnant healer had been as zealous as her archmage was adamant on insisting on Evangeline's daily examinations.

Mailin pursed her lips. "Oh, I am busy. Another team of

soldiers has just returned from Draedyn's Realm. They've brought three new survivors." Before Evangeline could utter a word, the healer tutted and motioned for her to remain seated. "But five broken ribs, a fractured hip, and lacerations that run deep enough to sever tendons warrant my daily attention, I think."

Evangeline flattened her lips, but she lifted her arms so Mailin could inspect her ribs. "My bones are completely mended, and the lacerations are nothing but faint scratch marks." It was extraordinary to say the least, but she had healed at a rate astonishing even to immortals. "You know this better than anyone," Evangeline huffed. "It is Declan you should examine."

In contrast to her phenomenal recovery, her archmage's wounds had barely knitted back together, and Evangeline knew the scores on his side—angry red welts—still pained him. He had somehow expedited her recovery at the expense of his own, through the incomplete mating bond between them. A bond Evangeline refused to complete.

Not when her own immortality was still in question.

Mailin's lips curved. "He has *you* for that, doesn't he?"

Usually, such a comment would have brought heat to her cheeks, but this time, Evangeline's brows furrowed as she stared down at her hands. "I can't heal him, Mailin. If I am Seelie, why can't I summon my healing energies?"

The moment Declan had carried her through Gabriel's portal, every sensation of magic had dissipated from her veins.

Mailin plopped onto the edge of the bed to sit beside her. "You've recovered from injuries that would have killed an immortal, Evie. That in itself is a miracle. And being in a realm not your own can't be helping with your powers." Mailin shook her head. "You know, I'd always suspected you carried nuances of Seelie magic in your blood . . . but I'd never expected you to be from the race that makes my own."

"I've always felt a sense of kinship toward you, Mailin." The halfbreed's magic soothed her like no other. "And now . . . I feel as I always have. Completely human."

As human as Evangeline Barre had always been.

No one could explain how she'd lost her immortality—no fae in recorded history had ever escaped the Abyss. Her sharp-tipped ears had returned to their rounded state, and her canines had receded. Apart from the bizarre rim of violet around her irises, there was nothing to indicate her Seelie roots.

Mailin huffed a laugh and pointed to the swirling symbol of shimmering gold etched over the swell of her bosom, just over her heart. "Even if you were human, Evie, you're no longer truly mortal. Not when you're mated to an archmage."

Evangeline clasped a protective hand over her mark. "Mailin . . ."

The healer waved a trivializing hand. "I know never to speak of this to another soul except Killian, Evie. You can trust me to keep the secrets of my liege . . . and my lady."

Evangeline swallowed the knot in her throat. "Thank you." The world might know her as Declan Thorne's lover, but until they figured out the ramifications of an archmage with a mate, she preferred it be kept a secret. "Besides, we aren't fully mated," Evangeline admitted.

Mailin raised a brow. "I've never heard of an incomplete bond before, Evie."

Evangeline parted her lips, but the air shimmered, and her archmage materialized in the middle of the room. He wore a faint smile on his lips, one that would quicken the beat of her heart—if not for the conflicting wariness in his gaze.

The crackle of the fireplace and the warmth of Declan's bedchamber melted away to be replaced by crisp spring air and the lighthearted chirp of cheery birds. Three silhouettes marched toward the copse of trees that marked the borders of Village Arns. Evangeline recognized one instantly, and a surge of elation had her gasping. Her eyes clouded. She whirled on her archmage and tugged him down for a sound kiss. "Thank you."

The arms around her tightened before they loosened ever so reluctantly. "Go on," he murmured, gruffer than usual.

Grinning, she pecked him again before turning around.

"Stefan," she called. The wind swallowed her words. "Stefan!" she yelled louder as she sprinted toward the trio.

"Evie?" Stefan's jaw slacked, but he broke off from the group to meet her halfway. He lifted her off her feet to give her a gentle spin before crushing her in a tight embrace.

"Railea's light . . . " He stared hard at her eyes. "The rumors are true? The Unseelie king . . . "

Evangeline only nodded.

Stefan blinked rapidly. "What are you doing here?"

"Declan brought me here to say goodbye."

At that, Stefan released her and glanced up warily. "He did?"

"Why didn't you tell me you were leaving today?"

Stefan's shoulders slumped. "I wasn't sure if you'd ever want to see me again. And . . . " He glanced up, and his shoulders tensed visibly. Evangeline turned to follow his gaze and pursed her lips in an attempt to curb the chuckle working its way out of her throat.

Her archmage stood at least ten paces away. And he was unnaturally expressive, wearing a glower he did not attempt to conceal. She projected her assurance, brushing up against his mind. Smiled when she felt the ice thaw.

She shifted her focus back to the man before her. "Why did you think I wouldn't want to see you? Didn't you think I'd want to say goodbye?"

"After everything I did . . . " Stefan hung his head, lips pressed in a thin line.

"Yes." Evangeline sighed, not eager to disregard his sins, no matter the chains that had once bound him. But neither could she disregard his attempts at bucking those chains. "But you also risked your own life by leaving those tips with Malcolm."

Stefan blinked as though astonished.

"You were Malcolm's anonymous informant all along, weren't you?" Evangeline cocked her head. "The reason he was so successful unearthing all those operators . . . until he decided he'd rather be a part of the operation instead of working against it."

Stefan swallowed, seemingly finding it hard to speak. "I'm surprised your archmage told you."

"Why wouldn't he?" She gave him a dry smile. "Declan also told me it was because of you he found me so quickly in Zephyr's palace."

Stefan released a long-drawn sigh. "I-I'm so sorry, Evie. I should never—"

Evangeline shook her head. "It's over, Stefan. Leave it in the past." She noticed the burlap bag slung over his shoulder, and a tiny knot formed in her chest. Declan might have pardoned the Hanesworths from a death sentence, but not without the punishment of exile.

"Where are you headed?"

Stefan feigned a nonchalant smile. "We don't know yet."

His eyes wandered to the couple, who remained at a distance. A woman and a man with their hands linked, finally reunited. Waiting for their son. A genuine smile lifted the corners of Stefan's lips. "But wherever it is, we'll be together."

Λ

Declan watched his little fire's shoulders droop as Stefan finally turned and broke into a loping run toward his family. Declan would spare her the sadness if he could, but it was better for the Hanesworths to begin anew in a land without the burden of condemnation.

From the copse of trees, Stefan turned to meet his gaze briefly.

The lands of Yarveric are fair. Declan arrowed the thought at the man. *Sonja Tuath is a just ruler.*

His thoughts were met with a ripple of gratitude and a low bow before the three melted into the forests.

"Stefan will find solace, little fire," he murmured into her ear as he warped up behind her. She turned to tuck her head beneath his chin and wrap her arms around his back.

"Thank you, Archmage," she murmured. He held her until she stirred in his arms. But when she looked up, her sunset eyes were still marred with melancholy. Needing to wipe the sadness from them, he linked their fingers together. "There is another place I wish for you to see."

"Where?"

Declan smiled. "A surprise."

She blinked at the sudden change of surroundings.

"This place . . . " Recognition filled her eyes with a watery sheen as she stared at the edges of what was once a thriving pond—now nothing more than a quagmire of peat, shallow grasses, and cattails. She toed off her slippers to walk barefoot until she reached a specific spot just before the marshy dip and sat down on the soft grass. She gazed up at him with a wealth of emotion in her eyes.

He smiled, pleased she'd remembered this place, *their* place, despite her still-incomplete memories. He stepped forward to join her, turning his head so she couldn't see his grimace as he lowered himself to sit beside her.

His wounds, though scabbed over, still ailed him.

"When I ascended, I used to come here every day, until the pond receded and the last fowl flew away," he murmured, running his knuckles over the curve of her cheek. "It was as though nature conspired with the fates to take the final remnants of you from me . . . and I was sure I'd never feel whole again."

"Oh, Declan," she whispered, her voice husky. She drew his face down and pressed soft kisses over his eyes before kissing his lips. On the psychic plane, her mind twined around his like a silken swath of sunlight breaking through a cold winter's day.

"Mate with me, little fire," Declan murmured, unable to help himself.

She shook her head. "We can't complete the bond. It has already weakened you." She flattened her lips in a grim line. "*I've* weakened you."

Undeterred, he leaned forward to press his forehead against hers. "You will always be my greatest weakness," he said, allowing himself to be lost in the sunset of her eyes. "And my greatest strength."

Her lips quivered.

"Be mine. I've been yours since the day you found me."

She stared up at him, her shallow breaths loud in the hush of the glade. A little sob sounded from her throat, and abruptly, she threw her arms around him.

"All right," she mumbled, the words muffled against his

chest.

Declan stilled. "All right?"

"If my uncertain immortality does nothing to faze you, Archmage . . . then I have no reason not to claim you," she muttered. Then she narrowed her still-watery eyes. "But I won't share you, Declan. No courtesans. No ayaris. Not for as long as I draw breath."

Declan gave a fervent nod. "Only you. For as long as *I* draw breath."

Tears brimmed in her beautiful eyes again, but her lips curved into a wobbly smile. "But if my immortality never returns, and I grow old and ugly, you don't get to change your mind."

The laugh rolled out of him, deep and rich. "Never." He tapped her nose. "I'll love you even if you're shriveled like a prune."

When her own laughter ebbed, it was quickly replaced by a sensual gleam that lit her eyes and shortened his breath. She gave him a little shove in the chest, and understanding what she wanted, he obeyed and lay back on the mossy bank. She went to her knees to straddle him on the ground.

"Archmage," she purred before lowering herself onto his chest to nip at his lips and kiss him till his powers surged and simmered beneath his skin, mirroring his need. "Tell me what to do," she whispered, and his heart hammered at the anticipation of wearing her mark. They were lost in a tangle of limbs when the sound of someone clearing his throat jarred them apart.

"Apologies, Lady Evangeline. Archmage." A forced cough.

Evangeline rolled off him with a gasp, and Declan reared upright. Scowled.

"Do you have a death wish, Gabriel?"

The guildmaster bowed low, but it was clear he was trying

hard to hide a smirk. "I thought to give you a report before I head back to the fae realm. And I wouldn't have . . . interrupted if I didn't need to leave. Imminently."

Evangeline, who had buried her florid face in Declan's chest, peered over his shoulder with obvious concern. "Have you any news of Zephyr?"

Gabriel shook his head.

"None, my lady. My men and I have been scouring the five realms, but we've found no trace of him." Gabriel's tone darkened. "Zephyr may have been a contemptible king, but his disappearance has not gone unnoticed in our realm. The noble houses are already rioting like rabid dogs while the princes are vying for power. The rich are plundering the royal coffers and the poor pilfering from each other."

Evangeline cringed. "The Unseelie princes are warring against each other?"

Declan shook his head. "Anarchy will draw out the worst in men." Personally, he couldn't care less if the Unseelie wiped themselves from the face of Ozenn's Realm. But he cared about Evangeline. And as his little fire was slowly, but surely, regaining her fragmented memories, he had to force himself to acknowledge that she might one day *want* to return to her own realm. Declan fought the involuntary shudder and nodded at Gabriel. "You don't need to do this. You no longer owe me a debt."

For the first time in two centuries, Gabriel surprised him. "After all you've done for me and mine, Archmage, I don't think I can ever repay my debt. I will be content to serve you"—he gave another nod in Evangeline's direction—"and yours, until the day Ozenn draws me back into the sand." The fae's solemnity ebbed as quickly as it came, to be replaced with a shrewd smirk. "For the right *sum*."

Declan's lips twitched. This Gabriel he recognized.

"Go, then. Do what you can to make peace, but do not stop hunting him." Declan would not rest until he saw Zephyr's corpse for himself. "And keep your ears open for the next Winter Court king. Zenaidus may be the heir apparent, but there will be others vying for the throne."

Gabriel curled his lips in disgust at the mention of Winter Court statecraft but nodded his agreement. "It has also come to my attention that some of the surviving soldiers from the battle have added to the whisperings of a Jilintree descendent. My sources believe the Unseelie princes are already seeking her."

Evangeline trembled.

Declan firmed his jaw. In a degenerate realm desperate for Seelie blood, Evangeline's existence could not be revealed. Especially not when her birthright made her a prized weapon that could make or break kingdoms.

"Silence all who fuel the rumors."

Evangeline's startled gasp derailed Gabriel's response. *Declan, there has already been too much bloodshed.*

Declan would put her on a pedestal, acquiesce to her every wish, pander to her every whim—but not when her safety was in question. Never again.

I would annihilate all of Zephyr's spawn and bathe in the blood of the entire Unseelie race if that were what it would take to keep you safe, little fire.

Evangeline's eyes were bleak when she met his gaze. But she didn't contest his statement.

Gabriel, seeming to sense the end of their private discussion, gave Declan a brief nod. "Consider it done, Archmage." The insurgent unfolded his arms and bowed. His violet eyes shifted to Evangeline. Softened. "My lady," he said with a reverent smile that had Declan narrowing his eyes.

The guildmaster turned to leave when Declan murmured,

"Gabriel."

Violet eyes met his.

"Thank you, my friend."

The words seemed to catch the Unseelie off guard, for the assassin stared. Declan stood and extended his hand to offer a warrior's greeting. Gabriel regarded him for a split second before a wide grin creased his face, and he accepted Declan's hand by clasping his forearm with his own. "You're welcome . . . friend."

Declan felt his own lips tug at the corners as he turned to scoop Evangeline into his arms. "And to think I once thought sparing your life was an imprudent act of benevolence."

Gabriel's startled laughter echoed in his ears as Declan warped Evangeline back into the hallway that led to his bedchamber.

It turned out to be a mistake. A woman loitered outside their door, deterring their entry. Evangeline, however, beamed. "Anaiya, what are you doing here?" she asked, shimmying out of his hold. As Declan battled the urge to nix decorum and warp Evangeline straight to bed, tiny hands tugged hesitantly at the hem of his coat.

Two big brown eyes stared up at him.

"Ach hage." The words were pronounced unevenly, the intonation off, but they were understandable. Her mother quickly corrected the child, "Arch-mage."

"Arc mage," Surin repeated studiously.

"My liege," Anaiya interjected with an anxious bow. "Please forgive her. She is still learning the common tongue."

Nodding at the woman so she would relax, Declan ignored the prickle of pain at his side and went down on his haunches to give the girl his full attention.

"Yes, little one?"

Like her mother, she had put on some weight, her brown

skin regaining an unmistakable sheen of health. Her eyes held no fear as she regarded him solemnly.

"Thank you," she said, and this time the words were clear. She thrust a hand at him, proffering a tiny fist.

Declan held out an open palm.

She dropped a colorfully braided band into his hand. The band was slightly haphazard, with obvious kinks. Studying it closely, he noted a black bead and a white one woven into the threads.

"What's this?"

She gave him a sweet, shy smile before tapping on the black bead. "You." She tapped the white one. "Evie."

Then she tapped the colored threads that wove the beads together. "Freedom."

THE END

Enjoyed Little Fire? Please consider leaving me a review on Amazon, Goodreads or Bookbub.

Want more?

Do you recall the scene where Declan decides to take the day off so he could spend it with Evie at the Capital? Ever wondered how their day went?

https://BookHip.com/HHXRWVD
Download your bonus short story, Courtship Capital and find out! The story comes after the first scene in Little Fire, Chapter 32.

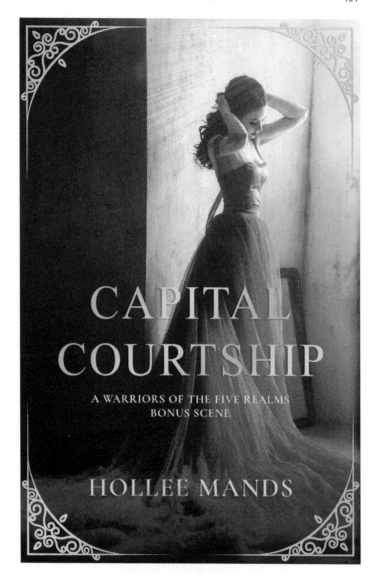

CAPITAL COURTSHIP

A WARRIORS OF THE FIVE REALMS
BONUS SCENE

HOLLEE MANDS

WARRIORS OF THE FIVE REALMS

LULLABY SCARS

(Warriors of the Five Realms Prequel)

*Want a full-length, standalone freebie? Sign up for my newsletter to claim your gift. **Lullaby Scars**' e-book is exclusive for my newsletter subscribers!*

He's the only man she's ever wanted. She's everything he can never have.

Killian's scars are all people see, but with his wretched past, he doesn't want them to look closer. He has long since resigned himself to live as an indentured slave to a powerful and capricious high mage —until a chance meeting with a temptress outside a brothel teaches him to *want...*

If only he hadn't asked her price for the night.

Lady Mailin's escape from her tyrannical father is so close she can taste it. All she has to do is to fake her magical prowess long enough for the high mage to sign a marriage contract and whisk her away. Then she'll lose him and start a new life. The last thing she needs is a tortured bondsman mistaking her for a woman who works on her back...

If only she could forget his gentle, callused touch.

When a stormy sea strands them together on Prison Island, Mailin and Killian's illicit desires may prove deadlier than the convicts out for blood. Or, worse.

They've spent their lives yearning for freedom. Can they survive long enough to make it last?

WINTER SUN

(Warriors of the Five Realms Book 2)

Finding each other was only half the story . . .

How does a small-town apothecarist fit into the dangerous world of an all powerful archmage?

You're about to find out.

Winter Sun is coming 30 November 2021.

Preorder now!

He'd do anything to keep her safe...except give her up.

Declan lost her once. Never again. He is an archmage. Fearsome. Terrible. Divine. Yet deadly whispers dare echo in his ear. None more threatening than those of his still-incomplete mate bond and his love's failing health. In a twist of irony, he must now protect his mate from the greatest danger she's ever faced...Himself.

Evangeline was raised to be an apothecarist, not an archmage's queen. She knows nothing of the subtle maneuverings of court life, and despite her awakened memories, she remains painfully human. Too human to claim an archmage for a mate. But Declan's contentious council and her questionable mortality aren't the only things she has to worry about. The secrets of her past are catching up, and even her all-powerful lover may not be able to keep her safe...

Winter Sun is the seductive sequel in the Warriors of the Five Realms adult fantasy romance series that will submerge you in a dazzling court of deadly secrets and deception lurking in every shadow...

ACKNOWLEDGMENTS

Ask any mother, and she will be likely to recall her firstborn's birth in lurid detail compared to her next child(ren)'s. It's not because moms are predisposed to love their first more than the rest (*as a fourth daughter, I sure hope not!*), but I believe the first is usually the most memorable.

Writing *Little Fire* was a bit like that. It was a story that had percolated in my brain for a good, long while. In 2017, I decided to write down some scenes. Maybe those voices would go away once they were written? Err…nope. They only got louder. Fast forward a few years…and here we are.

So if you've enjoyed *Little Fire* enough to spend more of your time reading this section, then the first thank-you goes to you, my **dearest reader**. Your escapism is my privilege and your enjoyment my prize. Thank you for gifting me precious hours of your life and sharing a story that is so close to my heart. Thank you for giving me a chance.

People say writing is a solitary affair and the magic of stories stems from the author's ability to keep her butt in the chair and her fingers tapping. Well, if writing is a lonesome pursuit, then publishing is a collaborative endeavor.

Little Fire would *never* have eventuated without these legends behind me:

Kelley Luna

You know how it's become a near-cliche expectation at the end of every book that the editor gets an honorary thank-you for all the good work they've done? Honestly speaking, Kels, your role in editing this manuscript is probably the *smallest* of your "contributions."

How could I say that?

Well, because the words "editing and proofreading" are woefully inadequate to describe what you've done for this manuscript and, more importantly, for me. You didn't just edit —you've championed and cheered and blessed every word with love. You didn't just proofread—you've bestowed painstaking hours, countless *days*, in vetting every line because that's just how much you care. You believed in the soul of this story, and you helped me polish it until it shone. You fuelled this author with encouragement, support, and laughter, and trust me, your unwavering friendship goes a *long* way in this season of her life. You've displaced a dark well of insecurity and filled it with confidence that enabled this book to eventuate.

So yes, your role as editor is by far your *smallest* contribution, and "thank you" is too small a phrase for your "help." Unfortunately, there are only so many words in the English language that convey gratitude. In an effort to emphasise my absolute adoration and appreciation, I'd like to say thank you in every language I know how: *Doh-jeh sai. Xie xie ni. Kamsiā. Terima kasih.* Thank you, Kelley. You've left more than your wisdom and fingerprints on Little Fire...you've left a little piece of your heart as well. And I will treasure it always.

Denali Day

You've always called me sweet, but that's because Messenger does well to mask my stubborn streak. And when it came to publishing my passion project, I believed I had to do things a certain way that could be nothing short of *perfect.* I'm guessing that's why He set you in my path. He knows I needed someone to help me ease back from the crippling quest for perfection so I could move on and keep growing.

And being nothing short of a force of nature, you couldn't have been more suited to the task.

You may not have been the first to read *Little Fire*, but I believe you were the first to truly fall in love with it. More, you're the first who *believed* it was worth more than a fledgling author's "practice" story. Without you, *Little Fire* would still be sitting in the dark abyss of my hard drive (because I'd still be fearful of the Google cloud stealing my data).

While you already know I have a great deal of esteem for your drive and determination, it has always been your blatant honesty that touches me the most. Thank you for always being unapologetically honest yet unfailingly gentle with me. Thank you for being the sort of friend I can run to with all my writerly (*and* non-writerly) woes and know that I'll get empathy, zero judgment...and in some cases, my head yanked out of my ass. Thank you for being my safe harbour amid the choppy waters of self-publishing.

Lyss Morgan

Thank you for critiquing the 2,653,738,839 iterations of *Little Fire* without complaint and with enthusiasm to boot. Your constancy and camaraderie in those early days were critical, to say the least. You've played an integral role in fostering my craft, confidence, and most of all, you made a world of difference in making this manuscript "real." :)

Courtney Kelly

Your attention to detail in *Little Fire* blew me out of the water! I will forever be grateful for your skill with plot inconsistencies and constructive story suggestions. More importantly, thank you for sharing your love for Evie and Declan long after you'd read the manuscript. Your support meant so much, and now your friendship means even more.

Liv Arnold

Thank you for being there for me when my writing was greener than grass. Thank you for all your kind words on *Little Fire* and, most of all, for sharing my publishing journey as well as yours. I am forever grateful knowing I can reach out any day, any time, and you're always there.

Natalie Murray

My first-ever "beta reader." I guess if I'd known better at the time, I'd have called you an alpha reader ;) I had no idea when I wrote the magic words "The End" the very first time that they would have meant "The Beginning" (or something to that effect, haha). It would not be an exaggeration to say that it was your exceedingly kind and encouraging words on a *far*-from-sterling draft that have spurred me to be a better writer.

Ivy Williams

You'll go down in history as the first reader to give me feedback that brought tears (of joy and disbelief) to my eyes. Thank you for the generosity of your time and simply just being amazing. Every author needs a reader like you.

Aimee Moore

Thank you for all your enthusiasm on *Little Fire*. I looked forward to each and *every* one of your emails because you have such a flair for making even the most mundane chuckle-worthy. Cheers with a cup of coffee ;)

Tina Emmerich

I've thought long and hard about where and how to slot you into this section of thank-yous and decided I haven't a clue. I've put many hats on you, haven't I? And you wear them all with ease. I suppose it would be easy to write a checklist of your many virtues for which I am thankful—chief amongst those being the care and consideration you take with each and every single comment—but I'd probably blow up the page. So I'll settle with a simple thanks, mate! Your analysis (yes, it was) and feedback on *Little Fire* were precious, but more importantly, your friendship is priceless.

And to my earlier readers—**Shantell, Trish, Anna, Danae,** and **Louise**—a resounding thank you! Your collective feedback, encouragement, and praise in those early days have gone far to shape *Little Fire* to its current form today.

A little something for the heroes of my heart...

And finally, a short ode to the people in my life who contribute nothing to the words but everything to my raison d'etre...and also, who doesn't like rhymes?

Dearest husband of mine,
A brilliant writer you will never be,
But that's fine,
Your contributions aren't for all to see,
And I suppose it shows in the way I shine,

Your love makes me grateful to be me.

Little master of my heart,
A disruptive force you are such!
Can't you at least let me pee alone and sleep apart?
Huggable bear always sticky to the touch,
Endless chatter and oh so smart,
Mommy loves you so very much.

Leaves may drop off trees in the fall,
But family will always be a brick wall,
Mommy, Daddy, and sisters one, two, three,
Thank you for always being there for me,
And to everyone else in my family tree?
I'm sorry but this rhyme is not long enough to accommodate
you all,
Luckily I know your love for me is not nearly so small.

Thank you for reading :)

ABOUT THE AUTHOR

Hollee Mands used to be that kid who sat at the back of the class, scribbling stories and doodling in dreary math work-books. Much older and still unrepentant, she's now determined to bring her imaginations to life through the keyboard. When she isn't squirrelling away time to write, read, or sketch, she is a communications consultant, wife, and proud mom to a tiny dictator who has the speech patterns (and physical energy) to rival a steam train.

She currently resides in fickle-weathered Melbourne and is a proud member of Romance Writers Australia.

Connect with Hollee
www.holleemands.com
@holleemands

Made in United States
Orlando, FL
07 September 2022

22130818R00288